Also by Madeleine E. Robins

The Stone War
Point of Honour

Petty Treason

A Sarah Tolerance Mystery

Madeleine E. Robins

TOR®

A Tom Doherty Associates Book
New York

PETTY TREASON

A Tor Book
Published by Tom Doherty Associates, LLC
175 Fifth Avenue
New York, NY 10010

www.tor.com

Tor® is a registered trademark of Tom Doherty Associates, LLC.

ISBN 0-765-34306-1
EAN 978-0-765-34306-2

First edition: August 2004
First mass market edition: June 2006

Printed in the United States of America

0 9 8 7 6 5 4 3 2 1

For
Eva Robins
Linda Robins
Ronda Robins
and
Juliette Clemente

with love

London, Fall, 1810

One

It is one thing, and a quite considerable thing, to be a lady. A true lady is a person of virtue and beauty, of accomplishment and talent, of gentle birth and rigorous upbringing. She inspires love in her suitors and obedience in her servants, and knows how to hold housekeeping and bully the butcher and chandler so cleverly that those persons feel it their privilege to serve her. The suggestion of strife oppresses her, and her pleasures are the mildest and most delicate. Her honor is a possession prized above rubies, and even the gentlest breath of scandal damages it forever. If adventure offers itself she understands that her reputation is at stake, and wisely settles for tedium. Or so the theory goes.

A gentleman, however, is not contained by prudishness. His sex licenses him, even encourages him, to seek out adventure and prove himself. There is no woman too low, no bottle too deep, no horse too fast or play too high, but there are gentlemen willing to swive, drink, race or wager. It is customary for a young man to prowl the fleshpots of London before he marries, to exercise his appetites to the fullest and slake them so that he does not appall the sensibilities of the Fair Flower he ultimately takes to wife. And for most gentlemen that is exactly what happens: each finds his favored dissipation—the bottle, the bootmaker, the bookmaker or the brothel—and falls violently in love for a time. And the passion runs its course and the young man is then suited for matrimony. Or so the theory goes.

But there are some gentlemen who find that giving rein to their desires only leads to the increase of those desires; and a man who lives for pleasure, and for the pleasure of being more debauched, more drunken, more spendthrift, more heedless, than his peers, is called a Rake. Young men with more money than sense who aspire to something higher than mere Fashion strive to be as thoughtless and wasteful as they may, ruining themselves pell-mell at drink, venery and gaming. But the true Rake has something more of imagination than of spendthrift waste, and his motto might well be "Because I wish it." Many Rakes combine considerable address and genuine thoughtfulness for the welfare of their tenants and aged parents, but it is also true that where the gratification of their wishes is concerned, they can be merciless. To be that man or woman who stands between a Rake and his desire—or as likely, comprises that desire—is not an enviable thing.

Of course, as in every other field of human endeavor, some men have more natural talent as Rakes than others. For every true Rake in London in the year 1810 there were likely a dozen pretenders to the title. The Dueling Notices in the weekly *Gazette* were peopled with those wounded or killed in pursuit, either of vice or honor. Spunging houses and debtor's prisons were likewise occupied by those who had been stripped of their fortunes by improvident congress with Rakes. As for women—those of both high and low estate were accosted with such regularity that it is surprising there were half the number of respectable females remaining in the nation. And the alleys and corners of gin-shops and taverns were lined with young inebriates whose ambitions outmatched their tolerance for drink.

Thus, Mr. Maurice Waldegreen, who was very drunk.

"Good God, I'm foxed!" he said thickly. "Cup-shot. Drunk as David's sow. No, drunker!" He giggled. "Drunk as . . . drunk as what?"

"A hippogriff?" his companion suggested politely. They had only met that evening, but Mr. Waldegreen clearly regarded brevity of acquaintance as no bar to friendship. His arm flung heavily across his new friend's neck, he leaned down until their faces were but a few inches apart. His breath was very foul.

"What's a hippogriff?" he inquired, his head weaving back and forth.

"Perhaps I meant hippopotamus?" his friend suggested, shrugging to shift the weight of Mr. Waldegreen's arm from collar to shoulder.

Mr. Waldegreen considered, tilting his head. Alas, as slight as this motion was, it overset him. Mr. Waldegreen stumbled, falling forward until he encountered, with every evidence of surprise, a wall of grimy brick. They had emerged only a moment before from a wine-shop into the icy November night, but the chill was not exercising a sobering effect on Mr. Waldegreen.

"Drunk as a hippogriff!" he announced, and groped his way down the wall until he was sitting in the mud and cobbles. His coat, which must have recently been clean and well tended, was wrinkled and dirty. His neckcloth had come untied and was stippled with wine, demonstrating that Mr. Waldegreen was not one of those dandies for whom elegance was a bar to dissipation. He leaned back against the wall and squinted up at his new friend. "Damn, what are you doing all the way up there?"

"Wondering where my hackney coach is." Relieved of Mr. Waldegreen's weight, his companion stepped back a pace and straightened the collar of her coat.

A careful observer—of whom there were none at that moment—would have discerned despite the darkness and her garb—breeches, boots, neatly tied neckcloth and a long, caped greatcoat from the Belgian tailor Gunnard—that Mr. Waldegreen's companion was young, female, and quite handsome. But Miss Sarah Tolerance had discovered that most people saw what they expected to see unless the truth of her sex was forced upon them. In more than three hours spent at Mr. Waldegreen's side, he had not focused his gaze upon her long enough to uncover her imposture. If their neighbors at the wine-shop they had just left had discerned her sex, none had seen fit to mention it. Miss Tolerance looked down at Waldegreen with amusement. "Are you comfortable, sir?"

"Aye, Frenchy, fine as frog hair," Mr. Waldegreen said. "Just a slight case of barrel fever is all. Don't know how, though. My father always said it wasn't possible to get drunk on Bordeaux—"

"Your father perhaps never encountered Bordeaux that bad. And of course, much is possible to a man of dedicated purpose."

Waldegreen snickered. "Dedicated purpose! Z'all clear to me! My father never 'preciated my dedi-dedi—" he belched loudly. "My dedi-cated purpose! Always wearing on about—" He belched again and took his head in his hands, as if all the less pleasant aspects of his condition had suddenly threatened to visit themselves upon him.

Miss Tolerance regarded him with a mixture of sympathy and impatience.

"How am I to get you home," she muttered. It had been a long night, she had necessarily drunk enough wine to pretend to keep pace with Waldegreen, and the thought of now having to raise the man's unreliable person to its feet and move him along the alley to Fleet Street did not appeal to her. "If the hackney's gone, how the Devil am I going to find another in this neighborhood?"

Mr. Waldegreen vomited. Miss Tolerance jumped nimbly to avoid being caught by the flow, and after a moment offered her handkerchief to the young man. He mumbled a thank you and mopped at his face. "Drunk as a hippogriff, Frenchy. How is it you're not?"

"A naturally more abstemious character, Mr. Waldegreen." She refused the return of the besmirched handkerchief, but added its cost to a mental reckoning.

He shook his head. "Mustn't call me that. Poggy, that's what you call me. That's what everyone calls me. 'Cept milord father." Mr. Waldegreen was clearly descending into the morose stage of drunkenness. "Milord father don't call me at all if he can help it. A fierce disappointment I am to milord father. Dammit, m'mouth tastes like a stable. Haven't a sip of brandy, have you?"

Miss Tolerance regretted that she did not. "I think perhaps I ought to go look out a hackney coach, Poggy," she said. "You'll have the Devil of a head tomorrow." She regarded her charge for a moment longer, then looked up and down the empty length of the alleyway. They were some paces away from the wine-shop in which she had found him, and its door was shut tight against the cold. In the chill post-midnight it was unlikely that Waldegreen would be troubled by idle passersby. She went down the lane to the corner of Fleet Street.

Finding a hackney, even on this thoroughfare, proved to be as thankless a chore as she had expected. It was a full ten minutes before she reappeared at the corner with the bulk of a disreputable coach paused behind her on the street.

"All right, Poggy," she began. Then stopped, when she saw three men clustered around Mr. Waldegreen. Miss Tolerance prepared for the worst—pushing her coat aside to free the hilt of her smallsword—but spoke with unruffled politeness. "It's kind of you to concern yourselves, but my friend will recover when I get him home, gentlemen."

The men turned to her, scowling. The man nearest Miss Tolerance appeared, by his attitude and appearance, to be the leader. He was short and extremely fat, his coat and breeches so tight that he gave the impression of being almost explosively compressed into his clothing. His several chins were forced up by the elaborate style of his neckcloth, and his face was shadowed by a small hat with a shallow, curled brim. The moon was not full, but there was some light from two torches flanking the door of the wine-shop from which Miss Tolerance and Mr. Waldegreen had lately emerged. She could see enough to know that the fat man meant her charge no good.

"Go away, boy." The fat man barely wasted a glance upon her. His voice was gravely, punctuated by audible wheezing. "This 'ere ain't none of your business."

She stepped forward. "I'm afraid I cannot do that, sir. I promised my friend's father I'd see him safely home."

"This 'ere ain't no business of yourn," the fat man said again. "Go 'ome."

Miss Tolerance continued to advance upon the group. The fat man's confederates, she saw, were trying to raise Mr. Waldegreen to his feet without success. Mr. Waldegreen, now unconscious, had apparently achieved a state of leaden pliancy which was defeating their efforts. The fat man tugged upon the shoulder of the tough nearest him.

"Bob, take the boy," he growled. "Sid, you get that one up *now*."

Bob, taller than his master by a foot and well muscled, pivoted away from Mr. Waldegreen and reached for Miss Tolerance. His coat gaped open, displaying a brace of pistols tucked in his belt, but no sword. Miss Tolerance made a rapid decision that Bob should not be permitted to get either of the pistols into his hands; she stepped into the circle of the man's arm, grasped her sword, and by unsheathing it, drove the pommel up into Bob's jaw with considerable force.

Bob fell like a stone, toppling onto the fat man.

"Sid!" The fat man disentangled himself from Bob and bent, wheezing, for the pistols in his hireling's belt. He was halted by the point of Miss Tolerance's sword, pressed into the folds of his neckcloth against the meaty flesh of his throat. The fat man straightened up, staring at her.

At his master's call, Sid had dropped Mr. Waldegreen and turned, cudgel in hand.

"Don't try it!" Miss Tolerance cautioned the man. "I should dislike to get blood on your employer's linen."

There was a moment of silent communication between the fat man and Sid, at the end of which Sid dropped the cudgel and stood still.

"I think it is time you left," Miss Tolerance said after a moment. "You needn't worry. If this gentleman cooperates he will come to no harm. You, sir, kindly dismiss your hound," she added for the fat man's benefit.

Under the curly-brimmed hat she saw the fat man's eyes move from side to side, as if surveying his options. Miss Tolerance was forced to encourage him with the slight pressure of her sword against his throat.

"Go home, Sid," the man said at last, with no good grace. "Wait for me."

Sid needed no encouragement. He turned and ran as his master watched, scowling after him.

"Yellowback coward." He turned his gaze to Miss Tolerance. "Who *are* you, boy?" the fat man growled. "There's no need for swords, you know. I just need a word or two with your mate here—make it worth your while."

"No, sir, I really think not. My friend's in no case to speak with anyone, and his father, as I said, is already making it worth my while to see his son safe home."

Miss Tolerance relaxed her arm somewhat, dropping her sword's point an inch or so from the man's throat. The fat man looked down at Bob, who lay across his master's boots, unmoving; clearly he would have no help from that quarter.

"Well," Miss Tolerance said. "We shall each of us have a chore getting our companions to their right places tonight. Unless you like to leave your minions littering the street?"

Mr. Waldegreen, still on his back on the cobblestones, stirred and belched. Moving with remarkable speed, the fat man pushed Miss Tolerance's sword aside, reaching for the pistols in Bob's belt. Without hesitation Miss Tolerance grabbed for the man's neckcloth and pulled up and twisted, overbalancing the fat man so that he flipped beetle-like onto his back beside Mr. Waldegreen. She stood over him with her sword again touching his throat.

"Now, will you tell me what this word is that you were so eager to have with my friend? Perhaps I can assist you." Miss Tolerance's heart was pounding, but she managed a tone of polite command, rather like that of a governess.

Evidently the fat man had never had a governess. Her tone did not encourage him to cooperate. He looked upward, studying Miss Tolerance's form with an expression of disbelief. "Christ," he said at last, a long slow hiss. "You're a female." His eyes bulged and his voice bespake revulsion. "What kind of unnatural bitch are you to parade about in man's clothes?"

"A Fallen Woman with a chore to do," Miss Tolerance said mildly. Her point remained where it was. "These clothes are far more convenient for my purpose than a muslin gown and kid slippers would be."

The fat man shook his head. "Abomination, that's what it is. Whore! No, lower than a whore! Wearing men's clothes, fighting like a man, standing the nat'ral order of things on its ear! And for the likes of *him*!"

"Do *his* likes make *my* dress worse, sir? I merely came to fetch him home from a several-days' absence and found you in the midst of what looked like a robbery. Or a kidnapping," Miss Tolerance suggested. "But—could it be that you are Mr. Haskett?" Her tone of polite surprise was not meant to convince.

The fat man's eyes shifted from side to side, then down to the blade of the small sword in Miss Tolerance's hand. "I'm Haskett," the man said reluctantly. "What of it?"

"Then you are the gentleman who has been attempting to extort money from Lord Pethridge on his son's account."

"Extort!" Haskett's eyes shifted back and forth agitatedly. "Not I! I'm the wronged one here," he protested. His tone became theatrically grieved and his speech finically genteel. "My family honor at stake! The virtue of a lady! You can't know the sort of man you are protecting!" Still lying on his back, Mr. Haskett twitched a tear into his eye.

"What melodrama, Mr. Haskett! As good as Drury Lane! I have, I think, a very good understanding of what sort of man poor Poggy is"—Miss Tolerance pushed gently at Waldegreen's foot with the toe of her boot. There was no response—"and I have as good a notion of what sort of man you are. I have been instructed to tell you that my client will not prefer charges or exact reprisal, providing you cease your blackmail scheme and go away. It's a good offer; I should take it, were I you."

Mr. Haskett eyed Miss Tolerance and made one last attempt. "You're a woman, surely you have some loyalty to your sex. You should understand!"

"Understand blackmail?"

"Understand the plight of a woman ruined! This scourer trifled with my sister, a sweet, good girl." Mr. Haskett warmed to his story. "Seduced her! Took her virtue and left her with naught to show for it but a broken heart. By rights the bastard should marry her. All I wanted was that he make provision for a woman he'd wronged." Haskett fixed Miss Tolerance with an oracular eye. "He'll wrong you in the end, missy."

Miss Tolerance laughed. "Will he? I should like to see him try it. Do you imagine I've lost my heart to Mr. Waldegreen? I thank you for your concern, but I'm not in the business of losing my heart."

Haskett muttered a speculation upon the business that Miss Tolerance *was* in.

"Nor that business either," she said crisply. "I am hired to ask questions, find things, and occasionally protect someone with more money than sense"—again Miss Tolerance tapped Mr. Waldegreen's foot with her own—"from being victimized." Miss Tolerance gathered up the skirts of her greatcoat in her free hand and crouched down at Mr. Haskett's side, the blade of her sword now lying across his stomach.

"As for the lady—by my count, my friend is the seventh young man of good family from whom you have attempted to extort money on her. And as she is neither a virgin nor your sister, your grounds for complaint are few. A magistrate friend of mine tells me that, were the matter brought to a court of law, you and the young woman would be the queen's guests on a ship to the Antipodes."

Haskett's jowly face seemed to swell in the moonlight. More than ever he appeared on the verge of explosion. "The scandal!" he sputtered.

Miss Tolerance shook her head. "Scandal? A young man sows his oats with a woman several years older who has been the mistress of a gambler and whoremaster since she was fifteen. She approaches him in the lowest sort of gaming hell and convinces him it is an exchange of mutual pleasures with no cost to either. I have witnesses to their meeting, Mr. Haskett. I suggest the next time your mistress tries this trick, she do it somewhere less public. Now," she slid her blade up to rest at Haskett's throat, then leaned across him to take Bob's pistols. "If you are clear on this, may I suggest we both get our companions home?"

Haskett, outgunned, nodded. Miss Tolerance rose, slipped the pistols into the pocket of her greatcoat, and watched as the fat man got clumsily to his feet, wheezing louder than before. Haskett looked down at Bob without favor, shrugged, and walked away.

Miss Tolerance leaned down to deliver a sharp slap to Mr. Waldegreen. He stirred slightly. One eye opened and shut.

"Frenchy? Where the Devil are we?" His voice was sticky.

"Outside Remsen's and about to take a hackney back to Bourdon Street, Poggy," Miss Tolerance said encouragingly. "Do you think you might stand up now?"

Mr. Waldegreen was optimistic about his ability to do so; it took Miss Tolerance several minutes to get the young man to his feet and thence to the hired carriage, whose driver Miss Tolerance suspected had watched the altercation in the alley without inclination to help either side. At this hour and in this neighborhood, it was enough that the carriage had waited.

I n Bourdon Street Lord Pethridge was waiting. He did not ask to speak to his son, who was in any case now insensible, but sent two footmen out to retrieve him from the carriage. Miss Tolerance he led into a small office. The chamber was rather more meagerly furnished than others she had seen: a desk, a chair, a second chair for the accommodation of visitors, a shelf of ledgers, a Bible, and one painting executed by an amateur hand upon a Biblical subject—not, Miss Tolerance noted to herself, the parable of the prodigal son. It was a room designed to inspire little hope in a visitor expecting benevolence.

In her dealings with him, Miss Tolerance had identified Lord Pethridge as a closefisted man with a superior sense of his own consequence, embarrassed by the need to seek her help, and therefore unfailingly impolite. He did not sit now, nor did he invite Miss Tolerance to do so.

"Well? Aside from the bringing the boy home, have you accomplished *anything*?"

Miss Tolerance responded to his words and not his tone. "Indeed, sir, the matter is concluded. Mr. Haskett, as we had anticipated, did attempt to contact your son this evening. I told him all I had discovered about his scheme. This, I believe, brought him to a full sense of its futility. I doubt you shall hear from Mr. Haskett again."

Pethridge nodded and cleared his throat, which miserly comment Miss Tolerance translated as *"Very good, well done!"* He took a key from his waistcoat pocket, unlocked a drawer in the desk, and drew from it a small coffer.

"Four days at three guineas a day?" Pethridge asked.

"And my expenses, my lord," Miss Tolerance said. "Totaling eight shillings fourpence. I can write you out an account of the monies spent if you like."

Lord Pethridge paused for a moment, caught, Miss Tolerance surmised, between the miser's wish for an exact accounting and the prude's wish to have the whole business done, and herself off his premises, with as much dispatch as possible.

"That won't be necessary," he said at last. Where Lord Pethridge's son was genially ill kempt, Lord Pethridge himself was a man so tightly controlled that his clothes appeared to be lacquered in place. Of the two, father and son, Miss Tolerance preferred the son. It was the father, however, who was her client, and she was polite.

"Thank you, sir," she said, as he pushed a pile of coins across the table. Pethridge, occupied in relocking the box and restoring it to its drawer, did not acknowledge her. When he looked up he appeared surprised to find her still there.

"If I might make a suggestion, sir? I think you ought to find some occupation for your son which is more useful than gambling and wenching."

"Occupation? He'll have occupation enough when he rises to the title and starts his way through my fortune! He clearly has no gift for responsibility."

Miss Tolerance put the coins in her pocketbook. "He's not likely to develop such a gift without practice, sir."

Pethridge did not deign to answer. Miss Tolerance took this as her dismissal, bowed, and started for the door. He stopped her.

"You'll speak of this to no one," he said, half command and half question.

Miss Tolerance smiled politely. "I should have very little custom if I could not promise discretion. I do not talk about my cases."

"Not ever? The whole world knows that you brought the Earl of Versellion to justice—"

"That the whole world knows it, my lord, is not my doing. When a murderer comes before the court he cannot expect to do so privately."

"You believe him guilty, then?" For a moment Pethridge's icy demeanor slipped, revealing vulgar curiosity.

" 'Tis not a matter of what I *believe*. I gave what I knew of the facts last month in court, under oath. Anything I merely *believe* is between me and my conscience. If you will pardon me, sir?"

Miss Tolerance bowed and left.

The hour was now very late. Miss Tolerance found that exertion and her meeting with Lord Pethridge had left her wide awake. She was reluctant to return to the silence of her home. She thought briefly of going to her club, Tarsio's, which at this hour was likely to be doing a brisk business. But she was still in her unconventional dress, and disliked to go to the club thus attired unless business was pressing. The management of Tarsio's was liberal in its views (as the only establishment of its sort to admit women as members, it had a need to be) and would not bar her from entry, but Miss Tolerance preferred not to advertise her affinity for men's garb. One never knew when the advantage of appearing to be something one was not would come in handy.

Not to Tarsio's, then. Miss Tolerance turned her steps toward Manchester Square and the brothel kept there by Mrs. Dorothea Brereton. It was a fogless night—rare for November—but dark. The law required that a light be hung at every door, but the lanterns and torches provided only a yellow smear of light at the doorsteps and did nothing to penetrate to the street or illuminate the passersby. And despite the hour there were people on the streets; mindful of the sorts of people they would tend to be, Miss Tolerance kept her hand lightly on the hilt of her sword. No one troubled her, however. Streetwalkers eyed her hopefully, then shrugged when she passed them by; twice she was aware of rhythmic shadows coupling in doorways. She walked up Davies Street, turned onto Oxford, and was near to Duke Street when she heard a woman cry out.

Miss Tolerance paused. She heard the cry again, clearly one of pain or anger—in any case, not something she was capable of ignoring. She turned to look down Oxford Street for the source of the voice.

A woman in an unseasonable muslin dress staggered out of an alley, pursued by a man. His clothes marked him as a gentleman; hers—the thin dress, cheap hat, and a limp, insufficient spencer jacket—marked her as a hedge-whore. Even in the dark, and at some yards' distance, Miss Tolerance could see that the woman's face was twisted in fear, and she moved forward to help. The woman—girl, rather, Miss Tolerance thought—bolted toward her.

"Please, sir! He'll kill me, sure!"

The whore reached Miss Tolerance and took cover behind her, cowering. One hand was cupped over her eye, and a smudged trickle of blood at her mouth explained her fear.

Her pursuer approached them at an easy pace; clearly he expected no trouble in reclaiming his prize. "Does the little bitch tell tales?" he called. His words were strongly accented but clear. French, Miss Tolerance thought. Not so often heard in London as the endless war with Bonaparte wore on. "I paid for what I have not yet received," the man said easily. "Come here, *belle*. We have business." He smiled broadly; his black brows knit downward, giving the smile a demonic character. Miss Tolerance's inclination to help the whore increased.

The girl was shaking her head. "I've changed me mind," she said. "You can have the coin back." She fumbled at a little purse hanging at her waist.

"But I have not changed mine," the man said, and made to reach around Miss Tolerance to take the girl's arm. Miss Tolerance shifted her stance and kept the girl away. The Frenchman did not like this: "Sir, this is nothing to do with you. If you do not wish to quarrel, I beg you will go your way."

"When I am certain the lady does not require my assistance, sir," Miss Tolerance said.

"The *lady*?" The man laughed. "The thing's a convenience, like a chamber pot."

Miss Tolerance set her teeth. "Find another pot to piss in, then."

Behind her the girl had managed to open her reticule and find the coin she sought. "Here! Take your money! There's some as like your kind of custom, but not me." She reached out her hand to return the money and the man's hand fastened upon her wrist.

" 'Twill be a matter of a few minutes, *belle*," the man said, and pulled the girl toward him.

Miss Tolerance had her sword out of its sheath and laid flat upon the gentleman's wrist. "As the girl has returned your money I believe your business is concluded. You should let her go."

The man looked at the sword, then into Miss Tolerance's face. His eyes narrowed, but he let go, stepped back, and dusted his coat off. He murmured something in French and turned away.

Miss Tolerance replied in that language to his retreating back. The man stopped for a moment but did not look back. Then he walked on.

The whore sighed. "Thank you, sir. A thousand times. If I'd known he was a foreigner I'd never 'ave let him come near me." Her tone changed. "If you'll let me thank you proper-like, sir—"

Amused, Miss Tolerance replied that that would not be necessary.

"No, really. No charge and all, sir. For the rescue."

"Go home," Miss Tolerance advised. "It's late, girl. Just—go home."

The girl looked confused. "Honest, sir. And I'm clean. For free, sir." She started to run her hand along Miss Tolerance's sleeve. Miss Tolerance stopped the hand with her own and pushed the girl away.

"Go home," she said again.

The girl took a few steps away, then turned back, puzzled.

"Was it what the foreigner said, sir? Did he say some lie about me?"

"About you? Not really. He said he did not understand the such a fuss over a blow or two to a whore."

"And what did you say, sir?"

Miss Tolerance smiled. "I said when someone fetches him a blow or two perhaps he'll understand it too."

The girl grinned. "I'll dream of that, then, sir. Not likely, though, is it?"

Miss Tolerance shook her head. "No, not likely. Good night." She turned toward Duke Street, grateful now that she was near home.

Torches burned at the large, fine house on the corner of Spanish Place in Manchester Square. When Miss Tolerance knocked, the door was opened at once.

"Miss Sarah! We'd not expected to see you this evening."

"Good evening, Keefe." Miss Tolerance entered the house blinking in the sudden light afforded by a chandelier and branches of candles liberally stationed around the front hall. It occurred to her, not for the first time, that a brothel such as Mrs. Brereton's must keep a chandler in business with the number of wax candles used there each week. "How is custom this evening?"

The footman considered. "Solid, but not bustling, miss. When the quality finish with their shooting parties up north and come back to town again, then we'll be on the hop."

"Passion is so seasonal a business?"

Keefe, who after nearly a decade at Mrs. Brereton's considered himself something of an authority upon the subject of brothels and their clientele, shook his head. "T'ain't the season, miss. It's the inconvenience. Not even the hottest buck's like to come two hundred miles from the shooting for his piece. He'll find a laundry maid or some obliging local girl to see to him until he comes back to London. And in course, them that stay in London at this time of year are not generally them that can afford a night at Mrs. Brereton's. Come December, when Parliament meets again, we'll see most of the government here."

"What a happy reflection upon the Nation." Miss Tolerance shrugged off her Gunnard coat but kept it draped over one arm rather than surrender it to Keefe. "Surely there must be some MPs who do not patronize this house?"

"Prigs," the footman said dismissively. "Chapel evangelicals."

There was a murmur of conversation from the front salon, and a laugh. Miss Tolerance raised an inquiring eyebrow.

"A couple of gentlemen haven't settled on their girls yet," Keefe said. "Not regulars. And—Mrs. B is—engaged."

Again Miss Tolerance raised her eyebrow. Mrs. Brereton, as owner and manageress of the operation, had only a few patrons and entertained infrequently.

"Marianne as well?" she asked.

Keefe nodded. "All that's in the salon is three girls: Emma, Chloe, and the new girl, Lizzie."

Miss Tolerance nodded. No one she wished to talk to. Fatigue, which had not touched her during her adventure on Oxford Street, suddenly came over her again.

"Perhaps I shall go down to the kitchen and beg a cup of soup before I go home."

"Cook will have kept something for you," Keefe suggested. It would have surprised Miss Tolerance to learn that she was something of a pet among the staff, one for whom favors large and small were often undertaken. It was not merely that she was liberal with her thanks, or that she gave generous tips whenever she was in funds; there was something about Miss Tolerance which commanded their imaginations. She was Mrs. Brereton's niece, and rented the tiny cottage which stood in the rear of the garden. She had the appearance and manner of a lady but had, like the women who worked above-stairs at Mrs. Brereton's, long ago lost her virtue and all the claims upon polite society to which it entitled her. Like the women above-stairs, she worked at all hours, and her work sometimes put her in peril. She had few friends and not even as much society as the whores, who when not employed spent their time in gossip and shopping.

"There was gooseberry tarts for the supper," Keefe said. "Tell Cook to put some out for you."

Miss Tolerance smiled. "Perhaps I shall." She stifled a yawn. "Or perhaps I shall forget my supper and go straight to sleep."

Keefe shook his head and looked as though he would offer advice, but did not.

"You think I should eat something, Keefe?"

"Miss Sarah, Cook would be hurt if you didn't take a little something, you being in the house and all."

"Ah, well. I must on no account ruffle Cook's feathers," Miss Tolerance agreed. She thanked Keefe for his care and set off for the kitchen in search of gooseberry tarts.

Two

Rising early the next morning, Miss Tolerance dispatched a note detailing her expenses, and a receipt, to Lord Pethridge. With the matter of Mr. Waldegreen and Mr. Haskett so profitably resolved, she was able to turn her attention to another pending inquiry. A wealthy brewer desired that she determine whether the fortune of his daughter's intended was as extensive as he claimed. Mr. Wheelock was short, stocky and mistrustful: "I'll be frank with you, miss: I fully expected Betty to be wed for my money by some down-at-heels nobleman, but this fellow says his pocket's as well lined as mine. I don't mind she's marrying *up*, as the phrase is—but I want to make sure the boy's all he says he is."

It took her several days to run to ground all her sources; she then had the pleasure of informing Mr. Wheelock that Mr. Colcannon's property was extensive, unmortgaged and, if anything, more productive than the gentleman had represented it. She turned in her account to the suspicious brewer, who sniffed as he read it and commented that his Betty had shown better sense than he'd ever expected of her. Miss Tolerance received her payment, and found herself at liberty.

It had been some time since she had last achieved this enviable state. Country-bred, she liked to keep busy as much from a preference for employment as for the sake of her pocketbook (although that object was a matter of constant interest; a Fallen Woman may count upon no one but herself for security in her old age). In the last few months she had been unusually busy, taking any task that was offered her. As she had lately been a witness in a murder trial of considerable notoriety, her star had risen sharply and several interesting opportunities had been offered her. It came as a shock to her to realize that there was nowhere she need be that day, no question to ask or goal to pursue. One day of idleness was delicious. Two days was enjoyable. Three was torture.

There were always a few matters of housekeeping and bookkeeping to attend to, but these barely filled the first empty day. The usual occupations open to a lady of leisure seemed singularly without luster. She enjoyed shopping as an occasional pastime. Her needlework was generally of the practical and not the decorative variety, and represented only duty. She was not addicted to reading for pleasure, rarely indulged in the theater, and only recalled how much she enjoyed musical performance when she found herself at one. She did not feel inclined to seek out the company of her small circle of friends; her two closest friends were Sir Walter Mandif, magistrate of Bow Street, and Marianne Touchwell, one of Mrs. Brereton's whores. Sir Walter was in the midlands for the hunting, and Marianne had professional constraints upon her time which Miss Tolerance was bound to respect. There was no one else she wished to call upon, and while Miss Tolerance spent part of each day at Tarsio's, making herself available to anyone who might look for her, no one did.

By the end of her third day of liberty, Miss Tolerance was aware of the imminence of a sort of mental languor which dismayed her. She had experienced this state only once before, after the death of Charles Connell, the man who had taught her to fence and had, coincidentally, ruined her. They had been living abroad when Connell died. She had fallen into a state of melancholy which nothing, not even the hazards of being English in French-occupied Belgium, had been able to pierce. She had slept for days on end; forgotten to eat; sat with a pen in her hand, poised to write to whom she knew not. It was only when her landlord threatened to turn her out, or worse, denounce her to the French authorities, that she had broken from this stupor and arranged to return home on one of the privateers which plied the waters between England and the continent.

Misliking as she did the idea of slipping into this drowsy fog, Miss Tolerance embraced a feverish routine of fencing drills. Her gender barred her from public practice at the *salles des armes* around town, and while she was known to several of the *maitres de fence* and sometimes went to work with them privately, it was not often enough to keep her skills honed. In warm weather she drilled up and down the garden; now it was too cold to work out of doors, so she pushed the furniture against the wall of her cottage and drilled, stocking-footed, across the room and back for hours until she was exhausted and the paper target she had pinned on the back of the door bristled with tiny holes. When she was done, she could spend an hour cleaning, filing and oiling her blade, by which time she had generally disposed of the better part of a day.

Out of deference to her aunt and other neighbors she forbore to practice with her pistols in the garden, and thus target practice generally meant retiring to some secluded place in the near-countryside. The unusually cold November weather made this a less than appealing notion, and Miss Tolerance did no more than clean and oil her pistols in the evening as she sat before the fire.

At the end of a fortnight Mrs. Brereton, having heard of her niece's activity, sent to invite her for tea. Miss Tolerance presented herself in her aunt's parlor quite careless of her appearance. Mrs. Brereton was never less than elegantly dressed herself, her short dark hair lightly pomaded and styled and her complexion improved by the discreet touch of the haresfoot.

"You look more hoydenish than usual, Sarah. Have you nothing better to do than thrash about with your sword all day?"

Miss Tolerance shrugged. "Apparently not, Aunt."

"You might help me with my bookkeeping," Mrs. Brereton suggested briskly. "You have an aptitude for it."

Miss Tolerance interpreted this suggestion as a part of the ongoing attempt by her aunt to interest her in managing the brothel. As the family to which both women belonged had cut them off entirely at the time of their respective ruins, each was the only relative who would acknowledge the other. Mrs. Brereton often spoke of someday transferring management of her business to her niece. Despite a face and figure that belied the fact, the madam was well into middle age, and could speak most feelingly upon the subject of advancing years and the property she would leave behind. That Miss Tolerance had no interest in assuming the role of madam, as she had resisted her aunt's attempts to interest her in turning prostitute, grieved the dynastic-minded Mrs. Brereton deeply.

"Ask Marianne," Miss Tolerance suggested. "She has a practical mind, and I'm sure she could do the sums."

"I don't want the girls involved in management of the house."

"Why not, Aunt? Have you something to hide?"

Mrs. Brereton's chin went up. "I built this house with my savings and my wit, both earned on my back. I run it as I see fit, and the girls in my house have no cause for complaint. I offer to make you a part of it because we are family—and because you've a mind for figures and for managing things. Marianne is just a whore."

"You limit yourself if you believe that, Aunt—"

Mrs. Brereton shrugged. "Then I limit myself."

They sat in Mrs. Brereton's private salon, a chamber expensively and handsomely furnished in the classical style favored by the former empress of France. A tray, upon which the remains of a light meal were evident, sat between them, and beyond that the *Gazette*, the sight of which reminded Miss Tolerance that she had not looked at a newspaper for more than a week. Half the windows in the room were still curtained, despite the advanced hour: Mrs. Brereton was of the opinion that sunlight was injurious to a woman's complexion. The remaining light, bright as it was on this clear day, did not dispel the chill between the two women.

Miss Tolerance filled the silence by checking the teapot, although she knew very well that it was empty. In recent months her relationship with her aunt, once easy and affectionate, had become awkward. Miss Tolerance could not trust her aunt to keep a confidence, and the necessity of guarding what she said made her cross in her aunt's company. Mrs. Brereton, for her part, treated her niece with the resentment common to those who have done wrong and dislike to be reminded of it. Miss Tolerance missed the communication of a six-month ago but had not the least idea how to restore it. Even maintaining a conversation with her aunt was now fatiguing.

"Have you any news from the warehouses?" Mrs. Brereton asked politely.

Miss Tolerance shook her head. Discussing bolts of dress-stuff would have been a safe topic, but her most recent intelligence from her wharf-side contacts had long ago been discussed with her aunt.

"The new figured muslins at Beady's is all that I have heard of recently. After the new year, when mantua-makers are planning for the season, I'm sure there will be more to hear."

"And more buyers to drive the prices up," Mrs. Brereton objected.

That appeared to be the final conversational coffin-nail. It was a fortunate moment for an interruption. Cole, the junior of the footmen at Mrs. Brereton's, entered and announced that Miss Tolerance had a caller.

"Here?"

"Aye, miss. I put him in the little salon, as it's unoccupied just now."

"Did the caller give a name?"

"Colcannon, miss. Matter of business, the gentleman said. Very agitated."

The effect of this intelligence upon Miss Tolerance was considerable. Curiosity and the hope of occupation energized her: Colcannon was the name of the young man whose finances she had investigated a fortnight before. So this was either the young man himself, or a member of his family. What reason could he have for calling? And why call at Mrs. Brereton's, when she kept up her membership at Tarsio's specifically to have an address to which inquiries could be directed.

Whatever the reason, she had no intention of talking to her visitor under her aunt's eye or in her aunt's house. This meant she must walk him to Tarsio's—or take him through the garden to her cottage, a place which she generally tried to keep free of business.

"I will be down directly, Cole." Miss Tolerance made a curtsy to her aunt and begged her leave.

"By all means, my dear." Mrs. Brereton, turning her cheek to receive her niece's kiss, was already reaching for the *Gazette*.

M r. Colcannon was a man of about Miss Tolerance's own age of eight and twenty, bandy-legged and stocky, as if he were not unacquainted with physical effort. He was neatly dressed in riding coat, buckskin breeches and plain-topped boots, all well made but none modish; his brown hair was worn longer than the fashion; his long, flat cheeks were as rosy as if he had just come from a brisk ride. Country-bred, Miss Tolerance knew from her investigation, and without any Town-polish to speak of. He jumped to his feet when Miss Tolerance entered the room, clearly anxious, and uncertain of what to expect.

Miss Tolerance dropped a curtsy; Mr. Colcannon bowed.

"I beg your pardon for coming unexpected," he said. "You are Miss Sarah Tolerance? I was told I would find you here—but this is not—that is—" He looked around the small room a bit wildly. "Perhaps I have—"

"Mr. Colcannon, if we have business to discuss, we will both be more comfortable speaking in my little house across the garden. Will you follow me, sir?" Miss Tolerance smiled and turned to lead the man to the conservatory at the rear of the house, thence across the garden to the door of her cottage. Mr. Colcannon had the appearance of one already bewildered, now grappling with a further confusion.

"You are—I was given to believe—" he stopped. "That is, I did not know you were a part of a . . ."

A mischievous impulse took Miss Tolerance. "You did not know you had been referred to a *pushing academy*, sir?" She used the vulgar expression deliberately to shock, hoping that with the worst out of the way Mr. Colcannon would speak more rationally, but she smiled kindly as she took the key from her pocket and opened the door to her tiny cottage.

Colcannon blushed. He nodded. "Perhaps this was someone's idea of a joke," he said. He followed Miss Tolerance into the cottage and looked about him, blinking. There was little enough to see: a table and several straight-back chairs, a settle on one side of the fireplace, the fireplace itself, walled in old Dutch tiles, and a cupboard of dark old wood. There were shelves on two walls that held an assortment of books and papers, and a second cupboard under the window opposite the fireplace. Candlesticks were grouped atop each cupboard; on the one next to the fireplace a small neat stack of dishes also stood. At the back of the room a narrow stair led to a chamber above.

Miss Tolerance's visitor recalled himself.

"You see me somewhat confounded," he said. "I was given the address of—that *bagnio*—and told that I might find a Miss Tolerance there, who was accustomed to make inquiries of a confidential nature. Perhaps it was naive of me, but it never occurred to me that you would be a—"

"A whore, sir?"

Colcannon nodded.

"Please rest your mind upon that point; I am Fallen and I keep this little house here because it is convenient for me, but I am not one of Mrs. Brereton's employees. I generally meet prospective clients at Tarsio's club, where I am a member—"

"Should I have gone there? I am sorry if I did this improperly, Miss Tolerance, but my business is very urgent. The man who sent me to you—"

"Who would that be, sir?"

"Mr. Gregory Wheelock."

"And what *did* Mr. Wheelock tell you about me, sir?"

"That you undertook investigation for a fee, that he had used you and found you reliable and discreet—more discreet then those men who advertise themselves as thief-takers might be. That you might be willing to, that is, that you, but I don't imagine—" Colcannon seemed in danger of lapsing into complete incoherence. Miss Tolerance rescued him.

"In what way may I be of assistance, Mr. Colcannon?"

Colcannon at last sat opposite Miss Tolerance upon the settle. The afternoon light from the window lit his face as he leaned forward to confide in her.

"It is murder, Miss Tolerance."

Miss Tolerance hid her surprise in an expression of polite interest. "Murder done, sir, or murder to be done?"

"Murder done, ma'am," Colcannon said. Then, as he realized
what she had asked, he sat back shocked. "You do not think I want
you to kill someone?"

"Not at all, sir. Perhaps it was the dramatic way in which you
spoke which startled me into imprudent speech. Even when the
matter *is* murder," she added, "it is more useful to me to hear the
tale without flourishes."

Colcannon nodded seriously, then sat regarding Miss Tolerance. After a few seconds he put his head in his hands and began
to rub his forehead, as if he could scrub away his troubles. Miss
Tolerance found herself growing impatient, and prodded him.

"So, there has been murder done, Mr. Colcannon? Might I ask
how it involves you?"

Colcannon was shocked. "I am not involved, Miss Tolerance.
How could you—"

Miss Tolerance spoke very gently. "Mr. Colcannon, will you
start at the beginning of your tale and proceed direct to the end? I
will save my questions until later, if you will save your agitation
and scruples. If I do not apprehend the matter I will be useless to
you. Please tell me what has happened."

"Do you not read the papers? The Chevalier Etienne
d'Aubigny, killed in his bed four days ago."

The last time Miss Tolerance had opened the *Times* had been
more than a week earlier. She had found the news depressingly
full of the Queen Regent's illness, reverses in the Peninsular cam-
paign, and the latest brangle in Parliament over the Duke of Cumberland's War Support Bill. Yet the name d'Aubigny was familiar
to her. A second's more thought and she had it.

"D'Aubigny is—was—married to your sister, I collect. That is
how you come to be concerned. Permit me to condole with you,
sir."

Colcannon nodded.

"Can you tell me the particulars? And may I offer you some refreshment?" Colcannon did not reply, but watched dumbly as Miss
Tolerance got out two glasses and poured a small amount of Jerez
wine into each. He tossed his back at a gulp and began his story.

"My sister Anne married the chevalier four years ago. He is the son of an excellent old French family of the *ancien regime*, quite important in France before the revolution. His family—an uncle and his mother and d'Aubigny himself—escaped and came to England when he was a boy. Here his prospects were quite different, of course. But he was educated in England, and his uncle had some influential friends. He was regarded as a promising man. And there was always the chance that, given the successful conclusion of the war, he might come into significant property in France. I tell you all this so you will understand that my sister was flattered when he began to particularize his interest with her. D'Aubigny's fortune had been lost in France, but there was nothing to suggest that he would not make his way in the world. His friends secured him a post in the government, and he still had the title. My father was alive then; he liked the match, and so did Anne. The settlements were made and the wedding celebrated."

"My felicitations. When did your family discover that they were mistaken in d'Aubigny?"

Colcannon frowned. "I never said—"

"Sir, when someone goes to such trouble to make it clear why a suitor was agreeable to his family, it suggests that there is bad news to come. Was the marriage not a happy one?"

"We thought it would be. Even a man who marries for money may make a good husband. But after a time . . ."

"The chevalier showed a different set of colors."

Colcannon nodded. His lips pressed together in a thin line.

"His death was then a release for your sister?" Miss Tolerance suggested sympathetically.

"Release? Had he fallen from his horse or died of a fever, even numbered among the casualties in the Dueling Notices, I should agree, Miss Tolerance. But he was beaten to death in his own bed and left among the bloody sheets for anyone to find. You may imagine how fearfully this has overset my sister—her nerves are not strong. Somehow someone gained entry to my sister's house and did this monstrous thing—and who knows but that they might not come back and serve her the same way?"

Miss Tolerance considered. "Is there any reason your sister should fear such a thing, sir?"

"A reason? You mean threats against her? No, who would threaten Anne? But such a murder is beyond reason; what might such a madman do? If the villain did not get what he wanted on his first visit he will surely come back again."

"The murder was a robbery also?" Miss Tolerance asked. "What was taken?"

Colcannon blinked. "I don't know that anything *was* taken. But the threat—"

"Your sister should hire guards for her house. Or you might hire them for her."

"And tell my sister she must live like a captive in her own house? While she is in mourning? And the authorities, the magistrate and his constables, make free of the house in their investigation, in and out with barely a by-your-leave, bullying the servants. Imagine how such people would rub along with hired guards! I must tell you, Miss Tolerance, I have only the smallest reliance that Bow Street will find the culprit in this killing, and until the murderer is found, how can my sister—indeed, how can anyone in the neighborhood—sleep sound at night?"

Miss Tolerance observed the man before her. He was plainly in earnest despite his overwrought expression. She thought back to what she knew of him: the only son, he had come into his fortune upon the death of his father three years before. He had, as she had told Mr. Wheelock, extensive estates which he managed well, and realized a fine income from them. And he was older than his sister, and had probably been taught that she was a fragile blossom in need of his protection. Whether Anne d'Aubigny was fragile or not remained to be seen, but clearly Colcannon was distressed by his sister's situation.

"Why do you place so little reliance upon Bow Street, sir? Some of the Runners are not genteel fellows; it is not a genteel calling. Yet it is, in the main, as honest and efficient an organization as you are like to find for the purpose in all Europe."

"I told you this seemed to me the work of a madman, Miss Tolerance. Can plodding effort hope to catch such a villain?"

"It may well—certainly better than no effort at all. But are you sure your brother-in-law had stirred up the enmity of a madman, sir? Are there no other reasons why he might have been slain?"

Colcannon considered. By his expression Miss Tolerance deduced that he was weighing his answer carefully.

"He was French," he said at last.

Miss Tolerance judged this a bad time to laugh. "There are a good number of émigrés in London, sir. Since most are not murdered in their beds, I cannot believe mere nationality is sufficient cause for so difficult and deliberate an assassination. And if the murderer was simply a madman who targeted Frenchmen in their beds, your sister is English-born and thus not in danger."

"Yes. I suppose you are right. It is neatly reasoned." Mr. Colcannon cocked his head and regarded Miss Tolerance anew. "I had wondered—that is, when I realized what this place was, I thought perhaps Mr. Wheelock had jested when he sent me here. Even before that, when he suggested I consult you. How could a woman do—provide—that is, the delicacy of your sex must surely constrain you in—"

Miss Tolerance, fearful that Colcannon would knit himself into such a frenzy of circumlocution that he would never reach the end of his sentence, spoke bluntly. "First, sir: *this* place is my house. I do not live in the brothel yonder, and while I am Fallen, I am not a prostitute. As for the rest, I have some skills which are uncommon for my sex, and a good deal of natural female curiosity. And I have a powerful need to earn my bread, preferably without becoming a whore myself." Colcannon was blushing again. She took a little pity on the man. "I could reassure you more fully if I understood the nature of the work you wish me to undertake."

"I want my sister safe, ma'am."

"I understand, sir. But safe from whom? If you think your sister is threatened, surely you'd do better to hire guards for her house."

"But for how long? Until Bow Street find the killer or decide they have looked long enough? What then? I want someone to find the killer, ma'am. Surely that is the only way to ensure my sister's safety and give her some peace."

Miss Tolerance sat back, turning her wineglass between her fingers. This was not her usual sort of commission.

"Did Mr. Wheelock give you to believe that such a task is within my abilities, sir?" she asked at last.

"Indeed he did. He said you'd had a notable success in the business of the Earl of Versellion—"

Miss Tolerance pursed her lips. "I set out to find a trinket in that case, sir, not a killer."

"But you found him, did you not?"

"I did." *At some cost to myself.* "But surely, sir, this matter is better left to the authorities?"

"I have already said, ma'am, that I place little reliance upon them. The constables—a pair of sordid brutes, looking to terrify my sister's servants! And the magistrate in charge seemed little better, bullying my sister as if she were a chambermaid. I tell you, Miss Tolerance, the man may be well-enough meaning, but he has no notion of how to proceed, other than scaring poor Anne."

"And you believe I would have better luck?"

"Mr. Wheelock said you performed quite thoroughly the task he gave you," Mr. Colcannon said. "Miss Tolerance, someone killed the Chevalier d'Aubigny. He moved in a number of circles, not confined to his own class. He was an émigré. He had a weakness for a certain class of female." He glanced toward the window through which Mrs. Brereton's house could be seen. "I need someone who can talk to Anne without scaring her to distraction, *and* to the sorts of people her husband was often among, and that Mr. Wheelock says you can do. I beg you, ma'am. Help my sister." He leaned forward again, extending his hand as if to take Miss Tolerance's own. She folded her hands in her lap, misliking the gesture.

"Mr. Colcannon, has it occurred to you that in seeking the killer I may unearth information that you and your sister would prefer to keep hidden? I do not bandy my clients' secrets about, sir, but it can happen that in the course of so serious an investigation secrets may come out. Will it suit you to have it so, if the killer is caught?"

"Whatever secrets you unearth could only be d'Aubigny's—I believe my sister is beyond being hurt by anything her husband did."

"You have not answered my question, sir."

Colcannon said, with a little stiffness, "You will follow your conscience. I would not expect you to do else."

Miss Tolerance nodded, but thought he still did not fully appreciate what he was promising. She came to a decision: she needed occupation, and this was certain to keep her busy.

"I will need, first of all, to see your sister's house, and to speak with her."

"I will go straightaway and tell her to expect you. When?"

"Tomorrow in the morning, if that is convenient. But we have not discussed my fee, sir."

Colcannon looked surprised.

"Would you not rather know beforehand? I charge three guineas a day, plus reasonable expenses, which I will detail for you."

The man shrugged off the figures as if they were unimportant. "Do you require earnest money or an advance?"

Miss Tolerance was tempted, but had found in the past that advance payment seemed to license her clients to plague her for details, impeding investigation with their inquiries into what she had done and what she was still to do.

"We will agree to trust each other, sir. If I find my expenses are high and I need replenishment, I will inform you." She stood and offered her hand. "You will tell your sister I will call upon her tomorrow at about eleven in the morning?"

Colcannon rose to his feet. He was only a little taller than Miss Tolerance, and looked directly into her eyes. "I cannot thank you enough, Miss Tolerance. I feel better in my mind already."

Miss Tolerance said something polite about hoping to justify his trust in her, and walked the gentleman through the garden to the gate which let onto Spanish Place. Colcannon repeated his thanks and bowed over her hand. Miss Tolerance curtseyed, said her farewells, then locked the gate behind him.

He had not told her the whole, she thought. Indeed, he had told her very little other than that his sister's marriage was unhappy and that he did not like the Bow Street officials set to investigate the case. Miss Tolerance had found that in general it was useless to implore her clients to tell her everything material to an assignment. They would withhold information, either from fear of embarrassment, a poor understanding of what the facts were, or because habits of secrecy (to call it nothing worse) impelled them to do so until it had been demonstrated to them that without truth she could accomplish little material good. She was not alarmed but intrigued by her sense that there were evasions and holes in Mr. Colcannon's narrative; the pattern of what he did not tell might prove more revealing than the information itself. And while holding back the truth now was likely to cost Colcannon more in terms of time and money, that, to Miss Tolerance's way of thinking, was simple justice.

Three

It was Miss Tolerance's experience that the virtuous women with whom she dealt treated her most often with stiff politeness. They were willing to avail themselves of Miss Tolerance's services but reluctant to expose themselves either to the contagion of her Fall or to the possibility that a husband or son would fall prey to her supposed enticements. Such women generally offered her commonplace tasks: follow an erring husband, redeem a bauble lost at play, catch a servant suspected of pilfering. These were all relatively minor chores which required little contact between employer and agent.

Never before had Miss Tolerance had to face a woman with the advantages of birth, breeding, and money in a role so like to become adversarial. But to parse murder, and so sudden and awful a murder, she would surely need to know the closest secrets of Anne d'Aubigny's marriage. Miss Tolerance woke in the morning wondering how best to persuade the Widow d'Aubigny to take one of the Fallen into her confidence. In the end she left matters to the silent persuasion of a well-made dress and impeccable boots.

The day was gray and drizzling, with a seeping chill. It was fortunate that Miss Tolerance's most respectable costume was warm: a walking dress of severely cut gray-blue twill, fur-collared coat, and neat half boots. Her long, dark hair she pinned up under a hat of moderate size and severe propriety. She looked like that which her upbringing had fitted her to be: Anne d'Aubigny's equal, a young matron of means, on the middle rungs of society, making a morning call. Shortly before her appointed hour she took up her reticule and asked Keefe to hail a hackney carriage for her.

The house of the late Chevalier d'Aubigny was located in Half Moon Street. The street around the house was thick with people of all conditions, despite the November cold; most of them appeared to have no business save to stand and gawk at the d'Aubigny house. If, as Miss Tolerance suspected, they hoped to find the lurid characters of crime writ upon the face of the house, they were disappointed. It was a small, pleasant old building of pink brick; the knocker had been taken down, and the crepe hung around the door bespoke everything respectable grief demanded. Miss Tolerance detected shabbiness in the matter of paint, but the brass was well polished.

She made her way through the crowd, knocked at the door, and presented her card, upon the back of which she had written a brief note to explain the purpose of her call. When the elderly manservant who took the card stood back to let her in there was a groan of protest from the crowd in the street: why did she gain entry to the murder house when they could not? The servant closed the door behind Miss Tolerance, sealing out the noise, and led her to the rear of the house and a small, neat sitting room. As she waited, Miss Tolerance noted further signs she ascribed to financial hardship: open spaces among the china figures on the mantel, and unfaded squares of the striped paper on the wall which had only lately been exposed to the sun. Ornaments and paintings had been removed and sold.

She became aware of voices from the hallway upstairs. Miss Tolerance heard first the rumble of a masculine voice, likely that of the manservant who had taken her card. A woman's voice, soft and high, answered; then another woman's voice, lower in pitch, broke in. They spoke for a few minutes more: there was no possibility of overhearing their words, but Miss Tolerance noted the tone and pondered the state of the d'Aubigny household.

"Miss Tolerance?" A woman stood in the doorway. She wore a

plain dress of dark gray stuff, and her hair was pulled back in an unadorned knot. There was so little pretense to fashion that Miss Tolerance wondered whether she had aimed to produce such a drab impression. She had a pleasant heart-shaped face with large gray eyes, a good figure, and a bearing which Miss Tolerance characterized as businesslike. Her age was perhaps a few years short of Miss Tolerance's own.

"I am sorry to have kept you waiting," the woman said. Hers was the lower of the two voices Miss Tolerance had overheard. It was difficult to tell where she had been raised: she appeared to have trained regional peculiarity from her speech, but did not affect the singular accent of a well-bred London dweller. "I am Mrs. Vose. I am lending Mrs. d'Aubigny company in this hard time."

Miss Tolerance returned Mrs. Vose's curtsy. "I hope Mrs. d'Aubigny will be able to spare me a few minutes. Her brother asked me to call—"

"It is very thoughtful of *madame's* brother, but I regret that she is unable to see anyone at this present moment. The shock and grief, you understand, have quite undone her."

"Indeed," Miss Tolerance said. "I wonder, then, if I might speak with the servants who were here on the night of—of the death."

Mrs. Vose appeared surprised. "Speak to the servants? Whatever for?" Her expression, which had been open and courteous a moment before, sharpened.

"Was Mrs. d'Aubigny not informed that I have been engaged to investigate the circumstances of the chevalier's death?"

Had Miss Tolerance announced that she had been hired to fly three times widdershins around the moon in a sewing basket, Mrs. Vose could not have appeared more thunderstruck.

"Investigate?" She looked Miss Tolerance up and down with deliberate rudeness. "What sort of fairy tale is this?"

"I assure you, Mrs. Vose, it is no fairy tale. I take it that Mr. Colcannon—"

Mrs. Vose interrupted. "You present a creditable imitation of a lady, but I apprehend now that you are some sort of adventuress. I cannot imagine what sort of advantage you think to gain from the unfortunate circumstance of the chevalier's death, nor how you persuaded Beak to let you enter. But I will ask you to leave now—"

Short of an incivility which might damage her ability to press further under Mr. Colcannon's authority, Miss Tolerance could not force Mrs. Vose to produce Anne d'Aubigny. She rose to her feet and took up her reticule. "I understand your reluctance, ma'am. When Mr. Colcannon has spoken with his sister I will return. He fears for her safety, and wishes the murderer caught as soon—"

Mrs. Vose sniffed. "Caught by a woman? Are you what they call a thief-taker?"

"*I* do not call myself a thief-taker," Miss Tolerance said coolly. "Say rather that I am accustomed to investigate privately such matters as my clients prefer are handled with discretion. I will return tomorrow and hope that Mr. Colcannon has convinced his sister of my earnest intent to assist her."

"You will find the answer no different tomorrow." Mrs. Vose pressed against the wall as Miss Tolerance passed, as if unwilling that so much as the hem of her gray dress should brush against the wool stuff of Miss Tolerance's own. The same man who had admitted Miss Tolerance appeared before her in the hallway and escorted her to the door with arctic authority, rather as if, she reflected, he suspected her of carrying off a silver spoon in her pocket.

Miss Tolerance took her leave thoughtfully.

The crowd outside the house was no smaller, and she suspected that many of them were examining her to see if the horrid glamour of murder had rubbed off upon her clothing or her person. She made her way through the crowd and walked for several streets, until she found herself in front of Tarsio's club, on Henry Street. Tea was what she needed, both to cut through the pervasive chill of the sunless afternoon and as an aid to organizing her thoughts.

Miss Tolerance was greeted at the door and admitted to the club by Steen, the hall porter. She and Steen were old friends, his amity ensured by her willingness to tip well for business steered her way. They exchanged the usual commonplaces about the November chill, and Steen offered the intelligence that there were several messages waiting for her at the desk. Miss Tolerance collected her messages and made her way to the Ladies' Parlor, on the first floor, where she ordered refreshment and found an empty writing desk. She wrote a note to Mr. Colcannon, explaining the result of her visit to Half Moon Street, and urging him, if he wished her to continue with her investigation, to convince his sister to cooperate. She also inquired about Mrs. Vose; that lady had inspired considerable curiosity in Miss Tolerance. Who was she, in what capacity did she occupy the household, and why was she so determined that Miss Tolerance must be chased away? For it seemed to Miss Tolerance that Mrs. Vose's outrage at her visit was not true ware but had been manufactured in order to make the visitor leave.

It was difficult to explain precisely why Miss Tolerance was certain of this. It was, of course, possible that Mr. Colcannon had neglected to prepare his sister for Miss Tolerance's visit; that would explain Mrs. Vose's manner to her. But as Colcannon had seemed so insistent upon the urgency of the matter this seemed to Miss Tolerance in the highest degree unlikely. Imagine, then, that a note communicating Miss Tolerance's investigation had, in fact, arrived and been read. Mrs. Vose might have been protecting the widow from an interview she believed would distress her, or from contact with a woman of damaged virtue. Why did Miss Tolerance doubt this was so?

She could not derive information from the conversation she had not quite overheard. Was it possible that Mrs. d'Aubigny had wished to speak to Miss Tolerance and Mrs. Vose had prevented it? Or that Mrs. d'Aubigny had dispatched Mrs. Vose a-purpose to send her visitor away?

The arrival of tea and a plate of biscuits put a temporary stop to these musings.

Miss Tolerance sent off her note to Mr. Colcannon's address and put her feet up, enjoying the warmth and smoky taste of her tea. She had been sitting so for perhaps half an hour when, hearing her name spoken, she looked up and saw Sir Walter Mandif in the doorway of the Ladies' Parlor, awaiting her invitation to join him. She rose and greeted her friend.

"But this is delightful! I had thought you away in the North. Will you take tea or a glass of wine?"

Sir Walter disdained tea in favor of something stronger, and Miss Tolerance gave orders for a bottle of claret, glasses, and another plate of biscuits to be brought at once.

"The shooting was poor, and there was too much business here for me to be absent long," he told her. "Would you believe me if I said I was homesick for London and my work?" His long, narrow face lit with a lopsided smile, as if quizzing himself as much as his auditor. He was a slight man, of no more than middle height, light-haired and fair, with a shrewd expression which emphasized his resemblance to a neatly turned-out fox. His dress, like his manner, was everything gentlemanly without ostentatious flourish.

"I would believe you have no gift for idleness," Miss Tolerance said. "But is there really so much business at this season?"

Sir Walter nodded. "The pickpockets and cracksmen of London do not take a holiday because I do."

"And yet I was told by my aunt's footman that her business was slower at this season."

"Two different classes of business, I think. Two very different classes of business, Miss Tolerance. The men who frequent Mrs. Brereton's are hardly like to be the same ones who are picking pockets on the Strand or staving in heads behind St. Paul's."

"Of course they are not, but they are the natural prey of those who pick pockets and stave heads, are they not?" Miss Tolerance took a sip of her wine. "On whom do they prey when the well-lined gentleman's wallet goes north for the grouse shooting?"

"Each other, of course. I beg your pardon; my profession makes a cynic of me. How have things been with you?" Sir Walter extended his boots toward the warmth of the fire. "Even at this season I imagine you are hard at work."

"I am, sir, but why did you think so?"

Sir Walter smiled. "Not much has changed in my absence: England is still warring with Bonaparte, the Queen is no nearer or farther from Death's door than she had been last summer, and man continues to mistreat his fellow man. That last should provide both of us with occupation."

Miss Tolerance agreed. "It puts us both in a horrid position, does it not, Sir Walter? How often do our livelihoods depend upon the misery our fellow man?"

"Indeed. Not even the West End has avoided violence of late. Even in Rutland the news of that murder penetrated. Indeed, the *Post* screamed of it; the *Times* was fairly restrained, but as the victim held a government post—"

Miss Tolerance nodded but did not immediately disclose her involvement with the d'Aubigny murder. She was curious to hear what Sir Walter had to say.

"—and as the murder comes so hard upon the heels of that business of Cumberland and Sellis in August—"

"Surely you do not think there is a connection?" The attempted assassination of a royal duke by his Corsican valet, who, when foiled, had fled, only to be discovered a suicide in his own chamber, seemed a markedly different affair from the murder of the Chevalier d'Aubigny.

"I suppose it's only the similarity of their being attacked in their beds that brings it to mind. But it has the public on edge. Gentlemen, to say nothing of royal dukes, are *not* supposed to be assassinated as they sleep. And when the public are on edge you may readily imagine that the magistracy hears of it."

"I can indeed." Privily, Miss Tolerance resolved to inquire about the movements of the Chevalier d'Aubigny's valet on the night of the murder. "Are you much involved in the case?"

"I? No, Bow Street was not called. The Great Marlborough Street Public Office has jurisdiction. I believe Heddison is the magistrate in charge. His constables are making inquiries."

There was something—no more than a pursing of the lips as he spoke the name Heddison—which suggested to Miss Tolerance that her friend Sir Walter did not place his whole confidence in the abilities either of Mr. Heddison or of the men who worked for him.

"Is an announcement to be expected soon?" she asked.

"It would be a fine thing. The coroner's inquest brought a verdict of willful murder but could not fix upon a culprit." Sir Walter raised his eyes from the fire to meet Miss Tolerance's own. He smiled, again lopsidedly. "The *Times* should have a report of it today."

"You will forgive me if I say that you sound . . . doubtful of progress. Is the case so difficult?"

"I have only the slightest acquaintance with the case," Sir Walter said. He pursed his lips, but this time he spoke further. "Heddison is a hardworking man, and I believe he is honest. But he has little imagination and a certain inflexibility of mind. I am not certain he has the mettle to solve such a case as this. And one of his constables is a man I should not like to have in *my* employ."

Miss Tolerance considered the constables who worked with Sir Walter to be as dubious a pair as could possibly be employed in the service of the Crown. To learn that there were constables who were still more dubious made her mind reel.

But Sir Walter was regretting his candor. "I should not speak so of officers of the law! Is it not shocking how completely a good fire and a sympathetic ear makes me cast caution to the wind?"

Miss Tolerance understood from this that she was not to make further mention of Sir Walter's reservations.

"I do not envy Heddison the case. Whatever he does is like to offend someone. My own business has been of the most pedestrian sort: pickpockets and cracksmen, as I said. A good deal of business, but not invigorating. What sort of work have you now? Did you defeat the blackmailer you told me of the last time we met?

"Oh, Lord yes!" Miss Tolerance had barely given Mr. Waldegreen's problem a thought after she had received her payment. "In truth I have been sadly idle for days. Look where you find me, dozing over the fire!"

"Idleness clearly becomes you," Sir Walter said gallantly.

Miss Tolerance frowned.

He apologized. "Would you prefer that I speak of nothing but crime and politics? I was concerned for you when I left Town. You have been working very hard, perhaps too hard. I am happy to see you with a little more animation."

Miss Tolerance flushed. Her first thought was to reject this very mild expression of concern; her second, that to do so would be churlish. "If I am more animated it is because I have work to do. If you had seen me in a state of idleness you would not be impressed. Indeed, I do not mean to be uncivil. I am out of the habit of having people fret over me."

"And I do not wish to burden you with my concern. Only that—no, I shall stop now. I would not make you the recipient of attention which is unwelcome to you."

"Not unwelcome, from a friend. But unaccustomed. And I hate that anyone would ever think there was something amiss with me."

"Oh, as for that," Sir Walter said carefully, "I suspect something has been amiss with you for some time. Since the trial of the Earl of Versellion, perhaps even from the night of his arrest."

Miss Tolerance studied her wine. "That was nearly a six-month ago. What could give you such an idea, sir?"

"When we met, there was a—a light in you that the events of Versellion's arrest left much dimmed. The trial could not but have given you pain. You have suffered a high cost for doing what was right. Testifying against—" He faltered.

"Testifying against my lover? I testified against Versellion because he had murdered an old woman. No amount of affection could excuse that. I gave my testimony and the jury their verdict. The matter is done. I must endeavor to forget it."

"I do not think you are so hard of heart," Sir Walter said.

"I cannot afford to be less so," Miss Tolerance replied. "I have my living to earn. Versellion . . . may I be frank, Sir Walter? After Connell died, I kept myself very guarded. I ought to have continued so. Of all men, why I allowed Versellion—"

"What, a man known for all those qualities best calculated to appeal to a woman of discernment: good looks, position, intelligence, charm—"

"A politician." Miss Tolerance spoke the word with distaste. "Bred to preserve his power at any cost."

Sir Walter examined his wine glass with interest, then took up the bottle and poured out the last of the claret. "You seem intent to doubt your own judgment. I must point out that in order to punish yourself you are painting Versellion more darkly than he deserves. Your own testimony secured his transportation. And as I believe that your relationship with him had begun some time before he committed the crime, how are you to be blamed?"

Miss Tolerance shrugged and smiled again, quite unconvincingly.

"You gave your testimony. I hope you will not continue to punish yourself," Sir Walter said. There was a little silence between them. Then he persisted. "I have spoken more freely than I ought, perhaps. I hope you will forgive it as the sincere concern of a friend. I should like to see that light I spoke of kindled again. But if you like, we will speak of it no further—except, you know, that if there is any way in which I may assist you—my friendship is very real."

A flush of feeling, compounded of gratitude and several other emotions less readily identified, swept Miss Tolerance. For a few moments she said nothing, striving to master the sudden constriction in her throat. She coughed, then raised her glass to him.

"Thank you, Sir Walter. That, at least, is a happy consequence."

They drank in silence broken only by the snap of the fire.

Sir Walter did not stay above an hour at Tarsio's. They spoke of matters of no personal consequence: there was a new bootmaker in Jermyn Street; the Duke of Clarence's mistress Mrs. Jordan had returned to the stage again; the Queen Regent's health was slowly declining.

This last had been a matter of public anxiety since June, when the Queen had suffered an apoplectic stroke. As His Majesty the King had been entirely mad for twenty years, and was now blind, deaf and sickly as well, the Queen Regent's health crisis had precipitated the nation into a state of vehement debate. Who could the next regent be? The Prince of Wales had been removed from the succession; the Duke of York had died heroically at the siege of Valenciennes. The succession was not open to debate: the Duke of Clarence was heir apparent. But the regency was in Parliament's gift, and every man in the nation, and most women, had an opinion upon the subject. Clarence's domestic liaison with Mrs. Jordan had left him with a half-score of little FitzClarences and the reputation of a profligate. As commander of Gibralter the next prince, the Duke of Kent, had bullied the men under his command so mercilessly that they mutinied; he had sunk himself so low in public esteem that his name was suggested only to declare him impossible. The Duke of Cumberland, never a public favorite, had also been touched with scandal upon scandal; the attack upon his life in August was only the latest. In fact, of all the brothers, it was Wales, the darkest horse, whose name came most favorably to the public lip. The prince had been struck from the succession upon his marriage to the Catholic widow Maria Fitzherbert, but that marriage had apparently settled him, and with Mrs. Fitzherbert now ten years dead—and dead in the delivery of a living and legitimate son, too—there were rumors that a restoration of the succession might be possible. Wales had legitimate heirs; he had rather fewer blots on his character than his nearest surviving brothers; he had been profitably employed, since the death of his brother York, in establishing and encouraging the military colleges which had considerably improved the quality and effectiveness of the army; and unlike Kent and Cumberland, he was believed to be neither too liberal nor too conservative.

Miss Tolerance amused Sir Walter with the thought that if Queen Charlotte really did recover, the careful plotting of politicians on both sides of the aisle would be thrown into disarray.

"You seem to relish the idea for its own sake."

"You know how little love I have for politicians."

"Then I must be glad I am a mere magistrate," Sir Walter said. "And a magistrate who must leave this pleasant company and return to his work." He rose and took his leave, and Miss Tolerance called for the *Times*.

As Sir Walter had suggested, there was indeed a report on the Coroner's Inquest upon the death of the Chevalier d'Aubigny. The witnesses were few; the first to be called was James Wandle, the surgeon who had observed the corpse.

"The chevalier had numerous bruises about the shoulders and neck, but principally upon the head, where he had been struck by some heavy object with such force that the bones of the skull had been shattered. I cannot tell which blow fell first, but from the absence of bruises arguing self-defense—that is, no apparent blows to the hands or arms—we may conjecture that the first blow or blows were to the head. The left parietal bone and the nose and left cheekbone had been smashed almost beyond recognition, with a concomitant loss of brain matter. The object with which these blows were struck would appear to be heavy and with a dull edge. It was not a blade. There is no evidence of any other wounds than those

*mentioned, nor of asphyxiation. The blows to the head would have
been sufficient to cause death."*

Miss Tolerance, finding herself unpleasantly affected by this dry
explication of horror, asked a waiter to bring in fresh tea. She read
onward. The statement of the officer of the watch was short and
businesslike, and suggested nothing of much use to Miss Tolerance;
he had been summoned, arrived, and found the man dead, whereat
he sent a message to Bow Street at once. He had not, apparently,
thought to examine the premises or the victim, whose appearance
"made me come over all faint." It was Miss Tolerance's surmise that
the officer, like most of his sort, was an elderly pensioner, half-blind
and half-drunk, and therefore of very little use. She read on to the
statement of Mary Pitt, the maid who had first found the body.

*"I went about as usual, lighting first the fires in mistress's room,
then the little salon downstairs, then back up to the master's room.
It was then about seven in the morning. Master didn't like to have
the fire lit early, for he was often out late, nor he didn't like waking
to a cold room. I went in quietly. I went straight to my work and
swept out the fireplace and laid the fire new. I had just catched the
fire and turned to leave when I saw it."* Here the witness began to
weep, but when asked if she wished to return later, she refused,
stating that she preferred to have the business done with at once.
*"First I saw that one of the bed curtains was all upon the floor. I
thought there would be a great to-do about that. Then I saw there
was spots on it, of blood. I felt near to swooning, and screamed, and
ran out of the room. Mr. Beak [the manservant] found me screaming
and went to look what had happened. Yes, I saw the master on the
bed. He was all over blood, most of it on his pillow under his head,
where there was great gashes, and brains all in the hair—"* Here the
witness was again overcome, and was excused by the coroner.

As well she might be, Miss Tolerance thought. She read the final testimony, from the footman, Adolphus Beak.

*"I was in the pantry laying out the breakfast plate when I heard
screaming. I went at once upstairs, and found Mary Pitt, almost*

*insensible, in the hallway a little way from Mr. d'Aubigny's room.
It was at first not apparent what had caused her distress, but when
I made out that some harm had come to Mr. d'Aubigny I went at
once to his room. I found the bed curtains much disarranged, with
one of them lying on the floor smirched with blood. Mr. d'Aubigny
lay in his sheets, much bloodied. He wore his nightgown; the
nightcap still clung about his head. I approached near enough to
the bed to see that he was not alive. I then ran from the room and
called to Peter Jacks, the underfootman, to fetch the officer of the
watch. I summoned Mrs. Sadgett [the cook] to assist Pitt, who was
still much affected by her discovery. When the officer of the watch
arrived I brought him to Mr. d'Aubigny's chamber. The doors were
always kept locked at night, after Mr. d'Aubigny had returned for
the evening. Most nights he returned before one in the morning.
On the night before the murder he came home by eleven, and the
house was locked up then. The doors were locked in the morning,
which I know in consequence of Jacks having to throw the bolt in
order to leave the house and fetch the watch."*

The coroner was reported to have thanked all the witnesses for
their time and cooperation in recalling an event so obviously distressing. The jury was charged and adjourned, and in short order
had returned a verdict of willful murder against a person or persons unknown, the obvious conclusion under the circumstances.
Still, the reports left Miss Tolerance with more questions than answers. The single most striking one, to her mind, was this: why, in
the testimony of these witnesses, was there no mention at all of
summoning to the site of the murder the person most closely connected to the chevalier: his wife, Anne d'Aubigny?

Four

William Colcannon called the next morning to escort Miss Tolerance to Half Moon Street personally. He apologized half a dozen times to her as they made their way to the d'Aubigny house, and wondered aloud who Mrs. Vose was. This struck Miss Tolerance as odd: the woman had seemed fully at home in the d'Aubigny household; the servants had evidently taken her word as law. How should the widow's brother not know Mrs. Vose?

"Were you not in the habit of visiting your sister, sir?"

They walked along Duke Street, which at this hour was thick with tradesmen seeking out the service entries of the great houses to which they brought food, flowers, casks of ale, and cases of wine and sundries. Miss Tolerance let herself seem to be watching a pair of carters carry a pianoforte, but observed her companion closely.

Mr. Colcannon flushed.

"I did not—that is, I am so much in the country, Miss Tolerance. It was not always convenient to visit."

Miss Tolerance nodded. "But you and your sister are on comfortable terms?"

"We are on most affectionate terms, ma'am." His tone was just short of protest.

"And you and your brother-at-law?"

Colcannon colored yet more deeply. "He and I—were not friends, if that is what you mean."

"You will pardon me if I ask why, sir?"

"I did not like his treatment of my sister," Colcannon said. "I know one cannot interfere between a man and wife, but it made it damned uncomfortable to visit and see Anne—" He broke off, his eyes focused on some scene in his mind.

"She was unhappy? What did the chevalier do to cause her unhappiness?"

"What did he not?" Colcannon said with bitterness. "You know, at the first their marriage seemed promising. It took nearly a year for d'Aubigny to change—"

"Change, or revert to previous behavior?"

Colcannon looked blank. "I cannot say. I did not know him before he married my sister. My father had inquiries made—"

"But they largely concerned his income and his prospects, I collect. Please go on."

"At first he seemed merely thoughtless, taking her for granted. Then he became discourteous, and in the last years, *brutal*. There is no other word for it. He humiliated her. He made fun of her country accent and how she ordered the household. If I took dinner with them he would mock what was served and what she wore and what she said—all in a tone which invited me to be scornful too. Anne told me if I tried to speak to him it would only make things worse. Finally I stayed away, Miss Tolerance. It is not to my credit—"

"But perhaps not to your discredit, either," she said.

"And there is worse." His voice dropped low. Miss Tolerance had to make an effort to hear him over the clamor of carriages and vendors around them. "When I visited her I saw—several times, I saw marks. Some on her wrists, twice on her neck: the marks of fingers, as if he'd held her down . . ." Colcannon paused to recover himself. "That was when I asked my solicitor what I might do to help my sister, but the answer was very little. Unless he beat her bloody on the steps of Parliament it is unlikely the law would have taken notice. And Anne would say nothing against him; she feared to do so, I think. He was the Devil to her."

An unpleasant idea had occurred to Miss Tolerance.

"Mr. Colcannon, had your sister any friend who might have shared your suspicions and, perhaps, taken steps to put an end to it?"

"Friend? Miss Tolerance, I don't believe my sister knows above a dozen people in the city. We grew up in Somerset; she married after a short season and set up housekeeping. She had very little time to forge friendships before her marriage, and I doubt she has done so since—" He stopped and turned to look at Miss Tolerance with dismay. "You do not use the word *friend* to mean a friendly acquaintance, I take it."

"I mean it in the sense of anyone who might feel strongly enough to take drastic action to help your sister, sir."

"You are asking if my sister had a lover."

Miss Tolerance maintained an attitude of polite inquiry.

"You have only to meet my sister to know the thing is quite out of the—"

"Mr. Colcannon, if the question could occur to me, you may be certain it will occur to Mr. Heddison and his constables. If you truly wish me to keep your sister safe you must be honest with me. You must trust me, as well, to keep anything I learn a secret. Might your sister have a friend who, even without her awareness, knew of her situation and thought to repair it?"

To his credit Mr. Colcannon appeared to weigh the sense of Miss Tolerance's words before he spoke. "I know of none," he said at last. "Indeed, when you have met my sister you will see how very unlikely such a thing is. It was d'Aubigny who . . . formed connections outside of his marriage. Nor were his liaisons discreet. He made certain all the world knew of them. My sister finally ceased to go into company to avoid the humiliation."

If that were so, Miss Tolerance reflected, the Widow d'Aubigny was more sensitive than half the wives in London. What had the girl expected, married for her fortune as she plainly had been? But was Colcannon aware of the motive his story suggested? There was no time to ask a question which would have doubtless offended her client: they had turned the corner into Half Moon Street, where the crowds were still jostling for a better view of the murder house. Indeed, as they approached the door they heard a heated conversation between the same manservant who had admitted Miss Tolerance the day before and a tall, flashily dressed man who stood on the step, waving his pocketbook about in a fashion she thought very ill advised.

"Only a little peek in the murder room," the man was insisting. "The lady wouldn't never know I been there."

The manservant rejected this plea with the air of one who has heard it before. He was firm, but as he recognized Mr. Colcannon he adopted an expression of more explicit outrage and rejected the offer again, more firmly. The thin man cast a bitter look at Mr. Colcannon and Miss Tolerance and turned on his heel, muttering that he had no doubt these 'uns would be admitted without payin' a shillin'.

Colcannon pushed past the gawker as if he were not there, greeted the servant by name (Beak, identified in the Coroner's Court as the chief manservant of the house) and started into the house. Beak admitted them, but not without giving Miss Tolerance a look of some disapproval. Again they were conducted to the room at the rear of the house, and Beak went to apprise the mistress of their visit.

In a few moments Anne d'Aubigny appeared at the door.

While brother and sister exclaimed over each other and embraced, Miss Tolerance observed the widow. She was a full head shorter than Miss Tolerance, fair and fine-boned. She lacked her brother's sturdy country manner and ruddy complexion, and might readily have been imagined the sister of the china figure on the table. The inky mourning she wore made the widow's skin look as sickish-white as parchment, and her eyes were pink as a rabbit's, presumably from crying. Miss Tolerance rose and curtsied.

"You called here yesterday," Mrs. d'Aubigny said. Hers was the first voice Miss Tolerance had heard the day before: tremulous and softly reproachful. Whom was she reproaching? "William?" The widow looked to Mr. Colcannon.

"Anne, may I present Miss Sarah Tolerance?"

Mrs. d'Aubigny bowed her head in a tiny acknowledgment, then turned to her brother and murmured something to him. From the rigidity of her carriage and Colcannon's red face, Miss

Tolerance thought Mrs. d'Aubigny was not pleased to find a Fallen Woman in her parlor.

Colcannon replied audibly. "I did not think of that, but indeed, it is exactly as she represented the matter yesterday. I am sorry if you dislike it, but I entreat you to speak with her. I think only of your safety—"

Miss Tolerance took pity on Colcannon's embarrassment.

"If I might speak a few words with you privately, I believe I can satisfy you as to my qualifications, ma'am. But I will first assure you that, whatever my status, I am not one of that professional sisterhood with whom I apprehend your husband was very familiar."

Anne d'Aubigny looked shocked. Miss Tolerance felt a moment of impatience, but kept her own expression studiously neutral. She waited. Mrs. d'Aubigny thought, then turned to her brother and said, "Willie, go away."

Colcannon left the room.

Mrs. d'Aubigny did not ask Miss Tolerance to sit. She stood just inside the door as if ready to run, waiting for an explanation she clearly did not believe would improve her opinion.

"You have a natural dislike of contact with that which is impure," Miss Tolerance began, "perhaps made greater by what your brother tells me was your husband's behavior. You must make up your mind to trust me, but I will tell you that, while I am indeed Fallen, I have never been a whore." Anne d'Aubigny flinched at the word. Miss Tolerance continued. "Indeed, I took up my profession to avoid being handed from man to man. I made what the world calls a mistake in whom I loved, ma'am. Perhaps I am wrong, but I imagine that mistake is one which might be familiar to you."

The widow twisted a handkerchief between her fingers. "What the world calls a mistake? You do not call it so?"

Miss Tolerance shrugged. "I know all the evils that attend a woman who has cast aside propriety for love. But there are many a man and woman joined by vows who have been less man and wife than . . . my seducer . . . and I."

"And yet you did not marry him."

"No, ma'am."

Anne d'Aubigny's frown deepened. "He had a wife?"

It was perhaps unreasonable of Miss Tolerance to resent this question. "I was not so lost to principle as that, even at sixteen! We eloped to the Continent, and marriage of a pair of English Protestants would have been difficult. But *he* was Catholic, which made the matter more complex, particularly because I did not want to be wed in the Catholic rite. It was the one quarrel we did not resolve before he died." The crux of the widow's objection occurred to her. "I can promise that I was not flaunted before a wife; I did to no woman what was done to you."

Mrs. d'Aubigny moved to the sofa and sat down. Tears stood in her eyes, and she appeared a little amazed.

"How could you know that?"

Miss Tolerance looked at the other woman with some kindness. "It is writ on your face for anyone with the eyes to see it, ma'am," she said. She passed over what Colcannon had told her; the widow would likely prefer to divulge the secrets of her marriage herself.

"I'm sorry." Anne d'Aubigny waved her handkerchief vaguely in the direction of an armchair, which Miss Tolerance took as an invitation to sit. "It has been difficult." She took another moment to master her emotions, then sat up and regarded Miss Tolerance steadily. Her blue eyes were reddened from crying, but as direct now as they had been guarded a moment before. "Will you explain what my brother has hired you to do, Miss Tolerance?"

"He wants me to uncover your husband's killer," Miss Tolerance said. She was startled by her hostess's sudden reversal, but much preferred this more rational woman and intended to get as many questions answered as she might before the widow sank into tears again. "He feels strongly that your safety depends upon it, and I regret to say that he places no particular reliance upon the civil authorities to do it."

Mrs. d'Aubigny sniffed, apparently sharing her brother's opinion of Mr. Heddison and his constables. "But why should my safety be in question?"

"The way this murder was done bespeaks great rage or fear or—perhaps madness itself behind that anger. Someone who killed from rage or madness once might return to do it again."

Mrs. d'Aubigny looked unconvinced.

"Perhaps more to the point for you, ma'am: once the murderer is uncovered, the constables will stop intruding upon your peace."

"But what can *you* do?"

Miss Tolerance smiled. "I can ask questions. I can take the answers I get and ask more questions, and perhaps come to an answer."

"The magistrate and his men can do as much," Anne d'Aubigny said.

"Indeed they can. But because I am who I am, I can ask them of a great many people, some of whom will not tell the constables what they will tell someone a little removed from the law—like myself." She smiled with a little humor. " 'Tis one of the ways in which my situation proves useful."

The widow considered. "You will want to ask questions *here*, I collect?"

Miss Tolerance nodded.

"And go among my husband's acquaintance as well?"

"I will."

"And you think you may get some good of it?"

"It is my hope, ma'am."

A peculiar mix of expression played across Anne d'Aubigny's pale face. Whatever the thoughts behind it, in the end the widow folded her hands in her lap like an obedient child determined to do an unwelcome task and bade Miss Tolerance ask what she liked.

Miss Tolerance took out a small bound book and the end of a pencil and asked the names and positions of the house servants. In a schoolgirl's voice to match her demeanor, Mrs. d'Aubigny recited the names: Adolphus Beak, the chief manservant; Peter Jacks, a second man who served to do heavy work and run messages; Mary Pitt, the housemaid; Sophia Thissen, a ladies' maid; and Mrs. Ellen Sadgett, the cook. There was in addition a laundress who came twice a week, Mrs. Sadgett's cousin, but Mrs. d'Aubigny could not remember her name. Did these servants sleep in the house? All except Mrs. Sadgett and the laundress: Mrs. Sadgett left the house after dinner was prepared each night and returned early in the morning to prepare breakfast. On the morning of her husband's death, Mrs. d'Aubigny believed Mrs. Sadgett had not been in the house above an hour.

"And where were you when you husband's body was discovered, ma'am?" Miss Tolerance asked.

The widow set her chin. "I was asleep."

If she expected Miss Tolerance to take exception to this answer she was disappointed. "Do you know what time your husband retired on the night prior to his death, ma'am?"

The widow gave a sniff that might have been supposed to express amusement. "I live a little withdrawn, Miss Tolerance. That night, like most nights, we dined, my husband left, I did a little sewing, the tea tray was brought in at half past nine, and I went upstairs directly afterward." She nodded in the direction of an embroidery frame that stood near the fireplace.

"You did not hear your husband come in in the night?"

"My husband and I do not share—did not share—a room."

"But someone would know what time your husband returned to the house," Miss Tolerance persisted.

"I imagine Beak would. Or my husband's valet, except that the last one left a sennight before. Jacks had been assisting Etienne until a new man could be hired. My husband spoke very feelingly upon the subject of Jacks' shortcomings."

Miss Tolerance had been wondering whether there would be mention of a valet. "You did not name the valet when you gave the servant's names, ma'am."

"Did I not? I suppose I didn't think of Norris after he left—he was hired away to Leicestershire."

"Had he any reason to dislike the chevalier, ma'am?"

Mrs. d'Aubigny shook her head. "You mean, could he have borne my husband a grudge? He was offered a good deal of money to travel out of the city. And even if he did dislike my husband, he was in Leicestershire when my husband died."

"The mail coach runs quite regularly to and from Leicestershire, ma'am," Miss Tolerance said mildly. "Your own maid also sleeps in the house?"

"Yes. In the servants' quarters on the top floor. Sophia retired after I did."

Miss Tolerance nodded, made note, and changed her tack. "You say that your husband went out most evenings. Do you know where your husband went on that night, ma'am?"

Mrs. d'Aubigny shook her head. "He rarely told me unless—"

"Unless?"

"Unless he thought he could cause me pain by doing so, Miss Tolerance." The widow pursed her mouth. "It pleased my husband to tell me about his women—their names and the things he did with them. I learned not to mind, or to give no sign that I minded, but even that did not please him. If he could not hurt me that way, he found other ways."

Half a dozen questions occurred to Miss Tolerance, but *Come back to them*, she thought.

"What were your husband's other pastimes?"

"All the expensive ones of gentlemen, Miss Tolerance. Gaming and sport and drink. The vilest of the Fallen—oh dear, I beg your pardon!" Her tone changed as she recalled to whom she spoke. "I did not mean—"

"Of course not," Miss Tolerance said. "Please proceed."

"Etienne was rarely home of an evening. He had friends among the émigré set. That French widow Touvois—"

Miss Tolerance blinked. D'Aubigny an habitué of Madame Camille Touvois' salon? It was not surprising that an émigré might be part of a circle hosted by another émigré, but nothing Anne d'Aubigny or her brother had said about the dead man had painted him with the sort of social, artistic or financial luster that would have made him welcome at one of the most celebrated— perhaps the proper word was notorious—liberal salons of the day.

Mrs. d'Aubigny continued. "He might have been there, or at his club, or in some horrid gaming den or with—with one of his women. Sometimes he said that there was work that kept him at Whitehall."

"Do you think that he lied?"

"I do not know. Perhaps not." The woman shook her head. A lock of pale hair came loose from her cap. "Why should he? I was not important enough to lie to."

Miss Tolerance could think of nothing politic to say.

"Ma'am, this question may be difficult to answer, but I ask you to consider carefully. Can you think of anyone who might have a reason to kill your husband?"

Anne d'Aubigny's mouth twitched into a peculiar smile. "Rather say, can I think of anyone who might not."

Oh, dear. "Ma'am?"

"I am sorry, Miss Tolerance. Such an answer is likely worse than no answer at all. But the women he—the women. And the men he gambled with—my husband was not lucky at play. I imagine he owed a great deal everywhere in town. It was often difficult to pay the tradesmen. Lately he'd had a little luck—a few weeks ago he came home and threw a fold of paper money upon my desk. He said there would be more, but there was not."

"Might he have borrowed that money, ma'am?"

"From whom? Oh, from a moneylender." Anne d'Aubigny looked off into the hallway as if seeking answers there. "But would a moneylender come into our house and kill my husband?"

A fine question, Miss Tolerance thought. Mrs. d'Aubigny, she saw, was beginning to lose the animation that had briefly energized the discussion. The chime of the gilded clock that stood alone on the mantel gave her an excuse to bring the interview to an end.

"Ma'am, I shall surely wish to ask other questions of you later, but I will not take the whole of your afternoon. I should like to see your husband's room, and then, may I speak with your staff?"

Mrs. d'Aubigny nodded. "If you wish. I shall instruct Beak. He will see to it."

"Thank you, ma'am. Two last questions, then, and I shall leave you to rest. Who is the Mrs. Vose whom I met yesterday? She is not one of the staff?"

The widow's cheeks flushed and she looked away from Miss Tolerance, toward the window, toward the fire, toward the door and, finally, to her own hands. "She is—that is, she's my husband's—his cousin."

Miss Tolerance understood that Mrs. Vose was likely not the chevalier's cousin nor any relation at all.

"And at what time that morning were you apprised of your husband's death, ma'am?"

This question appeared to retrieve the widow abruptly from

some place she had wandered in her thoughts. "I beg your pardon, Miss Tolerance?"

"I note from the reports in the paper that Mary Pitt found your husband, Beak sent Jacks for the watch, the watch came at once and examined him. No one mentions you, ma'am. Nor did the coroner have you testify. This argues a conviction upon his part that you had little or no useful testimony to share."

Mrs. d'Aubigny pursed her lips again. "I had taken a sleeping draught the night before, Miss Tolerance. I often have trouble sleeping, and when I have taken the draught I am rather thickheaded when I wake. I believe Sophia called me about nine o'clock in the morning, my usual time."

"*Two hours* after the body was found?"

"Yes," the widow said.

"Is that not rather odd, ma'am? Your husband had been killed in a dire manner here in your house, but the servants let you sleep after the discovery?"

Madame d'Aubigny's lips trembled. She pursed them again, seeking to control herself. "Sophia and the others are very protective of me, Miss Tolerance. What could I have done, half-asleep and addled by my sleeping draught? Wrung my hands and had hysterics? It may have been an error in judgment, but it was kindly meant."

There was that in the lift of her chin which said to Miss Tolerance that it was time to stop the interview. She rose and thanked her hostess.

"May I come to speak with you again?" Anne d'Aubigny nodded. "I thank you for your patience, ma'am." Miss Tolerance curtsied. "If you will ask your servants' cooperation in my inquiries I shall be grateful."

Mrs. d'Aubigny rose and took up the handbell. Beak appeared at the first ring as if he had been waiting by the doorway. The staff indeed appeared most solicitous of their mistress.

"Beak, Miss Tolerance wishes to see the—the room. Then she will have some questions for you and the others about the day of—" she waved her hand, then brought it back to her lips as if to contain the word *murder*. "It will please me if you will be helpful to her."

She did not wait to hear the man's "Yes, madam." She turned

back to Miss Tolerance, and this time offered her hand. "I must thank you for your efforts, Miss Tolerance. You will let me know what you learn?"

Miss Tolerance curtsied in lieu of agreement and took her leave. She had a good deal to think about.

Beak led Miss Tolerance to the first floor with a posture which suggested outrage. She was sympathetic: if for days he had been fending off strangers who wished to gape at the sight of the murder room, what was he to make of a woman who demanded—and was given the right!—to examine the room closely? She did not apologize aloud, but resolved to make her investigation as efficient as possible, to avoid antagonizing the man further. He might be of considerable help to her in the days to come; best not to lose his goodwill at once.

The chevalier's chamber was in the front of the house. It was a large, square room furnished in a heavy old-fashioned style. The drapes, now drawn and admitting wintry light, were a pale, frosty brown; the bed-curtains were of the same material. The bed itself had carved posts reaching nearly to the ceiling; there were a chest and garderobe in the same dark, carved wood. Miss Tolerance noted that not all the bed-curtains were in place; only the curtains at the foot and far side remained. From the description in the newspapers, Miss Tolerance surmised that the missing drapes had been smirched with blood and brains that no amount of laundering had been able to remove, and had been destroyed. There were neither sheets nor blankets upon the bed, and the feather ticking showed signs of an imperfect attempt to clean it. She gathered her skirt and dropped to one knee to examine the floor around the bed, and noted that sanding had not completely removed the stains there, either.

There were other commonplace furnishings of a gentleman's room: writing desk, chairs, fire tools, mantel clock, toilet cabinet. Everything was orderly and clean, but she had no idea if everything that ought to be in the room was there. The room was melancholy in its emptiness and very cold. When she exhaled, a plume of breath rose up before Miss Tolerance's eyes.

"There was nothing taken? Nothing missing from the room after—"

Beak shook his head. "Nor I found nothing extra, miss. You're wishful to talk to the staff, miss?"

Miss Tolerance sighed. They had quite reasonably wished to scrub away the marks of murder, but doing so had likely scrubbed away evidence that might have proved useful. *Would that I had seen this room that morning*, she thought. *Two weeks gone, now*.

"Thank you, Beak. I should very much like to speak to each of you alone."

Miss Tolerance spent the next several hours talking with the staff of the house in Half Moon Street, in a small room belowstairs usually reserved to Mr. Beak's use. Mary Pitt, the maid who had discovered the murder, was a plain, moon-faced girl who had clearly come to enjoy her role in this important drama. What she had to say did not materially enlarge upon the report in the newspaper, but Pitt recited her piece with considerable relish, and details Miss Tolerance suspected had been added as telling piled upon telling.

The cook, Mrs. Sadgett, was tall and thin, unlike many of her calling. She treated Miss Tolerance's interview as an insufferable interruption, giving her testimony with sniffs of aggravation, her lips pursed tight. When the master's death had been discovered she had been in the midst of her baking, she reported. She had arrived in the house an hour or more before Mary Pitt found the body, and gone straight about her business like a good Christian woman. When Miss Tolerance released her, Mrs. Sadgett left the room without a further glance at her interlocutor.

Sophia Thissen, Anne d'Aubigny's maid, was summoned downstairs by Beak. She was small—even shorter than Anne d'Aubigny, which made Miss Tolerance feel like a giantess—rosily plump, dressed neatly and without pretension in a brown stuff gown. Her eyes and hair were dark brown and her complexion dark; her vowels were Yorkshire with a veneer of London and gentility. She gave the impression that she might like to lean forward and straighten Miss Tolerance's collar or smooth back any lock of hair which was unwise enough to stray from her bonnet. When the maid had accounted for her own whereabouts on the night of the murder, Miss Tolerance asked the woman the same question she had asked her mistress.

"With your master dead in his sheets, why did no one think to wake Mrs. d'Aubigny until hours later?"

"He weren't *my* master. And what could poor little Madam have done?" The maid shrugged. "Mary Pitt was crying and carrying on, the house was all a-maze. And I had brung Madam her medicine the night before," she added. "The laudanum makes her sleep so deep it's hard to rouse her, and when she's waked she's addled and not much good for anything. It wouldn't have been a kindness. Had I waked her early she'd have had hysterics, and how would that have helped?"

Anne d'Aubigny might be correct that her staff was protective of her, Miss Tolerance thought, but her maid had more the tone of someone used to dealing with an idiot child.

"Did not the officer of the watch wish to speak to her?"

"I explained that Madam was *en dishabille* and not available yet. He was most agreeable about waiting."

That was a most peculiar way to manage an investigation, Miss Tolerance thought. Well, watch officers were not usually in the way of encountering full-blown murder in such a parish as this, and likely inclined to defer to persons of consequence. It might have been stupid of the officer, but it was not, Miss Tolerance regretted, unlikely.

"When you did wake your mistress and give her the news, what, exactly, did she say?"

Sophia shrugged again. "I don't recall exactly. *Oh no!* or *My God*, something like that. And then she wept. And then she bid me help her get dressed, for she knew there would be a great deal of business to attend to that day."

Miss Tolerance blinked. "Were those her words? A great deal of business?"

The maid shook her head. "That was the meaning of it, but I don't recall the words exactly." She glared at Miss Tolerance.

"Have you any idea at what time the chevalier retired that night?"

Sophia shook her head. "No, ma'am. I did my best to—to not to be close to the master, particularly in the evening. Not to speak ill of the dead, but—"

"I understand," Miss Tolerance said.

"You might ask Jacks. Sometimes he did for the master after Mr. Norris left."

Miss Tolerance dismissed Pitt and called for Peter Jacks. The footman could add little, however. On the evening of the chevalier's death he had let the master into the house at a little past ten. The chevalier had said he would see to himself, and sent Jacks off to his bed.

"What did you make of that?" Miss Tolerance asked.

"Miss?"

"Was there any reason why the master might have sent you to bed and seen to himself? He has not—you will forgive me—but he has not impressed me as the soul of consideration."

Jacks grinned for a moment, then recalled himself. "Master didn't make no secret that I wasn't up to his standards as a valet. Half the time he did for hisself at night, said he didn't want me racketing over him."

"And that night was one of those nights?"

"I suppose so, miss. He just said 'That's all, Jacks.' So I went to bed."

Miss Tolerance asked the footman to go over what had happened the next morning, but it varied little from what she had already learned. Jacks had been called from the kitchen by Mr. Beak to fetch the watch. "Glad to leave I was, too, with Mary Pitt bawling as loud as a trumpet. I ran out and fetched the old man back—"

"The door was locked until you left?"

"Oh, yes, miss. Tight as a drum every night. Mr. Beak locked it after master got in."

Miss Tolerance sent for Beak.

Adolphus Beak came into his parlor and made a little ceremony of seating himself opposite to Miss Tolerance, clearing his throat, and composing himself. He agreed that the testimony he had given at the Coroner's Court, reported in the *Times*, was correct. The house had been securely locked the night before, bolts thrown on both the front and kitchen doors. The windows in the chevalier's room had been undisturbed. The staff that slept in the house had been abed—he had personally locked the door to the servants' stairwell before he retired, to guard against kitchen pilfering.

"When you discovered the chevalier's body, your first act was what, Mr. Beak?"

Beak looked down his nose—a large, well-made feature, somewhat marred by a brown stain which indicated he was addicted to the use of snuff, but not so habituated in the use of his handkerchief. "I know what's proper, miss. I sent Jacks off to bring the watch."

Miss Tolerance was unmoved by the man's condescension. "Very proper. And he had to unbolt the door to do so, I believe? Which door was that?"

"The front one, miss. Didn't want to delay a second in Jacks finding the officer."

"Very right, Mr. Beak. But could not Mr. Jacks have used the kitchen door?"

"The kitchen door, miss?" Beak looked blank.

"Surely it had been unlocked when Mrs. Sadgett arrived that morning, to permit her entry to the house. Would that not have been quicker?"

The old man's face sagged at the import of the question was borne upon him. "I never did, miss."

"Never unlocked the door?"

He shook his head. "No, miss. I threw the bolt myself the night before, when Mrs. Sadgett left, but I never heard her knock that morning. Next thing I knew, she was in kitchen doing her breads."

He called for Mrs. Sadgett, who came in with an air of superlative annoyance. "The door locked? In course it were not, Mr. Beak. When I come that morning I just thought you'd brought in the milk—no, the milk seller come round a little while later. But that door was not locked when I got here, Mr. Beak."

Beak dismissed the cook back to her oven before he turned to Miss Tolerance. "Who unlocked it, miss?"

"Perhaps you should ask the others in the house, Mr. Beak. The answer may be quite simple."

But when Beak magisterially summoned each of the servants save Mrs. Sadgett back into his presence and put the question to them, the answer came back unexceptionally: none of them knew who had unlocked the kitchen door for Mrs. Sadgett. Miss Tolerance herself inspected the lock: an old-fashioned iron bolt that required considerable force to throw it; one would remember having bolted it. It was possible, Miss Tolerance reflected, that Beak scared the culprit from confession with his scowl of disapproval. But it was also possible that the door had been unlocked by some other party, including the chevalier himself. With a sigh at this conundrum she rose, gave her thanks to Beak, and suggested that she might come back again to talk. Beak conducted her up the stairs and back through the green baize door which separated the servants' hall from the rest of the house. In the hallway Miss Tolerance noted that a door which had been closed earlier now stood open, revealing a pleasant formal salon. She stopped, staring into the room.

"Is that a painting of your late master, Beak?"

The old man followed Miss Tolerance's glance. Upon the far wall, over a desk, was a portrait of a man, perhaps thirty years of age, with dark hair worn a little long, and dark winged brows. His features were handsome, and he was smiling, the smile perhaps intended to be pleasant; but the effect of those brows was to make him appear sinister. Upon second thought, Miss Tolerance decided that it was not a trick of the brows: the smile, and the expression in the eyes, *was* sinister.

"That is. A good likeness, too. He was a well-looking man, but the artist caught something about his eyes."

"Indeed he did," Miss Tolerance agreed, happy to turn away and follow Beak to the door.

She stepped out of the house and into the street, moving through the crowd, thinking. With all the doors to the house locked and no windows broken, the likely suspects would have been only those who slept in the house. With the kitchen door unlocked sometime between midnight and seven in the morning, the murderer might have been anyone in London. Anyone in the world.

Five

Miss Tolerance's interviews, which had occupied the greater part of the day, left her with generous avenues for inquiry. She returned to her cottage in Manchester Square with much to consider, and decided to pay a call upon her aunt. Mrs. Brereton, despite fixed rules against gossip between her employees with regard to her patrons, was quite variable in the application of this principle to herself. She had been in the past one of Miss Tolerance's best sources of information.

Darkness had fallen, and the brothel was discreetly bustling with activity. Miss Tolerance climbed the stairs to her aunt's apartment, nodding to the servants and employees as she passed, looking blankly past the faces of clients in the hall. She was considerably surprised to find Mrs. Brereton in her bed, being ministered to by her elderly abigail. Frost was fussing around her mistress, plumping pillows and laying hot bricks wrapped in flannel by her feet. The maid wore that expression, part disapproval and part delight, which is common to persons who believe themselves to be indispensable.

"A feverish cold she has, from not taking proper care. It's a scandal!" Miss Tolerance was not entirely clear what scandalized Frost: that a cold had had the temerity to strike her charge, or that

Mrs. Brereton was still ignoring her advice after all these years. "Look at her, at Death's door!"

Mrs. Brereton did not look very ill to Miss Tolerance's eye. She lay propped upon half a dozen laced pillows, and as her cap and nightdress were equally laced, it was difficult to tell where the pillows left off and the madam began. The only sign of illness Mrs. Brereton exhibited was a flush to her cheeks and a reddening around her nose from too-frequent recourse to her handkerchief.

"Don't be ridiculous, Frost, and stop fussing at me," Mrs. Brereton snapped. "For God's sake, get me a cup of tea and stop fluttering."

Frost glared at Miss Tolerance as if her mistress's behavior proved her point, and stalked out.

"A certain class of servant comes to believe that she is the secret mistress of the house," Mrs. Brereton said irritably. "I do not know why I suffer these pretensions."

"She does keep you looking remarkably fine," Miss Tolerance pointed out. She took a chair near her aunt's bedside. A silence fell between them.

"What brings you to me tonight, Sarah?" Mrs. Brereton asked at last.

"I'm in need of gossip, Aunt."

"Not about my clientele, I hope."

Miss Tolerance shook her head. "I know better than to ask such a thing. Someone nearer in line to a competitor, I think."

"Nearer in line? When is a competitor not a competitor? Very intriguing." Mrs. Brereton's eyes brightened. She sat up a little against her pillows and tilted her head encouragingly. "Who?"

"Camille Touvois."

"Good lord, she's no competitor of mine," Mrs. Brereton said. Her scorn was complete. "She gives *parties*. Chat-chat-chatter and bad wine and poets, heaven help us, holding forth on politics! That people meet there and go elsewhere for their liaisons does not make her *salon* into a house of assignation."

"I'm sure that distresses her nearly as much as it does you, Aunt. People meet there and go elsewhere?"

"Why else would they go? I understand that La Touvois has a knack for introducing people of like interests."

"Aunt, at the risk of exposing my naïveté, I wish you will plainly state what you are hinting at."

Mrs. Brereton rolled her eyes. "Molly to molly, Sarah. Bircher to birched. The old man who wants a young woman and the young woman who seeks a man just like her dear father—or granddad. From what I understand, she has a talent for discerning whose taste match; she introduces them and lets nature take its course."

"She is paid to do so?"

"Not in coin. But this one brings that one, and her gatherings are enlarged. I believe," Mrs. Brereton said offhandedly, "that her trade is in information and favors."

"But how difficult it must be to eat favors," Miss Tolerance observed.

Frost returned with the tea tray and bustled noisily for several minutes, pouring out tea and fussing over her mistress until Mrs. Brereton shooed her away impatiently. Then the abigail retired to the dressing room, glaring at Miss Tolerance. Miss Tolerance drank her tea.

"What about Camille Touvois herself? Can you tell me anything?"

Mrs. Brereton bristled as if her professional competence had been questioned. "Only a little," she said blandly. "Her family came here from France about the time she would have escaped the schoolroom, I think. She married another émigré—all of them as poor as rats, of course—and was widowed very quickly. The poor fellow was at Valenciennes with the Duke of York. Then she was someone's mistress—Lord, who was it? Whoever it was, he put her in society's way and she became acquainted with a vast number of the Opposition.

"So her sympathies—and her parties—partake of the liberal establishment?"

"Oh, I believe so, my dear," Mrs. Brereton said. While her own sympathies were as firmly in the Whig camp as Madame Touvois' were said to be, Mrs. Brereton's establishment took no notice of the political affiliations of its clientele. "But does this mean that Camille Touvois is tangled up in some inquiry of yours?"

Miss Tolerance shrugged. "Perhaps."

"Oh. Yes. Of course." Mrs. Brereton blew her nose. "You may ask me all you like, but you will tell me nothing."

"I was of the impression that you enjoyed being the one who knew everything about everyone. I do not ask you about your clients, and God knows you might always say to me, No, I cannot tell you anything. Would you prefer that I not come to you at all?"

"I would prefer that you stop punishing me!" Mrs. Brereton said angrily. "Every time you call on me you are everything polite and disapproving. You don't trust me."

Miss Tolerance was startled by the hurt in her aunt's voice. "I thought we had agreed—"

"You agreed you would talk of nothing substantial, whatever help I gave you." Mrs. Brereton blew her nose again. "Sarah, I made a mistake. Are you, of all people, going to hold that mistake against me forever?"

Miss Tolerance drew a sharp breath. "Aunt, you must understand—"

"I do understand. I was careless, and told something which put you at risk—"

"Careless?" Miss Tolerance struggled to master her anger. "In order to keep a client happy, you told him when I had gone on an errand. Only it was not me, but Matt Etan who went, and was followed and beaten to death. Perhaps you do not recall his body laid out in your parlor, but I do. I remember that it might easily have been me who was killed and not Matt."

"I could not have known—"

"Nor could I! Would I have let Matt take my place had I had any idea what waited him? Do you think I don't imagine what might have happened had it been me instead? At least *I* can use a sword . . ."

"So you blame me, that you need not blame yourself! I put the maintenance of my relationship with a client above the claims of kinship. I was not to know what would come of it. Matt's death— he should not have been out on your errand—" Mrs. Brereton went into a fit of coughing.

Miss Tolerance, who suspected her aunt of theatricality, was unmoved.

"I have learned my lesson, Sarah, and I am frankly tired of feeling every time we meet that you are scolding me!"

"It certainly is not scolding to watch what I say in your company. And I beg you to believe it is as difficult for me to do so as it is for you to accept that your mistake cost Matt his life. I must live with my guilt in the matter, Aunt, but so must you."

The two women glared at each other.

In the silence Frost's voice came from the dressing room. "Are you all right, madam? Miss Sarah, you'll remember that she is ill—don't you worry her!"

Miss Tolerance and Mrs. Brereton, with one look, came together to assure the maid that all was very well.

"*Don't* let her fuss at me," Mrs. Brereton murmured. She leaned back into her pillows as if exhausted. Miss Tolerance nodded.

"She is right, though. You're not well, and I have upset you. I'm sorry, Aunt Thea." She rose and kissed her aunt's cheek. Mrs. Brereton turned away slightly, but permitted the gesture. "Is there anything I can do for you?"

"Pour a little more tea, please." Mrs. Brereton watched as the tea was poured, and thanked her niece. Then she turned her face to the heavily draped window, as if trying to divine what weather lurked behind the curtains.

Miss Tolerance left her aunt to her conscience and her tisane.

In the morning Miss Tolerance dressed for riding in masculine garb and sent round to the stables to hire a horse. She set out for the Strand, noting as she rode that the citizens of London were taking on their winter conformations. Those with money maintained a slender silhouette, sealing the chill out with rich materials and furs, moving from houses where fires warmed every grate to carriages fitted out with warmed rugs and hot bricks. Those who could not afford such luxuries took on the appearance of bustling balls of wool, dressed in as many layers as they could contrive and barreling through the streets in scarves, shawls, and thrice-sold coats. Miss Tolerance sank her chin into the scarf wrapped loosely around her neck; the tip of her nose was likely red, but in that she was no different from every other Londoner out of doors on this day.

The neighborhood known as the Liberty of Savoy was, by ancient custom, a safe haven for debtors of all classes; a stink of desperation and compromise hung about its streets no less than the quotidian stench of sewage. Miss Tolerance guided her horse among the carriages, carts, street-sellers and pedestrians until she reached the Wheat Sheaf, a public house where the gleanings, she hoped, would include information.

Miss Tolerance was known here. The tapster greeted her with a look, a second look, and a nod of recognition. She ordered coffee and bread and suggested that Mr. Boddick draw something stronger for himself. He nodded acknowledgment, brought Miss Tolerance's refreshment, then liberally doctored a tankard of coffee with rum and nursed at it until he felt more communicative. It was then established between the two of them that it was indeed a raw day, that winter looked to be settling in for good and earnest, and that the poor soldiers off in foreign parts would be brutally cold that winter—if they didn't drown first in the torrential rains that were reported to have struck Portugal this fall. These preliminaries over, Miss Tolerance was able to inquire after Mr. Joshua Glebb.

The position Mr. Glebb occupied in the Liberty, and within the larger canvas of London generally, is difficult to describe. Gossip is too simple a word; informer both harsh and inaccurate; broker was perhaps the most apt term. It was Mr. Glebb's vocation to acquaint those who required financial assistance with all those ready to offer such assistance. That many of these lenders operated outside the bounds of the usury statutes did not trouble Mr. Glebb, a fervent believer in the virtue of an unfettered marketplace. Glebb had the ear of bankers licit and otherwise. There was very little he did not know about who borrowed from whom, and unlike Miss Tolerance, he did not scruple to share this information for a price.

Boddick drank the last of his coffee-and-rum, looked wistfully into the tankard, and allowed that Mr. Glebb was likely to take up his usual place in the back of the room within the hour. As the fire was warm and the coffee drinkable, Miss Tolerance greeted this news without dismay, ordered more coffee for herself, and directed the tapster to refresh his own. Mr. Boddick carried on a one-sided conversation regarding politics; Miss Tolerance drank her coffee.

Mr. Glebb appeared some five and forty minutes later, trailing three petitioners of varying class and desperation. He recognized Miss Tolerance and conveyed with a nod that he would be happy to speak with her after his immediate business had been dispatched. He then spread his coattails and settled himself with a sigh at the table nearest the fire. He was a short, elderly man built upon pyramidal lines: a long, narrow head and negligible chin, a pair of shoulders only a little broader, and a spreading paunch ill concealed by a neat dark coat. The fashion for high shirt-points and elaborately tied neckcloths did not reduce this triangular illusion. Age made Glebb's movements stiff and painful, and no amount of attention with his handkerchief could expunge the bit of milky white spittle in the corner of his mouth, or the clear drop that seemed always poised to fall from his nose. Miss Tolerance watched as Glebb dealt with one, then another, then the last of the waiting supplicants. He then waved Miss Tolerance over; she thanked Mr. Boddick for his company and went to join Glebb.

"Haven't seen you here in a while, miss. Not come to borrow, I take it?" Glebb's voice was dry and hoarse.

"No, sir. I find myself quite beforehand with the world," Miss Tolerance said pleasantly. "I should like the favor of a few minutes' conversation, however."

"Oh, aye, talk is cheap—in course, information comes dearer. But *you* know that." Glebb raised a hand to beckon to the tapster. "Hi, you, Boddick! Coffee and a pie here, if you please."

Miss Tolerance took a seat across the table. "Do you pay rent, that they let you inhabit this corner of the room, sir?"

Glebb shook his head. "I'm good for business. Particularly later in the day, when people drink a little courage before they talk with me. But that's not your question. What is it you need to know?"

"Is the name Etienne d'Aubigny—the Chevalier d'Aubigny—known to you, sir?"

Glebb drew his brows together and pursed his lips in a caricature of thought. "Frenchman name of Dobinny—" He did not bother to essay Miss Tolerance's pronunciation. "I've heard nothing of a Frenchman by that name going to the cents-per-cent. And if I don't know it—"

"He has not been on the lookout for funds," Miss Tolerance finished. "Not among the reputable moneylenders, in any case," she added.

"Oh, I'd 'a heard about it if he'd gone to the sharks, as well," Glebb said firmly. He slid his hand across the table, palm up, but Miss Tolerance was not done with him.

"No such Frenchman has been pawning or selling off his goods?"

Glebb considered. "Such a Frenchman might 'a done in the past—but I take it you want something more recent? Nothing worth noting. I could ask about, but it will cost you."

Miss Tolerance smiled politely. "Of course. 'Tis only fair."

Glebb looked up to nod as Boddick brought his pie and coffee. "I know the name, though. Outside of the financial area. Can't recall why."

"It might be because the man was murdered. His widow believes the murderer could have been an unhappy creditor."

Glebb engaged himself in the demolition of the pie before him. When he looked up at Miss Tolerance at last he said indistinctly, "That don't make sense."

"Why not?"

Glebb swallowed his mouthful and explained patiently. "It's what you call recourse, miss. When a gentleman defaults of a debt, even the lowest Jew may call the bailiffs in and seize 'is property. Or take the matter to court and send the fellow to a spunging house—all it takes is shillin' for the warrant. But once the man's dead, may be harder to collect. If you do see any of your money, it's like to take far longer. Ideal-like, you want your debtor in the top of health and of a disposing mind. P'raps a gullgroper might send someone to roast your toes if you was late chronic-like, or break a bone or two. But *killing*—that's not about debt."

"Debts of honor—" Miss Tolerance began, half to herself.

"Oh, well, yes." Glebb was disapproving. "Gentlemen and them, they're all for blowing each other's head off for a farthing. It's not the way of good business."

"It wasn't a duel, in any case. The man was beaten to death in his own bed."

Mr. Glebb nodded and tapped the side of his nose with one short finger. "In 'is own bed? Beat to death? That's why the name's familiar, then. That West End business. Look to the household, I say. A wife, a child, a servant. Who else'd have so easy a chance?"

Miss Tolerance opened her pocketbook, took out several coins and slid them across the table.

"I'm grateful for your help, Mr. Glebb."

"Well, aye. Come find me any time. I'm always here." Glebb pushed the coins off the edge of the table and into his hand. "And I'll ask about for word the gent was deep in to the sharks," he promised.

Miss Tolerance had gained the street when a thought occurred to her and she returned to the Wheat Sheaf's tap-room again. Glebb, brushing crumbs from his coat, eyed her without comment.

"When you make your inquiries regarding the chevalier, Mr. Glebb, would you ask as well about the size of his debt to tradesmen and the like? Thank you!" She left with Glebb staring after her, clearly weighing the scope of the task she had set against the money he would be able to charge for it.

Shrugging her way out of the door into the sour fog which was, even at this hour, beginning to drift in the street, Miss Tolerance considered. The d'Aubigny household had shown all the signs of life lived chronically beyond means: the missing objects which had most likely been pawned or sold, the patchy condition of the servants' livery, the house in a good neighborhood but with paint cracking and shutters askew. Miss Tolerance made a silent wager with herself that the Widow d'Aubigny was missing jewels which had come with her into the marriage and were now reposing in pawnshops. But if Glebb could find no indication that d'Aubigny had borrowed money from professionals accustomed to lend it, whence would the money to support that household come? It seemed impossible that the man hadn't borrowed money from someone.

Miss Tolerance's horse was still in the custody of the grubby child she had paid to watch it. She dodged a cart barreling by at a speed certain to throw the unspeakable contents of the gutter up in an odorous spray, then crossed the street to where horse and boy waited. She flipped the boy a coin, mounted the hack, and started west.

Perhaps the chevalier had borrowed money from a private source, a friend or business associate. Anne d'Aubigny had suggested that only a moneylender would have advanced her improvident husband money, but it was clear to Miss Tolerance that the widow had not been in her husband's confidence. Perhaps d'Aubigny's superior in the Home Office would know, although Miss Tolerance had little confidence that such a person would share the information with a Fallen Woman who appeared on his doorstep asking questions. Regretting that she would have to return home and change from the relatively warm breeches, coat and greatcoat that she wore into more feminine garb, Miss Tolerance turned the hack toward Manchester Square again, to render her costume and her self unexceptionable to the clerks of the Home Office.

An hour later Miss Tolerance had achieved a highly respectable appearance calculated to suggest impoverished female virtue and bereavement without directly claiming either. Her dress was of dark gray wool, her dark blue coat was untrimmed, and she had removed the crimson ribbons and feather cockade which had formerly given her bonnet a rather dashing appearance. This costume, together with a posture and attitude which suggested anxiety at war with necessity, she hoped would gain the confidence of the Home Office. She hired a carriage to Parliament Street and began her impersonation there on the street, staring anxiously into her reticule and paying the driver with a collection of small coins, parting with each one with a slight frown of distress. Firmly in character, she entered the building and asked the porter for the office of Mr. Etienne d'Aubigny.

The porter looked distressed. He bade her sit and scurried off down the low-ceilinged hall. Perhaps the man was afraid she did not know of the chevalier's demise and feared feminine hysterics; certainly he had gone to place the problem in more senior hands. A few minutes later the porter returned with a tall square-headed gentleman who asked her business with the chevalier. Miss Tolerance gave rein to her considerable sense of mischief.

"My poor dear cousin sent me," she began. "The widow, poor thing. Quite distraught. I—" She stopped and applied a handkerchief to her eye as if to stop a show of grief. "Poor Cousin Anne! So much business to resolve! So many callers, so many letters to write! I only hope my small assistance may be useful to her. Indeed, when I left, she told me—"

This was apparently credential enough for the gentleman, who dismissed the clerk and invited Miss Tolerance into his office. Miss Tolerance took a seat opposite the desk, which made her the full recipient of drafts from which her host's chairback protected him.

"Now, then," the gentleman said. He settled himself at his desk. "I am Sir Andrew Parham. How may I assist you, Miss—"

Miss Tolerance disregarded the implicit invitation to give her name. "Sir Andrew, so very kind of you to see me. My poor cousin Anne asked me—'tis very hard to speak of it, such a horrid, untimely death, and of course everything left every which way. But her husband's affairs, perhaps you might know, I'm sure the poor chevalier reposed the greatest confidence in you—"

From the expression on Sir Andrew's face he had not much liked the poor chevalier. "That is very gratifying," he began.

"You see, there it is," Miss Tolerance rattled on. "Men always know so much more than they tell their wives. My poor dear cousin—so distraught!—is trying to discover who—that is to say, if you could help us learn—I imagine that—"

"Madam, if you would tell me how I may help you," Sir Andrew said encouragingly.

"Ah, men are always so businesslike! You see, the chevalier told Cousin Anne that he had borrowed money from someone in his office, but she can discover nothing, and no one has come forward, and she does consider it a debt of—of honor, and asked me to particularly inquire—"

Sir Andrew raised an eyebrow. "D'Aubigny borrowed money from someone in *this* office?"

Miss Tolerance pursed her lips and nodded. "That is what we believe, sir, and if you—"

"I hardly like to say this, Miss—" again the pause for a name, which Miss Tolerance again ignored. "The men at d'Aubigny's level in this department are men with their ways to make. If the chevalier borrowed money here it was more likely to be a sixpence than a guinea. He certainly knew better than to approach *me*," he said sternly.

"Oh, of course, sir. But we thought—and with the poor chevalier such a promising man, and certain to rise in the service—"

Irritation, Miss Tolerance was pleased to see, was now plainly written on Sir Andrew's face. She continued, "—Quite certain to make his fortune, for he was such a *clever* man—"

"Yes, well—"

"—And only recently he came into money—my cousin was certain at first that it was a prize of some sort for his superior work, but then she thought that it must have been a tiny loan against his expectations. Expectations that have been so horridly dashed—and how is she to manage now? That money is all gone, of course. Such a—"

"I hope Mrs. d'Aubigny's jointure was protected against any depredations—" Sir Andrew began. He had begun to regard Miss Tolerance with a kind of horror.

"Of course it was, the soul of honor the chevalier was, as I'm sure you know, and my uncle, Cousin Anne's father, you know, quite properly saw her jointure tied up sound as can be! I don't mean to take up your time, dear Sir Andrew, but perhaps you know who the dear chevalier's particular friends in the office were? Poor dear Anne says he was so popular that he frequently stayed out of an evening—I am only just come to London, and the pace of life is quite unsettling to a country mouse such as I am. But with Cousin Anne so very overset, and so many details to be seen to—and the poor dear chevalier such a paragon in every—"

"Quite," Sir Andrew broke in. "Madam, I regret to tell you that the chevalier, so far as I could observe, had no particular friends in this office. He made no push to attach anyone here in that way, and while his work was competent he was by no means the rising star his wife imagines him. As for his evening activities, I can tell you that there were reports that the chevalier played very deep, and was involved with Persons that this office regards without favor. In fact had the chevalier not died in this unfortunate way, he was likely to have been reprimanded in the strongest possible terms, and warned that his continued employment with this office would be imperiled by those connections."

Miss Tolerance burst into tears. Which is to say that she buried her face in the handkerchief and let her shoulders shake.

"Oh, how horrid!" she gasped. "That I should have to tell these things to my poor Cousin Anne! Oh!"

Sir Andrew, aghast at what his ire had led him to say, rose and took her hand, patting it anxiously. His hands were square, meaty, and covered with dark hairs. "My apologies, Miss—" Still he had no name for her. "I had not meant to speak so bluntly, but—"

"And his connections—these people you speak of! What must they be, to have brought down such a threat of censure!" Miss Tolerance sobbed again and permitted her hand to remain in Sir Andrew's clasp. "But if it is to one of them that the chevalier applied for money—have you no name to give me, sir?"

Sir Andrew appeared appalled by the idea. "Name? I only know—no, ma'am, I really know nothing to help you. Mrs. d'Aubigny might apply at his clubs—he was asked to leave Brooks', but was still a member of the Tarsio, I believe. Or among his own countrymen in England. But has she no relative—no *male* relative who might more properly take on these inquiries for her?"

Miss Tolerance shook her head.

"Ah. Well, I regret, Miss—I regret that I truly cannot be of more help. I send my condolences, of course, and a collection is being taken up here to help defray the—that is, the final expenses—but you see, that is, you understand . . ."

Miss Tolerance understood very well. She got to her feet, still partly hiding behind the handkerchief, withdrew her hand, and sniffed. "Oh, yes, Sir Andrew. And I do thank you for your time and your kindness in seeing me, particularly as it seems my cousin's husband had quite deceived—oh!" Another paroxysm of false tears. "But that's of no account now. I shall simply tell my cousin that you could not tell us who might have loaned the chevalier money. Poor dear Cousin Anne does not need to know the rest, do you think?"

Sir Andrew, his relief poorly concealed, was guiding Miss Tolerance toward the door. "I think you show excellent common sense. There, now. I shall have Hemmings procure a hackney coach for you, shall I?"

Their farewells were accomplished with relief on Sir Andrew's side and a good deal of sodden gratitude on Miss Tolerance's. It was not until she had reached the confines of the carriage that she permitted her shoulders to straighten, and succumbed to the laughter which had threatened to destroy her imposture.

She was not surprised that the chevalier had not been well liked, or liked at all, at his office. His propensity for deep play was known there, and his losses as well (had his luck been better, she doubted his job would have been threatened). As to his memberships in Tarsio's and Brooks' clubs: the wonder was not that d'Aubigny had been cast out of Brooks' but that he had been admitted at all. Miss Tolerance would very much have liked to speak to someone at Brooks', but she had no contacts there. This made it very simple to know where her next destination must be. She rapped on the carriage roof and ordered the driver to take her to Tarsio's.

As the coach approached Henry Street, Miss Tolerance saw Steen, Tarsio's night doorman, heading toward the club. She rapped at once for the driver to stop, called out to Steen to hold a moment, and paid the fare. Steen, a little surprised to be hailed in the street by an apparently respectable woman, brightened when he recognized Miss Tolerance, and agreed at once to her request for a few minutes' conversation before he reported for work.

"It will not make you late, will it?" she asked. "I should dislike to put you in trouble with Mr. Jenkins."

Steen assured her that he usually arrived early, and that the club's manager would, in any case, wish him to accommodate one of the club's favorite members. Miss Tolerance privately doubted that Mr. Jenkins would be concerned with accommodating her unless a coin found its way to his pocket.

"Now, miss, how can I help you?" Steen asked politely, when they had settled by the fire in a nearby tavern which catered to upper menservants.

"I need some information about one of Tarsio's members," Miss Tolerance said.

"A *member*? Ah, miss, you know I can't!"

Miss Tolerance was familiar with the rules of a game which required that Steen must proclaim his unwillingness to betray the secrets of his workplace, and that she must overcome his scruples with a soothing application of silver. "Since the member is deceased, Steen, and I am investigating his death, I honestly think even the chevalier would not blame you for rendering assistance. Perhaps this will assuage your honor?" She slid a coin across the table.

Steen did not look at the money, but placed his hand over it and regarded Miss Tolerance with an expression of sincerity. "Then it's the Frenchman you're talking about?"

Miss Tolerance nodded. "The Chevalier d'Aubigny. I cannot think why I never knew he was a member."

"Kept different hours from you, miss. Only come late in the evening, for the deep play. He wasn't the sort to come chat in the Ladies' Salon. One of the burgundy-and-guinea set, so to speak."

"Who else makes up that set?"

Steen looked uneasy. "There's a good number of 'em, miss. Can't name 'em all."

"Of course not. But had he any particular friends or cronies I should speak to? Always keeping your name and the name of the club from the conversation, of course."

Steen considered. At last, "Another Frenchman, Beauville—they was thick, miss. At play and drinking. And w—I overheard them talking some times about—" The man reddened. "Talking about the girls in that cat-smart in Green Street, too."

"Cat-smart?"

"*You* know, miss. Mrs. Lasher's." When Miss Tolerance did not immediately understand he continued with a tone of desperate embarrassment. "A birchery. A whipping house. They was talking about how—*agreeable* Mrs. Lasher was, and another called Jenny Striker. There was another Frenchy, a woman, they spoke of too, but she didn't sound like a whore."

"Camille Touvois?" Miss Tolerance suggested.

"Madame Too-wah," Steen agreed. "They seemed to think she was a rare bit."

"So I have heard," Miss Tolerance agreed. "Would you by any chance have Mr. Beauville's direction, Steen?"

The footman shook his head. "Mr. Jenkins would know, a-course, but I don't know he'd give it to you."

Miss Tolerance agreed that that was highly unlikely. "Can you tell me anything more about Mr. d'Aubigny?"

"Not much, miss. He wasn't an openhanded fellow, nor an agreeable one, that I can say. Brimful with consequence. I wouldn't wish no one to die the way he did, but I can't say I'm bothered that he's gone."

Miss Tolerance noted that this appeared to be the universal sentiment in the matter. Steen pocketed the half crown Miss Tolerance had passed to him, hoped they would see her soon at Tarsio's, and took his leave. Miss Tolerance, reflecting that each new turn seemed to limn the chevalier's character more grimly, decided that she must pay ɔcall at Mrs. Lasher's in Green Street.

This, she reflected, had become a highly instructive afternoon.

Six

M iss Tolerance was no innocent, and was familiar with the
general run of brothels in London, but she had never before
set foot in a house exclusively run for the pleasure of flagellants. It
was a pursuit which baffled her: if one was neither a criminal nor
a schoolchild, what possible reason could there be to be whipped?
She had not been caned since she was seven or eight (although her
father had threatened it, upon learning of her love for Charles
Connell), and certainly she had never sought such punishment.
Her first impulse was to return to Manchester Square to take up
the armor of her masculine garb, but to do so would be to lose the
momentum of inquiry she had achieved. She left the coffeehouse
and walked to Mrs. Lasher's. Whatever the character of the house,
she reflected, its address suggested that it catered to the gentry. Indeed, when she reached the address Steen had given her, she
found the trappings of respectable commerce not unlike those at
Mrs. Brereton's establishment: well-maintained property, polished brass, and a doorman in clean livery.

Miss Tolerance applied to see the brothel's manager.

"Mrs. Lasher's occupied, miss." The doorman, with condescension suited to the household of a duke, looked Miss Tolerance

up and down and made it plain he was unimpressed with what he saw.

Miss Tolerance smiled politely. "Then perhaps I may wait for her. I only need a few minutes of her time." She patted the reticule at her side meaningfully. "I would be very appreciative."

With a boldness that belied both her drab, respectable costume and her pleasant demeanor, Miss Tolerance planted herself in the foyer. It was smaller than that in Mrs. Brereton's establishment, and less lavish in its appointments, but the smells were predominantly of beeswax and blacking, and it was well lit.

"I shall wait here." She took a straight-backed chair stationed outside a withdrawing room and smiled up at the doorman, who was obviously perplexed by the novelty of this visit. He left her alone in the hallway; Miss Tolerance could hear tones of urgent conversation beyond the stairs. After a few minutes more a hard-faced older woman in unrelieved black appeared before Miss Tolerance and asked her business. Miss Tolerance had her measure at once, and met cold dismissiveness with authority.

"I need a few minutes of Mrs. Lasher's time, on urgent business. No, I am afraid I cannot trust the matter to anyone else. No, I shall stay here until she can see me."

The woman sniffed, went away, and returned after a quarter hour, when she appeared surprised to see Miss Tolerance still there. She left again, returned after another quarter hour or so, and this time asked Miss Tolerance to follow her. She led Miss Tolerance up the stairs. Whatever the specialty of the house, Miss Tolerance reflected, the fundamental noises and comments audible through the closed doors seemed much the same as at Mrs. Brereton's. The woman on the landing above, in a costume like a Hussar's uniform, complete to the tall shako on her head, carrying a riding crop, was novel.

"In here," her escort said. Miss Tolerance brought her attention back, murmured her thanks, and went in. She found a plump older woman seated on a sofa, gently dabbing with a sea sponge at welts on the back of a younger woman who sat, naked from the waist up, beside her. A tray at her feet held a basin of blood-stained water, another sponge, and several jars of ointment. Both women were chatting unconcerned, as if such wounds were not worth commenting upon—and in this venue perhaps that was so. The older woman spared a glance for her visitor, then returned to her work.

"Mrs. Lasher?"

The older woman looked up again. She wore a frilled cap perched on brazen hair, and a girlish dress which displayed too much well-worn bosom. The half-naked girl stared at Miss Tolerance curiously but seemed unself-conscious in her own undress.

"I'm Mrs. Lasher." The woman lisped slightly. "Are you come looking for work? If you are, I must tell you at present we have all the girls we need. Unless you have a *specialty*." She looked Miss Tolerance up and down, much as the footman had done.

"I haven't come seeking employment, ma'am."

The madam's face hardened. "Then what? Come to beg me to send your man home?" Her tone was mocking. "I'll tell you what I've told others, girlie: if your man got at home what he gets here—"

"I'm sure that's all true, ma'am, but I'm afraid you misread me. I merely require information about one of your late clients."

"Information?" Mrs. Lasher put the sponge aside and began to dab the girl's welts with a greenish salve. She took her time, finished her work, draped a robe gently over the girl's shoulders and wiped her hands. "You'll do, Jen. Off you go." She waited until the girl had departed, then turned back to Miss Tolerance. "And who would *you* be?"

"I am Miss Tolerance, ma'am. I've been asked to inquire into the death of one of your late patrons."

Mrs. Lasher's small black eyes narrowed. "A death? We've had no death here."

Miss Tolerance hastened to reassure her. "Of course not, ma'am. But I was told that the Chevalier d'Aubigny—"

A look of mingled apprehension and relief crossed the madam's face. "Oh. Him. You'll pardon if I got a little wary, missy. A woman in my business is prey to all sorts of rumors. Truth to tell, since I heard the chevalier'd got killed I've half expected someone to come round. I never expected it would be a woman, though." She looked at Miss Tolerance with renewed curiosity. "Why ain't it the Runners? How comes a female to be poking around in this business. Tolerance, is it?"

"Yes, ma'am. Sarah Tolerance. I earn my living asking questions." Miss Tolerance smiled politely. "Am I correct that the chevalier was one of your patrons?"

Mrs. Lasher nodded. "Was. 'E started out to come regular." Having established an equality of footing, her pretense to genteel speech diminished. "We weren't quite what was 'e was lookin' for."

"Indeed, ma'am? How so?"

The older woman leaned forward confidingly. "Some men come here, they want to be lashed, scolded, taken down a bit. Some want to do the whipping. They all want to *play*. The chevalier, though, what he really liked was too rich for our blood. A real brute, 'e was. I had to keep a girl in the room to chaperone, otherwise 'e'd go too far. 'Ad is own gear for it and all—"

"Gear?" Miss Tolerance's imagination failed her.

"Aye. A regular kit he had, and would pay well to use it. Not just whips, neither. Most of my girls wouldn't, not after one time with 'im. At the last I had to tell 'im 'e was welcome for a civil whippin', but we couldn't tolerate the rest. That was the end of 'im and us. I hadn't seen 'im in near a year. You'll hear the same story at all the birching houses in town. We talk among ourselves, see. That's how 'is sort ends up: thrown out of the quality houses and having to find poor girls that's desperate enough to take his money. Now the chevalyer, 'e set a woman up for his private use."

"Did he?"

"Din't she come around 'ere about a month ago and tell me herself, asking could I use 'er some time? 'E run out of money, I imagine. Josie's a good looker and willin', and if she was good enough for the chevalier, I figgered she'd do for us."

"A month ago? Before he died, then."

"Must have been," Mrs. Lasher agreed.

"What about the chevalier himself? Can you tell me anything about him?"

Mrs. Lasher shrugged and her raddled chest heaved. "A lordly one, wasn't he, nothin' too good for 'im." She rose, clearly feeling the interview was at an end.

Miss Tolerance thought back to what Steen had told her. "Was he ever accompanied by a friend, Mrs. Lasher?"

The madam pursed her lips in a parody of reticence. "I dunno as I should say. The chevalier's dead, and never mind to 'im. But—"

"Let me try again. I was told that the chevalier came here with a Mr. Beauville. Do you know where I might find him?" Miss Tolerance took up her reticule as she spoke. The gesture was not lost upon Mrs. Lasher.

"'E and the chevalier was thick as thieves," she agreed. "Though Mr. Beauville's tastes din't run so rich. When Josie's here 'e comes to see her—for a bit of civil fucking, mind, and nothing nasty. We don't take names and addresses, miss."

"Perhaps I might speak to Josie, then."

Mrs. Lasher shook her head. "She don't live on the premises. Sees 'er callers by appointment, you might say. Can't say when she'll be back."

Miss Tolerance asked for Josie's address but received only a frown. Miss Tolerance did not press. For the moment Mrs. Lasher had said what she was comfortable saying. It would not do to lose her good will and future cooperation. Miss Tolerance opened her reticule and extracted a note.

"I hope I may call upon you again some time, if further questions arise."

Mrs. Lasher looked at the note and pursed her lips. Finally she nodded. "Will you find your way out? I've some tidying to do here."

Miss Tolerance nodded, curtsied and left.

Night was fully fallen when she emerged from Mrs. Lasher's. She had accomplished a good deal that day, but there was one intriguing path of inquiry left to her: Miss Tolerance was obliged to admit herself strongly drawn, by private curiosity as well as necessity, to investigate the chevalier's association with the salon of Madame Camille Touvois.

About Madame Touvois Miss Tolerance knew only what was repeated as *on dit* in her aunt's establishment, or reported in the social notes of those gazettes that covered the *moyen*, as well as the *haut ton*. She knew, for example, that Madame Touvois occupied a set of rooms in Audley Street and, for her evening parties, kept them filled with a lively mix of poets, politicians, pamphleteers, peers, painters, playwrights and women of all sorts. She knew there was frequently music, or the reading of poetry; that essayists and pundits were said to polish their epigrams there, and the conversation was reputed to be wide-ranging, vigorous, and radical in tone. She did not imagine it would be too difficult to insinuate herself into such a gathering.

Miss Tolerance returned to Manchester Square to dress for the purpose. It took some ingenuity to devise a costume fashionable enough for such an evening but not so fashionable as to draw attention. Upon this errand she was determined to stay in the background, whence her best observations might be made. She settled upon an evening dress of moss-green silk, a particular favorite of hers. With her dark hair pinned up with a beaded ornament and her warmest cloak wrapped around her, and armed with no invitation but her own wit, she set out for Audley Street.

She gained entry to the party without much ado, mingling with a crowd as they entered the building. Once inside she left her cloak with a weary attendant at the door and proceeded in to the party.

The apartment was made up of several large rooms, all quite crowded. By the evidence of plates and cups already emptied and abandoned throughout the first room, Miss Tolerance understood a refreshment table to be located further in. She assumed the hopeful expression of one in search of sustenance, which gave her license to move through the party without the need to speak to anyone. A group of writers expounded upon the perfidy of publishers; a throng of somberly dressed men debated the government's handling of the war, their boisterous pessimism fueled by gin punch. An intense young man with a soft collar and sloppily tied kerchief attempted to attract her attention. A young woman in sheer silk and deep décolleté was arguing passionately upon the subject of girls' education with a man whose eyes did not once rise above her collarbone. A tall, spare man of middle years was listening to the views of a substantially younger man with very bad skin; they appeared to be debating the War Support Bill and whether it would cause outright starvation among the peasantry;

the older man kept his hand on the younger one's shoulder, kneading it possessively, and it appeared his thoughts were upon hungers which would not be solved by a good harvest.

It was, all in all, very much what Miss Tolerance had expected.

In the last and largest of the rooms she found a table piled with cakes, fruit and savories, and a man dispensing cups of punch and lemonade. Across from the refreshments a group of men were clustered; from the center of the group distinctly feminine laughter issued, cutting through the masculine noise. Casually Miss Tolerance worked her way to the edge of the crowd, whence she saw a woman holding forth with great animation upon the crimes of the current French regime. This, Miss Tolerance surmised, was her hostess, Madame Camille Touvois.

"—The property of the poor? May the Good God preserve us from sentimental optimists! The poor have no property! The only right the poor have in France, Mr. Allen, is to provide more fodder for the cannons."

Madame Touvois turned to hear a murmured question, then threw back her head in a great laugh. She was not a beauty, Miss Tolerance observed. Her features were irregular, her hair was sandy-colored and coarse—from the sheen of candlelight upon it Miss Tolerance gathered it was unruly and had taken a generous amount of pomade to subdue—and her skin a little sallow. However, she was amply supplied with that confidence and vivacity which made beauty inconsequential. Her eyes were handsome, dark, and compelling. Her mouth was small and neatly shaped, with small white teeth. When she smiled, Camille Touvois looked as though she were poised to bite something.

Or someone, Miss Tolerance thought.

She drew back from the crowd and made her way back to the refreshment table, where she took a cup of lemonade and a plate of pretty, flavorless iced cakes. Armed and disguised by these items, Miss Tolerance took a seat and observed all who came and went from the circle around Madame Touvois. The hostess liked to hold court, and that suited Miss Tolerance exactly. Tonight she wanted to observe rather than act, and was grateful that the press of guests made this possible. But in the course of an hour she observed little more than she had in the first five minutes: Madame

Touvois was a lively, informed speaker who preferred her own opinions to those of the majority of men around her. What fascinated Miss Tolerance was that each man hung on her acerbic utterance, apparently convinced that Madame Touvois's darts were directed at some other fellow, not at himself.

Miss Tolerance grew restless. She rose and began a circuit of the rooms again. While the conversation was lively, she did not find it compelling. What was the use of arguing over the wisdom of the government doing this or that when the government plainly meant to prosecute the war and govern the nation without recourse to the opinions of Madame Touvois' guests? And how seriously could one take a poet after hearing him argue the merits of sonnet forms and bootblacking in almost the same sentence?

"You have enjoyed yourself this evening?"

Miss Tolerance turned to find Madame Touvois herself examining her with an expression in which amusement seemed to take the greater part, but the tone of her question had been all solicitousness. Although she was known to be an émigré it was her manner of speech, rather than an accent, which suggested that English had not been Camille Touvois' first language.

"Indeed, ma'am," Miss Tolerance said. "I have never heard so many deep thinkers speaking with such authority!"

"Authority, yes." She leaned forward confidingly. "Between us, mademoiselle, my guests come for the table, and the drink, and most of all to hear themselves speak. There are a few who are clever, but the rest—" She shook her head.

It was so exactly what Miss Tolerance had been thinking that it took her a moment to respond. "Then why invite them, madame?"

"Why, to hear *myself* speak!" Madame Touvois looked delighted with herself. "At least I have the consolation that someone is speaking sense."

Miss Tolerance put on an expression of mild shock.

"Surely, ma'am, Mr. Southey and Mr. Cobbett—"

"Poets?" The woman shrugged. "No poet should be permitted to have ideas beyond meter and rhyme. Now I have shocked you. How very bad of me."

"Oh, no, certainly not." Miss Tolerance's tone suggested otherwise.

"Mademoiselle, you have me at an advantage, for you have guessed that I am Camille Touvois, and I do not know you. But wait—" She put her hand out in a theatrical gesture. "I do know you!"

"I do not think so, ma'am."

"I do," Madame Touvois said positively. For a moment she said nothing more; Miss Tolerance suspected she would wait until she saw some disquiet on the part of her guest. It became her own goal to show no such emotion. After an awkward moment of silence Madame Touvois repeated, "I know you. But not from my evenings. Shall I tell you how?"

Miss Tolerance smiled politely.

"I saw you speak at the trial of the earl. Versellion. Edward Folle."

"You were in the gallery, ma'am?" Miss Tolerance strove to keep strong dislike from coloring her voice. She had testified against Versellion with outward composure, but she had come to loathe the audience that crowded the gallery. They treated the trial as a gala or a pantomime, bursting often into laughter, cheers, or catcalls.

"Indeed I was, every day! 'Twas your evidence convicted him. It's a clever thing to bring a peer down, my dear. I commend you."

"I did not bring him down, ma'am. He did that himself."

Madame Touvois' smile broadened; the disquieting quality increased. It was as if the woman felt she had the upper hand in the conversation and was waiting for Miss Tolerance to acknowledge it.

"Did he so?" she asked. "So, what brings you to us tonight, Miss—I regret that I cannot recall your name." She moved, Miss Tolerance thought, from one manner to another; from polite disbelief to polite inquiry, each attitude a little more theatrical than real.

"Did I not give my name, ma'am? It is Sarah Tolerance."

"Tolerance? What a curious name." It seemed Madame Touvois's habit to leave something unstated—in this case, the fact that her name marked Miss Tolerance as a Fallen Woman—to unsettle her guest.

" 'Tis a good old English word," Miss Tolerance replied evenly, "and a quality I aspire to." She was conscious of a pang of excitement, as though at the beginning of a fencing match. She must be entirely upon her guard with this woman.

"Whatever your name, I am delighted that you have come. But why should a—what are you? A thief-taker? What does a thief-taker in my *salon*?"

"Even a thief-taker may read poetry, madame, or have an interest in the arts or politics. I was curious about these parties, to which so many interesting people come."

Madame Touvois sketched an ironic curtsy. "I am delighted that the company entertains you. Then I need not fear that a woman who has brought down one criminal is on the prowl for more?"

A cat with a mouse, Miss Tolerance thought. Her jaw set; she was no mouse.

"Oh, I seek no criminals unless I am hired to do so, ma'am. Merely enlightenment. Why? Do you suspect your guests of villainy?"

"These?" Camille Touvois scanned the room, her eyebrows raised as if to invite Miss Tolerance in on the joke. "Villainous verse perhaps? Malicious government? Criminal arrogance? I doubt it. Most of these gentlemen could not summon up a backbone shared between them." She turned back to Miss Tolerance, observing her through narrowed eyes. "But with one of my regular *habitués* so recently dead, I cannot help but wonder when a woman such as yourself turns up upon my doorstep."

"A guest, dead? What, this evening?"

For a moment some strong emotion was evident in Madame Touvois's expression. As quickly as it had come it was gone, and the bland, slightly predatory smile was in its place. "Is he so soon forgotten? What a sad thing is mortality! But surely your *profession* requires you to be a little more *au courant*, my dear—"

"The requirements of my profession are necessarily elastic, madame. But you were speaking of the dead?"

"Etienne d'Aubigny. He used to come and listen to the poets hold forth. Much as you have done this evening."

Madame Touvois was watching Miss Tolerance closely.

Miss Tolerance impersonated bemused incomprehension. "Take

me with you, madame. Are you saying that attendance here was the cause of his death?"

"What, talked to death?" Camille Touvois laughed. "No, rather, bludgeoned, if the newspapers are right. As M. d'Aubigny was known to visit me, I wondered if you had not been sent by Bow Street."

"I do not work for Bow Street, ma'am."

"Do you not?" Madame Touvois' smile became acute. "I should like to know for whom you do work."

"When I am working, my client's identity is confidential."

"So you are not working tonight, mademoiselle?"

"I am enjoying myself this evening," Miss Tolerance said, and realized that it was not untrue.

"I am happy to hear it," Madame Touvois said. "I wonder—" she trailed off provocatively.

"Yes, madame?"

"I wonder how one becomes *what you are*." The emphasis, and the thinly disguised insult behind it, did not elude Miss Tolerance.

"An agent of inquiry?"

"Yes, I should like very much to know how an Englishwoman of good birth becomes an agent of inquiry."

Miss Tolerance recognized a bolt meant to draw her into some indiscreet comment. She only smiled. "Oh, I am sure someone could tell you that story. I make no secret of my past, madame."

"But you have some questions about mine, I think, Miss Tolerance. You must come some afternoon and I shall give you tea. Perhaps we may exchange confidences."

To what advantage Miss Tolerance might have turned this invitation she could not know. At that moment Camille Touvois was interrupted by a manservant who murmured urgently into her ear. She nodded and turned back to Miss Tolerance.

"A special guest has arrived and I must greet him. You must remember: tea and confidences, Miss Tolerance."

Before Miss Tolerance had risen from her curtsy Madame Touvois was gone, leaving Miss Tolerance with a sense of breathlessness, as if she had just completed a brisk fencing match. She had no idea whether she had won, lost, or drawn, but she was left with a lively curiosity about the identity of the special guest. It was not kept a secret. Within a moment the manservant stepped to the doorway and cleared his throat.

"His Royal Highness, the Duke of Cumberland!"

Cumberland? Was it possible the announcement was a jest? Of all the royal dukes, why would the violently conservative Cumberland show himself in this hotbed of talky radicalism?

Miss Tolerance, like all the other women in the room, dropped into curtsy at Cumberland's entrance, all a-maze.

She had once met Cumberland's eldest brother, the Prince of Wales. Her impression of Wales had been of a good-natured man, quite possibly a clever one, who disguised his wit with a manner both informal and friendly. Watching from behind lowered lashes, she noted that Cumberland had neither of those qualities: his eye was sharp and intelligent, but there was a malicious light in it. His air was disdainful and condescending; he appeared to view his fellow man, or at least that sample gathered at Madame Touvois', as he might a collection for curiosities from the Antipodes. In looks, too, he was unlike his brother: he had his brother's height, but was thin where Wales was corpulent, handsome in a cold way, but marked with several still-livid scars. From the attempt upon his life in August, Miss Tolerance thought.

Cumberland let the room remain in obeisance for a full minute before he motioned the guests to rise again. From the appearance of his manner to Camille Touvois, and hers to him, he was on cordial terms with the hostess.

What had Sir Walter said? D'Aubigny's murder had come hard on the heels of the attack upon Cumberland. It had been the similarity of it, that both men had been attacked in their beds, which brought the two together in his mind, a similarity he had then dismissed. But it appeared that Cumberland and d'Aubigny were connected by the common thread of Madame Touvois. What would Sir Walter say to that?

Miss Tolerance meditated upon these questions for some time, until she grew restless. Cumberland held court in the first room, with Madame Touvois at his elbow. The hostess had ceded her position at the center of the evening to the duke, and made herself his faithful audience. The rest of the party seemed inhibited by his presence: many of the guests Miss Tolerance had marked as government men departed, and a good number of the poets as well. Where earlier the party had seemed largely male, now the balance had changed. Many of the women who were left appeared to be parading themselves before Cumberland, quite as if . . . The women were indeed parading, Miss Tolerance realized, hoping to catch the duke's eye. He looked at each one but appeared in no hurry to make his selection. Madame Touvois stood at his elbow, apparently commenting upon each woman who went by.

The *salon* had suddenly taken on the character of a market, and Miss Tolerance had no interest in being mistaken for part of the commerce. She was just about to take her leave when she saw Madame Touvois smile encouragingly at one of the women, who advanced to join her at Cumberland's side. Miss Tolerance had met the woman, but on that occasion she had been dressed in a stuff gown with her hair pulled tightly back. Now she wore a dress of rosy silk, banded with gold embroidery, and her hair fell in pomaded curls from a Grecian knot. There was nothing about her to suggest the courtesan except, perhaps, her bearing and a knowing smile. Her look appeared to please Cumberland, who returned her smile and nodded.

Mrs. Vose, whom Miss Tolerance had met in Half Moon Street the first time she had called there, seemed as much at ease in Camille Touvois' drawing room as she had in the d'Aubigny parlor.

As Cumberland had evidently made a choice, the conversation in the room started up again. Miss Tolerance had had enough, and more than enough to think about. She collected her cloak and requested that the porter fetch her a chair. The noise was as loud behind her as it had been when she arrived, and she found herself thankful of the chance to think in the icy night air.

Seven

Miss Tolerance hoped for nothing more than to go home, have a cup of soup or a dram of whiskey, and fall into her bed. She had the chairmen deliver her to Manchester Square and Mrs. Brereton's house, the better to wheedle supper from Cook, but was greeted there with trouble. Cole opened the door, saw her, and turned his head to summon someone else forward.

"I was hopeful you'd come through the house tonight!" Her friend Marianne Touchwell, in a plain gown and apron which made her look more like a worried farmer's wife than a popular *fille de joie*, came forward and took Miss Tolerance's arm. "Give me your cloak, please. I wish you will come see your aunt; she's not well at all." Miss Tolerance was less alarmed by the words than by the uncharacteristic anxiety which she saw in her friend's light eyes, and the crease of a frown between her brows.

Miss Tolerance did her best to shrug off her exhaustion. She followed Marianne up the stairs, noting that while the business of the house went on as usual, Cole admitted gentlemen to the house with an expression of gravity not unlike Marianne's. Miss Tolerance, who had never known her aunt to fall prey to more than a head cold, grew apprehensive.

Mrs. Brereton's room was hot and close; the windows were

tightly shut and curtained, and the bed hangings were drawn. Mrs. Brereton slept in the center of the large bed, lost in a tumble of sheets and blankets. Her cheeks were flushed. She frowned deeply in her sleep and, as Miss Tolerance watched, made a feeble motion with one hand as if to pull the covers off. Her maid, Frost, pushed the hand away, pulled the covers back into place, and returned to sponging Mrs. Brereton's forehead with a damp cloth.

"Aunt Thea?" Miss Tolerance said quietly. "Aunt?" She went to the bed and bent to kiss her aunt gently on the forehead. Her skin was damp, warm but not frighteningly so: she smelled of rosewater.

"The fever is not high," she said to Marianne.

"But she don't rouse, not even to piss. Twice we've changed the sheets. I've never seen her like this."

"What does the doctor say?"

"She doesn't want the doctor." Frost, on the far side of the bed, put up her hand and the cloth as if signaling *Halt!* Her lips were as pursed as her patient's. "I'm taking fine care of her."

"Of course you are," Miss Tolerance agreed. "But I really think—"

"We don't need a doctor," Frost said again. She glared at Miss Tolerance and Marianne. *Lord, it needs only this,* Miss Tolerance thought. Her aunt's appearance worried her more than the maid's jealousy.

"How long has my aunt been like this?"

Marianne answered. "Since early this evening. A matter of five or six hours. We have twice given her powders, but nothing seems to help. Frost has been with her constantly."

"I am sure she has." Miss Tolerance smiled at Frost. The maid scowled. "Does my aunt have a doctor she prefers?"

"She's consulted with Sir George Hammond once or twice, I know."

"Have Cole send for him," Miss Tolerance ordered.

"We don't want the doctor," Frost insisted. She wadded the cloth in her hand and dropped it into the basin as if throwing down a gauntlet.

"Perhaps you don't," Miss Tolerance agreed. "But I shall feel very much better if Sir George looks in. At very least he will praise your excellent care—and tell us if there's anything else we should be doing."

"Madam won't want—"

"Perhaps not, and she may scold me when she recovers. In the meantime, Marianne, please ask Cole to send for Sir George."

Marianne left with a look of gratitude. Miss Tolerance sat down to wait at her aunt's side, and Frost fixed her with a look so arctic it should have returned Mrs. Brereton's temperature to its normal state. Miss Tolerance closed her eyes.

M iss? Doctor's come."

She wakened from her doze. Looking at the clock upon the mantel, Miss Tolerance discovered the hour was well advanced—it was almost eight in the morning. At what time she had fallen asleep she did not know, but Miss Tolerance rose now to greet Sir George Hammond. He was tall, lean, and younger than his title suggested, but he wore an expression of professional compassion which Miss Tolerance found comforting. After an exchange of courtesies, Sir George advanced upon the bed and stood for several minutes, holding Mrs. Brereton's hand and observing her face. He turned back to Miss Tolerance.

"Have you a sample for me?"

It had not occurred to her to have a sample of urine ready, but Frost had evidently expected it. Still scowling, she took a glass jar from the table and passed it to the doctor.

"Thank you," both he and Miss Tolerance said at the same moment. Sir George went to the window and pulled a curtain back a little to examine the color of the urine in the light; he smelt it, dabbed a finger in and licked it thoughtfully, swirled the jar around for a moment and examined it again.

"The influenza," he pronounced. "The fever is not dangerously high, but her unresponsiveness does inspire concern. However, as there is no rash, I don't think we need fear that her earlier condition has returned. What have you given her?" He asked the question equally of Miss Tolerance, Frost and Marianne, who had followed him into the room.

"Two doses of Dr. James' powders," Marianne said.

The doctor nodded thoughtfully. "Fever does not appear to be the chiefest concern, but if that excellent remedy has not brought some relief we must try another. Well." He sat at Mrs. Brereton's writing table and took up pen and paper. "I shall prescribe a draught which should do the trick. But you must open these windows and give the poor woman a little fresh air. Bathe her with rosewater every hour until the fever breaks. She may have barley water—all she will take—and gruel, if she wakes hungry. As for the rest, when she is quite recovered from the influenza I want her to see a surgeon; I shall leave you the name of a fellow with some experience with her old ailment." He wrote a name on another piece of paper.

"She seen someone for it," Frost said flatly.

"Fine, fine. But it never hurts to take extra care." Sir George did not appear ruffled by Frost's rudeness. "Well, then. Take this to the apothecary. Every four hours, one spoonful in wine. I shall look in again tomorrow." He bowed toward a space between Miss Tolerance and Marianne and started for the door. Miss Tolerance went after him.

"Sir George, you said something of my aunt's condition?"

The doctor nodded. "A common enough one in this profession, my dear."

She could not mistake his meaning.

"When I last saw Mrs. Brereton I gave her Mr. Warringe's name, but never heard that she had seen him. If she has been physicking herself, or going to quacks, it is possible the affliction is still with her."

Miss Tolerance nodded. "But you think Mr. Warringe can cure her?"

The doctor shrugged. "No cure is certain, but I will tell you that your aunt is more likely to be cured with proper care than by some of the peculiar remedies advertised for the pox. If I could but persuade the ladies of your profession of that—"

Miss Tolerance straightened her shoulders. "My aunt's profession is not mine, sir." She forced a smile and offered her hand. "I shall see to it she calls upon your surgeon. Thank you for your call."

He paused before he took her hand. "If you are not—what your aunt is, how is it you are here?"

"She is my aunt, sir," Miss Tolerance said.

"Your family-feeling is to be commended," he said drily. He shook her hand briefly, then left.

K eefe was dispatched to the apothecary. Frost, frowning, permitted the windows to be opened a few inches, as the doctor had ordered it, but refused to leave her post for refreshment. Marianne and Miss Tolerance went downstairs to break their fast. Miss Tolerance was shortly aware that the servants—from Keefe to the girl who brought their coffee—were looking to her for their orders. Mrs. Brereton kept no housekeeper; she was accustomed to making virtually all domestic decisions herself, and did not take the staff into her confidence.

"I cannot think what to tell anyone, other than that they should carry on," she said to Marianne. "If I were not here, who would give the cook her orders or—do whatever must be done?"

"No one," Marianne said flatly. "We'd cobble along best we could."

"But surely you know more than I do—"

Marianne nodded. "But Mrs. B wouldn't want me to take it upon myself."

"Well, I will take that upon *myself*. If I ask you to manage things here while my aunt is ill, the order comes from family, and must therefore be unexceptionable." Miss Tolerance added with humor, "And I do not ask, I implore it. Think how much better everyone will feel, knowing someone is in charge!"

"But you—"

"Not I. I have other matters to attend to. Keefe!"

The footman, returned from the apothecary, presented himself.

"Miss Marianne will have the ordering of the household until Mrs. Brereton is able to take matters back into her hands," Miss Tolerance said. "Will you let the others know?"

"But Miss Sarah, oughtn't you—"

"No," Miss Tolerance was firm. "And no one with a jot of sense would think I should. But I'll look in again this afternoon to see how my aunt goes on."

"Very good, Miss Sarah," Keefe said.

Marianne looked regretfully at her coffee. "I suppose I had best talk with Cook," she said. "And I suppose that for the next few days I shall have to say *adieu* to most of my followers. If Lord Marton should call, Keefe, or Mr. Waxworth—" she went from the room, instructing the footman on which of her clients she would accept while Mrs. Brereton was ill. Miss Tolerance finished her coffee before she could be joined by any of the brothel's clients or employees, and fled to her cottage.

M iss Tolerance washed and dressed herself in breeches and coat for riding and took up her hat and Gunnard greatcoat. When the stables had sent round her favorite hack she started off for the Liberty of Savoy again to hear what Mr. Glebb had been able to learn. As if to atone for the last week's dreary skies, the sun shone strongly, piercing the perpetual coal haze and taking an edge from the cold. Miss Tolerance arrived at the Wheat Sheaf before Joshua Glebb, and again took refuge and coffee with the tapster, Mr. Boddick.

As the Wheat Sheaf received the London papers, Mr. Boddick followed the progress of the Peninsular War closely. A veteran himself, he was energetic in denouncing Bonaparte and his generals, but just as vociferous regarding the stupidities of England's recent conduct of the war. As Miss Tolerance drank her coffee, Boddick reviled all parties—the government, the military, and God—about equally. He was particularly bitter about Wellington's apparent refusal to chase the French forces out of Portugal after his victory at Busaco.

"Only one victory since summer! That's not much for man nor nation to 'ang 'is heart on! Specially not when them in Parliament's looking to bleed a starvin' nation in Wellington's support."

"The troops must be provisioned," Miss Tolerance said mildly, curious to see upon which side of this issue Boddick came down.

"Aye, and indeed they do. Nothin' takes the heart out of a soldier more than being hungry, miss. But this War Support Bill? Three bad harvests, with the common folk starvin' in the countryside, and still His Royal Grace of bloody Cumberland's made damned sure that him and his noble pals won't pay a groat toward keepin' thesselves safe."

"Mr. Boddick, you sound positively Republican," Miss Tolerance said, smiling.

"Heaven forfend, miss. But that War Support Bill's a grand way to stir up sympathy for Bonaparte, if you ask me. Folk who ain't been abroad and don't know is likely to think they'd be in no worse case did Boney win. Well, miss, I marched through Holland with Cornwallis; I know what the French done to the countryside."

"I, too," Miss Tolerance agreed. She and her lover Charles Connell had been in Belgium in 1800 when Brune's armies had taken the country. She was under no illusion that the French force was the army of liberation Bonaparte styled it.

"Britain never fails in a clinch, miss. We'll pull through and put Bonaparte down; who else is there to do it?"

Miss Tolerance sipped her coffee as Boddick disposed, one by one, of each of the nations of Europe, suggesting their fates if the war were lost, and again if it should be won. His predictions were fascinating and lurid. Finally his opinions ran down and, apparently abashed at his own vehemence, the barman apologized if he had spoken too strong, and began to polish his taps. Miss Tolerance finished her coffee and pleased herself by imagining the effect Boddick would have had upon the political theorists at Camille Touvois' salon.

Joshua Glebb arrived shortly thereafter. Established in his accustomed place, Mr. Glebb informed Miss Tolerance that he had made her inquiries.

"Now, here's a thing," he said thoughtfully. "I've asked around among all my acquaintance. Your chevalier, he owed money right enough, to a dozen tradesmen and, near as I can tell, all the sharpers in the clubs. Liked to live well, Moosoor Dobinny did; coat from Weston and breeches from White and Thomas, wine from James and Son and snuff from Freiborg and Trayer. Whoever kept 'is household practiced tuppenny economies—second-best bit of beef and mutton stew for the servants' hall—but that can't have helped much. And since you asked, he did sell off paintings and gew-gaws about town. But then that stopped."

Glebb took a long and grateful draught of coffee and poked a stubby finger into the pie Boddick had brought him. A rich scent of beef and onion rose up with the steam thus released. Glebb sniffed appreciatively and took up his fork.

"What stopped?" Miss Tolerance asked.

"The selling off," Glebb mumbled through his pie. "Same time as some of the tradesman's duns was paid off. I suppose the gaming debts was covered as well—I can't know about them. But here's a thing," he said again. The soft folds of skin under Glebb's chin shook as he chewed and considered. "No one loaned 'im the money. Not bank, not cents-per-cent, and not gullgroper. That money didn't come from no one I know—which is to say, it didn't come from no one."

"What about gaming? Could his luck have changed long enough for him to have discharged his debts?"

"I didn't hear of it. The question occurred to me, so I asked it, too. It ain' natural, money just appearing and I can't trace it. It ain't what I like."

Miss Tolerance gave this outburst of professional pride a moment of respectful silence. Then, "Could he have borrowed money from a friend, or someone not in London?"

Glebb nodded. "That's my suspicion, miss. Maybe he has an old auntie was an easy touch? All I know is, your Moosoor Dobinny owed money to all and sundry, and then he didn't, and no one in the moneylending line in London helped him to do it. Now," he added. "A man's time is worth something, miss."

Miss Tolerance nodded. "It is, Mr. Glebb. Thank you." She felt for her pocketbook and handed him a bank note. "I hope that will be sufficient."

Mr. Glebb regarded the note affectionately. "Handsome, miss. Very handsome. Well, I think that concludes our business." He looked over her shoulder. Miss Tolerance understood by this that her time was at an end, and deferred to a squat, swarthy man who was awaiting Mr. Glebb's attention.

M r. Adolphus Beak, who opened the door to the d'Aubigny house, recognized Miss Tolerance at once despite her unorthodox dress. The crowd outside was only a little reduced from what it had been a few days before.

"Do they never go home?" Miss Tolerance asked.

"When they do, others come in their places, miss," he said. "All of them crazed to see the place where murder was done. Shameful." Beak eyed Miss Tolerance's attire as if to include it in his pronouncement.

"Quite. But I have come to see your mistress." Miss Tolerance said. "Will you tell her I am here?"

Beak started as if regretting his moment of familiarity. "Madame is upstairs in her little parlor. Will you follow me, please?"

Miss Tolerance followed.

Anne d'Aubigny's parlor was indeed little: a small, square chamber at the front of the house. Unlike the salon downstairs, the parlor did not appear to be missing anything by way of mantel clock or painting, but that might be because there was so little one might reasonably have sold. Miss Tolerance had the impression that the room had been furnished with odds and ends of furniture not wanted elsewhere in the house. It was certainly a dreary room: the drapes were half-drawn, occluding the winter light, and no candles had been lit. The widow herself was seated by the fire with a book of sermons in her hand, open but face down.

"Miss Tolerance, ma'am," Beak said, and bowed himself out of the room. Miss Tolerance waited for a moment; Anne d'Aubigny appeared lost in her thoughts.

"I hope I see you well, ma'am?" Miss Tolerance advanced and bowed.

"Oh." Mrs. d'Aubigny appeared to return from a place very far away. "Oh, yes, thank you," she began, and made a halfhearted attempt to rise. As she dropped into her chair again the widow focused at last upon her visitor. Her surprise and dismay at Miss Tolerance's costume was no less evident than Beak's had been.

"I apologize for coming to you in this peculiar dress, but it is convenient for those days when I must call in some of London's less genteel neighborhoods."

"Oh," Mrs. d'Aubigny said again. "But surely you must meet more ill use in that—in those—"

Miss Tolerance smiled. "On occasion. But not so much that I

would give up the option to dress this way. It gives me greater freedom in moving about the city."

"Freedom," Anne d'Aubigny repeated, as if the word were an exotic one. She recalled herself and asked how Miss Tolerance's inquiries were faring.

"Well enough so that I have new questions for you, ma'am. I spoke to a source who tells me that while it was well known that your husband had recently come into funds, the money was not loaned to him by any banker or usurer in London."

A line appeared between Mrs. d'Aubigny's brows. "How could this person know such a thing? Not loaned by anyone in the whole of London?"

"It is this gentleman's livelihood to be acquainted with all the people in London who are in the business of lending money. I am confident that when he says this, it is true. He did wonder if perhaps your husband had borrowed money from a relative or friend privately, or from someone outside of London, where he has fewer contacts."

"My husband has no relatives living, not in England—and if any are alive in France, I am sure they are in no case to loan him money."

"That does leave us with a puzzle," Miss Tolerance said. The widow had not yet invited her to sit, and it was difficult for her to maintain a confidential tone when she stood over her client in a pose which must emphasize, not their common femininity, but the distance between them. "I confirmed with his superior at the Home Office that the chevalier was unlikely to have borrowed money from anyone there. Had he any friends not in London—"

"I don't know where it came from, nor where it went—except the little that he gave me to pay the household expenses." The widow lowered her head sulkily. "Why is this money of such importance?"

"It is a mystery, and such must always command attention. And it was you who suggested that money might be the motive for your husband's murder."

As Miss Tolerance watched, Anne d'Aubigny shook off her sulks. "I have forgot my manners, Miss Tolerance. Please sit down. You are quite right, of course. I did say that. But I cannot tell you what I do not know—and that is whence Etienne received that money."

"I understand. And frankly, ma'am, I do not think that money alone could inspire so violent a crime. There was rage in the act which killed your husband, ma'am. Rage or madness."

The widow shuddered. "You may imagine how I have thought about this, Miss Tolerance. Indeed, I have racked my brain for some idea, and still I have none. No one in my household told you anything of use, I take it?"

"Nothing immediately useful, no. It is quite a large household for only two people, isn't it?"

Mrs. d'Aubigny smiled wanly. "We keep too many servants. That will have to change. For our circumstances a maid, a man, and the cook should have been sufficient. But Beak came with the hire of the house, and Mrs. Sadgett as well. Etienne thought the desirable situation was worth the expense; I think he believed that a large household gave him more consequence as well. But Beak is too old to do half of what we would ask of a footman, and so we have Jacks as well. And Mary Pitt. And my Sophie has been with me since—"

"Please, I did not mean that you must account for your household to me, ma'am. Only, it is a great many people, even with your husband's valet gone. And what of Mrs. Vose, ma'am, whom I met on my first visit here?"

Anne d'Aubigny's countenance grew bleak. "She is my husband's cousin."

Miss Tolerance's attention was caught by a perceptible pause between the last two words. "Did you not tell me your husband had no relatives now living?"

"I meant he had none living who would be able to lend him money," Mrs. d'Aubigny said. "I have no—"

What the widow did not have, Miss Tolerance was not to learn. In that moment Beak announced the arrival of Mr. William Heddison and Mr. Boyse, of the Greater Marlborough Street Public Office. Beak waited for instruction.

Mrs. d'Aubigny turned to Miss Tolerance. "The magistrate! Must I see him? He plagues me every day."

"I think you had better see him," Miss Tolerance said gently. "If you do not, he will certainly take it amiss."

Mrs. d'Aubigny nodded, and Beak turned to invite the law into the widow's parlor.

Having heard her friend Sir Walter's opinion of Mr. Heddison, Miss Tolerance was curious to meet him. However, the widow had a right to meet with the man privately, and so she told her.

Anne d'Aubigny shook her head with the first evidence of strong emotion she had given all day. "Please don't leave me! He glares at me so, it frightens me!"

Miss Tolerance nodded. She did not voice the thought that what the widow regarded as harsh treatment, someone less fortunately situated by way of birth and fortune might regard as extraordinary politeness.

Beak returned with Messrs. Heddison and Boyse following. Heddison was a short, plain-dressed man with close-cut gray hair and a wide, thin mouth pressed into an expression of impatience. He had the air of a man who will do his duty but expects no joy from it. His companion was at least twelve inches taller than the magistrate, and so broad that his waistcoat, which was a reddish-brown suggesting the customary red of the Bow Street Runners, strained across his gut. Silvery-white hair fell over his collar, and his round face was smallpox-scarred and red; the color, Miss Tolerance suspected, was only partly from the November wind. As the men entered the room, Heddison looked directly for Mrs. d'Aubigny; Boyse, on the other hand, squinted about him as if appraising the worth of the furnishings. He walked on the balls of his feet, which served to make him loom menacingly. Miss Tolerance was reminded that Sir Walter had said Heddison's constables were men he would not want in his employ.

She and Mrs. d'Aubigny rose to their feet. Heddison bowed to Madame d'Aubigny and Boyse bobbed his shaggy head in a way to suggest the courtesy. At the same moment both men became aware of Miss Tolerance's presence, and of her dress. Boyse appeared to shrug off the company of another person of whatever appearance; Heddison started a bow in her direction and stopped, as if uncertain what he beheld.

"Miss Tolerance," Anne d'Aubigny said. "May I make Mr. Heddison and Mr. Boyse known to you?" Miss Tolerance realized with amusement that the widow was enjoying the magistrate's confusion. She bowed to the men and took her seat. "Miss Tolerance has been engaged by my brother to look after my interests."

"Your interests, madam?" Heddison thought about this for a moment. Then, "I know your name. You're the woman that testified in the matter of the Earl—"

"I am, sir," she said.

"And you are acquainted with a colleague of mine, Sir Walter Mandif?"

Miss Tolerance nodded.

"We have met. He spoke of you," Heddison said thoughtfully. "I hope you do not plan to obstruct my investigation."

What had Sir Walter said of her, Miss Tolerance wondered. "It is the farthest thing from my mind, sir. Mr. Colcannon feared that Mrs. d'Aubigny might be in danger, and asked for my help."

"Danger?" Heddison scoffed.

"A violent murder took place in this house, sir. Until we know why and who did it, we must consider Mrs. d'Aubigny at risk as well."

Heddison stared at Miss Tolerance blankly for a moment, then turned abruptly to Madame d'Aubigny. "I have some questions to put to you, ma'am. Do you wish this person to stay?"

Anne d'Aubigny nodded. "I have no secrets from Miss Tolerance, Mr. Heddison."

The magistrate took a seat, unasked, leaving Mr. Boyse to stand behind him, looming like an unshaven tower. The constable sniffed deeply, rubbed his nose with the back of his hand, then wiped that hand on his breeches. When he looked upon the widow he scowled.

"Well, then." Heddison began with a series of unexceptionable questions: when did Mrs. d'Aubigny retire on the night of the murder, who had bolted the doors, at what hour were the doors customarily unlocked again, did her husband ever lock the door to his own chamber—all questions Miss Tolerance herself had asked. From Mrs. d'Aubigny's rote response, this was not the first time Heddison had asked them either. The widow sat with her hands in her lap like a child before a harsh preceptor, clearly fearful that at any moment a mistake might bring her a scolding or worse. Miss Tolerance judged it time to add a word.

"I beg your pardon, Mr. Heddison, but may I add something you will like to know?"

The magistrate turned to face her with the same expression he might have worn if the pantry cat had spoken to him.

"It appears that the kitchen door was unlocked when the cook arrived on the morning after the murder."

"*Un*locked when the cook arrived?" he repeated.

"Yes, sir. All the servants swear they did not unbolt it. Which suggests that someone else did." Miss Tolerance did not want to point out that if the servants had not done so, that left Mrs. d'Aubigny and the chevalier as the likely culprits. She did not like the possibility that could suggest to Heddison.

"The old man, Beak, may have forgot to bolt it in the first place, or may have forgot that he unbolted it in the morning." Heddison turned to Anne d'Aubigny again. "Do you know how that door came to be unlocked, ma'am?"

"I, sir? No, I could not say."

"Could not say? Someone in your household may have let a murderer in and you cannot say? You expect that I will believe that?"

Anne d'Aubigny's lips trembled. "I do, sir. I am afraid—" she attempted a joking tone. "I am afraid I do not even know what sort of lock the kitchen door has. I could not swear to its mechanism."

The magistrate may have doubted this, but Miss Tolerance, having seen the staff's protectiveness, found it credible if unfortunate.

Heddison cleared his throat. "What of your door, ma'am?"

"My door?"

Heddison nodded. "Was your chamber kept locked at night, ma'am?"

Mrs. d'Aubigny shook her head. "My door has no lock, sir."

"No lock?"

"No lock, sir. My husband had it removed. He said such a thing was—had no place in the household of a gentleman."

In the light of what she had learned of d'Aubigny's character, Miss Tolerance thought this a very sinister piece of information. Mr. Heddison seemed to regard it only as proof of gentlemanly eccentricity. He did ask a few pointed questions about the state of the d'Aubignys' marriage—never quite asking if it had been a happy match. Mrs. d'Aubigny twisted her kerchief and looked from time to time at Miss Tolerance, who could only smile encouragingly.

At last Heddison rose to his feet.

"I will talk to your manservant. Thank you, ma'am." He bowed curtly in Mrs. d'Aubigny's direction, ignored Miss Tolerance, and left the room with Mr. Boyse, sniffing, just behind him.

Anne d'Aubigny turned to Miss Tolerance as if to finish a conversation only just interrupted. "You see? What is one to make of such treatment? One would think they believed I had left the door unbolted."

Miss Tolerance shook her head sadly, wondering how best to make Anne d'Aubigny understand her peril. Plain speaking was surely her best course.

"'Tis worse than that, ma'am," she said quietly. "They think you may be the murderer."

Eight

Believe me the murderer?"

Miss Tolerance closed her eyes and took a breath. *She is an innocent*, she thought. *No one has ever thought worse of her than that she drank up all the nursery cream or took two sweetmeats from the dish instead of one.* She opened her eyes and spoke quietly.

"I had hoped you understood, ma'am. You are threatened, not only by the real murderer, but by the chance that you may be the Crown's best suspect. The law considers the murder of a man by his wife worse than mere homicide—the punishment is a terrible one. It is why I beg that you take your situation seriously. Your brother believes your greatest danger is from an attacker; my fear is that Mr. Heddison may decide that you had cause and opportunity to kill your husband yourself."

Mrs. d'Aubigny stared at her hands, curled in her lap. "Do you think I could do such a thing?" she asked. In the black mourning dress and cap, in this ill-lit room, her pallor was almost luminous. She appeared even smaller than Miss Tolerance knew her to be. "Do you think I overpowered my husband?" Her voice shook. Another moment and she would likely be in full hysterics.

Miss Tolerance knelt by the widow's chair and took her hand.

"Please believe, ma'am, that I do not think you are the murderer. But you are best served by the truth with no varnish upon it: Mr. Heddison very likely considers you a suspect in your husband's death."

"And what—what is this terrible punishment? Are not murderers hanged? What could be worse than that?"

"Burning," Miss Tolerance said baldly. She let this intelligence sink in for a moment before she went on. "You understand now why it is imperative that you tell me anything which may be helpful in my investigation."

Madame d'Aubigny nodded and allowed herself to be seated again.

"You were going to explain Mrs. Vose's presence in your house, ma'am. Since I have recently seen her at the *salon* of Madame Camille Touvois, you may imagine that my curiosity is considerable upon this point."

Anne d'Aubigny began to twist her handkerchief.

"Miss Tolerance." Her voice was very low. "In order to explain, I must confide in you certain things I do not want—I had rather die than see spread."

"Rather die?" Again Miss Tolerance felt a pang of impatience. "That is too easily said. Please believe I will do my best to see that the secrets of your marriage are not broadcast. However, if it is a choice between upending those secrets or, by my silence, conspiring in your execution, you will understand that I have been hired to keep you alive. Please, ma'am, who is Mrs. Vose?"

"She was my husband's mistress." Mrs. d'Aubigny twisted her handkerchief until it was a hard gray line between her fingers. "You had probably guessed that. But—how am I to make you understand her true role here, Miss Tolerance? My husband meant her to be a humiliation to me, but she was often a friend. A protector."

"A protector?"

Anne d'Aubigny pursed her lips as if to contain strong emotion. "Yes. I am not so foolish—no longer so foolish—as to believe her actions were entirely disinterested. I'm sure she had some benefit in taking my husband's attention from me; I only know that when she came to him he did not—"

"He did not come to *you*." Miss Tolerance nodded soberly. "Please forgive my plain speaking. I have learnt a little of your husband's tastes—and that he made himself unwelcome with them, in the very houses that cater to such interests. If they, who are accustomed to a measure of brutality, would not tolerate him, I can only imagine his behavior to you. But you say he brought her *here*?"

Mrs. d'Aubigny nodded. "She said her lodgings were not suitable."

Miss Tolerance could well imagine what Josette Vose's lodgings were like. "I can certainly understand your loyalty to her while your husband lived. I am less able to fathom why I found her here, the first morning that I called. You were not come together to mourn the chevalier, surely?"

"Mourn? No." Mrs. d'Aubigny sniffed at the absurdity of the idea. "But Josette came to condole with me, and asked if I would like her to stay for a day or so. She was kind to me, Miss Tolerance; I had come to depend upon her. You saw how she protected me—even from you! But after a few days she left us—said it was better that way."

"I see." Miss Tolerance reflected upon Anne d'Aubigny's peculiar knack for awakening sympathy and protectiveness. She herself had felt it; why should not Josette Vose, to whom she was more intimately connected? Still, that woman who had dismissed her from the house, and whom she had seen paying court to the Duke of Cumberland, did not much accord with the image of a tender mother hen.

"When was the last time Mrs. Vose was in your house before the murder?"

The widow shrugged. "A day or two before, I think."

"She was not in the house on the night of the murder?"

Anne d'Aubigny looked at Miss Tolerance blankly. "She did not tell me so."

A peculiar answer, Miss Tolerance thought. Then she recalled that the widow had taken a sleeping draught on the night of the murder, and had even slept through the discovery of the body.

"Did your servants mention her?" she asked.

Madame d'Aubigny shook her head.

The Coroner's Court had not mentioned the presence of Mrs. Vose either, Miss Tolerance thought. She was left with the sense that there was a question she had not yet asked. Unable to frame that question, she went on.

"You understand that this information will change my investigation. Did you tell Mr. Heddison of the chevalier's relationship with Mrs. Vose?"

Anne d'Aubigny shook her head, her eyes very wide. "She was here the first day he called—we said she was my cousin. How could I tell Mr. Heddison what she—what she is?"

"How could you *not*?"

"But why should it matter? Josette said—"

Miss Tolerance bit her lip. She could well imagine any number of things Mrs. Vose might have said. "I understand your gratitude to Mrs. Vose—I'm sure she is blameless." In fact, she was sure of no such thing. "But those around her might not be. If she had an admirer—or a pimp, or a brother who resented the chevalier's attentions? You must write Mr. Heddison and tell him of Mrs. Vose's true relationship to your husband."

The widow's lip trembled. Miss Tolerance leaned forward in her chair and took the other woman's hand, holding it in a strong grasp. "I would not say you must do this if I did not believe it necessary to your safety," she said. "I will go and speak to Mrs. Vose myself. Do you know where she lodges?"

Mrs. d'Aubigny pulled her hand from Miss Tolerance's. "I believe she said she lived near Marylebone Road. It might be Knox Street, but I am not certain. Please, Miss Tolerance, it distresses me to trouble Mrs. Vose, who has been so good to me—" Her breath was coming fast, and the handkerchief in her hands was impossibly twisted.

"All I intend is to talk with her, just as I did with Beak and Mrs. Sadgett and the rest," Miss Tolerance said soothingly. She permitted a few minutes of silence to pass in hope that the widow would recover herself. When Anne d'Aubigny's breathing had slowed and her pallor was tinged with pink, Miss Tolerance said, "I have two more questions and then I will leave you. Are you acquainted with a friend of your husband's, a Mr. Beauville?"

Miss Tolerance had the sense that Mrs. d'Aubigny had braced herself for a more difficult question. "I know his name, and I believe my husband was often in his company, gaming and at sport, but we never met. I understand Mr. Beauville is an émigré, like my husband."

It was no more than Mrs. Lasher of Green Street had said.

"You would not know his direction?"

Mrs. d'Aubigny shook her head. "I knew that Beauville was his intimate. And that they shared a fondness for the same amusements." Her tone was bitter. "Otherwise, I cannot help you."

"I'll run him to the ground one way or another. Perhaps Mrs. Lasher—she keeps the establishment I mentioned to you—can be persuaded to be more forthcoming."

"Mrs. Lasher knew my husband well?"

"Well enough to describe him and his habits tolerably well. She said he was so devoted to his amusements that he was accustomed to bring his own kit of—" Here Miss Tolerance stopped, unable to define what such a kit would have contained. "It is my understanding that the chevalier had a collection of implements for use with women like Mrs. Vose."

"The box." Mrs. d'Aubigny's eyes had closed. She nodded.

Miss Tolerance looked at the widow, shuddered and damned her own stupidity. A blow was one thing; but somehow she had not believed d'Aubigny could practice the worst of his cruelty upon his wife. Had she thought Anne d'Aubigny was naive? She swallowed bile and asked as gently as she could, "Can you tell me anything about it?"

Anne d'Aubigny spoke without inflection. "The box was made of rosewood, I think. It had come over from France with the family. It was lined with red silk. In it he had . . ." She shook her head. "I do not know where the box is."

"Is there any reason you know of that the box might be material to my investigation?"

Mrs. d'Aubigny shook her head. Her eyes were still closed. Miss Tolerance waited in silence while the widow regained her composure.

"Perhaps that is all I need trouble you with today, ma'am," she said at last. "It is only my real concern for your safety that made it necessary to speak of such distressing things."

"I understand, Miss Tolerance. I appreciate your kindness." She ran her hands over her cheeks to wipe away any evidence of tears and rose to make her farewell. "You must come to me with any other questions you have."

Miss Tolerance curtsied. "I will, ma'am. Thank you."

A last glance as she left the room showed her the widow seated again, staring thoughtfully at the fire. The book of sermons lay forgotten at her feet. As she went down the stairs Miss Tolerance reflected, not for the first time, that whoever had killed the Chevalier d'Aubigny had done the world a considerable service.

There was still enough light left to admit of a visit to the area of Marylebone to seek out Mrs. Vose. Miss Tolerance pulled the collar of the Gunnard coat closer to her face against the rising wind and hailed a hackney carriage. She gave the jarvey the direction of a tavern she remembered in that area. Miss Tolerance liked taverns; they were hotbeds of useful gossip, often with keepers who were not particular with whom they shared this largesse. She settled back in the carriage, an old, ill-sprung specimen smelling of piss and chypre, and tried to piece together what she had learned.

She was frankly curious to meet Mrs. Vose again. On the first meeting the woman had made little impression upon her except as a barrier to her task. In a sober gown and close-dressed hair she had looked more like the housekeeper Miss Tolerance had taken her to be than a courtesan specializing in the more exotic branches of Eros. The woman she had seen at Camille Touvois' was more in that line, gowned and jeweled and glowing in the golden candlelight, coming forward to curtsy to the Duke of Cumberland with an expression half salacious and half speculative.

There is a considerable distance between an émigré civil servant and a royal duke. Mrs. Vose had certainly set her sights high since taking leave of the Chevalier d'Aubigny.

Miss Tolerance considered.

Anne d'Aubigny had said that Mrs. Vose's last visit to the Half Moon Street house had been a day or two before d'Aubigny's murder. But Mrs. Lasher had said that a woman called Josie, lately d'Aubigny's mistress, had split with him some weeks before his death. If Josie and Josette Vose were one and the same, which seemed to Miss Tolerance's mind a logical assumption, then what had brought Mrs. Vose to Half Moon Street a fortnight after the relation between herself and d'Aubigny had been severed? And why would the woman come back to the house after the murder? Anne d'Aubigny might believe it to be disinterested kindness on Mrs. Vose's part, but professionally Miss Tolerance did not place much reliance upon disinterested kindness.

Mrs. Vose was not known at the first alehouse Miss Tolerance tried. At the second, a small, dark room lit by a sullen fire, a few lanterns hung up too high to do much good, and a quantity of greasy yellow candles, the barman agreed that he did know a working woman by name of Josie Vose, who lived with two others in a similar line of work in rooms on Balcombe Street, near Boston Place. Miss Tolerance gratefully slid a coin across the bar and left the Queen's Head. It had been warmer in the alehouse, but only slightly so.

A crowd of boys hovered on the corner of Boston Place. A few held brooms and looked hopeful as Miss Tolerance passed; the others were content to dance in the cold, beating their arms against their sides and commenting loudly upon passersby. Miss Tolerance beckoned to the nearest of the crossing-sweeps, a fair, grubby, red-nosed boy of about seven years, and asked him her question.

"Do I know 'er, sir?" the boy croaked.

"Know 'oo?" one of mates asked, crowding in. In a second Miss Tolerance was surrounded by the boys—seven or eight of them— all offering to give directions, sweep the street, call a chair for the "gentleman."

The name Miss Tolerance had given the boy was murmured among them. "Josie Vo-sie," one of the boys chortled, and several of them began to chant the name. So much, she thought drily, for circumspection and a quiet interview with Mrs. Vose.

"A penny for the one who sweeps my path," she offered firmly. "And"—she raised her voice slightly—"tuppence to the one who brings me to Mrs. Vose's rooms."

That quieted the noise. The boys who held the brooms jostled each other, pressing forward to get her custom. In most of the others she recognized a speculative expression which suggested they were wondering how to cozen tuppence from this well-heeled mark. Miss Tolerance chose the first boy to sweep the ordure and muck from the crossing. Then, with another look at the boys, she beckoned to one whom she noted was looking, not at her, but at a building across the street and several doors distant. The other boys protested loudly as the boy pushed forward.

"You know Mrs. Vose?"

"I know a Josie, got a lot of names." His eyes stayed upon Miss Tolerance's face. After a moment they widened, and he looked around him to see if anyone else had discerned her sex.

Miss Tolerance called his attention back. "What does this Josie look like?"

"Pretty, like. Clean, for a whore—"

"Yah, you'd know, woun't you? Your mam and sister is whores!" one of the boys said cheerily. This started a small riot of amusement.

The boy ignored them. "She got dark hair, and dresses fine some times. Other times she dresses like—like t' parson's mother."

Miss Tolerance nodded. "Show me." She gave the sweep his penny and held out her hand to the other boy, and after a moment he slid his own, cold, moist and filthy, into it. They left the crowd of boys behind, crossing Balcombe Street and entering a building opposite. The boy led her into a public hallway that was lit only by a lantern on the ground floor, then up two flights of narrow stairs.

"That's 'er door," he said. He held out his hand for his reward.

Miss Tolerance put two tuppenny pieces into it. "A reward for prompt service and discretion," she said. "You might want to go out the back and give your friends the slip."

The boy snorted. "Yeah, I might. Ta, miss. Sir, I mean."

He was gone, and Miss Tolerance knocked on the door. It was opened immediately by a young, fair-haired woman in a work gown and several shawls. She had a scarred lip and the squint of nearsightedness, and the scent of gin hung about her. Miss Tolerance asked for Mrs. Vose.

"Who? Oh, right. Josie. She don't go much by that name round a' here, sir. You come on in, I'll see if she's to home."

"What name does she go by?" Miss Tolerance asked, escaping from the dark hallway into a somewhat brighter room.

"Mostly called Josie Whipsmart in these parts. 'Mrs. Vose' is for her gentry followers." She gave Miss Tolerance a coquettish look. "My name is Susie Lickmettle, dearie. In case Josie don't give you what you want."

"And my name is Sarah Tolerance, Mrs. Lickmettle. You said you would see if Mrs. Whipsmart will see me?"

Expressions of dismay, revelation and disappointment chased across the woman's face. Then she laughed, called Miss Tolerance a caution, and left her for the moment. In her absence Miss Tolerance looked around, noting that the room was tidy and fairly clean, lit with tallow candles which had a reek of mutton fat, and showed evidence of occupancy by several persons.

"Miss Tolerance?"

The woman Miss Tolerance knew as Josette Vose stood in the doorway. She wore a dark green wrapper and an expression of surprise. Her feet were bare.

"Mrs. Vose. Or am I to call you Mrs. Whipsmart?" Miss Tolerance bowed.

"Oh, Vose will do, as that is how we began." Josette Vose motioned Miss Tolerance to follow her into the next room, while Susie Lickmettle pushed past her to return to the outer room, sat down by the grate, and took up some knitting. Miss Tolerance followed Mrs. Vose into a room which, like the first, was well ordered, if very crowded. There were three cots against the wall, two wardrobes, two chests, and a single chair, all crammed into the room. On one of the cots a woman slept heavily. The square blue gin bottle near her outstretched hand suggested that she would not wake to interrupt their conversation.

"So you've smoked me," Mrs. Vose said coolly. She waved Miss Tolerance to the chair and seated herself on the nearest cot. Today she was neither the severe duenna of Half Moon Street nor the glittering courtesan of Camille Touvois' salon. Her dark hair was parted and swept smoothly in a soft knot at the nape of her neck. When she leaned forward the green wrapper gaped at the neck, showing several inches of white chemise.

"It only required a little willingness to ask questions," she answered.

"And you hope I'll answer some of your asking." Mrs. Vose's chin thrust forward militantly. "Why should I?"

"Perhaps to help your friend Anne d'Aubigny? Or to oblige me in hopes that I'll not inform His Highness the Duke of Cumberland of your connection to a scandalous murder? To keep me from telling Bow Street that your relations with the late Chevalier d'Aubigny were more carnal than cousinly? Or possibly because I can reward you generously if you assist me."

"All excellent reasons."

"I forgot to include, of course, your fondness for the late chevalier."

Mrs. Vose gave a snort of laughter. "Of course. *Poor* Etienne." She leaned back against a pile of cushions in an attitude of sensual relaxation. "Ask your questions."

"I will, thank you. When did you last see the Chevalier d'Aubigny?"

"A little more than a fortnight before his death. We were both at Madame Touvois' salon. That's where I met him: Madame Touvois is a knacky matchmaker."

"So I have heard. There was nothing between them?"

Mrs. Vose seemed to find the question funny. "Nothing and everything," she said. "What is the expression? Thick as thieves. Not for fucking, though. It was the challenge, each one trying to get the upper hand of the other. It drove him mad that she wouldn't take him at his own estimation—"

"And that was?"

"As a dangerous man. Which he could be, I can tell you that. And it drove her mad that no matter how she abused him, he kept trying to have the mastery of her. As good as a play, it was, to watch them together. I think they were beginning to tire of the game, though."

"Why do you think so?"

Mrs. Vose shrugged. "Something in the way Madame Touvois looked at d'Aubigny. Nothing more than that."

"Even the most exciting relationship may grow stale after a while." Miss Tolerance added, as if upon the same thought, "And you were his mistress for how long?"

Mrs. Vose did not miss the jibe, but appeared more amused than angered. "A little more than a year, until he ran out of money."

"Ran out of money?" Back to d'Aubigny's finances again! "When did that happen?"

"As I said, a few weeks before his death. There was never any illusion of true love, Miss Tolerance. A man of d'Aubigny's sort knows what he is, and pays for his pleasure. When *he* could no longer pay, *I* would no longer stay." She smiled as if the rhyme pleased her.

"Now that is curious, Mrs. Vose; at about the time you say you were leaving the chevalier because he said he could not afford you, he was paying all the debts he had racked up around town—with money whose source I cannot find. I was hoping you could suggest such a source."

"I? I could tell you a great number of things about the chevalier, Miss Tolerance, but where he got his money ain't one of them. I thought he had married all the money he owned."

"You knew some of his intimate friends, I presume. None of them might have loaned him the money?"

"None of them was monstrous intelligent, but neither was they stupid enough to loan money to D'Aubigny. He spent it far too easily on what amused him."

"Then I may assume that his inability to pay you what you wanted was because you no longer amused him?"

"No, you may assume no such thing. His play had got too rough for me. It's a thing that happens with some men like him: after a time the old games don't get a rise in 'em. They want more. According to my thinking, a rise in the stakes demands a rise in payment. The chevalier and I disagreed upon the point, and we parted company. I had thought it was simply because he hadn't the silver."

"And you went to work for Mrs. Lasher in Green Street."

"You are well informed."

"You are kind to notice it. It is curious, though, that Mrs.

d'Aubigny swears you were in the house only a day or two before the chevalier's death."

"She is mistaken."

"Ah," Miss Tolerance said. "Yet, given the friendliness of her feelings for you, I am surprised that she should make such a mistake. And then, after the chevalier's death, you went back to the house?"

"I felt sorry for her."

"How kind of you," Miss Tolerance said drily. "There was no other reason?"

"What a suspicious mind you have, Miss Tolerance. The little missus is a lost soul—her marriage was her great disaster. It deprived her of friends and fortune and innocence, all at once. It wasn't hard to be friendly to her—grateful for crumbs, she was, after a year or so of M'sieur d'Aubigny. When I heard of d'Aubigny's death I thought she'd be overset, so I went to her."

"How kind."

"Wasn't it?" Mrs. Vose laughed. "Don't think me a paragon, I beg you. I went by as soon as I'd heard of the murder, and the poor little missus wept and begged me to stay. Like a soggy kitten she was, curled up crying upon my shoulder. How could I refuse her? And to tell the truth, she needed a bit of protecting, those first few days. The staff was all in a tear—as how should they not be?—and her brother had filled them with tales of murderers waiting under the bed to kill them all."

"You don't believe in murderers under the bed?"

Mrs. Vose shook her head, all levity gone. "The chevalier wasn't a man much liked. If someone came to kill him, the job was done. I doubt anyone is waiting to kill again in that house."

"I am of the same opinion," Miss Tolerance agreed. "The question remains, however, who *did* kill him?" She spoke with rather more force than she had intended.

"I did not," Mrs. Vose said firmly. "I have no idea who might have."

Miss Tolerance believed the truth of Mrs. Vose's first statement, but not the second. The woman knew more than she said, and she suspected someone.

"For a man so unpleasant, it is curious how many people have not the first idea who might have killed him."

Mrs. Vose smiled politely. The two women sat for a few minutes listening to the snoring of the drunken woman on the cot a few feet away. At last Miss Tolerance rose to her feet. Mrs. Vose stopped her with a hand on her elbow.

"May I ask you a question now, Miss Tolerance? How is it you style yourself Miss rather than Mrs.? You do not pretend, walking about the streets in such an outfit, to be anything other than Fallen?"

"No, ma'am. But I do not pretend to be a whore, either."

"Was that supposed to sting?"

Miss Tolerance thought. "Perhaps it was," she said. "I have little patience with half truths. They are ineffective guardians, and generally serve to wave a flag that something has not been said. This discussion would be far more profitable for both of us if you dealt straight with me."

"Perhaps," Mrs. Vose said. "But profit is not the only motive for a woman in my position—despite your obvious belief. What does it profit a woman that she gain thirty pieces of silver and a broken neck?" She rose from the bed. "Now, Miss Tolerance, I must send you away. I have business in Green Street this evening, and it is high time I was dressed and on my way. Perhaps you will come again some time and we can continue this discussion."

She offered her hand. Miss Tolerance put a ten-shilling note in it.

"If you ever decide to speak plain truth, Mrs. Vose, I hope you will let me know."

"It is unlikely, but I shall remember." Josette Vose folded the note thoughtfully.

"Do you really fear for your life?" Miss Tolerance asked at the door.

"Always," Mrs. Vose said. "This is not a safe world for a woman alone."

Nine

It was dark when Miss Tolerance emerged from the house on Balcombe Street, and an icy rain had begun. Miss Tolerance pulled her hat down low and the collar of her greatcoat up higher and began to walk toward Marylebone Street, looking for a hackney carriage. There were, of course, none to be had. It was not a great walk back to Manchester Square, and she set her mind to it, thinking less of the interview just past than of a change of clothing and a cup of warm soup and a good fire. There was little light on the street, and the weather had driven most foot travelers inside for their suppers. She turned south on Baker Street and plied her way steadily along the dark streets to turn again on Blandford Street.

She did not hear her attacker until he was just upon her.

She had been walking with her head down against the rain and her hands in her pockets, trying to make connections between Mrs. Vose's testimony and other facts in the case. There was a long low rumble of thunder which all but swallowed the scuff of boot leather upon the cobbles just behind her. She raised her head, her right hand already pushing through her coat for the hilt of her sword, when she was circled by strong arms that pulled her backward, all but off her feet. The man—it was undoubtedly a man from the strength and size of him—was taller than she and heavy, with a sizable gut against which the arms pinned her. Without thought Miss Tolerance raised her foot and brought the heel down hard; at the same moment she drove her elbow back with force.

The man *whuffed* at the blow but did not release her; her heel, which had come down on nothing more useful than an icy pavement stone, hurt. She raised her foot again and brought it down again, this time hitting her target squarely.

He swore, dropped one arm, and staggered back. Miss Tolerance pulled away, her hands free now, and made to draw her sword, but the man had raised his own hand and dealt her a blow across the face with enough force to knock her onto her back upon the stones. Her head hit a set of stone steps hard, and her hat went flying across the flags.

Miss Tolerance thought dizzily, *Either he does not know I am a woman or this fellow is no gentleman.*

As if to confirm her judgment the man kicked viciously at Miss Tolerance's side. The Gunnard coat took the worst of the first kick, but the second one landed squarely upon her ribs with such force that it rolled her over onto her knees. He tried a third kick, but Miss Tolerance, kneeling, grabbed for his boot. She did not catch it, but the man lost his balance avoiding her hand and fell back several steps. Aching for breath, Miss Tolerance rose to her feet and wheeled around to face the man.

She could see nothing of his face: a scarf was wrapped around the lower half, and his hat obscured the eyes and brow. He regained his balance and jammed one hand into his pocket urgently. Seeking a weapon, Miss Tolerance guessed, and reached into her pocket for her own pocketknife, which she kept for fighting close in. Her hand was briefly fouled in the folds of her coat, and her assailant lunged at her, blade in hand. Miss Tolerance sidestepped the thrust and brought her left arm down so strongly that his knife arm was thrown off and the knife flew into the shadows. Both she and her attacker followed the trajectory of the knife; she recovered first and swept a kick at the man's shins which, in a stroke of luck, caught him just behind the knee, taking his legs out from under him altogether. The man fell backward, hit his head with an audible thud, and rolled until he lay, face down, half in the gutter. Miss Tolerance, her knife finally in her hand, looked down at her fallen opponent.

Miss Tolerance inspected him gingerly; his hat was still jammed onto his head, hiding his face, and she could not tell if he was conscious or not. After a moment she decided he must be stunned; lying in a puddle of icy water with rain rolling down his neck was too uncomfortable a position for imposture. She reached down, gasping at the pain along her ribs and in her head as she did so, and attempted the roll the fellow over to get a glimpse of his face.

A shout came from the far end of the street. "Oy, you fellow! What are you doing?" The shouter raised a lantern as if its thin light could illuminate Miss Tolerance and her opponent. The watch.

Miss Tolerance assessed her alternatives quickly. Stay, and perhaps be believed when she explained that the man had attacked her, but more likely be taken in by the watch and spend the evening showing off her bruises and hoping she would be believed— particularly if her attacker were brought along to tell his side of the story. Or run, and hope to sort out the trouble another day.

She turned and ran, vanishing into the shadows as quickly as the icy street and her bruises allowed.

K eefe's face, when he opened the door, told Miss Tolerance a good deal about her own appearance.

"Holy God, Miss Sarah! What happened?"

"Footpad," she said tersely. "For God's sake, Keefe, don't make a fuss. I'll be right enough shortly." But she knew her shudders of cold and shock could be seen even through her greatcoat. "How is my aunt?"

"I'll call Marianne," he said. Not quite an answer. "You go into the blue salon, miss. There's a good fire there, and no one about right now. I'll have Cook send up some soup and wine."

Miss Tolerance permitted herself to be steered from the hallway to the first floor and the blue salon which had, as promised, a fine fire. She took off her Gunnard coat, gasping as she did so. Keefe took the sodden greatcoat and said nothing. Miss Tolerance's thanks were as much for his tact as his service. She sat gingerly in a chair by the fire and gratefully felt the warmth seep into her. She was aware of stickiness along one side of her face, but application of her kerchief to the most painful site slowed the bleeding, and she was able to sit, relaxed enough, waiting for her soup.

An uncertain number of minutes later, Keefe returned with Marianne.

"What's happened to you, then?" Marianne asked calmly.

Miss Tolerance tried to smile. The effort was not particularly successful. "Footpad," she said again. "Like a stupid flat, I was caught unawares with my hands in my pockets. It's nothing. It will pass."

Marianne rolled her eyes and asked Keefe to leave the tray he had brought. Miss Tolerance realized it bore, not food as she had hoped, but a basin, bandages, and several jars of ointment.

"Marianne really, there is no need—how is my aunt?"

Marianne shook her head. "First things first. We must see to you. Thank you, Keefe. If you would bring the food up in a quarter hour? Now"—she turned back to Miss Tolerance—"let's have a look at the damage. No, don't bother to push me off. Do you think because you were caught off your guard you cannot ask for help? A broken head needs attention no matter how you come by it." She ran careful hands along the crown of Miss Tolerance's head, discovering several considerable lumps but no bleeding.

"Well, your brains got a rattling, I don't doubt, but they're all in a piece."

Miss Tolerance inclined her head in acknowledgment, or would have done had the gesture not caused such pain. Seeing this, Marianne insisted she shed coat, waistcoat and shirt so that the state of her ribs might be ascertained. She made clucking noises at the bruises on her friend's left side.

"It's a good thing your breasts were bound. You'd likely have broken ribs otherwise. Nasty fellow that was." She took up a pot of salve from the tray.

"He was," Miss Tolerance agreed. "But about my aunt?"

"In good time, Sarah. You look like you was run down by the stagecoach." Marianne wrapped a bandage several times around Miss Tolerance's chest, tied it off, and handed her a dressing gown. "Mrs. B ain't going to change while you get yourself patched up. And patched," she said judiciously, examining her friend's face, "is just about the right word for it. Didn't care what he did to your face, did he?"

"I don't think care for my looks was his first objective, no. How bad is it?"

Marianne had wet a rag and begun to sponge carefully at Miss Tolerance's brow and cheek. "Black eye for sure on the right, maybe two," she said. "I don't think the nose is broken—no, still straight, there's luck. A good lot of blood, though. Ahhh, there we are." She pressed upon the spot to which Miss Tolerance had lately applied her gore-soaked handkerchief. "Nasty deep gash, that. Looks as though it was torn—did your bruiser wear a ring? We'd best to have the surgeon sew it up for you."

Marianne's matter-of-fact pressure on the cut had hurt enough to cause Miss Tolerance to see sparks. She waited until her dizziness passed, then attempted to assure her friend that the surgeon would not be necessary.

"Don't be an idiot, Sarah. He's upstairs with your aunt. It won't take a moment to have him down to see to you. And here is your soup." Marianne took the tray from Keefe and dispatched him to summon the surgeon.

"Now will you tell me how my aunt is?" The fire had at last warmed her through, the soup smelled comfortably of chicken and barley, and she was aware of a pleasant drowsiness to which she could not yet succumb. "Why is the surgeon here?"

"Doctor suggested she should be bled tonight and tomorrow morning. The fever's almost gone now, and she's sleeping—"

"Has she roused at all?"

Marianne shook her head. "Not yet. She began to stir a bit this afternoon, murmured a little, but with no words I could make head or tails of. The doctor—he shakes his head. He won't say he's worried, but he did say the fever alone wouldn't be enough to knock her to pieces this way."

Miss Tolerance frowned at her soup. "So the doctor knows nothing except she should be bled. What do you think?"

Marianne shrugged. "I do not know what to make of it. A fever-ish cold, which is certainly what it appeared she had, ought not to—but here is Mr. Pynt." She rose and curtsied to the surgeon.

Miss Tolerance, tired enough to feel that her disabilities ought to be catered to, did not rise.

Pynt was a man of middle years and middle size with highly starched collar points which required him to turn his whole body in order to view Miss Tolerance's wounds. He took the seat which Marianne had vacated, wiped his hands upon his kerchief and gingerly touched the gash on Miss Tolerance's forehead.

"How came this to happen?" he asked. He clearly disapproved of ladies with wounds that smacked of the prize ring.

"I mistook the cellar steps for a door. Does it require the needle?" Annoyance worked against warmth and exhaustion. Miss Tolerance felt suddenly more awake.

"I would say so, madam. Although 'twill leave a scar no matter how it is treated."

"Then perhaps it ought not be sewn?" Marianne suggested.

"I did not say that. I merely did not want to give rise to expectations in the young woman that her looks would not be affected by the surgery."

"If that is your only concern, sir, then pray get on with the business. I do not live by my looks." Miss Tolerance turned away long enough to finish drinking her soup. Pynt observed that a medicinal dose of spirituous liquor was likely to be more helpful to his patient.

"Perhaps later," Miss Tolerance said, and turned back to the doctor.

The procedure took no more than ten minutes, but it was more painful than Miss Tolerance had expected. Because she had taken the surgeon in dislike, she managed not to make a sound. At the end, when she inspected the inch of tidy stitches, she had to acknowledge that the surgeon knew his business. Mr. Pynt washed his hands and instructed Miss Tolerance to bathe the wound frequently and rub on a little of a salve he would send round, in hope of avoiding infection. He bowed to both women and took his leave, promising to return in the morning for Mrs. Brereton's second bleeding.

Miss Tolerance sat by the fire for a while longer, feeling tired and weak. At last she went upstairs to look in on her aunt, whom she found deeply asleep. The rigidity which had characterized her earlier repose appeared to have passed off, and Miss Tolerance was hopeful that perhaps the doctor's advice and the surgeon's ministrations would prove correct. She stayed but a few minutes, then wrapped herself in a shawl pressed on her by Marianne, and went downstairs and through the garden to her own little cottage. Someone had gone across and laid and lit a fire, and the downstairs room was warm. She had been drowsy earlier; now Miss Tolerance was aching and wakeful. She poured a glass of the spirituous liquor earlier prescribed by the surgeon and drank it in thoughtful silence.

A mong the other talents and qualities which had informed Miss Tolerance's choice of occupation, she was a fast healer. Even so, she woke in the morning aching fiercely from head to toe, and resolved to beg some arnica from the cook, who kept a well-stocked shelf of household simples and salves. She had just put her kettle on the fire when the kitchen maid, Jess, arrived at her door with the mail and a message: Mrs. Brereton had awakened.

The rain had stopped, but the sky was dark, and a brisk wind set the branches of the trees dancing against her window.

Someone had cleaned her Gunnard greatcoat and the other clothes she had removed the night before; Jess had left them folded upon her table. Miss Tolerance felt no need for men's dress today, and put on her blue wool gown and a warm shawl. She did not look in the mirror when she pinned up her hair; she knew her face was swollen, and could imagine the extent of the discoloration. Why wound her vanity with the sight? She pulled the shawl up tightly and stepped across the garden to visit her aunt.

She found Mrs. Brereton propped upon pillows, irritably instructing Frost to stop trying to feed her gruel and to bring her strong tea, toast, and eggs. Frost looked as though she was not certain whether to be cheered or chastened by this uncivil treatment.

"My God, Sarah, you look as though someone had taken a stick to you!"

Miss Tolerance bent carefully to kiss her aunt. "Someone did. I am happy to see you looking so much better, Aunt Thea."

"You ought not to be. I sleep for a day and what happens? Doctors and surgeons given the run of the house and one of my whores authorizing an extra dozen of claret to be put out in the dining room! What were you thinking?"

"I was thinking—as were Marianne and Frost, and everyone else in the house—of your health, ma'am. The doctor's treatment does seem to have done you good."

"Good? Bled twice in twelve hours and forced to drink gruel?" Mrs. Brereton frowned. "And about that other: I understand you gave Marianne free rein over the house."

"Hardly that. I did ask the staff to go to her for instructions while you were ill. Now that you are awake, she will of course want to tell you all that has been done—"

"Sarah, I told you I didn't want to involve one of the girls—"

"Yes, you did, but I could not manage your house and my own business, and I did what I thought was best. You may scold me later for all my faults, Aunt, but I am not up to a lecture just now, nor do I think you are up to delivering one. Again, I ask: how are you?"

Mrs. Brereton shrugged oddly. "I am awake, the fever has broken, and I do not understand what all the fuss was about."

Before Miss Tolerance could attempt to explain to her aunt why her too-sound slumber had frightened the people around her, Cole announced Sir George Hammond. Miss Tolerance retreated to a chair by the window; she had no wish to explain her bruises to the doctor. Sir George entered, smiling at his patient.

"This is much more as I would see you, ma'am. How do you do this morning?"

Mrs. Brereton might have liked to scold the doctor, but the habit of charming men kept her from doing so. She smiled. "I am very much better, sir. I understand I have you to thank for it, but I do not understand why everyone in my household was in such a terror. A feverish cold—"

Sir George took her wrist and counted her pulse before he answered. "The cold itself was nothing, ma'am. It was your stupor which was worrisome. I see *that* has passed off." Again he smiled. Again Mrs. Brereton smiled in return.

Flirting, Miss Tolerance thought. My aunt is recovering.

She watched as Sir George went through a practiced routine, relating a bit of court gossip while he examined Mrs. Brereton. "You will not have heard, ma'am, that the *Times* reports that the Duke of Clarence has been to the Queen's bedside . . ."

When he had finished his story Sir George gave his opinion that Mrs. Brereton was on the mend. "There is a little weakness in the muscle of your left hand and arm—you will perhaps have observed it?—but I expect that will pass off shortly. You need not be bled again—rest and good food will do the rest. I'm sure I can rely upon you for that," he said to Frost, who pursed her lips and nodded. "Now, ma'am, I'll call on you again in a day or two, just to see how you are going on. No excitement, no callers, no midnight galas. A week in bed and then we shall see how you do." He bowed over her hand as though he might have kissed it, and left.

Mrs. Brereton sagged back into her pillows. "A week in bed! I cannot afford it!"

"Ma'am, we don't want to fall sick again—"

"You can afford to die, Aunt?"

Frost and Miss Tolerance spoke at the same moment. Mrs. Brereton sniffed.

"What a fuss over nothing. Well, since you are in league against me I will stay in bed. But I want Marianne to come to me at once and tell me all that has happened since I was ill. And no more gruel! Tea and eggs. At once."

Mrs. Brereton glared at both of them. Frost left to summon Marianne and eggs. Miss Tolerance was about to leave when her aunt called her back.

"You might have been more involved," she said irritably.

"I was involved: I put Marianne in charge," Miss Tolerance said reasonably. "I place the greatest reliance upon her good sense, and I had business of my own to attend to."

"Yes, I can see that. For God's sake, Sarah, ask Cook for some raw beef to put on your face. Look at yourself!"

Reluctantly, Miss Tolerance glanced in the glass. The swelling was, in fact, not quite so bad as she had imagined it. Her right cheekbone and eye were a rich plum color, but on the bridge of her nose and her temple the bruising was already paling to a mottled yellow. Above her right eyebrow there was the neat arc of stitches in black silk, an inch long.

"Do you like this lace with my dress, Aunt?" she asked.

Mrs. Brereton was not amused. "Don't play with me, Sarah. You may turn your nose up at whoredom, but at least no one beats my girls—"

"Not every whore is fortunate enough to be in your employ," Miss Tolerance said, thinking of Etienne d'Aubigny.

"Even if you did not wish to . . . to practice, you could be a fine manageress. Look at the danger you face! Please consider—"

"But Aunt, I like my hazards," Miss Tolerance said calmly. "Or at least, I don't mind them too much. I enjoy what I do; I should not enjoy being the manageress of a brothel half so well."

Mrs. Brereton snorted. "Enjoyment. What is enjoyment when—"

"Enjoyment, Aunt, is what is left after survival. Let us not quarrel; I am very glad to see you so much recovered." She surprised herself with the catch in her voice. "I hope you will not see fit to scare us all this way again." She bent and kissed her aunt again. "Now I must be about my own business. I'll call in on you later."

Her niece's emotion seemed to move Mrs. Brereton. "Dear girl," she said shakily, "get some steak for that eye, I implore you!"

M iss Tolerance meant to ask the cook for arnica and beef-steak, but was forestalled. Cole met her at the foot of the stairs to tell her she had a caller: Sir Walter Mandif was waiting in her cottage.

"As he's called so often, I thought you would not mind," Cole said apologetically. "Somehow one don't like to put the law to wait in the parlor with the other guests."

Miss Tolerance nodded, but privately wished her friend Sir Walter had chosen any other morning to call upon her. She was certain her appearance would bring another scolding upon the unsuitability of her work, and she was in no mood to hear it. She walked into her cottage set to do battle, and was disappointed.

Sir Walter rose and bowed as she entered. She saw his eyes widen at the sight of her bruises, but he said nothing about them.

"I came to hear what you thought of Will Heddison," he said. "I understand you made an impression upon him."

Miss Tolerance took a seat. "Did I really? I thought him far too occupied in bullying Anne d'Aubigny to take much notice of me."

"Bullying?"

"I would call it that. He barked at her as if she were a truant kitchen girl—which might be suitable for a Cheapside fishwife, but seemed a harsh treatment for a girl just widowed. Does he truly consider her a suspect?"

"He did not tell me so," Mandif said. "I will say, from the little I have learned of the case, one cannot rule out the possibility—"

"One could if one had seen her," Miss Tolerance said. "She barely comes up to my chin, and hasn't the courage to say *boh* to a mouse, let alone kill a husband. The idea that she might overcome him—"

"From what I understood, d'Aubigny was asleep," Mandif pointed out. "It takes very little courage or strength to overcome a sleeping man."

Miss Tolerance frowned. "It would take a considerable deal of strength to bash out the brains of a sleeping man."

"Who else would you propose in her stead? The front and kitchen doors were locked, the servants locked in to their quarters, and yet the man was slain."

"But the kitchen door, as it happens, was unlocked at some point." Miss Tolerance explained the matter to Sir Walter. "So anyone might have come in from the street."

"You're not suggesting a passing marauder simply seized the opportunity to go in and dash out the brains of a complete stranger?"

"Of course not. But it does suggest an alternative to Mrs. d'Aubigny, does it not? And she was drugged and asleep when her husband was killed. I suppose Mr. Heddison did not tell you that."

Sir Walter smiled. "Heddison is only doing his duty. The doors to the street were locked, so the widow and the servants are suspects because they had opportunity. The servants were locked into their quarters, which leaves the widow. She was drugged and asleep—but you must admit that one can feign taking a sleeping draught and pretend to be asleep—"

Miss Tolerance opened her mouth to rebut, but Sir Walter held up his hand. "I truly did not come to pick a quarrel with you; I thought you would be interested in the opinion Heddison formed of you. He sought me out in Bow Street and asked me if I thought you likely to impede his investigation."

"He asked me the same question. Of course not. I consider it more likely he intends to impede mine."

"I can relieve him upon that point, then," Mandif said.

Miss Tolerance frowned. "Sir Walter, I know our acquaintance is not of the longest duration, but surely you know me well enough to know—"

"I know you to be an honorable woman. But your sympathy, when roused, is particularly vehement, and it is possible—"

"I gave my lover up to Bow Street," Miss Tolerance said. "I sat in the witness box and gave testimony which saw Versellion convicted of manslaughter and transported for life. I think you may rely upon me to go against my own sympathies in the cause of justice."

"Of course," Sir Walter said. "Of course. But you did not tell me you had been employed in the d'Aubigny business."

"You know I do not like to mention my clients unless I must."

"So I had to learn it from Heddison? That put me at a disadvantage, and—to put it in the most baldly practical terms—you cannot look to me for assistance when I am hampered in my work."

"I do not look to you to be of assistance to me," Miss Tolerance said, stung. "I did not think that was the basis of our friendship. If the fact that I did not tell you at once that I was involved in the d'Aubigny matter caused you trouble with Heddison I am very sorry for it. I should certainly have told you if you had asked."

Sir Walter raised a brow. "Am I to ask if you are involved in every criminal case which arises in London? No, no—" He stopped her protest. "That was unfair of me."

There was a long, awkward silence. Miss Tolerance mended the fire, but the heat did little to cut the chill between them.

"So," Sir Walter said at last. "Have you made any progress with the case?"

"Are you asking for yourself, or Mr. Heddison?" The moment the words were said Miss Tolerance regretted them.

"I am not a go-between. I asked as a colleague. Out of friendship."

"Of course you did, and I apologize. The knocking I took last night seems to have scrambled my ability to be civil. I did not mean to imply that you were Heddison's spy." She attempted to answer his question. "Except that he has misread Anne d'Aubigny, Heddison seems a rational enough man. I *can* see why you said you would not have his constables working for you. Or at least, the one I met."

"Which was that?"

"Mr. Boyse. Large and bloodthirsty."

" 'Tis not his size nor his bloodthirst in particular that I deplore, but—I should steer clear of him. His partner is merely a foppish climber; Boyse I cannot help but feel is only opportunity's reach from criminal himself. Heddison denies it; he believes the man's size inspires dread and makes him more effective. And in default of proof, I must defer to my colleague's judgment."

Miss Tolerance considered this and busied herself making tea.

"You don't trust Heddison's lieutenant, and yet you do trust his judgment that Anne d'Aubigny is a credible suspect."

"Logic suggests that she must be considered. I say no more than that. Thank you." He accepted the cup Miss Tolerance extended to him. "Have you a more reasonable suspect?"

"As near as I can see, half of London might have wanted the wretched man dead."

Sir Walter's brows rose. "Half of London?"

"He had a broad acquaintance, but I have yet to speak to anyone who actually liked the man. He owed money everywhere. His work for the Home Office was apparently indifferent. His only true gifts appear to have been for venery and brutality."

"He sounds unpleasant, but not deserving of murder."

"When was murder ever a matter of desert?" Miss Tolerance asked. "D'Aubigny kept some high company; he was a frequenter of Camille Touvois' salon, and I myself saw one of the royal dukes there a few nights ago. I must call upon Madame Touvois again—"

"But you will wait until you have recovered somewhat from your injuries? I do not like to say anything, but it appears someone got the better of you. I should not like to think it could happen again."

Miss Tolerance smiled. It hurt to do so. "I appreciate your concern, Sir Walter, and your tact. A footpad attempted to get the better of me. The fact that I am here suggests that he did not. I was careless, nothing more."

Mandif put down his cup, the tea in it untouched, and rose. "That is unlike you." He extended his hand to her. "I hope you will be more careful, Miss Tolerance. I value your friendship; I dislike that anyone should hurt my friend."

Miss Tolerance curtsied. "Your friend got what she deserved for letting her attention wander. That will not happen again."

When Sir Walter left, Miss Tolerance turned her back on a deep longing to return to her bed. Instead, she wrote a note and brought it to the house to ask that it be delivered to Madame Touvois' rooms in Audley Street. She stopped in the kitchen afterward for arnica, then returned to her cottage, where she applied compresses to her swollen face and awaited a reply. It came within the hour. Miss Tolerance put aside the liniment and compresses and made ready for a visit in Audley Street. What Camille Touvois would make of her bruises, Miss Tolerance did not know. It would be instructive to find out.

Ten

For her first visit to Madame Touvois, Miss Tolerance had dressed as an unexceptional guest at an informal evening party, to suit her purpose as observer. Today, with the marks of a brawl unmistakable upon her face, she could not pretend to be unremarkable. Miss Tolerance decided to meet Camille Touvois as brazenly confident as possible. She outfitted herself in a seldom-worn gown of china-red twill with narrow ruffles of white lace at the throat and wrists. The simplicity of the tailoring argued respectability. The vibrant color suggested its lack. The effect of the whole, worn with a gray bonnet trimmed with red ribbon, was pleasantly bold.

Miss Tolerance presented her card to the maidservant who admitted her. She was ushered into the second of the rooms in Madame Touvois' apartment, where there was a good fire. Madame Touvois rose from a chair by the grate to greet her visitor; as Miss Tolerance stepped further into the light and the livid bruises on her face became unmistakable, Madame Touvois' eyebrows rose. Miss Tolerance curtsied and thanked her hostess for her invitation to call; neither woman mentioned the bruises, and Miss Tolerance took the chair to which her hostess gestured.

Madame Touvois turned to a tray at her elbow upon which were a decanter, a pair of glasses, and a plate of rather shopworn biscuits. She wore a gray-green dress, with a heavy shawl looped over her elbows which moved gracefully as she poured wine and offered a glass to her visitor.

"You wished to talk," Madame Touvois said.

Miss Tolerance smiled politely and took the glass. The room, which she had seen only in candlelight and filled with people, was not improved by the addition of daylight. The ceilings and windows were high, the drapes heavy; there was gilding upon the woodwork and the furniture was handsome, but Madame Touvois and her servants were clearly indifferent to dirt. The windows were smoky, the gilt worn thin, and there was a taste of something stale and musty about the air.

"The day is dark, is it not?" Madame Touvois suggested.

"It is indeed. And windy as well."

"And you have come to speak with me about the Chevalier d'Aubigny's death."

Miss Tolerance inclined her head.

"You do not ask how I know it?"

"But you knew that on the evening when I visited your *salon*, Madame. As for how you knew it, I imagine Mrs. Vose told you. Or perhaps the man who followed me from my interview with her." Miss Tolerance brushed a finger across her cheek to indicate her injuries.

Madame Touvois looked sympathetic. "A man followed you from an interview? But such a thing must be an everyday event in your profession!" Then, with only the appearance of changing the subject: "I cannot tell you how gratified I was to receive your note, Miss Tolerance. Surprised and gratified."

Miss Tolerance feigned misunderstanding. "Because I was followed home, ma'am?"

Madame Touvois blinked. Her smile became fixed. After a moment she went on. "Because I have been so very interested to speak more with you. You must know I am very curious about your so-interesting profession."

"As am I in yours, ma'am." Miss Tolerance looked at the wine in her glass but did not drink.

"Me? I have no profession. I am merely a woman with a taste for artistic society, and sufficient jointure to entertain widely."

"You do yourself no credit, ma'am. The woman whose *salon* is talked of everywhere, and which attracts such visitors as a prince of the blood, is not an hospitable widow but an artful hostess."

"You flatter me, Miss Tolerance." Camille Touvois smiled.

"Certainly not, ma'am. I confess I was surprised to see His Grace of Cumberland here," Miss Tolerance continued. "I would not have thought the company to his taste."

"I believe His Grace honors us through a wish to understand his liberal enemies."

"Indeed?" Miss Tolerance's tone bespoke polite disbelief. Would the prince, who commonly referred to even the mildest exponents of the Whig party as *canaille*, mix with common poets and civil servants out of mere curiosity? Given Cumberland's reputation, she thought it more likely that La Touvois had lured the duke there with the promise of handsome women—of which there had certainly been a number.

"Now, Miss Tolerance, I believe you have some questions to ask me."

"About what, ma'am?"

"About the Chevalier d'Aubigny," Madame Touvois reminded her.

"Is there something you wish to tell me?" Miss Tolerance's instinct was that a direct question to Madame Touvois was likely to yield a flat lie. Her aim was to annoy the woman into admission, if it was possible. "My recollection was that you had some questions for *me*." She was gratified to see that she had confused Madame Touvois.

"I had—"

"You wished to know—what was your phrase?" Miss Tolerance mimed recollection. "Oh, yes: how one would become what I am."

"Oh, dear. I hope you did not take offense at my harmless curiosity, Miss Tolerance." From her tone, Madame Touvois hoped quite the opposite.

"Not the least in the world, madame. I value curiosity; it is a staple of my trade. I can easily answer your question if you like."

"I *should* like to know," Madame Touvois said with studied earnestness.

" 'Tis easily told. I fell in love with a man when I was young. I was ruined. I did not like the usual career available to women like myself, and so I found another one."

"But that does not tell me how you became what you are?"

"And what is that?"

Madame Touvois considered. Miss Tolerance had the impression that, for a moment, all artifice had fallen away and the woman was striving to put into words something difficult to articulate. "A woman who moves through a man's world. A woman without regrets. A woman who does not capitulate." She looked directly at Miss Tolerance with an expression that was reflexively admiring, as if by admiring these traits in Miss Tolerance she hoped to make it clear that they were hers as well.

"Now you flatter me," Miss Tolerance said coolly. "I am only a woman with her living to make. Some do so on their backs. I choose to do it on my feet. I have regrets; I simply cannot afford to indulge them. As for capitulation—why, if I had capitulated to the man who attempted to kill me yesterday, I should not be here enjoying this conversation."

She smiled at her hostess. Silence descended.

"You know that Etienne d'Aubigny was a very unpleasant man," Madame Touvois said at last.

"That seems to be an understatement," Miss Tolerance replied.

Whatever Camille Touvois had expected, it was not Miss Tolerance's bland agreement. She gave a low, delighted laugh.

"You are right. He was well-looking enough. He had some charm and, from what I am told, some—" She paused thoughtfully. "Some gifts of invention. But he was not generous, which might have commended a man of his tastes to his playfellows. And he vastly overestimated his own intellect."

"With you, ma'am?"

"Oh, certainly. He was the sort of man to match wits with everyone he met. Since most people have not the wit of a kitchen cat, *M. le Chevalier* had convinced himself he was a very clever fellow."

"But he was not?"

Madame Touvois smiled at some private thought. "Not in the end, no." She shook her head. "I believe he came here at first in order to be amused by the company—will it amuse *you* to know, Miss Tolerance, that most of the men who come to my parties believe that they are political theorists and patriots? It is easy to laugh at them."

"So d'Aubigny came at first to laugh—and stayed?"

"Because of Mrs. Vose, of course." Madame Touvois did not bother to deny the connection. "He was the sort of man who likes to dominate—a room, a conversation, a woman. Among her other gifts, Mrs. Vose is the sort of woman who will permit herself to be dominated. For a fee. They dealt very well together while he had money."

"So she had told me. You would not have any notion of where the chevalier's money came from, would you?"

Did Madame Touvois frown? "Why, I thought he had married it. Some poor little girl with countrified vowels whom he kept locked away at home. Certainly he could not have bought his boots on what the Home Office paid him."

"In the days before his death, the chevalier apparently settled most or all of his debts, which is intriguing, since he had been unable to do so before. And he did not borrow the money," Miss Tolerance added. "Not from banks or moneylenders. I was wondering if you knew of any particular friends who might have loaned d'Aubigny a substantial amount of money."

Again, Miss Tolerance had only the impression of a frown on Camille Touvois's face. "I doubt anyone would be so foolish as to loan M. d'Aubigny money, Miss Tolerance. They would surely never have seen it again."

"For some people that is not the first consideration," Miss Tolerance said. "Else the Dukes of Kent and Clarence would have been forced to rusticate long ago."

"Yes, but there is no cachet to lending money to a man like *M. le Chevalier* to offset the insult to one's pocket."

Miss Tolerance nodded. An idea occurred to her. "Perhaps it was a . . . a forced loan?"

"Do you suggest robbery, Miss Tolerance? *M. le Chevalier* had

far too high an opinion of himself to take to the—what is it called?
The high toby."

Miss Tolerance, in the grip of a theory whose logic grew more
convincing with each second, shook her head. "I was not suggesting he had turned highwayman, madame. But consider: an unpleasant man who likes to dominate rooms and conversations and
women, who imagines himself very clever indeed, a man who
must constantly expect to hear the bailiff's knock, but has no re-
sources to pay his debts of honor, let alone his butcher's dun. If
such a man got hold of a secret, might he not use it to his advantage?"

"*Chantage?*"

"Blackmail, yes. It would answer a good many questions."

"But where would he have got such a secret? Even his most optimistic superiors at the Home Office would not have entrusted
secrets of state to a man like d'Aubigny."

"As his superiors knew he was gambling and traveling in a
questionable set, you are likely correct. But I was not imagining
d'Aubigny would traffic in secrets of state. I think it must be
blackmail and not treason that was his goal."

"Why is that?" Madame Touvois paused to refill the glasses.

"As you say, his work was not likely to provide him with information that could have commanded money. And, too, with all the
unpleasantness of which it appears the man was capable, I have
not heard that he was ungrateful to the nation which took his
family in. You are an émigré, Madam. Would you betray England?"

"What a question!" Madame Touvois pursed her lips. "Perhaps,
then, d'Aubigny learned a secret in one of the birching houses—"

"You think he threatened to expose a patron? But would that be
such a dire exposure, ma'am? When you consider the sorts of dis-
sipations with which many of our leading men are credited, mere
birching seems rather tame. But let us suppose that your notion is
correct." Miss Tolerance nodded amiably and tasted her wine. It
was very dry. "Using a secret learnt in a whorehouse creates a sort
of reciprocal effect: did he try to blackmail one party, he might be
blackmailed in return. But a person who can turn tables on his

oppressor is less likely to resort to murder himself. And, of course, I am looking for a murderer. Therefore, I am looking for someone who could not exert a reciprocal pressure on his black-mailer."

"Nicely reasoned, Miss Tolerance. Except, you appear to argue away every venue where the chevalier might have learnt a valuable secret."

"Do I? I wonder if perhaps he learned something in the drawing room of a friend."

"Here? Should I resent the implication, Miss Tolerance?"

"Not in the least, ma'am. I have no wish to offend you. Yours is, after all, not the only drawing room to which the chevalier was a visitor. Nor can you be expected to control what your guests murmur to each other out of your earshot."

That, Miss Tolerance thought with some satisfaction, was a palpable hit. She was not certain which her hostess disliked more: the assertion that there was something in her circle that she could not control, or the reminder that hers was not the only *salon* of note in the city.

"But perhaps lesser drawing rooms would not yield the sort of visitors capable of supplying *M. le Chevalier* with his needed cash," Madame Touvois countered. "But you see how I am confused! Do I truly wish to convince you that mine is the only house in which the chevalier might have blackmailed another of my guests? Of course I would have been horrified had that been so." She fixed Miss Tolerance with guileless regard.

"I am certain of it, ma'am." Miss Tolerance returned her look. "But you have been generous with your time. I must not trespass on that generosity further." She stood, took up her gloves and reticule. "Thank you, ma'am. It has been very informative to speak with you."

"Good afternoon, Miss Tolerance. And pray—" Madame Touvois tilted her head solicitously. "Pray do take care that no more men follow you home from your interviews."

Miss Tolerance left Audley Street convinced in her mind of three things: that Etienne d'Aubigny had found relief from his financial troubles in blackmail; that Camille Touvois had been aware of it; and that she had also known of the attack upon herself. Now all she needed was proof.

F rom Audley Street she shouldered into an icy wind to walk to the d'Aubigny house. Closed carriages plied the streets, but there were no idle strollers out. She found herself one more scurrying figure amid erranding maidservants and footmen. The gutters were inches deep in half-frozen muck, but crossing-boys were scarce, all hiding from the cold regardless of the pennies they might have made. In Half Moon Street it appeared that cold had diminished the thrill of notoriety in some who had thronged around the house—the crowd in the street was notably thinner.

But there was something else: as she neared the house she was struck by a familiar and unpleasant smell of sewage, more noisome than usual even for the London streets. Somewhere behind the houses a privy was overflowing.

Miss Tolerance took her handkerchief from her reticule and held it before her nose, where it slightly lessened the awful smell. She knocked upon the door of the d'Aubigny house and was greeted by Beak, who blinked once at the sight of her injuries, then admitted her with an expression of studied blankness.

"Mrs. d'Aubigny is out," he said. "She is expected to return shortly, however. If Miss would care to wait in the back salon?"

Miss decidedly disliked the notion of waiting in the back salon, which overlooked the garden: she had concluded from the evidence of her nose that it was the d'Aubigny backhouse which required cleaning. Perhaps she could use the time more profitably.

"I will wait, thank you, Beak. But before I sit, I should like to look again at the room where the chevalier—" She paused out of respect for Beak's sensibilities, which appeared to her much tried by events.

Beak's understanding seemed to encompass both her business purpose and the stench from the yard; clearly he would not want to sit in the back salon himself. "Madame did say you was to be cooperated with. I suppose there could be no objection." He turned and was about to lead the way up the stairs when the younger manservant, Peter Jacks, appeared and said something in

Beak's ear, of which Miss Tolerance made out only the word "goldfinder." From this, and the expression of relief upon Beak's face, she apprehended that a man had arrived to clean the privy. Beak muttered something to Jacks and turned again to the stairs, motioning Miss Tolerance to follow. She did, musing upon the dire financial straits which would have led Anne d'Aubigny to neglect so vital (and inexpensive) a service until matters had reached a crisis point.

The chevalier's chamber was as cold and untenanted as she remembered it. From the fact that the drapes were still missing from the bed, Miss Tolerance concluded that they had been destroyed. There was a rime of dust on the top of the chest; after the initial effort to remove the signs of violent death, perhaps no one in the household wanted to clean here.

Whereas the first time she had examined the room Miss Tolerance had wanted merely to see the murder scene and had not expected she would find clues that the diligence of Bow Street had missed, now she had a specific question in mind. If the chevalier had been a-blackmailing, he must have had proofs to use as leverage. If the murderer had sought, but not found, evidence which rendered him vulnerable, it must still be there to be found. Where would a man such as Etienne d'Aubigny hide his secrets? It took only a few minutes to look in the most obvious places—the writing table, the drawers of the chest and the garderobe, the small box which proved to hold a case of razors. If d'Aubigny had hidden something in any of those places it was gone already.

Miss Tolerance shivered. No one had lit a fire in the room since the chevalier's death. The fire tools she had noted upon her first visit to the room stood orderly by the grate. Miss Tolerance examined the fireplace, wishing for a convenient romantic article such as a trap door or secret cupboard, but found none. The grate had been swept, a fire neatly laid but unlikely to be lit anytime soon. The brass fittings shone dully.

Something caught her eye. She dropped to one knee—a little clumsily, as the red dress was not designed for such a movement—and tried to prize the bit of something white that had been caught in the pinched joint of the grate. She lamented that she did

not have a knife with her with which to work the thing loose—
and then Beak was at the door.

"Mrs. d'Aubigny has returned, and asks that you join her
downstairs in the back salon, miss."

Miss Tolerance sighed, rose to her feet and started after the
manservant. As they reached the stairway she saw Anne
d'Aubigny below her in the hallway, handing her coat and bandbox to Jacks. The widow looked up, saw Miss Tolerance, nodded
slightly, and began to say something.

There was at that moment a considerable noise from somewhere in the rear of the house, the sounds of persons both male
and female shouting. Madame d'Aubigny was drawn away to
the conflict and Beak all but ran down the stairs to find out what
had disturbed the peace of the house. Miss Tolerance, no less curious, followed down the stairs and to the rear of the house,
through the green baize door which separated the worlds of servant and served, and stopped on the stairway just outside the
kitchen.

An interesting tableau was there. In the doorway to the
kitchen garden stood a short man, amply padded against the
cold, with a filthy smock over all, high boots, and gloves. He was
pocked and toothless, and would have been ugly even had he
been clean and well dressed, but the mark of his profession was
everywhere upon him, rendering him repellent. Further, the
smell which had penetrated the house was concentrated in his
presence. The privy-man stood in an attitude of combat with
something, perhaps one of his tools, tucked under his arm. The
cook, Ellen Sadgett, stood in opposition to him, a rolling pin
clutched in one hand as if to smite him if he despoiled the cleanliness of her kitchen. Beak advanced upon them, ready to chastise
both for making such ado. Beside him Anne d'Aubigny stood,
watching.

The privy-man was yelling, "Well you'd better let me talk to
someone, you oul' besom! What I got 'ere ain't just the wrecking
of a perfectly good jakes—it may be vallable! What it was doing
down there, backin' matters up, *I* can't say."

"You get right out, you smelly varmint, or I'll—" Mrs. Sadgett waved her rolling pin menacingly. "I don't care what you 'ave there. Madame's not to be bothered by—"

"Mrs. Sadgett!" Beak roared over both. "And *you*!"

"Willis, sir." The privy-man happily turned to report to masculine authority. "A man in my position is liable to all manner of abuse, and if I finds something looks as it might be a' value, I'm bound to turn it over as soon as possible. I don't want no misunderstanding about that, sir. I keep nothing what ain't mine, no matter where I finds it. Not to mention your jakes will back up do you go heavin' furniture into it!"

Willis reached under his smock and produced a handkerchief, incongruously white against the stains of his smock. He shrugged the object under his arm forward and wiped it all over with the handkerchief before extending it toward Beak.

"What's a thing like that doing in your cesspit is what I want to know," Willis scolded, and bounced the thing at arm's end by way of emphasis.

Beak regarded the object with revulsion. It was a wooden box, perhaps two hands high and four hands broad, about the size of the box in which Miss Tolerance kept her own writing materials at home, but of a far more aristocratic origin. Mr. Willis' ministrations had barely lessened the crusting of filth on it, but she could see that the box was carved upon the lid and sides; there was a brass latch on one side.

Anne d'Aubigny gasped and stepped forward as if to examine the box. Then she crumpled to the kitchen floor in a profound faint.

The effect upon the occupants of the room was electric. Mrs. Sadgett forgot about the privy-man and dropped to her knees, fluttering over her mistress. Beak hurried forward, barking for Jacks' assistance, then for Mrs. Sadgett to leave over fidgeting and fetch Madam's vinaigrette. Mr. Willis, apparently much gratified by his effect upon the household, dropped the offending box upon the table and hurried forward to give advice, being careful not to rub against any of the kitchen furnishings. Within a moment Jacks had appeared and gathered up Mrs. d'Aubigny. With Beak leading the way they started up the stairs, followed by Mrs.

Sadgett, who waved a bottle Miss Tolerance assumed to be *sal volatile*, and Mr. Willis, giving helpful suggestions. For a moment Miss Tolerance was left alone in the kitchen.

And there, upon the table, was the box.

She took up one of Mrs. Sadgett's kitchen cloths and used it to wipe the worst of the muck from around the latch. It lifted easily, and in a moment the box was open to her. It was a nice piece of workmanship; despite its immersion in the privy, the box's contents were dry and clean, although disordered. With one finger Miss Tolerance carefully pushed the contents from one side to the other, examining them and the box. As Anne d'Aubigny had told her, it was lined in red silk, worn napless in spots and specked, here and there, with rusty flecks. There were several silk scarves and what looked at first to be a number of whips but proved, when she took it up, to be one whip with many ends, each finished with a small lead weight. Imagining the impact of this object upon tender flesh, Miss Tolerance shuddered. Below the cat was a case with six tiny pearl-handled blades, one still wearing a brown stain of blood. There were several lengths of heavy silk cord, and some other objects the use of which Miss Tolerance could only guess.

Miss Tolerance poked through the box's contents until she reached the bottom, a matter of a minute or so. What she did not find were letters or evidence which might have been used for blackmail. She returned the cat and scarves to the box. The filth on the box's exterior, and the sight of the box's contents, acted unpleasantly upon Miss Tolerance's stomach. She was almost grateful to be interrupted by the sound of approaching footsteps.

"Please, Miss." The abigail, Sophia Thissen, stood in the doorway, looking not at Miss Tolerance but at the box. "Madame asks will you join her in the rear parlor."

Miss Tolerance closed the lid of the box and stepped away from the table.

"I'll see to that," Sophia said. "Madame would not like to have it sitting out."

She was certainly correct in that, Miss Tolerance thought. She noted that Sophia recognized the box and understood its contents—which made sense, for certainly Sophia must have been the one to patch up Anne d'Aubigny when her husband had finished disporting himself. *Perhaps I should talk a little with Sophia Thissen,* she thought. *What she knows of the late chevalier's life is like to be unflattering but informative.*

"I shall go up, then." Miss Tolerance wiped her hands on a clean towel—alas for Mrs. Sadgett's orderly kitchen—and went past Sophia to the stairs. Some prudent instinct caused her to turn and instruct Sophia to put the box somewhere safe, just in case. "Perhaps I shall need to look at it again," Miss Tolerance told her, and went upstairs.

In the hall Miss Tolerance met Mr. Willis, apparently quite pleased to have started such a fuss, with Mrs. Sadgett following him to the kitchen and maintaining a steady flow of expostulation. In the back parlor Anne d'Aubigny sat in an armchair, eyes closed, the pallor of her faint beginning to recede. A decanter stood at her elbow with an empty glass next to it.

"Are you recovered, ma'am?" Miss Tolerance asked.

"Nearly so, Miss Tolerance. You must think me very weak and easily overset!" Anne d'Aubigny essayed a smile. It did not convince.

"Not at all. You had sustained a shock." She waited for a moment, then asked, "May I sit, ma'am?"

"Oh, yes. Of course. Forgive my shabby manners, Miss Tolerance, and—good Heaven, what has happened to you? Are you all right?"

Miss Tolerance put her hand to her cheek as if to remember her bruises. "Please don't think of it. I had a bit of trouble on my way home last night, that is all." Ready to talk of anything but her injuries, she asked the first question that occurred to her. "Was it you who put the box in the necessary house, or Sophia?"

Anne d'Aubigny gaped.

"It takes very little to come to that conclusion, and to hit upon the reason. It must have been painful to you to know it was in the house."

The widow nodded.

"Wholly understandable, if perhaps a little ill-advised. Now, let me tell you of my progress, and ask you some questions quite unrelated to the box." Miss Tolerance took on a soothing note of false heartiness, like a nursery maid calming a child with a cut finger. "It is the belief that you are awake to the whole of your husband's character that encourages me to speak freely. I think the chevalier was blackmailing someone, and I believe that when I learn who it was, we will know who killed him. If I'm right, the murderer can have no designs upon your safety, which should give you some ease, at least."

Miss Tolerance watched as Anne d'Aubigny took in the whole of this intelligence and considered it. At last she smiled a crooked smile.

"My poor husband. He will have no character left at all. You say you have questions, Miss Tolerance?" She sat very straight in her chair, with her hands folded in her lap, as she had done when questioned by Mr. Heddison.

"Only a few, ma'am, and you need not fear them. Did your husband have a safe or some other place he might have hidden blackmail proofs?"

"At his desk, in the library. He had a locked box. I thought it held things like the lease to this house, and his passport, perhaps a little money. When he died I looked for it but could not find it—"

"You did not inquire of—"

Miss Tolerance's question was interrupted by the sound of heavy footsteps in the hall. Beak was thrust into the room, his mouth open. The massive form of Boyse, the constable who worked with Mr. Heddison, pushed past him and stopped, legs spread as if he were establishing a claim upon the space. A smaller, younger man in a bright blue coat was just behind him, frowning at Boyse.

"I beg pardon, ma'am—" the second constable began, but Boyse cut him off.

"In the name of the King, we're here to bring you to the Public Office, Anne Dobinny, for questioning in the willful murder of E-ten Philleep Dobinny. You come along quiet with us, ma'am, and I shan't have to put the irons on you."

Eleven

Anne d'Aubigny gaped up at Boyse.

"There has been information laid against you, ma'am," the second man said.

"Ah, shut it," Boyse said out of the corner of his mouth. The slighter man, whom Miss Tolerance took to be Mr. Greenwillow, Boyse's partner, stepped back.

"Who has laid the evidence?" Miss Tolerance asked without much hope of a reply. The constable was not required to answer, and in practice the law often preferred to keep the accused ignorant of their accusers.

Boyse said nothing, but glared at Miss Tolerance and ran his hand through his fringe of white hair, cupping the back of his head gingerly. She turned to Mr. Greenwillow and asked the question again.

"I couldn't say, Miss. Mr. Heddison sent us to bring Madam Dobinny in for questioning."

"But I have answered every question that has been put to me," Anne d'Aubigny said. She looked around her a little wildly, as if seeking the person or thing which would contain this new threat.

"That may be so, ma'am. But Mr. Heddison sent for you and

you're bound to come. You may wish to tell your maid to pack you some necessaries to send 'round."

Mrs. d'Aubigny got unsteadily to her feet and looked to Miss Tolerance.

"Can they do this? Must I go?"

The constables turned their attention to Miss Tolerance as if her opinion would shape their actions as well as the widow's.

"I am afraid they can and you must, ma'am," Miss Tolerance said. "If you go now, I will follow with Sophia and we will try to see that you are made comfortable. Then we will set about refuting this information." She let her tone speak her opinion of the evidence. "Where will you take her?"

Boyse grinned. "Don't know as it's much business of yours."

"If we are to fetch Mrs. d'Aubigny some necessities, surely we must know where to bring them to her."

The slighter constable spoke up. "The Public Office, Great Marlborough Street. You know it? I imagine you'll find her still there."

"Thank you, Mr.—Greenwillow?" The constable nodded. "And after?"

"If she's held over in custody—"

"*Held*—?" Anne d'Aubigny had been watching Miss Tolerance. Now she turned back to the constables with the look of someone who has woken from nightmare into horror.

"—she'll be sent to Cold Bath Fields, most like," Greenwillow finished.

"Held over? *Imprisoned*? Miss Tolerance, can you not help me? How can they think—" Anne d'Aubigny put her hands out before her as if wondering if they, independent of their owner, could have done murder.

Miss Tolerance did her best to appear authoritatively reassuring. "They do not know you, and if someone has given information which is wrong, they are still bound to make inquiries. Whatever the evidence is, ma'am, I will find it out. Gentlemen, it appears"—she cast a pardonably hostile eye upon the constables—"it appears that you have been taken in. 'Tis but a matter of learning how, and refuting this evidence. Do you wish me to contact any of your friends, ma'am?"

Mrs. d'Aubigny shook her head. "Only my brother. I couldn't bear to have anyone else know—"

"They'll know soon enough," Boyse said flatly. He seemed pleased. "Newspapers is been howling their heads off at Mr. Heddison to find the culprit. They'll be celebrating that the streets of Lunnon are safe again." He looked down at Anne d'Aubigny's slight form and even he appeared to find the idea ludicrous.

"Ma'am, do you have a cloak or a coat? A bonnet?" Mr. Greenwillow seemed to wish to offset his partner's ill manners.

As if he had waited only this cue, Beak appeared.

"I am going out, Beak." Mrs. d'Aubigny said the words as if she was asking a question. "If you will desire Sophie to bring my brown wool cloak with the sable—oh, no. Not that one. The black cloak, please, Beak."

Beak reappeared in a moment with Anne d'Aubigny's cloak, and a bonnet and gloves as well. Miss Tolerance helped the widow tie the ribbons of her bonnet, and lowered the heavy mourning veil to shield Anne d'Aubigny from the worst of the prying eyes.

"Can you not take her out the kitchen door?" Miss Tolerance suggested. "So she needn't be ogled by the crowd?"

Mr. Greenwillow by himself might have said yes, but Mr. Boyse shook his head, and Anne d'Aubigny turned to Miss Tolerance. She drew herself up and squared her shoulders to face the ordeal ahead of her.

"Never mind, Miss Tolerance. If you will bring Sophia to me, and let my brother know what has happened?"

"Of course."

Greenwillow led the way from the room and out the door to the street, where a noise issued from the crowd—Miss Tolerance could not tell if it was a roar of approval or a groan of dismay. Anne d'Aubigny stopped in the door for a moment as if the noise frightened her, then was prodded forward by Boyse, whose bulk blocked off hope of retreat to the house. Beak held the door, watching as his mistress was taken away. His face was blank, but it was not the studied lack of reaction common to well-trained servants. Mr. Beak clearly did not know what to feel or think in the face of such overwhelming calamity. He had "come with" the lease of the house, Miss Tolerance recalled. It was likely he had never encountered so grave a loss of countenance to his establishment before. Murder, arrest, perversion, all in *his* house. Poor Mr. Beak.

Miss Tolerance waited as Sophia Thissen packed a valise for her mistress, advising her to include nothing of great value, since it was likely that most of what she sent would be stolen. She then wrote a terse note to William Colcannon explaining what had happened. She did not anticipate with pleasure her next meeting with her employer, particularly if his sister were in fact remanded to custody for prolonged questioning. The notion of Anne d'Aubigny given over to the hospitality of the Cold Bath Fields prison—which, while newer than the other prisons in the Fleet, was quite as harsh as any of them—was not at all a happy one.

In Great Marlborough Street, Miss Tolerance applied at once to speak with Mr. Heddison, while Sophia asked for her mistress, to convey the valise she had brought for her. Miss Tolerance was directed to a bench against one wall to wait. From there she watched as the abigail attempted to gain access to her mistress from a clerk who was determined that she should not prevail.

"But the constables said I was to bring Madam her case—" Sophie's vowels partook more richly of the Yorkshire moors as her dismay increased.

"No orders was given to me, Miss, and wivout orders I can't allow *Madam* to 'ave noffing off you." The clerk was young and snub-nosed, his hair just a little too long, his cuffs and high shirt-points slightly soiled. He wore a good coat of a slightly foppish cut; used, Miss Tolerance thought, but stylish enough to march with the fellow's good opinion of himself. He looked not very much older than the street-sweeps who had crowded around her in Boston Place, and just as capable of bullying someone he perceived as weak.

"You come 'round later if you like, or you can sit over there. P'raps in a while someone will come take that vallis off you."

Sophia, Miss Tolerance was amused to see, was not to be bullied. As short and plump as she was, she looked down at the seated clerk with the hauteur of which only an upper servant is capable. "No one is going to take this *valise* from me, young man. It will go into Madam's hands, if I have to sit here all night."

The young man looked down for a moment, then regained himself. "Suit yourself, then, *miss*. Your Madam can do wivout her smellin' salts and lace kerchiefs for all of me." He leaned forward and grinned unpleasantly. "Wos it like, then, to work for a murderess?"

"I wouldn't know," Sophia snapped. "My lady's no murderess. What is it like to work for persecutors of—"

Miss Tolerance judged it time to intervene.

"It is interesting, sir, that you should call the lady a murderess when she was only called in to answer questions."

The clerk looked irritably over at Miss Tolerance. "She'll be arrested too, I don't doubt," he said firmly. His eye had taken in the quality of Miss Tolerance's garments; he adjusted his tone to something more like civility.

Miss Tolerance rose, put a hand on Sophia's shoulder, and motioned the abigail toward the settle. "Indeed. You sound very certain. What could have convinced so astute a fellow as yourself?"

"Mr. 'eddison says—" in those three words Miss Tolerance heard the certainty of hero worship—"she's the best suspect he 'as."

"Indeed," she said thoughtfully. "What evidence has he against the woman?"

"She was there, wa'nt she?" he asked reasonably. "And wimmen is always murdering their 'usbands, an't they?"

From the settle Sophia spoke up, outraged. "It's more like Madam would ha' been murthered by him!"

Miss Tolerance shook her head at Sophia, who sat back against the settle, still seething. "There were a number of people in the house that night," she said reasonably. "And if women often kill their husbands, there's nothing to say that this particular woman killed that particular man."

The clerk tossed off this reasoning. "Don't matter. Mr. Boyse talked to someone's got the goods."

"Did he?" Miss Tolerance smiled politely. "Well, Mr.—"

"Cotler," the clerk supplied.

"Well, Mr. Cotler, this is all very interesting. Now." She took her pocketbook from her reticule. "We must agree to disagree about Mrs. d'Aubigny's guilt until the evidence against her becomes public. In the meantime, Mr. Greenwillow specifically asked that Miss Thissen"—she inclined her head toward Sophia—"bring Mrs. d'Aubigny some belongings, in case the questioning goes on for some time. Surely it cannot hurt to tell him that we are here."

She placed a half-crown on the table. Mr. Cotler looked at the coin for a moment, then shrugged.

"I can ask, miss. When spoken to civil-like," he added for Sophia's benefit. He rose, pocketed the coin, and disappeared down the hall.

Sophia was specific in her comments upon Mr. Cotler's character, and upon Miss Tolerance's bribe.

" 'Twas expedient," Miss Tolerance said without shame.

Five minutes later, Mr. Greenwillow appeared with Cotler just behind him.

"No one can see Mrs. Dobinny just now, miss," he told Miss Tolerance. "I can take the case in, if you like. Or you could wait," he said more generally to Sophia and Miss Tolerance, "to see if she's remanded into custody. If she is—"

"Is it likely?"

Greenwillow nodded. "There's considerable evidence against her, miss."

"May I ask what that evidence is, Mr. Greenwillow?"

The constable shook his head. "You know that's not the way, miss."

"I cannot even ask what information your partner was supplied?"

Greenwillow looked a little shocked, and glanced once at Mr. Cotler, who blushed and looked away.

"Should I tell you that so you can find a way to say it ain't so?"

"If the information is wrong, ought not Mr. Heddison to be apprised of it?" she asked reasonably.

Greenwillow might have been impressed by this reasoning, but stood firm upon the common practice of the office. "That may be so, ma'am. But it's not the law's way to give sensitive information to outsiders—even were you a man and a lawyer, miss, I wouldn't tell you. I can say that it don't look very good for her."

"Let me speak with Mr. Boyse, then," Miss Tolerance suggested.

Greenwillow shook his head. "I wouldn't do that, miss. He's a bit of a rough diamond, John Boyse is. I doubt you'll learn anything of him."

"At least ask him if he will speak to me," Miss Tolerance pressed. "I am a citizen of this parish, more or less, asking a question of a constable. What could be more reasonable?"

The constable thought, shrugged, and went down the hall with an air which said that Miss Tolerance had made her bed, and must now be prepared for whatever she found in it. He returned after a few minutes with Boyse just behind him. The big man approached until he was so close that the swell of his belly was but inches from her own frame; so close that Miss Tolerance had to cramp her neck not to look up at him.

"What do you want?"

Miss Tolerance inclined her head politely. "A few minutes of your time, sir. Is there somewhere where we may speak with privacy?"

"Why?"

"Because I dislike broadcasting my business to the four winds," she said, still politely. She looked around to take in Greenwillow, Sophia Thissen and the clerk, Mr. Cotler. "I have some questions to ask; are you certain you wish to answer them before an audience?"

Something passed briefly over Boyse's face: a look of concern. He recovered himself and sneered. "How do you know I'll answer your questions?"

"I don't. But if you do not, it suggests that there is something you fear in the answers, and I shall have to investigate *that*."

Boyse crossed his arms on his chest and looked down at Miss Tolerance. She was a tall woman, but he was at least a head taller than she. Speaking to him was rather like addressing a bad-tempered mountain. "Ask your questions. Here and nowhere else."

"Very well. I understand that you have evidence against Mrs. d'Aubigny?"

The constable smiled. "I do."

"May I ask what that evidence is?"

"You can ask if you like." The big man smiled. Miss Tolerance understood at once that she would get nothing from him except by trickery or payment. She was not ready to try the latter in the hallways of the magistrate's court.

"Physical evidence?" she essayed.

"Might could be," Boyse said easily. His eyes were steady; Miss Tolerance was certain that he lied.

"Or perhaps some poisonous nonsense that was whispered to you in a tavern somewhere. Yes, I suppose that is more likely. There are many men who would say anything for a part of the forty-pound murderer's bounty."

Boyse's eyes flickered. Had she hit upon it? "Whatever it is, I ain't telling you."

Miss Tolerance trod carefully. "If someone had told a Canterbury tale in hopes of getting his part of the bounty—well, I'm sure Mrs. d'Aubigny's brother would pay just as well for the truth. You might let your informant know it."

Boyse considered for a moment and then, apparently by decision, glowered at her. "You suggesting a bribe? Right here, in front of witnesses?" Boyse's face was red. He swept his arm out to include Cotler and Greenwillow.

"Not in the least, sir. I'm sorry you should imagine it. Like you, my object is only that the truth be known." Miss Tolerance smiled politely and did not back away, although the constable's looming, wrathful presence was oppressive. "You can tell me nothing? I shall have to see what I can do for my client elsewhere."

"I ought to have—" the constable began. He broke off, running his hand through his hair again, and looked crestfallen. Then he turned, growled something to Greenwillow, and stomped back down the hall. Miss Tolerance did not stay him; she was now reasonably sure that the information upon which Heddison intended to base his case came from a paid informant. If she could discover the source she could discredit the informer or his information. Physical evidence in hand would have been harder to discover and disprove.

She turned to Mr. Greenwillow, who had watched the interview blank-faced.

"*You* believe that matters do not look well for my client?"

Greenwillow appeared surprised to be appealed to. "Aye, miss. And you should know that if she's held over she'll need—"

"Money." Miss Tolerance called Sophia over. "Take my purse, Sophia. If, as Mr. Greenwillow fears, they do not finish their questions tonight, Mrs. d'Aubigny will need to pay garnish at the prison."

"Garnish?"

"Fees. For food and a bed and a little privacy," Miss Tolerance explained. "Anything that this doesn't cover, you may promise that Mr. Colcannon will pay for."

"But where will you be, miss?" Sophia asked a little wildly. Greenwillow looked uncommonly interested in the answer.

"There are some people I need to speak with," Miss Tolerance said coolly. "As it appears we are to meet with very little cooperation here, my time is better used elsewhere, learning what I can of this spurious evidence. When you see your mistress, Sophia, tell her I hope to have her home again very shortly. With all the goodwill in the world, sir, I must say that this has been very badly done."

Greenwillow's natural sympathy for the widow had put him off his guard. Now his posture straightened and his expression was glacial. "You may think so, miss," he said. "We are only doing our duty."

Miss Tolerance left the Public Office to find that night had fallen. She was in a restless mood and longed to walk some of that energy off, but she was not dressed to walk through darkened London streets, or to defend herself should someone make another attempt upon her. She stood for a few minutes on the steps of the building, thinking what next to do. At last she hailed a hansom and directed it toward Covent Garden and Bow Street. Her first case must be to find out the nature of the information which had convinced Heddison to bring Anne d'Aubigny to Great Marlborough Street. The quickest way to do that was to enlist help. She was not certain, however, that help would be easily secured.

At the offices of the Bow Street Magistracy, she was led away from the public hall and taken down a long, low-ceilinged hall-way to a small square chamber. The room was gloomy, lit by two lamps whose light reflected off the dull white of the walls. In the center of the room was a large table; a straight back chair was set before it and there were two more chairs against one wall. A large chest stood against the wall, its top open, disclosing stacks of paper and ledgers. On the table papers and books were strewn, and amid this chaos Sir Walter Mandif was at work covering a page with his neat, square script. He looked up as she entered.

"Miss Tolerance! I am delighted to see you." Sir Walter's smile lit his narrow, foxy face. "What brings you here? I do not recall that you have ever called in Bow Street before." He put down his pen, covered the inkpot, and rose to his feet.

"I have never had a need to before." Face to face with Sir Walter, Miss Tolerance was surprised by a welling up of anger. She knew it was unlikely in the highest degree that Mandif had even known of Anne d'Aubigny's detention: the little communication there was among the magistrates and public offices of London was reputed to be more suspicious than collegial. No effort was made to work together or share information and, given the rewards mandated by Parliament for the conviction of murderers, Great Marlborough Street was unlikely to inform Bow Street or Whitechapel or Hatton Gardens of how its investigations fared. Miss Tolerance knew it was irrational to feel that Sir Walter *should* have known and *should* have told her, and yet she did feel that way.

"This afternoon Anne d'Aubigny was taken by Mr. Heddison's constables and brought to Great Marlborough Street for questioning."

"I am sorry to hear it," Sir Walter said.

"So was I. For that matter, I expect she was as well. Mr. Heddison's tame constables will not tell me what the evidence is that convinced Mr. Heddison to take such a step—"

"It must have been convincing—"

"To a man who was already half-convinced, I don't doubt it was."

Sir Walter frowned. "Do you believe this information is unreliable?"

"I do. I think someone has laid information in hopes of sharing in the damnable murder-bounty." Sir Walter's mild shock at hearing such language from her heightened Miss Tolerance's own irritation.

"That may be so, but have you proof that the information is wrong?"

"I do not know what the information is, so I cannot refute it! But everything I know of Mrs. d'Aubigny says that the information must be wrong. Good God, Sir Walter, I could as readily believe a nursing baby guilty of treason as I can believe Anne d'Aubigny killed her husband. She doesn't even know how her kitchen door locks."

"That, in itself, is not proof infallible that she is innocent," Mandif said lightly.

Miss Tolerance refused to be humored.

"I mention it only because it is indicative of her—" She sought the word. "Her childish reliance upon everyone around her. This is not a woman who would commit murder; she would have no idea how. And in any case, she was drugged asleep when her husband died. But this is beside the point, Mandif. If Heddison has such faith in Mrs. D'Aubigny's guilt, why does he not make the evidence known? Because it might blow a hole in his neat case and force him to do the work to catch the real killer."

"That is a very weighty accusation against a seasoned magistrate."

She had offended him. Miss Tolerance drew a long breath.

"I mean no disrespect to the man or his office. But, Sir Walter, you said that *you* were not certain that Heddison was up to the pressures of this investigation. How easy might it be to throw Anne d'Aubigny to her fate on the basis of a casual information from an unnamed source! And they marched her out of her house before the mob. The mob roared! It was a fine show, so fine I doubt anyone is refining overmuch about the truth. But I was hired to be Mrs. d'Aubigny's protector, and this information stinks of falsity to me. If I am too hot, I apologize. But until I know what the evidence is, I shall not know how to refute it."

"Ah." Sir Walter sat down and crossed his arms. "You have come in hopes that I can learn that for you."

Miss Tolerance drew a breath and nodded. Her smile was apologetic. "I'm afraid that is so."

"You know it would be difficult for me to do so. And Heddison would not appreciate it if I did tell you."

"Does that mean that you will not do it?"

"I mean that it will be difficult. And that it will render any future attempts of mine to discover information—on my own account or on yours—more difficult if Heddison believes I betrayed professional confidences to you. You may wish to think if you want to spend your coin in this fashion."

Miss Tolerance spoke slowly. "I would not ask this if I did not consider it absolutely necessary. If I did not believe Anne d'Aubigny to be innocent. I see no objection to spending my coin in such a cause. But if you think my judgment is so questionable—"

Sir Walter's eyebrows, so fair they were almost invisible in the lamplight, drew down in a frown. "I do not wish to offend you. But what you ask will have repercussions, and I wished to make that plain. The next time—"

"The next time will take care of itself," Miss Tolerance said flatly. "Please, Sir Walter. I pressed at Great Marlborough Street, but your friend Heddison could not be spared to speak to me. I have no legal standing, no way to pressure or bribe my way in." She sniffed. "You may think Boyse is corruptible, but I assure you that he is not corruptible by *me*."

"I am delighted to hear it." Sir Walter smiled, and for a moment Miss Tolerance felt a return of something like their usual cordial understanding. After several minutes of thought he nodded, as if making a resolution to himself. "Very well, Miss Tolerance. I will do my best to learn what the evidence is. I will send a note round to Manchester Square if I can discover anything."

Miss Tolerance smiled. "Thank you, Sir Walter. In the end, it will mean a greater credit for Heddison, you know. He would not want to be known for having the wrong person in custody."

"I imagine he would not," Mandif agreed drily. "May I give you a glass of wine and ask how your aunt does?"

Miss Tolerance was guiltily aware that she had not thought of

Mrs. Brereton all day. "I have not been back in Manchester Square since I saw you this morning."

"You have been very busy."

"And I have not the temperament for the sickroom." Miss Tolerance shook her head. "No wine, thank you, Sir Walter. Now that you have reminded me of my duty, I must go home and inquire after my aunt. You will let me know what Heddison says?"

Sir Walter stood. "I will. I hope you will not place too much reliance upon my ability to ferret out the informant. Heddison and I are not friends, and he may look askance at my curiosity; the habit of professional secrecy dies hard between the magistracies."

"You have told me that you will do what you can. I place every reliance upon that." Miss Tolerance smiled with warmth and offered her hand. "I am sorry if my anxiety for Anne d'Aubigny should have—"

"Your enthusiasm is one of your greatest charms." Sir Walter bowed over her hand.

Miss Tolerance flushed. "I look to hear from you." She took her hand from his and turned for the door. Mandif called her back.

"What will you do if the information truly implicates the widow?"

She shook her head. "I'll do what I must. But I am sure it cannot. Thank you, Sir Walter." She curtsied and left him.

The light from the house on Manchester Square glowed in the dark street as Miss Tolerance alit from her hansom carriage. She did not trouble to walk around the corner to Spanish Place, but knocked on the door and was admitted by Keefe. Song of a particularly riotous sort issued from one of the parlors. Miss Tolerance rolled her eyes and inquired after her aunt; Keefe informed her that Mrs. Brereton appeared to be on the mend, and had left word that her niece should call in the morning. Miss Tolerance thanked Keefe and was about to proceed toward the garden steps when she was stopped by a crowd of merrymakers who erupted into the hallway, surrounding her. The men looked alike in dark coats and pale breeches, the evening uniform of the fashionable male; the women, all recognizable as Mrs. Brereton's whores, wore a variety of garb from formal evening dress to transparent chemise. The entire party appeared in a state of merriment, playing a parody of that nursery staple, blindman's buff. First among them was Miss Tolerance's particular friend, Marianne Touchwell.

Miss Tolerance was uncomfortably aware that she might be mistaken for one of the whores. She felt as well some awkwardness at the sight of her friend, flushed and laughing, playing at using her fan to protect her from the importunities of one of the men. She did not often encounter Marianne at work.

For a moment Miss Tolerance stood still in the midst of the merrymakers, as if inaction itself could differentiate her from the crowd. This subtlety—and the fact that Miss Tolerance wore a coat and bonnet and not the Hellenic draperies of some of the whores—was lost on one fellow, who came up behind her and snaked his arm about her waist, attempting to slide his hand into her coat and tweak her breast. Miss Tolerance reacted more quickly than thought: she had the man's arm twisted behind his back before she recalled where she was and whose business she was depressing. The game abruptly stopped.

"I beg your pardon, sir," she said at once, and released the man. "I'm afraid you startled me. I did not think—"

"Didn't think?" Chloe, one of the whores in the crowd, pushed forward. "I should say not, Miss Sarah! My poor Mr. N, are you quite all right?" She fluttered around the man, who stood rubbing his arm. He had caught sight of her bruised face, and stared in fascination.

"I quite understand, miss—" He paused. "I ought not, that is; I mistook you—"

"Quite understandable," Miss Tolerance said. "I did not hurt you?"

"Really, Miss Sarah!" Chloe put her arm about her patron's shoulder and ran a caressing hand across his shoulder. "Don't you fret, Mr. N. It's quite—"

Marianne pushed through the crowd. "That's all right, Chloe. He wasn't to know that Miss Sarah isn't one of us—" This to Mr. N, who was now watching Miss Tolerance with some interest. "And she was naturally startled, being . . . embraced in that fashion. I'm sure there's no hard feelings to either," she finished briskly, and extracted Miss Tolerance from the crowd, pushing her brusquely down the hall.

"I am sorry," Miss Tolerance murmured. She was very aware that several of the gentlemen were still staring after her. "Should my aunt ever ask, you have now seen an excellent demonstration of why I do not yield to her pleas that I join the house."

Marianne grinned. "I shall be sure to tell her. But in the morning; Frost says she's sleeping now. Are you well? You look tired." Her eyes shifted back and forth as she examined Miss Tolerance's face.

" 'Tis only the cold and the bruises, and an eventful day. A night's sleep will put me right. Your party looks for you." Miss Tolerance shrugged away from the concern in her friend's voice and looked over her shoulder to the hall, where two gentlemen, one fair and one dark, were still watching them.

"My Mr. C and . . . well, I hope the other one hasn't taken a fancy to you! No, Lisette's come for him," Marianne noted approvingly.

"Do not let me keep you. I'm for my own bed." Miss Tolerance, oppressed by the emotions of the day, was as good as her word. She returned to her cottage, went up to bed, and even without recourse to that notably soporific text, Mainley's *Art of the Small-Sword*, she was very soon deeply asleep.

She waked in the dark, sitting upright in her bed without any notion of what had pulled her out of sleep. She listened intently and let her eyes adjust to the darkness. Was that footfall downstairs? Now there was a soft, billowing sound. Moonlight could not penetrate the clouds, but the light from Mrs. Brereton's house across the way danced on the frame of the tiny window that overlooked the garden.

No. Not from Mrs. Brereton's house. At the same moment that smoke began to curl under her door, Miss Tolerance realized that the orange light that danced on the window lit the upper sill only: it came from below. Miss Tolerance grabbed for what clothes she could find—a pair of breeches, a waistcoat—and pulled them on over her shift. She did not open the door of her room; with a fire belowstairs, she might die trying to escape by the stairs. She opened the window next to her bed and looked down, seeing the orange glow of fire through the window below. There was a tree bough perhaps five feet from the window, but it would be a hard enough task to climb through; jumping to the tree and climbing down would be impossible. She resigned herself to the drop and, taking hold of the sill above, put first one foot, then the other, out the window. She began to lower herself down. It was a tight fit, particularly at the hip, and required some careful placement and replacement of her hands. After a few moments she hung from the lower sill, feet braced against the side of the house, looking down.

It seemed as good a moment as any to start a cry of "Fire!"

There are few actions one can take in London which will evoke a more immediate response. After her second cry Miss Tolerance dropped to the ground; when she had regained her feet again people had already begun to run from the back of Mrs. Brereton's. Keefe, at the forefront, had a bucket of water to hand. Behind him came various men in different states of dress or its lack.

Miss Tolerance looked in the window on the first floor of her cottage; the blaze was in the center of the room, directly under the spot where her bed stood. Before she could note more than that, she was jostled out of the way by Keefe, who dashed the first bucket of water through the door and turned to take the next one. Miss Tolerance took a place in the line and was very busy for a few minutes. She did not begin to feel the cold until the fire was put out, when she realized with dismay that she was all amuck from exertion and soot and soaked through with water. She could barely feel her bare feet in the icy water. Shivering, she turned to thank the men who had come to help her—including the man who had accosted her earlier, and was quite pleased to have played the hero as part of his evening's pleasures. All of them, servant and client, demurred thanks. Marianne, who appeared in a prosaic dressing gown, invited all back into the house where hot water and hot drinks were waiting for them. It appeared that the crisis was over.

Miss Tolerance went into the cottage to examine the damage. The fire had been remarkably contained, burning, as she had noted, directly under her bed. That this was ten paces from the grate suggested that the fire was not the result of a flying ember. More to the point, Miss Tolerance saw, were the remains of several charred pieces of furniture: a chair, the dish cupboard, her writing box, and several ledgers, piled in the middle of the room at the fire's center. The fire had been set. Someone had apparently intended her death.

Miss Tolerance turned back to the house, conscious of a queasiness born of ebbing excitement and a new, deep sense of menace. She looked up at the face of Mrs. Brereton's house, which appeared entirely as usual. Or almost as usual: in one of the upper windows a man stood, looking down at her. In the light from the windows below she could see that he was fully dressed and unsmirched by soot or smoke. He was the fair-haired man who had watched her speak with Marianne earlier; and as their eyes met, the man inclined his head in acknowledgment and smiled broadly.

Twelve

Miss Tolerance spent the night in Mrs. Brereton's servants' quarters; the better bedchambers were, by the nature of the house, at a premium. The room in which she slept was tiny but clean and quiet; Miss Tolerance locked the door and slept soundly. In the morning, bathed and in a morning gown borrowed from Marianne, she presented herself in Mrs. Brereton's room.

"What *are* you wearing, girl?" Mrs. Brereton had so far recovered from her indisposition that she was seated at her table with her ledgers and writing box to hand, a tray of chocolate and toasted bread at her elbow. She still wore a heavily laced dressing gown and cap, and gave no sign that she meant to go downstairs that day.

"Marianne loaned me the dress, ma'am—we differ somewhat in the matter of breadth and height." In fact she had had to sash the dress twice, and it displayed considerably more ankle than was fashionable. "I have not yet had a chance to inspect my own clothes. You may have heard I had a little excitement in my cottage last night."

"Of course I heard. Of all people, Sarah, I would not have expected you to be careless with fire." Mrs. Brereton poured chocolate into her cup; Miss Tolerance noted that she did it with particular care and one-handed. Her left hand rested in her lap.

"I was not careless, Aunt. I made no fire last night; the only candle I had was by my bed and I extinguished it before I slept. The fire was set." Miss Tolerance offered this information without heat. Mrs. Brereton pursed her lips thoughtfully, then sent Frost to fetch another cup for Miss Sarah.

"I don't drink chocolate, Aunt," Miss Tolerance pointed out.

"Don't be stupid, girl. I don't want Frost to hear this. The fire was *set*?"

"There can be no doubt. Half my parlor furniture had been shifted to the middle of the room, and the fire was lit there. I think it was meant to kill me."

Mrs. Brereton stared at her niece. "My God."

"Indeed."

"Someone climbed the wall, do you think? Some enemy you have made in doing your work?"

"I have not inspected the garden for any sign of an intruder, and unfortunately, after the crush in the garden last night to put the fire out, I doubt that any tracks I might have found will be legible this morning. Still, I shall look. I might have better luck trying to determine who would want me dead."

"Who would not?" The question seemed to have been asked without irony, in the spirit of inquiry. Mrs. Brereton sipped at her chocolate and gazed at her nonplussed niece.

"Good Lord, Aunt; while I may have a few enemies, I suspect most of those would prefer to see me horsewhipped than burnt."

"In your profession—" Mrs. Brereton began. She stopped and said thoughtfully, "I suppose the two with the greatest cause to wish you dead would be Versellion and his cousin."

Miss Tolerance shook her head. "Versellion is on his way to Australia, if he is not there already. Henry Folle was hanged a fortnight after his trial. I think we can acquit them both. As for the rest—I cannot think of anyone else who would so dislike me as to desire my death."

"Well, who then?" Mrs. Brereton put her chocolate cup down and looked at her niece. Gradually her eyes widened and she sucked air through her teeth. "You think it was someone here."

"What?"

"It is perfectly clear to me. You mean to lay some new crime at my door. All right, then. Whom do you suspect? What is your evidence?" Hectic color mottled Mrs. Brereton's cheeks; her eyes were wide and angry. Miss Tolerance felt a pang of concern, remembering how recently her aunt had risen from her sickbed.

"My dear Aunt Thea, I have laid nothing at your door. I said that I did not know I had made so deep-dyed an enemy as would set my house on fire. Please calm yourself; this kind of vehemence cannot be good—"

"You will go to your tame magistrate and involve him, and have my patrons taken up and ruin my business, is that it?"

"That is not it at all, ma'am. Good God! Where did this idea come from?

Mrs. Brereton regarded her niece suspiciously. "If you haven't thought it yet, you'll come to it sooner or later."

A rattle from the dressing room suggested that Frost had returned from her errand but was waiting tactfully for a moment less fraught in which to enter.

"Aunt, I promise you I had no thought of it at all. The fire was set by someone, but as to whom, I cannot say at all. Certainly I have nothing I could lay before a magistrate, and even Sir Walter Mandif—I collect it is he you mean by my tame magistrate, although I don't care for that label any more than he would—would require a good deal more proof than I can offer at this moment. I hope you know I would do my best to keep your house untroubled by the matter."

"Of a certainty you would. My clientele—" Mrs. Brereton took up the pot again and poured chocolate into her near-full cup so awkwardly that the lid of the pot dropped into the cup, breaking it and spraying chocolate over the papers and her dressing gown. "See what you have done!" She half rose from her chair, dabbing at her stained lace.

Miss Tolerance suppressed the impulse to respond in kind. "Let me help you, Aunt."

"You've done enough!" Mrs. Brereton snapped. "Frost! Damn that woman, where is she?"

On cue Frost appeared in the doorway, murmured soothing remonstrance, and began to clear away the mess.

"Aunt, please be calm. This excitation—"

"'Tis all your doing, Sarah. Had I known when I took you in what sort of trouble you would bring upon my house . . ." Mrs. Brereton sat back in her chair, panting.

Miss Tolerance regarded her aunt with distress. She felt as one might in a dream, as if she had stumbled into a conversation scripted beforehand, without any idea what her proper part was to be. For several minutes she said nothing, only watching as Frost took away the tray and returned with a fresh dressing gown for her mistress. In the same time Mrs. Brereton's breathing slowed, and Miss Tolerance decided she might safely speak again.

"Dearest Aunt Thea, I have never wished to bring trouble into your house. As to who set the fire, I cannot possibly say; I have not even been out to the cottage this morning. Let me ring for more chocolate—"

"Stop fussing!" Mrs. Brereton ordered, but her color was more nearly normal. "Frost will get me more chocolate, won't you, Frost?"

The maid nodded, straightened her mistress's collar, and gave Miss Tolerance a look of proprietary triumph: *See who is indispensable in this household?* Then she swept serenely from the room again.

"I shall go, then," Miss Tolerance suggested.

"Go? From the house?" Mrs. Brereton looked shocked. "I don't want that, Sarah!"

"No, ma'am, nor do I. I only mean to go across and look at the damage to the cottage and see what repairs will be necessary."

"Oh." Mrs. Brereton's relief was manifest. "Well, then, I suppose you ought to do so. And for the love of heaven, take someone with you to carry out your clothes and clean them. The sooner you're out of Marianne's castoffs, the better. What room were you put in?"

It was as though the entire argument had not happened. Mrs. Brereton was now looking at her niece with some of her usual fondness.

"I slept upstairs in the servants' quarters, ma'am—I did not wish to put one of the staff out of a room—"

"That was very thoughtful of you, my dear, but I think we can put you in the little yellow room at the end of the hall for a night or two, until your house is put to rights." Mrs. Brereton turned her face for her niece's kiss. "Run find out where Frost is with my chocolate, there's a good girl."

Miss Tolerance did as she was bid.

Cole accompanied Miss Tolerance across the garden to inspect the cottage. The foul smell of charring was everywhere, but the fire had not done great damage. There were water and ice everywhere on the kitchen floor; the table, cabinet, writing box and chairs which had been at the center of the fire were of course beyond repairing, but the room itself seemed sound. The floor beneath the fire was charred and would need to be replaced, and the whole room would require a quantity of whitewash. Miss Tolerance regarded the black mark of fire on the ceiling with a frisson of horror; how easily she might have burnt to death! It certainly appeared, from the placement of the fire just under her bed, that that had been someone's objective. But why?

Miss Tolerance forced herself away from the sight of the charred ceiling and went upstairs to her room. She pushed her bed from its accustomed place and examined the floor beneath it. Two of the boards were discolored and seemed to her to sag when she trod on them. She would need to have a joiner in to look at the floor—or rather, the ceiling below. And more whitewash, she thought. The mark of smoke, and the gritty stench of fire, was in everything. She opened the wardrobe, gathered up all her clothes save for a suit of men's clothing, her boots, and her Gunnard greatcoat, and gave them all to Cole to give to the laundress. With sufficient water and soap, she hoped, they could be salvaged.

She changed into her masculine clothes, hoping that exposure to fresh air would take the worst of the smell from them, and returned downstairs to look again at the furniture which had been piled up and set afire. One rail-backed chair, seemingly whole, crumbled when she tried to pull it away. The remains of two of her work ledgers sat under the chair, and Miss Tolerance spent several minutes trying to divine their significance: one was a set of her household expenses from several years earlier, and the other contained notes from her first cases in '07. She could not ignore Mrs. Brereton's suggestion that the arson had been accomplished by someone attached to a former case, but nor did she believe the fire had been set to destroy the ledgers. Why not simply carry them away instead? It seemed to her that her death, or at least the destruction of her house, was what had been intended. The ledgers were not clues, but tinder.

Her fears regarding the footprints in the garden proved correct; the half-frozen mud looked as though an army had passed across it in the night. Examinations of the gate in the garden wall proved that it was locked; nor did the ivy which covered the wall appear bruised, as it would have done had someone climbed in or out of the garden. She must consider that her arsonist had come from the house or had a key to the gate—a highly disturbing notion.

Miss Tolerance quit the garden and found Marianne in one of the parlors, knitting placidly. She returned the borrowed gown with thanks.

"Is it bad out there?" Marianne tipped her head in the direction of the cottage.

"It might have been a very great deal worse," Miss Tolerance said. "I shall need a joiner, and some whitewash. And I shall have to see what I can find in the used-furniture warehouses, once the repairs are made. But the structure is sound."

"That's luck," Marianne said. "And how are *you*?"

Miss Tolerance smiled. "Alive, for which I am most grateful. Particularly after having seen the damage and imagining what might have happened had I not waked up."

"What did wake you?"

"There were sounds. Footsteps downstairs just as the blaze was set off," Miss Tolerance said flatly.

"Good God! Do you know whose?"

She shook her head. "I must find out, mustn't I?" she said lightly. "One question I do have: there was a gentleman in the group last night, one of the dancers?" Marianne nodded. "Of middle height, fair-haired, blue coat, neckcloth a bit askew. He was standing with the fellow who was waiting for you, watching us talk. Later—I don't know who he went up with, but they were in a room in the back on the second floor—"

"Oh, yes. Mr. Beauville. He don't come often—his custom is better suited to the whipperies. Bit of a bully-boy, and fancies himself a bit, as you may have noticed. What does—Sarah? What?"

Miss Tolerance had begun to laugh.

"All over London I was prepared to go to find the man, and here he is on my doorstep! What a convenience! I have been longing to ask him some questions about an inquiry. It's such a convenience it makes me wonder: did he come seeking me?"

"If he did, he made a very expensive job of it. Played in our revels a bit, as you saw, spent the night with Lisette, drank deep, didn't blink when Keefe gave him the reckoning. I don't like to disappoint you, Sarah, but it certainly appeared that his aim was pleasure, not—"

"Not me." Miss Tolerance finished. "He didn't ask anyone about me? Lisette or one of the others? I find it hard to trust a coincidence that is so . . . coincidental. Did most of your patrons last night come into the garden to help with the fire?"

Marianne nodded. "Fire's a serious business. There was likely a few that didn't—in the throes, belike, or too old or feeble. But most of them. Didn't you see?"

"I did. And was most grateful to all of them. But I did note that Mr. Beauville was not among them. Was he seen inside before the alarm was raised?"

"You never think he lit the fire!" Marianne raised a skeptical eyebrow. "What reason would he have to do it?"

"I don't know," Miss Tolerance said frankly. "I have been eager to speak to him—he may have some information about a recent murder. Beyond that, and the fact that he is—what was it you said? A bit of a bully-boy? I know nothing worse. Perhaps he has something to hide and feared I would come too close."

"If that's so, 'twould be a stupid thing to set a fire, wouldn't it? I mean, why draw attention to yourself that way?"

"If he believed I would die in the blaze, who would know the connection? I saw him looking down from the window last night after the fire was out, and I swear he looked amused. As if it all was a great joke."

"A joke?"

"Not one I find amusing."

This line of thought was interrupted by Cole, who informed her that the laundress had been put in possession of her clothes and was shaking her head with professional dismay as she prepared to go to work.

"She instructed me to say she could promise nothing. But I think she likes the challenge, Miss Sarah." He also offered her two letters which had come for her that morning. Miss Tolerance thanked him again for his heroic assistance the night before, and for the morning's more prosaic help, and examined the envelopes.

The first was from William Colcannon. He had learnt of his sister's incarceration and was on his way to Cold Bath Fields Prison; would Miss Tolerance do him the kindness to meet him there— no, he would call upon her—no, he would meet her at the Public Office in Great Marlborough Street. She was left with no particular idea of where she was to meet the man, but a very good idea of his state of mind.

The second note came from Sir Walter Mandif:

> I have spoken with Heddison and contrived to learn something of the evidence against your client. Aside from the matter of motive, which I understand to be rather more substantial than the usual reasons a wife might wish her husband dead, Mr. Boyse interviewed a man named Millward who says Mrs. d'Aubigny approached him in hope that he would kill her husband. The man apparently refused, and thus raised Mrs. d'Aubigny's ire. Heddison has asked Boyse to bring Mr. Millward in (it seems this interview took place in a pothouse) so he may hear the story himself. Although I am sure you will wish to interview Mr. Millward, I have no description to give you, nor could I discover the pothouse where they met, Boyse having drunk rather deeply in the process of attaining the statement.
>
> I know this will not please you. I trust, however, that you will take this information at its value. I have exhausted, for the moment, my influence with Heddison, but if there is any other way in which I can assist you, I beg you will let me know.
>
> Your faithful servant—

"Perfection!"

"You don't look it." Marianne bound off a stitch.

"Sir Walter informs me that my client has been taken up for questioning on the word of a man one of the constables met in an alehouse—and as the constable was too foxed to remember which house, or what this witness looked like, I have little hope of discovering him."

"Well, that is the way of these things." Marianne shrugged. "Although if the informant was hopeful of the reward, you'd think he'd have given the constable his direction."

" 'Tis vague, yes. And another thing that's too convenient. I do not believe for a moment that Anne d'Aubigny could have tried to hire this Millward. How would she find the sort of man who would entertain such a proposal? But that leaves me with the vexed question of why this Mr. Millward would lay false information."

"The reward," Marianne said practically.

"Well, yes. But if he's risking a charge of perjury for money which will be paid only after conviction, why not give his address to the constable?"

"P'raps he has an ax to grind with Mrs. d'Aubigny and wants to bring her down."

"Yes, perhaps. But if Millward is honest, why seek out a constable in a tavern rather than present himself in Great Marlborough Street?"

"The sort of man gets approached to do murder is mayhap not the sort of man wants to see the inside of the Public Office."

"You would be surprised by the sort of deep-dyed rogues who hang about the Public Houses telling outrageous lies in hope of making five pounds," Miss Tolerance said. "It is all too convenient. No description of the man, no idea even of which alehouse. And if this Millward is never found, his testimony cannot be contested."

"You think he's one of those lying rogues."

"It hardly matters what I think. The magistrate won't release Mrs. d'Aubigny unless this man's statement is refuted. My strong mistrust of Mr. Boyse—the constable who took the statement—is unfortunately not evidence of wrongdoing."

"Well, you've got yourself a proper coil," Marianne said placidly.

"I do. And I shall not unravel it sitting here. But before I go: Marianne, have you noticed any change in my aunt since her illness began? I went up to see her just now and she was—odd."

"She's been a mite touchy, yes. I suppose it chafes her not to be downstairs and managing everything."

"Touchy?" This seemed an indifferent word to describe Mrs. Brereton's erratic mood.

"But she is much recovered, you know. The doctor says the weakness in her arm is wearing off nicely, and we have only to keep her from overdoing when she does leave the sickroom."

Miss Tolerance nodded, not wholly satisfied. It was possible, she thought, that she was simply viewing her aunt's behavior with sensibilities affected by the stresses of the last several days. Marianne seemed confident that Mrs. Brereton was recovering well. She must put her faith in that, take up her greatcoat and hat, and herself off to Cold Bath Fields Prison to meet with William Colcannon and Anne d'Aubigny.

Cold Bath Fields Prison was a squat gray stone structure in Farrington Road. It was newer than its more celebrated neighbor prisons of Bridewell and Newgate, but was in no regard a dainty accommodation. Miss Tolerance found William Colcannon pacing the street opposite the prison gate, working himself into a state of extreme excitement. His long, earnest face was ruddy with distress, and he looked as if he had slept in his clothes. He barely looked at Miss Tolerance, but at once laid the blame for his sister's detention at her feet.

"I hired you to keep her safe! Imagine my shock to receive your note, writ in the coolest way possible, as if it were an everyday occurrence that a woman of one's family should be hauled off to Newgate—"

"Cold Bath Fields," Miss Tolerance murmured under her breath. She struggled to subdue a contrary spirit which wanted to respond to his panicked outrage with dry humor. "I am sorry if my letter seemed to you out of tune with what has happened. I hoped, by taking a calm tone, to encourage you to remain calm likewise. I am more affected by these events than I appear, but I assure you, your sister needs you to be in command, to deal with the gaolers politely but firmly—to act, in fact, as thought the whole matter is merely a stupid mistake. Which I firmly believe it is," she added.

Colcannon drew a long breath and closed his eyes. When he opened them again he appeared to have mastered his emotions.

"What must I do to help? Is there anything I *can* do?"

"Have you been to visit your sister yet, sir?"

"Not yet. I did send a purse of money to her, as you suggested."

"We must hope it reached her and purchased her some comfort last night. This morning we should first speak to the gaoler and do what we can to secure Mrs. d'Aubigny comfortable accommodation and food. I sent her maid with *my* purse last night, and told her to promise more money in your name if necessary. It will be expensive—I'm told you can spend as much a night for a decent room in prison as at Claridge's Hotel."

Colcannon looked mildly shocked, but murmured his assurance that he would pay whatever was required to see his sister comfortable.

"Then take out your handkerchief—the stench inside will appall you until you become used to it—and let us see what sort of night your sister passed."

Inside the gates of the prison they were met, not only by the smell of which Miss Tolerance had spoken, but a sudden hush, as if a woolen cloak had been cast over the whole establishment. Prisoners at Cold Bath Fields obeyed a rule of silence—or disobeyed it at their peril; after the clamor of the street, the difference was remarkable. Miss Tolerance and Mr. Colcannon went first to the Warden's office, where, after a brief interview with the gaoler, Mr. Colcannon secured for his sister a more pleasant room with a window facing away from the common area of the prison and offering some untainted air; a lamp, a fire, a bed with clean sheets, and some decent provisions. The extortionate hire of these modest accommodations being arranged for a week, Miss Tolerance and Mr. Colcannon were permitted to pay an additional fourpence each to visit Mrs. d'Aubigny.

As they walked down the corridor Miss Tolerance remembered

one last detail. "What of her fetters?" she asked the man who was escorting them.

"Oh, she paid for them when she was brought in, miss. Nice light ones, more like bracelets, you might say, hardly half a pound each. She'll have passed the night quite comfortable."

Miss Tolerance thanked the man. She did not look at William Colcannon's horrified face.

Anne d'Aubigny had been quartered in a low-ceilinged, white-washed room with no more than five other women who had arrived too late to be put into permanent quarters. They found her sitting upon the bandbox Miss Tolerance had last seen in Sophia Thissen's hands; this served to keep her from sitting on the filthy floor, and to protect whatever remained in the box from Madame d'Aubigny's cellmates. Miss Tolerance noted to Mr. Colcannon's credit that the face he showed his sister was full of cheerful optimism and sympathy. Anne d'Aubigny was likewise composed; only a slight tremor in the hand she extended to Miss Tolerance suggested the effort it took to maintain that composure.

Mr. Colcannon assured his sister that she would soon be very much more comfortable, and asked if there was anything she wanted from her home. Anne d'Aubigny asked for her workbag. "One could go mad from lack of occupation here."

"In the ordinary way, they'd put you to picking oakum or some other redemptive task," Miss Tolerance said. "But your brother has paid to save you that, at least for now."

Anne d'Aubigny nodded absently, as if the prospect of ruining her hands plucking apart old rope for use in caulking ship bottoms did not trouble her in the least.

"They kept asking me about a man named Millward," she said. "I told them I knew no such person, but they insisted I should remember him. Have you any idea—"

"It appears that Mr. Millward told one of the constables that you asked him to kill your husband." Miss Tolerance spoke the words with no emphasis at all, watching for reaction.

Colcannon and Mrs. d'Aubigny looked at her, shocked.

"I know little more than that, but I intend to learn enough to prove this Millward a liar. Do either of you have any notion who this man could be? Do you know of anyone who would have reason to say such a thing?"

"To lie about me?" Anne d'Aubigny shook her head. "His name is not familiar, and—I should not know where to go, how to—"

Miss Tolerance nodded. "Of course you would not. Mr. Colcannon, do you know the name? Is there anyone you can imagine with a grudge against your family who might—"

"Good Christ, no!" Colcannon said loudly. The other prisoners in the room tittered.

"I beg your pardon, sir. I did need to ask. And I entreat you to keep your voice low—any one of your sister's companions might sell anything she overheard to the law as testimony. So: it seems that I must not only discover who killed the chevalier, but who this Millward is and how he features in the crime. Ma'am"—she turned back to Anne d'Aubigny—"can you give me no idea of how to reach Mr. Beauville?"

The question appeared to confuse the widow. "Mr. Beauville? But what has he to do—"

"I am not certain." Miss Tolerance had decided not to say anything about the fire in her cottage. "I shall not be certain until I have spoken to him. Perhaps he will have some insight into your husband's death. I should certainly like to know if he spent any part of that evening in your husband's company, and at what time they parted."

"You do not suspect him?"

"I must, perforce, suspect everyone, ma'am. At least until I know better."

"But Beauville was my husband's friend."

Miss Tolerance nodded. "So it appears. But your husband seems to have been a man who cultivated drinking companions rather than bosom friends."

"They drank and sported together. They were members of a club—"

"Tarsio's," Miss Tolerance agreed. "I've made inquiries there. If you—"

They were interrupted by a rise in the mutters and whispers of the other prisoners in the chamber; one of the gaolers had returned and was stepping through the crowded room to Madame d'Aubigny's party.

"Beggin' your pardon, missus," he said. "Magistrate's sent 'is men to bring you back to Great Marlborough Street. More questions."

Anne d'Aubigny looked around her a little wildly. "More? But I've told them—"

The gaoler, a beefy man with rheumy dark eyes and a lugubrious mouth, shrugged and bent to unlock the chain which attached Anne d'Aubigny's fetters to an iron staple. "Is what they sent me up for: fetch you down and hand you over. You never mind about your things," he added. "Your man here's paid for a nice room, neat as widow's lodgin'. We'll move your box back there and you'll have everything comfortable for your return."

Both Mrs. d'Aubigny and her brother turned to Miss Tolerance. She felt a momentary quiver of impatience, shrugged it off, and nodded to the pair. "Go along," she counseled Anne d'Aubigny. "Do your best to answer their questions. Your brother will speak to his solicitor and learn what the law can do for you and I shall work to turn up this Mr. Millward. I'm sure you'll not be here long."

Miss Tolerance took Mr. Colcannon's arm and steered him from the room; Anne d'Aubigny and her gaoler followed after and farewells were said in the corridor. Mr. Colcannon was much affected by the parting, and Miss Tolerance found it necessary to guide him through the crowd at the prison's entrance. They paused at the crowds' edge to draw a breath of cold air, deliciously clean after the prison. Then she escorted him to his carriage, which waited in Farrington Street. There, he gave vent to his outrage. Miss Tolerance permitted him to rant for a few minutes, then briskly informed him that he would feel very much better when he was doing something to help, and advised him again to speak to his solicitor.

"And I have a good deal to do myself, sir. If it is not out of your way, might I ask you to drive me to Henry Street? And perhaps we may discuss a little business as we go?"

Colcannon handed Miss Tolerance into the carriage and seated himself, looking apprehensive. His relief, when he realized that Miss Tolerance meant only to ask for an advance of monies for her expenses, was patent.

"I am afraid I am a little more out-at-pocket than I had expected, sir. We could not have foreseen—" she waved her hand to indicate Cold Bath Fields Prison and its attendent fees.

"Good God, not at all, Miss Tolerance. It is we who are in your debt. My poor Anne. How much have you spent thus far?"

Miss Tolerance named a figure and Colcannon doubled it, putting a sheaf of paper money into her hands. She put the money in her pocketbook and they rode in silence to Henry Street.

She was greeted at Tarsio's by Steen, who took her aside at once, saying, "Thank God you come quick, miss. He's still here." Miss Tolerance knew not what to make of this greeting until Steen explained that he had sent a note to her house not an hour past.

"Your Mr. Beauville is here, miss. In the gents' cigar-room."

"Is he so? There's a stroke of luck—in a chore that has thus far been singularly lacking it. I hadn't even seen your note." She took out a coin and pressed it into the footman's hand. "The Gentlemen's Smoking Room?"

"Aye, miss. But you can't go in there, not even dressed as you are."

Miss Tolerance was well aware of Tarsio's rules regarding the mixing of the sexes on club premises. "Of course not. But I can invite Mr. Beauville to take glass of wine with me in a private parlor. If a parlor is available?"

"Yes, miss. Number six is empty just now. I'll ask Corton to invite him up, shall I?" Tarsio's rules, primarily intended to protect the reputation of the establishment, specified that men and women might mingle in the Ladies' Parlor or the Little Card Room; the rules likewise forbade women in the Gentlemen's Smoking Room and men in the Ladies' Withdrawing Room. What went on in the private parlors was, of course, the business of no one but the participants.

Miss Tolerance ascended to the parlor on the second floor, a small, cheerful room with a fire already lit, ordered wine and cakes, and sat back to wait. This was her second too-convenient brush with Henri Beauville, and she placed no faith in its accidental nature. Mr. Beauville, who for a week had been difficult to find, was now all but throwing himself in her path. Why? Perhaps he had information to share with her. But whether it was information in which she could place her trust was another matter entirely. If the man had set the fire in her cottage the night before, might he now be meeting to warn her with a promise of worse to come?

A tray with wine and biscuits was delivered and left on the table at Miss Tolerance's elbow. A moment after, Corton appeared in the doorway and bowed Henri Beauville into the room, indicated Miss Tolerance to him, and departed. Miss Tolerance rose, bowed to her visitor, and invited him to sit. She thought, from the expression on his face, that M. Beauville was attempting to reconcile the woman from Mrs. Brereton's hallway with the person standing before him in breeches.

"Monsieur, we have not met formally. My name is Tolerance."

Beauville bowed. "Madame."

"Mademoiselle," Miss Tolerance corrected, and took a seat.

"What is it you wished to speak about, mademoiselle?" Beauville had a light, melodic voice and a pleasant suggestion of an accent. He eyed Miss Tolerance from boots to a crown in a way she imagined was meant to intimidate.

"I thought, given the good fortune of finding you here today, that perhaps you wished to speak to *me*," Miss Tolerance said mildly. Beauville's eyes moved to her face. "When someone I have been seeking for a week twice appears at my doorstep, as it were, I must consider that a possibility. No? Ah, well. Perhaps you have heard that I am investigating the death of *M. le Chevalier* d'Aubigny? I am everywhere assured that you were a friend of his."

"Poor d'Aubigny," Beauville said without a note of regret. "A very sad end. Yes, we were friends."

"Perhaps you have an opinion as to why he was murdered, sir?"

"How can one know such a thing? He was not an easy man, Etienne. He could be—harsh." He lingered over the word as if it bore contemplation.

"The world is harsh. Is that alone a reason for murder?"

Beauville shrugged. "D'Aubigny was not a conciliatory sort; and he was expensive."

"And yet, before he died, he paid his debts. Even the tradesmen's bills."

"Did he? Do you think he expected to die?" Beauville asked.

"I can only guess. You knew the chevalier. Do you think so?"

Beauville shook his head. "We were engaged for the evening at Madame Touvois' two nights later. He was looking forward to it."

"And you have no notion how he found the money to pay his debts, sir? As you say, the chevalier was expensive."

"Not the least in the world." Beauville waved a hand airily.

"When was the last time you saw him, sir?" Miss Tolerance took from her pocketbook a scrap of paper and the stub of a pencil and scribbled thoughtfully. Beauville watched her for a moment before he answered.

"He and I spent the earlier part of the night of his death at a cockfight in Bankside, but we left early—before ten. He had an engagement with his mistress."

"Which mistress is that, sir?"

"The same one as always. The only one who put up with d'Aubigny's pleasures."

"Mrs. Vose? Do you know where?"

Beauville raised an eyebrow. "You have been thorough. Yes, with Josette Vose. And at his house, I imagine. Her accommodations would not have suited him."

"And yet she says that they were quits with each other a fortnight or more before his death."

"Josie's never quits with anyone with money." Beauville slouched in his chair and regarded Miss Tolerance critically. "These clothes go better with the damage done to your face than the gown you wore last night."

"And I had been fancying that the bruises were fading," Miss Tolerance said. "I'm afraid the fire in my little house left most of my other clothes unfit for wearing. To return to the subject, sir: after this sporting event, where did *you* go?"

"A whorehouse. I don't recall which one; they're all alike, and I am more flexible in my pleasures than poor d'Aubigny." Beauville leaned forward. He was not a big man, and rather mild-featured, but his shoulders were broad and at this proximity and in this posture he appeared slightly menacing.

"There is no one can place you there that evening? Perhaps someone at Mrs. Lasher's establishment in Green Street?"

Beauville's mouth contracted for a fraction of a second. He said again, "You are thorough."

"One must be, in my profession. Well, sir?"

He blinked. "Well?"

"Did anyone in this brothel see you there, or were you by yourself the whole time?"

"Not by myself. But whores, like whorehouses, are all much alike."

"Doubtless whores feel much the same way about the men they service," Miss Tolerance said blandly. "I only have a few more questions, sir. Have you seen Josette Vose since the murder? Or Camille Touvois? I did not see you among her guests when I was there the other night."

Beauville leaned further forward and showed his teeth. "I do not hang about Madame Touvois' neck, mademoiselle."

Irritated by these attempts to intimidate her, Miss Tolerance leaned forward also, until she was close enough to feel his breath upon her face. She smiled. "How fortunate for you. I imagine that would be a very uncomfortable place to hang."

Beauville blinked, then sat back, wheezing with laughter. "You are right, without a doubt. As for Mrs. Vose, she's far too busy being taken up by royalty these days, from what I hear. Have you any other questions, mademoiselle?"

"Just two. Have you ever met a man named Millward?"

"Millward? I do not believe so." Beauville let his theatrically honest expression drop. In consequence, Miss Tolerance believed him. "And your last question?"

Miss Tolerance took a sip of wine.

"What amused you so much last night about the fire in my house?"

Thirteen

Mr. Beauville studied the sleeve of his coat. He had reacted to her mention of Mrs. Lasher's flagellary; he had distanced himself from Camille Touvois. But to this question Mr. Beauville evinced a studied lack of reaction which piqued Miss Tolerance considerably.

"Is that what happened?" Beauville asked at last. "I observed a great ado in the garden."

"Yes, sir. I observed you observing, and you were mighty amused by what you saw, I thought."

"The scurrying of my fellow man always amuses me," Beauville drawled. He looked up from his coat sleeve and grinned like a dog.

"Does it? I find the willingness of my fellow man to keep my house—and the rest of London around it—from burning to the ground to be more laudable than amusing," Miss Tolerance said. "I am rather surprised that when the alarm was sounded you did not join the scurrying yourself. You appear to be a hale enough fellow."

"I was occupied."

"Indeed? May I ask how?"

"Fucking the jade I was with."

"Quite reasonable." Miss Tolerance did not oblige him by re-acting to his language. "It is interesting, is it not, that when I saw you observing your fellow man you were fully dressed, even to your neckcloth. The sight gave me the oddest notion."

"Yes, mademoiselle?"

"It could not be that you set the fire yourself, sir?"

If Miss Tolerance had wished to remove the grin from his face she had succeeded in her object.

"Why should I do such a thing?"

"I really do not know. Do you?"

"I was with a whore. You may ask her."

"I'm sure Lisette will commend your performance, sir. And I will, of course, ask her. As to why you decided to grace Mrs. Brereton's house—where you have never been a frequent patron—on the very night when someone tried to roast me in my bed, I shall simply have to reserve judgment."

She rose to her feet.

"I thank you for your time, Mr. Beauville. Now I must take my-self off to Mrs. Vose's."

"Mrs. Vose's?"

"Investigation is an additive and subtractive process, sir. If I add your testimony to Mrs. Vose's and subtract what I know to be untrue, I may perhaps come upon a clue to the chevalier's death. So it seems I must talk a little more with Mrs. Vose." Miss Toler-ance rose and bowed. "I thank you very much for your time, sir. If anything else occurs to you, I hope you will let me know of it. A note here will always find me."

She left the room before Beauville had time to rise. She would have liked to have seen the effect of her final shot, but felt strongly that its effect relied on her leaving before he could respond. Miss Tolerance left Tarsio's quickly and stepped onto the street, invig-orated as if she had spent an hour fencing in a *salle*. As she walked north toward Balcombe Street, however, the invigoration faded and her footsteps slowed until she found herself stopped on the corner of Oxford Street, thinking. She had two immediate tasks: to find the chevalier's killer, and to secure Anne d'Aubigny's re-lease from Cold Bath Fields Prison; discovering who had set fire to her cottage came after those. The Chevalier d'Aubigny was unlikely to become more dead; his wife's situation, however, could very well worsen if no steps were taken. Before she could convict Beauville, Miss Tolerance must first impeach the mysterious Mr. Millward. With a little regret, Miss Tolerance turned south toward Covent Garden and Bow Street.

The Brown Bear had been for nearly half a century the chiefest public house catering to Bow Street's officers and their private counterparts, the thief-takers. Since the inception of the seven Public Offices patterned upon Bow Street, many of the constables of those offices also came to the Bear, to drink, brag and gossip. Miss Tolerance had been to the Bear once or twice before, and knew enough about the competitive nature of law enforcement to be certain that no Runner or constable would willingly share information with anyone who might reap the statutory rewards before himself. She was also aware that the patrons of the Bear regarded her not as a colleague but as an annoyance, an unfeminine abomination. They were unlikely to be charmed, or paid, for information. She did not hope to learn anything about the case against Anne d'Aubigny, but thought she might gain some insight into the habits of John Boyse.

She slipped into the Bear and went directly to the bar. Even now, not so long after noon, the small room was thick with custom, and the air with wood and tobacco smoke. At one table half a dozen Runners, distinguishable by the red waistcoats of their office, were arguing over their coffee. Further from the door there was a similar group of fellows, less noisily refreshing themselves and watching the Runners' table with something she construed as envy. At the bar a woman stood polishing glasses. Iron-gray hair curled under her cap and framed her square-jawed face. She was heavy and poorly corsetted; from the way she shifted from foot to foot, Miss Tolerance surmised that her feet and her back felt the strain of her work very much.

"Aye, sir. What can I get for you?" the woman asked.

Miss Tolerance put a silver piece on the bar. "Ale, please."

"Please. That's nice," the woman said comfortably. "Most a'

yon paragons of the law don't say please nor thankee. Here you are, sir."

She slid a pewter mug across to Miss Tolerance and filled it from an earthenware jug. "Brewed fresh. You taste that, now."

Miss Tolerance did, and smacked her lips. It was very good, and she said so.

"Polite and knows good ale. Wish we had more of your custom here," the woman said. She took a handful of coins from her pocket and began to pore over them nearsightedly to discover the proper change.

"Keep it, please," Miss Tolerance said.

Rather than endearing her to the woman, this seemed to arouse her suspicion. "And what?" she asked.

"Not much. I was curious to know if a constable named Boyse comes in here for a drink."

The suspicion on the woman's face deepened. "You a friend of his?"

"Mr. Boyse? I shouldn't think he had any friends," Miss Tolerance said.

The woman snickered. "You're right there, sir. But you won't find 'im here. He does his drinking nearer to his own Public Office—don't come in here unless it's to pick a fight. Which I'm grateful for, as you may imagine. If you're wanting of Mr. Boyse, look in Oxford Street at the Duke of Kent. I've a friend married to the barman there, she's mentioned Boyse more than once."

"Not with favor, I gather?"

The woman shook her head. "I'd stay clear of that 'un were I you, my lad. Unless you want your face more bashed about than 'tis already."

"Actually, I'd happily stay clear of Mr. Boyse. I'm looking for a friend of his, a Mr. Millward."

The woman shook her head. "Don't know the name. What's he look like?"

Miss Tolerance shrugged. "I don't know. And I've a need to find him without Mr. Boyse learning of it." She reached for her pocketbook. "If you happen to hear of a Mr. Millward, I would be very grateful—"

The woman put a hand on Miss Tolerance's arm. "Keep your money, boy. 'Fit happens I hear of this Millward, and 'fit happens I get word to you, you can give me a little something then." She rubbed an affectionate finger on the heavy cloth of the Gunnard coat. "I never had a fancy for brown hair, but even with them bruises there's something agreeable-like about you." She took her hand away. "Millward? 'F'I hear aught of him, where shall I let you know?"

Miss Tolerance bit her lip to keep from smiling. "You can send a note to me at Tarsio's Club in Henry Street," she said. "Address it to Miss Tolerance. I really would be most appreciative, ma'am."

The barmaid's brows drew together and she squinted, examining Miss Tolerance's face closely. Then her face lit with a lopsided grin; it appeared she was not one to hold a grudge. "Damn, took me in proper, you did. Well, my eyes ain't what they was. Very well, Miss T. 'F'I hear of Millward, I'll send to Tarsio's to let you know, and you can pay from that wallet. But do you try the Duke of Kent, too." She turned away, chuckling.

Miss Tolerance, smiling herself, left the smoky, hospitable warmth of the Bear.

The Duke of Kent shared a narrow street front with a stairway to the two upper stories of its building. Once inside, Miss Tolerance perceived that the alehouse was considerably larger than its front suggested. The room described an L, with a massive greasy fireplace on the right wall which looked as if it had not been cleaned since the time of the last King Henry. In contrast to the venerable fireplace, the furnishings of the tavern gave the impression of great impermanence; the bar itself was merely a few boards laid atop sawhorses, with half a dozen barrels stacked behind, each with a label scrawled on in chalk: bitter, new ale, apple beer and the like. The clientele of the Duke of Kent gave an equal impression of rough-hewn unsteadiness. It was not the most disreputable public house Miss Tolerance had ever seen, but neither was it an inviting spot in which to take refreshment. Miss Tolerance shouldered her way through the crowd with as good an impression of masculine impatience as she could muster, and took a place at the bar. When the sullen barman turned to her she ordered apple beer and tried not to notice that the man barely wiped the pot before he tapped the cider into it.

"Thank you," she said, and dropped a coin onto the bar. It fell on its edge and began to roll along the rough surface, but the barman was evidently familiar with the phenomenon, and caught the coin before it fell off the edge of the bar.

"We're fixing things up," he said in tones of grudging apology.

Miss Tolerance nodded. "Is Mr. Boyse in this afternoon?" she asked.

The barman turned to take another order, then shook his head. "Not yet. Mayhap this evening, around about ten or so. Come in most nights when he's off duty, like."

"A regular, then?"

The barman pulled off a pot of ale and pushed it in the direction of its recipient. "What you want with Boyse? 'E's not the sort a young gent like you ought to be mixing with."

"I've no wish to mix with him," Miss Tolerance agreed. "In fact, I'm not interested in Boyse at all—only with a friend of his named Millward."

The barman looked to one side and then the other and began to swipe at the surface of the bar with his apron. "Wouldn't say Boyse 'ad no friends, like. Even that nancypants mate of 'is don't drink with 'im above twice a month."

"Mr. Greenwillow?" Miss Tolerance suggested. "So you don't know of a man named Millward?"

"What am I?" The barman left off polishing the uneven surface of his temporary bar and looked square at Miss Tolerance. "I don't ask no one's name. Look, you. If I did know of this 'ere Millward—"

"I would make it worth your while." Miss Tolerance slid her hand inside her coat to suggest payment of a sum sufficient to loosen the barman's tongue. "I believe Mr. Boyse was drinking with him two nights ago. They made quite a batch of it, from what I hear."

The man shook his head. "Two nights ago? They weren't hard-drinkin' here. Boyse come in, sober and full of hisself as usual, and took up straightaway with Betty Strokum, like he does when he's in funds. They supped a while, had a few tots of gin, then left."

Miss Tolerance took another sip of her apple beer. Despite the unpromising surroundings, the cider was crisp and potent. She considered. "Together? And how long was Mr. Boyse here?"

"Look," the barman said firmly. "I don't know who you are or what you want. Boyse is a constable—I don't want no trouble here."

"I promise you: tell me the truth, whatever you know of it, and I'll pay you well. If all goes as I hope, you'll never hear from me again."

There was a thoughtful pause while the barman drew another pot of ale and received payment for it. Then the man leaned forward over the bar, close enough that Miss Tolerance could see the rheum in his bloodshot eyes and smell tobacco and juniper berry on his breath.

"Boyse come in about eight that evening. Soppin' wet from the storm, of course, but sober as a judge when he got there. Like I told you, 'e was here wiv Bet a few hours, then they left, Bet with her tongue in Boyse's ear. After that? Ask Mrs. Strokum, if you want to know what Boyse was doing. That's all I can tell you, in truth or safety. You'll oblige me by moving' along, then, sir," he added loudly. "We don't want troublemakers at the Duke of Kent."

"Right, then," Miss Tolerance agreed as loudly. More quietly she asked a last question. "Where might I find Mrs. Strokum, sir?"

The barman laughed, apparently genuinely amused. "Look on any corner hereabouts. Handsome mort, yellow hair and a red dress. She's got no teeth in the front—makes it convenient-like, see?"

Miss Tolerance blinked, then laughed. She put a half-crown piece flat on the bar so that there was no chance of its rolling away, then turned the collar of her Gunnard coat up, tucked in her muffler, and went in search of Mrs. Strokum. She did not believe she would have much luck at—she checked her pocket watch—three of the afternoon. Still, she walked in an expanding circle around the Duke of Kent, looking for a blonde woman with a convenient lack of teeth, wearing a red dress. A few streets away from the tavern she came upon a whore in an ancient bottle-green velvet coat, leaning against an iron fence and calling drunkenly to passersby. Despite the coat and a patchy fur tippet wound round her throat, the woman's teeth were chattering so hard it made her offers of pleasure hard to understand. Miss Tolerance noted a rosy chancre at the corner of her mouth and shuddered.

"Mrs. Strokum?"

The whore's head turned so quickly she nearly lost her balance. "I can do you better than she, sir," she said.

Miss Tolerance sighed. "No doubt. But I have a specific need to talk to Mrs. Strokum. Do you know where I may find her?"

The woman cackled and glanced around her; as she did so she kicked at something—a square blue gin bottle near her foot. "Why should I send you to Bets when I got you here, young gentleman?"

"Because I will pay you to do so—and given that your lips are as blue as that bottle, I'd suggest you buy yourself something warm to eat." And see a surgeon and get yourself cleaned of the pox that's eating your face, she did not say. Seen close to, the woman was likely Miss Tolerance's age, but she looked far older. Miss Tolerance was aware of a sudden unlikely desire to take this poxy sister in tow, get her cleaned and fed and doctored. As well try to drink the ocean dry as save all the whores in London from their fate.

"Let's see the color of your money, then," the woman said. She stepped closer to Miss Tolerance, weaving on her feet, and belched so foully it was all Miss Tolerance could do not to reel away.

"All I need to know is where to find Betty Strokum," Miss Tolerance said. She took a handful of coins from her pocket and selected a half-crown, which she held firmly between her thumb and forefinger. "If you please?" she prodded.

The whore shrugged petulantly. "Down there—" She pointed along Eastcastle Street. "Two streets down. I saw her half an hour ago, draggin' a gent into the mews. She's likely done with 'im now. Or 'e with 'er." She snatched at the coin and would have missed it but that Miss Tolerance pressed it into her hand.

"Thank you. Eat something hot," Miss Tolerance advised again. The woman had already turned away in the direction of the Duke of Kent. At least, Miss Tolerance thought, while the money lasted she would be drunk inside, near a fire.

She picked her way along Eastcastle Street. Clouds were beginning to thicken overhead, giving the streets and pedestrians a gray cast. Underfoot the sludge in the gutters was beginning to ice over, and the crossing-sweeps looked more interested in picking pockets than clearing a path through the muck. The mews the hedge-whore had indicated opened onto the street through an arched gateway, but the gate itself had long ago rusted out of use, and the alley leading to the stables was lined with crates and barrels and rotting bales of straw. Miss Tolerance suspected it had been some time since any horse had been stabled there.

She misliked walking blindly into any alley, particularly one which seemed providentially designed to hide attackers. She pushed back the skirt of the Gunnard coat, put her hand to the hilt of her sword, and advanced slowly. Thin gray sunshine lit the left side of the alley and left the right in shadow; once off the street the rattle of carriages and horses and handcarts abated a little; the quiet increased a sense of dreadful anticipation. She heard something, rustling and a mutter of voices, ahead and to the right around the corner. Cautiously she stepped forward, peering into the shadows. Against the dirty brick wall she saw a man's shirted back; his pants were dropped to reveal pale buttocks, pumping furiously. Miss Tolerance blinked and realized that the splash of color that framed the man was a red dress, rucked up waist-high.

She retired to the street.

Some few minutes later the man left the alley, calling some rude pleasantry over his shoulder. He saw Miss Tolerance waiting at the gate and called out cheerily, "I primed 'er for you, mate!" as he continued on his way. Miss Tolerance did her best to banish all the unfortunate images this called to her mind, and stepped back to meet Betty Strokum.

As the barman at the Duke of Kent had said, she was missing her front teeth, top and bottom, which gave her smile a quality of idiocy at odds with the shrewdness of her eyes.

"My, ain't I the popular one today?" Mrs. Strokum said pleasantly. The red dress which had lately been hitched up and splayed

around her patron was now back in place, the bonnet which covered her blonde curls only slightly askew. "What's *your* pleasure,
dear?"

"I was wondering if you would like a bowl of stew," Miss Tolerance suggested.

The whore looked as if she had not understood. "Stew? To do
what with?"

Miss Tolerance's imagination failed her. "To eat, ma'am. I am
hungry. Are you?"

"You offerin' to buy me dinner?" Mrs. Strokum looked her up
and down and apprehended what her sister down the street had
not. "You're female."

"I am. I've a few questions to ask, and am happy to pay for answers—but I'm also cold and hungry. Would you like to dine,
Mrs. Strokum?"

The woman made a face, half amusement, half disbelief. "Why,
certainly, Your Highness. So kind of you to ask." She caught up
the skirt of her red dress, righted her bonnet with a tap, and swept
past Miss Tolerance out of the mews. Once on Eastcastle Street
Miss Tolerance took the lead and turned left, away from Oxford
Street and the Duke of Kent.

Mrs. Strokum tried to stay her. "There's a place I know—" she
began.

"Where you are well known, I collect? For our purposes, m'am,
I think you will prefer a more anonymous spot." Miss Tolerance
firmly led them several streets to the east before she began to look
out for a public house. Several times Mrs. Strokum suggested gin
houses they passed, but Miss Tolerance wanted the whore sober
and of a reflective mind for their talk.

At last she found a neat chophouse of rather better character
than the neighborhood that surrounded it, and steered Mrs.
Strokum through the door. She chose a table well away from the
door and the one grimy window onto the street, and settled Mrs.
Strokum at it. The girl who came to serve them looked rather
sniffily at the whore, but evidently had decided that custom was
custom, and did nothing worse than explain that there was no
stew, only mutton soup with barley, or joints of beef or mutton.
Mrs. Strokum's eyes lit greedily; she ordered a beef bone and

bread to soak up the juice. Miss Tolerance made do with a bowl of soup.

Mrs. Strokum went about making herself comfortable, removing the several wool shawls with which the upper part of her body had been wrapped. The shawls she draped over the back of her chair, trailing on the greasy floor; her red gown, which must once have been a handsome morning gown, had been cut down in front to display highly compressed breasts which looked as if they might burst across the table like weapons. Mrs. Strokum patted at her hair, straightened her bonnet again, quite uselessly, then leaned across the table toward Miss Tolerance, further compressing her breasts.

"Now, darling, what's to do? What's so dire we can't talk about it at the ol' Duke a' Kent?"

"Shall we wait until the food comes?" Miss Tolerance suggested.

"Suit yourself." Mrs. Strokum shrugged. "Nasty weather, ain't it?"

They discussed the savagery of November for several minutes more, until the serving girl brought the food. Mrs. Strokum wasted no time in applying herself to the beef. Miss Tolerance stirred her soup and considered.

"I understand you're a friend of Mr. Boyse's," she said at last.

As she had feared, the greedy light in Mrs. Strokum's eyes dimmed, replaced by apprehension. "I don't make no secret of it," she said. "What's it to you?"

"I only need to know if you were with Mr. Boyse two nights ago, and if you are acquainted with a gentleman named Millward."

Mrs. Strokum's face hardened. She leaned back, picked up the beef bone in her fist as if it were a club, and raised it to her lips. The missing front teeth meant that she had to gnaw the bone using her side teeth, which gave her a savagely wolfish look.

"Happen I was with 'im. What then? I don't keep count a' who I'm with here and there."

Miss Tolerance pushed her bowl away and leaned forward herself. "Mrs. Strokum, I have a witness who puts you some time in Mr. Boyse's company on that evening. I merely need to know for how long, if he spoke with Mr. Millward, and where I might find this Millward."

"You know Mr. Boyse?" Mrs. Strokum asked. Miss Tolerance nodded. "Then you know he ain't the sort of man you want to peach on. 'E finds out I been a talkin' of 'im behind 'is back—"

"I shan't tell him. Only help me find this Millward—" Miss Tolerance took out a purse and let the gentle clink of coins on the table speak for her.

The greedy light returned to Mrs. Strokum's eyes. She thought for a moment or two, then seemed to come to a decision.

"That Millward, would it be, um, Tom Millward? Skinny fellow? Prig?" At Miss Tolerance's blank look: "Gent in the receiving line?"

Miss Tolerance shrugged noncommittally. "A fence? It might be."

"I didn't see 'im that night," Mrs. Strokum said flatly. "And Boyse was with me most of the night—left at dawn's turning." She regarded Miss Tolerance as if this would be unwelcome intelligence. "There. So there's naught you can pin on 'im."

"I see," Miss Tolerance said gravely. "You're certain?"

"As the grave," Mrs. Strokum said, and gnawed sideways at the bone.

"And this Millward? Where might I find him?"

Mrs. Strokum shrugged. "Dunno. Here and there, I 'spect."

"He is a receiver of stolen goods; does he work with any particular dips or footpads?"

Mrs. Strokum shrugged again. Clearly she was not going to volunteer more.

Miss Tolerance took up her pocketbook and slid a half-crown toward the whore. If Mrs. Strokum had hoped for more, she appeared philosophical. Miss Tolerance rose and paid the shot, then came back to the table.

"If you remember anything further, you may leave a message at Mrs. Brereton's house in Manchester Square. You know of it?"

She might have been talking of St. James's. Mrs. Strokum's eyes lit. "Know it? You from there? D'you think you might put a word in for me there? I'd like fine to get off the streets, and I'm a good worker. I can do a dozen men a night, maybe more if needful."

Miss Tolerance contended briefly with the image of her aunt confronted with the overripe and underbred Mrs. Strokum. "I do not recruit for Mrs. Brereton," she said. "But you can get a note to me there, if you wish."

Mrs. Strokum did not seem to take the rejection amiss. "I could do that, could I write a word," she agreed. "I 'spect you and I are quits, darlin'. Thank ye for the dinner."

Miss Tolerance did not smile until she had gained the street. Betty Strokum had mistaken Miss Tolerance's purpose in asking about Boyse's whereabouts; thinking to provide an alibi for his actions, she had instead raised a question as to whether Boyse had talked to the informant at all.

I t was Miss Tolerance's custom, when searching for a person of illegal profession, to inquire first of all with that person's colleagues who, in the highly competitive venue of London, were likely to track the progress of their rivals closely. There were, however, so many receivers of stolen goods in London that one could not have a single resource—a Joshua Glebb—of whom to inquire. Should she look in the area of Oxford Street, near to the Duke of Kent? No; the barman at the Duke of Kent, who had a broad acquaintance with local characters, professed not to know Millward, which suggested that he fenced his goods in another district. But which district?

At last she decided to call on a professional woman whom she had found had rather more acquaintance than the general run of receivers in the central part of the city. She hailed a hackney coach and gave a direction in Shoreditch. The afternoon was now growing late; she was sure to find Mrs. Nab at work.

The hackney deposited her in a narrow street lined on both sides with ramshackle wooden houses. The varying heights of these buildings, and the fact that they had apparently been built without recourse to the carpenter's plumb, gave the street the look of having been knocked askew. Here and there a lantern burned by a door, the light abetted by the cold glow of the moon above the rooftops, visible for the first time in several nights. The street was busy; people were fetching home food from cookshops

or tucking brown bottles of ale inside their coats with more ten-
derness than they showed the children who followed after. Miss
Tolerance threaded her way through the crowd, counting houses
on the left side of the street. She entered the fifth one, stepping
over a drunk snoring in the doorway, and proceeded straight back
to a door in the shadow of the stair. The occupant of the rooms behind the door evidently expected visitors: a chair and a tiny table
stood on one side of the door, and a rush light glowed sullenly in
a jug. Miss Tolerance ignored these amenities and knocked on the
door.

A child, a girl of eight or nine, quaintly dressed in a shabby
dress and clean apron, her cap tied under her chin and her hair
spilling down her back, opened the door halfway.

"Is Mrs. Nab in?" Miss Tolerance inquired.

"I'll see, ma'am. May I tell her who's inquiring and what
you've brung?" The girl's accent was so deeply Cockney as to
defy orthography.

Miss Tolerance gave her name and the assurance that she
would take only a few moments of Mrs. Nab's time. The girl
dipped a tiny curtsy, closed the door, and returned a moment later
to inform the visitor that Mrs. Nab would be pleased if Miss Tolerance would walk in.

The first room was well lit, and Miss Tolerance saw two more
girls of six or seven, similarly attired, busily picking over piles of
clothes—mostly silk and linen handkerchiefs—examining each
item and folding it neatly. At the rear of the room a boy of like age
in old-fashioned knee breeches and a clean white shirt was looking over a tray of pocket watches, holding each to his ear and
shaking it gingerly. Mrs. Nab's fences-in-training. It seemed to
Miss Tolerance that no keeper of an orphanage or poorhouse
could have a better-ordered set of charges working with more
laudable industry.

Mrs. Nab was in the rear chamber. The room was dominated
by a large chest made of dark wood and piled high with such an
assortment of silver plate that that side of the room glowed in
the candlelight. Mrs. Nab herself sat at a desk in the center of
the room, examining a row of glass-and-silver bottles and de-
canters. She was a comfortable-looking woman of middle years,

wearing a blue worsted dress and apron, with a plain cap neatly containing her iron-gray hair. Her face was ruddy but her expression was placid—hardly what one would expect of a master criminal.

"Come in, Miss Tolerance, come in. Tabitha, tell Arabella she may put some sausages on for supper by and by." Mrs. Nab waved the girl out of the room. "What can I do for you?" Despite her cozy appearance, Mrs. Nab's manner was all business. There was no chair for Miss Tolerance to sit in; she suspected Mrs. Nab preferred to keep her clients standing, and likely to take the first price offered for any item they brought to her.

"I won't take your time, ma'am. I merely wanted to ask about a competitor of your—"

"Not asking for a reference, are you?" Mrs. Nab raised an eyebrow.

"No, ma'am. Only a direction where I might find the fellow. I simply need to ask him a question or two."

"Where was you when such and such happened? I won't be thanked for getting a *competitor* into a quizition with the law." Mrs. Nab picked up a decanter of cut glass and held it to the light.

Miss Tolerance shook her head. "The man I want has already spoken to the law; I merely want to ask him about his evidence."

"So this competitor's peached on someone else?" Mrs. Nab said. "And who are we speaking about? All this 'man in question' such-and-such don't tell me naught."

"I was told his name is Tom Millward. I know only that, and that he is a receiver."

Mrs. Nab turned the decanter in her hands. The candlelight threw tiny rainbows across the bridge of her nose.

"Millward? Millward? What's 'is territory?"

Miss Tolerance shrugged. "I don't know. I was hoping you might tell me."

"And you're certain-sure he's a receiver? Because I thought I knew most of my *competitors* in this neighborhood, and a goodly number of 'em about town, and I don't know that name a-tall."

"That was the name I was given," Miss Tolerance said. "Perhaps he's new to the business."

"Anyone new of consequence I'd ha' heard of straightaway.

Not a whisper of anyone by that name have I heard. I'd go back to them as give you the name, my dear."

"Perhaps another neighborhood—"

"P'raps." Mrs. Nab's tone offered little hope. "Ave you 'quired of Noah Abraham in Southwark?"

Miss Tolerance shook her head. "I came to you first, ma'am."

"Right flattering, that is. I'm sorry I can't offer you no more 'elp than that, dear. I don't know of no one named Millward, Tom nor any other, as is receiving. You talk to the Jew in Southwark, why don't you? He's perhaps got a broader 'quaintance among 'is own people—though Millward don't sound a Hebrew name, does it?"

Miss Tolerance agreed that it did not. In the interests of maintaining a good business relationship, she gave Mrs. Nab a token payment and requested that if she heard anything of Millward she get word to her at Tarsio's.

"A'course, a'course," Mrs. Nab said. She had taken up a silver pitcher and was examining it closely.

Miss Tolerance took her leave, went out past the industrious children with their stolen goods and, after some walking, found a hackney carriage to take her to Southwark.

By ten that evening Miss Tolerance had been from Shoreditch to Southwark to Whitefriars to the back parlor of a chophouse just off the Knightsbridge Road. Not one of the receivers she spoke to would admit ever to having heard of Tom Millward. Either all of them were so fearful of Millward (or Boyse) that the lure of financial interest had no power to pry information loose, or she had been given false coin by Betty Strokum. One might almost think Tom Millward did not exist at all. What the law would make of that, and what bearing it would have upon Anne d'Aubigny's case, was a very interesting question indeed.

Fourteen

Cold and tired, Miss Tolerance entertained a vision of home: a cup of soup, her slippers, and the novel she had borrowed from Marianne, to lull her to sleep. Then she recalled that home, at this moment, meant the yellow bedchamber at Mrs. Brereton's, with a borrowed nightshift and slippers. The comfortable image of her cottage was exchanged for the notion of the more luxurious but less cozy chamber surrounded by other rooms in which Mrs. Brereton's business was being pursued. Did her door have a lock? she wondered.

It was easier, thinking of the cheerless luxury which awaited her, for inspiration to strike her as she reached the corners of Audley and Green Streets. Miss Tolerance's face ached with cold and the healing of her bruises; the stitches on her forehead itched distractingly, but she was very near Mrs. Lasher's establishment. Some useful bit of information might yet be salvaged from the evening. Miss Tolerance knocked at the door of Mrs. Lasher's, inquiring for Josette Vose or, failing that, for Mrs. Lasher herself.

The footman, looking no farther than Miss Tolerance's Gunnard coat and topboots, displayed no awareness that he had seen her before. She found herself being treated with the respect accorded a potential customer: Mrs. Vose was not in the house at present, but he would inquire as to Mrs. Lasher's availability. He left Miss Tolerance in a small parlor near the door, where she waited, warming her hands at the grate.

When the door opened it was Mrs. Lasher herself who swept in.

"Good evening, sir! I hope you'll tell me how we can—"

Miss Tolerance turned from the fire. She observed that the madam was handsomely dressed in purple jaconet and a spangled turban, scented to high heaven and preparing to offer the hospitality of the house. She observed, too, the moment when Mrs. Lasher recognized her visitor; her smile hardened and cordiality departed as if it had been blown from the room.

"You? Wallace said you was a *customer*. What are you doing in that rig-out?"

Miss Tolerance bowed. "It is convenient when I go about Town on certain errands. How do you do?"

"Errands." Mrs. Lasher dropped into a chair and waved at Miss Tolerance, indicating that she might seat herself. Her expression was less one of shocked dismay at the unconventionality of her guest's attire than it was of dismay that a fat fee would not be forthcoming. "Should have known something wasn't right. Single man, come all on his own without a such-and-such sent me, never been here before. What do you want?"

"I was hoping to talk to Mrs. Vose."

"She's not here." Mrs. Lasher seemed far more delighted than the mere chance to thwart Miss Tolerance would explain. "On a very important call she is, with everything fine about 'er. Silk sheets and silver pisspots, and French wine too, I've no doubt. All of the best with His High—with my Lord Such-and-Such." She rubbed her hands together greedily. "Quite covered in laurels. Brings distinction to the house. And perhaps custom, as well."

Miss Tolerance added a few facts and came up with a human sum which gave her a cold start. "The Duke of Cumberland."

Mrs. Lasher frowned. "How did you know?"

"You all but had the Royal Warrant: by appointment to His Royal Highness. Beside which, I was there when Mrs. Vose was presented to the Duke. I had not realized until now that she had won her point with him."

Mrs. Lasher preened as if the conquest were her own. "Well, as you already know, I suppose there's no 'arm in speaking of it. She won 'im complete, Josie did. Like I said: everything fine about her. 'E likes it all kept quiet, though. I s'pose 'is family shouldn't like to have it bruted about; 'e's had enough scandal this year, and the public don't much love 'im to start with—"

"You find his money lovable enough."

"Well, why shouldn't I? I'm a woman of business. Mind, I ain't seen a penny yet. I have my hopes—but that's neither 'ere nor there." Mrs. Lasher pulled herself up short. "You didn't come about Cumberland, did you?"

"You're quite right. And for what it's worth, I doubt I shall remember a word of what you said on the subject," Miss Tolerance lied reassuringly. "I was actually wondering if you could recall if Mrs. Vose was here on the evening of eighth November."

"What you want to know that for?" Mrs. Lasher asked.

"I've been told two different stories, and knowing where Mrs. Vose was on that night would help me to know who was lying."

"I told you, Josie ain't one of the house girls. She works when she likes—"

"But surely you must know which evenings she is here."

"Of course I do. I run a business, miss. Just because it's a whorehouse don't mean I don't need to keep accounts."

Miss Tolerance smiled sympathetically. "Of course not. There are so many things to keep count of. My aunt, Mrs. Brereton, seems to be aware of the smallest expenses—"

"Your aunt? Mrs. Brereton of Manchester Square?"

Miss Tolerance nodded. "Her ledgers are the most painstaking imaginable—"

"Mrs. Brereton's ledgers?" Mrs. Lasher appeared torn between awe and rank curiosity.

"Oh, yes. Sea sponges and tea cakes and wax candles. Laundry and livery and victuals—but I needn't recite to you the sorts of expenses a first-class house incurs. She doesn't spend a penny out of place. And knows to the minute the time each of her employees spends with a customer."

Mrs. Lasher nodded sagely. The spangled fringe of her turban released a waft of unpleasantly musky scent. "You must do, that's for certain."

"So you see, I was sure you would be able to tell me if Mrs. Vose had been here on the evening I mentioned," Miss Tolerance finished.

Mrs. Lasher sucked on her teeth and thought. "She wasn't 'ere that night," she said at last. " 'Ad a meeting with her old keeper—the chevalyer you were inquiring after the other day. Now I remember, I was a mite anxious she might decide to go back to 'im."

"She did not, I take it."

Mrs. Lasher shook her head. "Never fear that. It seems 'e was just as nip-farthing as ever. They couldn't come to terms, and she left before ever they got to business, so she made no money that night. She slammed right out the kitchen door, she said, like a scullery maid. Swore she'd never go back there while 'e lived."

"And nor did she," Miss Tolerance murmured.

"Now, Josie won't want you queerin' her pitch with Lord Such-and-Such," Mrs. Lasher warned, suddenly recalling discretion. "All this talk about the chevalyer—"

"My dear madam, you've only confirmed for me what Mrs. Vose would doubtless have said herself." Miss Tolerance extended her hand. "My aunt would so appreciate the courtesy you have extended me."

"Would she?" Mrs. Lasher asked. "Well, she should, I s'pose. Professional courtesy, like. Not but what—you're not one of 'ers, are you?"

Miss Tolerance shook her head. "No, ma'am."

"Pity. But why—" Mrs. Lasher's puzzlement set her fringe to dancing again. "Then why do you care where Josie was—oh." Mrs. Lasher's intellect was calculating rather than imaginative. "That night you asked about, that's the night 'e was killed. But Josie wouldn't—she never did—"

"My dear Mrs. Lasher, calm yourself. I am not looking at Mrs. Vose as a suspect. As I said, someone else had told me she had an appointment with Mr. d'Aubigny—we had as well include his name in the discussion—and I merely wished to confirm it, so I can understand how much of the informant's word I can trust."

Mrs. Lasher's face had pinked remarkably. Now the color began to ebb. "Well, if that's all," she said slowly. "That's twice now you've winkled something out of me. I should remember you're a slippery one, but I suppose it ain't done no damage this time. Because I do know for a fact that it couldn't ha' been Josie."

"Do you, ma'am?"

"Oh, yes. When the papers come out with 'Horrid Death' all over them, she sounded a bit regretful-like. Told me about runnin' out the house and going back to her room in Balcombe Street without a penny to show for it. Said she'd suspected the chevalyer'd go for his little wife after she left, but principle was principle and without money she wasn't going to stay. Did say that whoever'd killed Dobinny done the wife a service, which made me wonder if perhaps one of the servants done it. Josie said none of them 'ad the brass to kill a rat. Nor the widow neither—Josie said she was always dosed full of laudanum by the time tea was brung in. I'll tell you what I think." Mrs. Lasher leaned forward. "I think it was *spies*."

"Really?" Miss Tolerance was polite. "Why would a spy—for the French, I presume?—kill one of his own countrymen?"

"That's the thing, isn't it? But the chevalyer was a government man, and worked for England now. There's no accounting for what a foreigner will do."

There was a tap at the door and a woman—the same dour, black-dressed woman who had brought Miss Tolerance to see Mrs. Lasher on her last visit, looked around the jamb. "Mrs. Lasher, Mr. Barto—" she caught sight of Miss Tolerance. "There's a question with Annie's gentleman."

At once Mrs. Lasher was upon her feet, all business and with a face full of wrath. Miss Tolerance rose also and hastily thanked her hostess.

"Will you tell Mrs. Vose that I do need a word with her?" Miss Tolerance called out. "She can find me at Tarsio's—"

With a nod of the prodigious purple-and-gold turban that might have been assent or, as likely, dismissal, Mrs. Lasher was gone.

Miss Tolerance went home to Manchester Square with a good deal to consider.

S he lay wakeful in the yellow room for a long while that night, distracted by the feeling that she had at least one answer within her grasp and had yet to take it up. When she was wak-

ened in the morning by the homely noise of Jess, come to light the
fire, Miss Tolerance lay abed for a time in the grip of an idea
which had occurred to her as she slept. At length she washed,
dressed in one of her newly laundered gowns, attempted to visit
her aunt (Frost, with a pursed smile, sent Miss Tolerance away
with instructions to come back at a decent hour when Mrs. Brereton was actually awake) and went to the kitchen to beg a roll and
coffee from Cook.

At half past ten Miss Tolerance started out for Oxford Street.

The Duke of Kent public house had not long been open for
business when Miss Tolerance arrived there. She wore her blue
wool gown and cloak, a sober enough costume for such a venue,
but the barman hardly bothered to look at her, let alone wonder
what a single woman of respectable mien was doing in his establishment. He was a different fellow from the one she had spoken
to the day before; he produced the coffee she ordered and returned to polishing his taps with sleepy indifference.

Miss Tolerance slid a half-crown piece along the bar but kept
one gloved finger upon it. "Has Mrs. Strokum been in this morning?" she asked.

The barman blinked and turned to examine Miss Tolerance
more closely.

"What's a mort like you want with Betty?"

"She and I were talking yesterday. I have recalled a question to
ask her."

"You 'ave? And how do I know she's wantin' to talk to you?"

Miss Tolerance smiled. "You don't. But do I look a dangerous
sort to you? I only want five minutes of her time. Is she likely to be
in her usual spot?"

"This hour, she's likely asleep." The barman shrugged and
turned away.

"Perhaps. But perhaps I could make it worth her while to wake
and speak to me." Miss Tolerance slid the coin back and forth
upon the rough-hewn bar in subtle rhythm. The barman was not
unmoved by this music.

"She's got a crib over the chandler on Goodge Street. If she's
sleeping home, that's where she'd be." The man slid his hand toward Miss Tolerance's.

Miss Tolerance lifted her finger from the half-crown. The barman put his own atop it and slid it across the bar and into the pocket of his apron.

"You don't look like a whore."

"No, I don't," Miss Tolerance agreed.

"You're not one of them Ee-vangelical Ree-formers?" He spoke with distaste.

"Hardly. Mrs. Strokum's soul is her own concern and none of mine."

"Well, that's all right, then," the barman said. He turned back to the taps and Miss Tolerance swallowed the last few watery sips of her coffee in silence.

The chandler's on Goodge Street was not a prosperous business, nor did the building which housed it appear to be a prosperous one. The shop window was flyspecked and badly illumined, and the structure itself sorely wanted a coat of limewash. In the cramped hallway which led upstairs, the scent of beeswax was overwhelmed by the less pleasant smells of tallow, sweat, and a whiff of chamberpot. When Miss Tolerance knocked at the door at the head of the stairs it was opened at once by a bony old woman with rheumy eyes.

"The doxy?" She pointed down the hall and slammed her door shut.

Miss Tolerance turned and went along the corridor. She knocked firmly for several minutes, and was about to decide that Mrs. Strokum was not at home, when she heard a thump inside the chamber. A moment later there was the sound of someone fumbling with the latch.

The door opened an inch. An eye, blackened and swollen, appeared in the space. Miss Tolerance was not certain that the owner of the eye could, in fact, see enough to discern who it was.

"Mrs. Strokum?"

The eye blinked and a ribbon of mucus filmed it. "Christ, an't you done enough damage?" Miss Tolerance could not see enough of the person behind the door to be certain it was Betty Strokum, but the tone—and the words—persuaded her that it was.

"What has happened to you?" she asked.

"What d'you think?" Mrs. Strokum stepped away from the

door, shoving it open as she turned her back. "You might as well come in and see your 'andiwork."

Miss Tolerance's heart sank. She did not pretend incomprehension. "Boyse?"

"In course, Boyse. *You bin a-talkin' of me, Bet*? he asks. And before I can say yea or nay, I'm beat to the bone. I shan't be able to work today or tomorra."

The whore turned to face Miss Tolerance. Both her eyes were blacked, and the right side of her face was purple with bruising; her nose was flattened. She wheezed and lowered herself gingerly into her chair. Miss Tolerance suspected that Mrs. Strokum had broken a rib or two as well. Miss Tolerance raised her hand to her own fading bruises as if the sight of Mrs. Strokum's had worsened her own pain.

"I am so sorry." It was quite inadequate.

"I tried to tell 'im I 'ardly said a word but to give 'im a alibi. 'E wasn't listening. *Bin a-talkin' of me, Bet*? he asks. Then this. What did you do, go off and tell half a' Lunnon what I told you?"

Miss Tolerance shook her head. "I never used your name. In fact—" she thought back to the conversation she had had the night before. "I don't know what I could have said to anyone that would have set Boyse upon your trail. I went to several fences of my acquaintance, looking for Tom Millward."

Mrs. Strokum glared. "And that 'splains it. You stupid bitch, there ain't no Millward."

"No Millward."

The whore nodded; a moan and a wince suggested what the gesture had cost her. "I played along, made 'im up to get rid of you. If Boyse learns I been talking to you again—well, I been beat before, I know the difference between a man means to kill and a man that don't. Next time you'll find me dead."

Miss Tolerance nodded. If Millward was a fiction she could readily believe that Boyse would kill the doxy to protect his secret. Looking at Betty Strokum's bruises, so like her own, she felt a twinge of guilty sickness which she covered with a decisive manner.

"We shall have to keep you safe, then," she said briskly.

"*What*?"

"Get your coat and hat. I shall take you somewhere you can stay for a few days until I have dealt with Mr. Boyse."

"What, simple as that?" Mrs. Strokum stared at Miss Tolerance. It was difficult to parse her expression; the bruises made it unreadable. "How'm I to earn my keep, hidin' away? And you—how do you know I'm not lying now?"

"Why would you lie? For fear of Boyse? Did he tell you to do it? I cannot see his purpose. He wants it to be believed that he got information from a man named Millward on Wednesday night—but the barman at the Duke of Kent said Boyse spent the best part of the evening in your company. You tell me Boyse was in your company but did not see this Millward—but obligingly tell me Millward is a fence. Yet not one person in the receiving line I spoke to recognized the name Millward. The barman at the Duke of Kent didn't know the name, and he's a fellow recognizes his custom. So even before I found you yesterday, I was upon my way to doubting Boyse's story."

"Well, I'm not going to help you peach 'im," Mrs. Strokum said. "I've no ambition to be dead."

"I've no ambition to see you dead. If you can dress yourself"— the woman wore several flannel shawls over her shift—"I will take you somewhere where you will be safe. It might even prove to be a profitable stay for you."

"What's the use?" Mrs. Strokum whined. " 'E'll find me out. I'm dead."

"If you stay here you certainly are," Miss Tolerance agreed. Her patience was wearing thin. The red dress Mrs. Strokum had worn the day before hung from a nail in the wall. Miss Tolerance plucked it down and held it out. "I will avert my eyes," she said.

The other woman gave a snort that might have been amusement, followed by a gasp of pain. "Ain't that genteel of you," she said. "But I'll need my corsets."

Within an hour Miss Tolerance was at the door of Mrs. Lasher's establishment. Mrs. Strokum, heavily veiled, stood a pace or two behind, caught somewhere between awe at the brothel's elegance and disbelief that she would be admitted thereto. Miss Tolerance gave her name to the footman and the two women were shown to the parlor. Within a quarter hour Miss Tolerance had arranged at an extortionate rate to have Mrs. Lasher provide room and board for "Mrs. Smith" for a few days.

"I didn't think to see you again," Mrs. Lasher said. "This is on the same business?" She had assessed Mrs. Strokum with a glance and adopted her plummiest genteel accent.

Miss Tolerance smiled. "I cannot say what the business is. My purse will have to do my talking for me. And I require absolute secrecy."

Mrs. Lasher eyed Mrs. Strokum without favor. "You don't think I want it got about that that's the sort of woman I keep here?" she asked. From her disapproval one would have thought her the wife of an archbishop, at least. "I'm more afraid your Mrs. Smith will announce herself to my clients."

"I don't think you need worry about that," Miss Tolerance told her. "She is as fearful of being found as you are of having her associated with the house. Give her a room and a bath and I'm sure she'll stay out of your way."

Just to be certain, however, Miss Tolerance took Mrs. Strokum, now called Mrs. Smith, aside and reminded her of the peril in which she stood should the constable Boyse find her out.

"No bloody fear," the woman said. "I'll keep to me cot and say my prayers until you say it's safe to come out again." She smiled her peculiar toothless smile, began to curtsy but winced and thought better of it, and followed Mrs. Lasher's dour assistant out of the room.

M iss Tolerance went then to make a report of her progress to Anne d'Aubigny, and, as importantly, to see how that lady had fared in her new accommodation at Cold Bath Fields. She paid the visitor's fee, stepped from the clamor of a crowded street into the enforced quiet of the prison halls, and was led along a dim, low-ceilinged corridor halfway around the prison. "She's to be taken back for more questions after a while," the guard warned her, and unlocked the door.

Anne d'Aubigny sat by the room's small, square window, obscured by the glare of light behind her. Miss Tolerance curtsied, stepped into the room, and heard the door close and lock behind her.

"Good morning, ma'am. I hope you passed a tolerable night."

The widow nodded listlessly.

Miss Tolerance looked about the room. It was only half a dozen paces deep and wide, with a cot set in one corner, a trunk in the other, and the table and two chairs set in the middle. The trunk, Miss Tolerance assumed, stood in stead of a wardrobe. For the rest, there were three sticks holding half-burnt candles, a few books including the Bible on the floor by the bed, and a workbag with a 'broidery frame and silks spilling out of it on the table. It was hardly a pleasant room, but it was clean.

Miss Tolerance took the empty chair across the table from her client.

"I have, I hope, good news. I believe I shall be able to refute the information which was the cause of your arrest."

Anne d'Aubigny nodded. "Thank you."

Miss Tolerance misliked the hopelessness of her tone. "I beg you will not lose heart, ma'am. I know this is a hard time for you, but it will soon be over, and you safe at home again."

"Safe." The widow sounded the word vaguely, as if it made no sense to her. Miss Tolerance felt that prick of impatience which touched so many of her conversations with Anne d'Aubigny.

"You are frightened and uncomfortable, nor can I blame you. But your situation could be much worse. I am working to have you released as soon as possible. They cannot proceed against you unless you give your consent to be tried."

"They will press me if I do not cooperate." While it was true that one could not be tried without consent, and while English law forbade the sorts of torture said to be practiced wholesale on the Continent, it was not uncommon to wring a confession or consent to be tried from a recalcitrant prisoner by pressing.

"Nonsense," Miss Tolerance said briskly. "You're a beautiful young woman with money and good family, imprisoned on poor evidence. Mr. Heddison would not countenance—"

"It was he who said it. They will press me—"

"They say so only to frighten you."

"Then they succeed. Mr. Boyse very helpfully described what pressing is, when Mr. Heddison was called from the room." The widow's detached voice all of an instant quavered. "They strip you naked. They put you on a granite table and pile stones on you until your—your organs are flattened, or burst from your body. He said the effect was rather like that of a carriage wheel crushing a squirrel."

Miss Tolerance silently damned Boyse to a Hell of her own devising. "They have not enough evidence to make them sure of a confession. They will not press you—"

The widow grimaced. "They told me over and over that my birth and money and family will not protect me. That within a day or so, if I do not consent to trial or tell them how I killed Etienne they will press me until I beg to tell them." She laughed bitterly. "I thought with Etienne dead my troubles were over."

"I beg you will not say such a thing to the magistrate!" Miss Tolerance could only imagine Heddison's opinion of such a statement.

"My husband beat me and said it was his right. The law will kill me and say it is its right."

Miss Tolerance rose from her chair and knelt at the widow's feet, taking her hands in her own. She spoke slowly, as she might have done to a child. "I promise you, I shall not let that happen. I am very near to exploding the evidence against you. Once you are free again I will find who killed your husband, and the whole matter will be behind you. Remember that and be brave."

Anne d'Aubigny nodded. Unshed tears made her eyes bright, but her expression was childishly courageous, as if she placed her entire faith in Miss Tolerance's ability to rescue her. Certainly Miss Tolerance was the only rescuer to hand, but she found that regard both touching and unnerving. She rose briskly, meaning the action to inspire courage in both herself and her client.

"I must be about your business. I want to consult with a friend—if I can secure his assistance it will doubtless speed your removal from this place. I know that cannot come too soon for you. Are you well? Have you everything you need?"

The widow nodded again. "William came early today, and said he would return tonight to dine with me. Having a little privacy, and the freedom to walk about a little in this room, has been restorative."

"I am sure the food is not what you are used to—"

Mrs. d'Aubigny shrugged. "It hardly matters." Then, as if fearing she had been ungrateful, she smiled. "Thank you, Miss Tolerance. It is a comfort to know you are working for my good."

Miss Tolerance curtsied. "Good morning, then, ma'am. I hope the next time I come I shall have better news."

M iss Tolerance took a chair to Henry Street, established herself in Tarsio's Ladies' Parlor, and wrote a note to Sir Walter Mandif, begging to know when she might call upon him for advice. She ordered a pot of tea, her universal restorative, and sat with paper and pen, seeking to make sense of what she knew. At the outset it was difficult to put the image of Anne d'Aubigny out of her mind. It was not surprising that the widow seemed even more fragile in her new surroundings; with all the advantages of accommodation, board and treatment that money could secure for her, she was still a prisoner. It was a sort of treatment no gently reared young woman could imagine.

Of course, her marriage had given Anne d'Aubigny some experience in dealing with situations unimaginable to most gently reared young ladies.

Miss Tolerance mused, drank her tea, and scratched notes to herself.

The matter of "Millward's" testimony she thought she could dispose of fairly quickly. Without that against her, Heddison must release Anne d'Aubigny from Cold Bath Fields Prison. Then the real matter before her—the finding of d'Aubigny's killer—could proceed. And what did she know of that?

Etienne d'Aubigny had come into a sum of money shortly before his death, with which he had satisfied his debts. He had suggested to his wife that there would be more money to come—but whence it was to come she did not know. Miss Tolerance did not place any credence in Anne d'Aubigny's suggestion that an angry creditor had killed the chevalier. She had suggested to Camille Touvois that d'Aubigny's money might have come from blackmail, which certainly provided a motive for murder. But who might his victim-killer have been?

D'Aubigny's friend Beauville said that d'Aubigny had left him early on the night of his death, gone home to keep an assignation with Josette Vose. He himself had gone to a brothel, but could not remember which. She could ask at Mrs. Lasher's and at Mrs. Brereton's, two houses she knew he had visited, but doubted that she would learn anything useful in either place.

Josette Vose, who had broken with d'Aubigny over money, had met with him on the night of his death and—if Mrs. Lasher was to be believed—quarreled and left. She would need to talk to Mrs. Vose to confirm this story; it contradicted Mrs. Vose's earlier statement that she had not seen d'Aubigny for several weeks before the murder. If d'Aubigny was still alive when Mrs. Vose left, it was possible that her being there at all was just an unhappy coincidence. Possible, but how likely?

Miss Tolerance was conscious of a strong, instinctive mistrust of Beauville, and a conviction—which she was well aware might be based in dislike—that if d'Aubigny was involved in blackmail, Camille Touvois was likely to know who his victim was. Miss Tolerance suspected, with no more proof than she had of her feelings about Beauville, that Josette Vose knew more than she had said of d'Aubigny's murder, but she did not believe the woman had done the murder herself. All ideas, none of them based upon anything more than instinct.

I used to require rather more in the way of evidence, she thought to herself. *Still, if I cannot trust my own judgment, I am in a sorry way to do business.*

She returned to the idea of blackmail. If d'Aubigny had blackmailed someone he would need to have proofs of some sort which he would have kept hidden. If the murderer had not found the proofs, they might still be hidden in the house at Half Moon Street. She closed her eyes and tried to imagine where a man such as d'Aubigny might hide such a thing. His library, perhaps, or—

"So I find you here." A pleasant voice broke her concentration. Miss Tolerance opened her eyes to the sight of Sir Walter Mandif smiling at her. "I came to learn how I could be of assistance."

The idea which had been forming in Miss Tolerance's mind

was lost. She rose up, curtsied, and begged that her visitor would join her.

"I had no thought that you should seek me out," she apologized. "I know you are particularly busy. I meant to come to you—"

"So your letter said. But I felt a strong wish to get up and away from my desk. Court does not meet again until later this afternoon, so I gave myself the pleasure of calling upon you." Sir Walter took the cup of tea Miss Tolerance offered to him. "How is it I may assist you?"

Miss Tolerance smiled. "At the very least, I need your guidance. Can you tell me how best to go about impeaching Mr. Boyse's testimony against my client?"

Sir Walter raised an eyebrow. "You wish to impeach the constable, not his source? I hope you understand that that will incur considerable ill will from the magistracy—"

"The magistracy, saving yourself, does not bear me any great love now. But if one of the magistracy's officers is bearing false witness, I should think they would prefer to know of it."

"Perhaps so." Sir Walter sipped his tea.

"Perhaps? Sir Walter, would you not prefer to know if you had a dishonest man working for you?"

"I would, yes. But, my dear Miss Tolerance—" Sir Walter passed a hand over his face. "I may not like Boyse, or want him in my service, but he is an officer of the court. He has Heddison's trust. And the law gives its officers a good deal of latitude in the matter of how they gather evidence—"

"Surely the law does not permit its officers to invent witnesses and their testimony," Miss Tolerance said firmly.

Sir Walter looked at her. At last, "You have proof of this?" he asked.

Miss Tolerance sniffed. "It had never occurred to me before how much easier it is to prove someone's existence than nonexistence."

"Meaning there is no proof." Sir Walter put his teacup down on the table near at hand and pressed his hands together, rather as if he intended to pray.

"It is not that dire; certainly what I have learned convinces me. May I tell you?"

"I wish you will, else I shall not know how to advise you."

In a few short sentences Miss Tolerance reviewed her investigation with Sir Walter. The magistrate listened without interrupting, with so fixed and thoughtful an expression that Miss Tolerance could not be certain what he made of her tale.

"You believe that Boyse made Millward out of whole cloth," Sir Walter said at last. "Because a prostitute who wished to give him an alibi told you that he was with her, and saw no one named Millward, on the seventeenth night?"

"Because she later told me that there was no Millward at all. That, coupled with the fact that no one—not Mrs. Nab or Noah Abraham or Black Wiggin in Creel Lane—had heard of him. The idea is rather confirmed by the fact that he beat Mrs. Strokum savagely when he learned she had spoken to me. And consider: how would a woman like Anne d'Aubigny know to find a man like Millward?"

"You did tell me that the family was pawning things—"

"I think someone was, but I doubt it was the widow herself. And if it was she, would she not go to her jeweler or banker to sell her trinkets? I'm not certain she would know how to find a pawnbroker, let alone an assassin! And supposing that she *did* go looking for someone to kill her husband, how would she avoid making a great wonder of herself, looking for a man like this Millward? What did she do, ask a barman if he knew anyone who could oblige her with a murder for hire? I wish you had met Mrs. d'Aubigny. I think you would understand why I find the whole notion so ridiculous."

"I believe that you believe in her, and that carries great weight with me. But—"

"I have not convinced you." It cost Miss Tolerance some effort to keep her tone even.

"Even if the prostitute—Mrs. Strokum—is telling the truth, and Boyse did not meet with Millward that night, all your story tells me is that she invented the Millward she sent you chasing. Why should not Boyse have met with the real Millward that night?" Perhaps he saw the frown Miss Tolerance struggled to hide. "I am only attempting to explain the construction I believe Heddison could put upon the matter. The law would generally prefer to believe that the law is honest."

"I'm sure the public would prefer it as well! Sir Walter, no one I spoke to who saw Boyse that night saw him with anyone other than Betty Strokum. When did he meet with Millward, then?"

"Why must the interview have been so late at night?"

"According to the information you gave me, Boyse reported that he had spoken to Millward at a tavern the night before the arrest, but could not remember what he looked like, which tavern it was, or any other particular than his information against the widow."

"Boyse would not be the first man to spend an afternoon in an alehouse instead of about his duties."

A memory fell into place in Miss Tolerance's mind. With a pardonable expression of triumph she said, "But I saw him and Mr. Heddison that evening in Half Moon Street, at the widow's house. He was sober then, and the barman at the Duke of Kent—and how should he not remember the alehouse he most often visits, no matter how drunk he is?—said he was sober when he came in at eight o'clock of that same evening. And he joined Betty Strokum there, and stayed with her until cock's crow the next morning. When did he see Millward in all that time? When did he become so drunk that he could not remember the place or time or any other particular except Millward's story?"

"Perhaps after cock's crow," Sir Walter began.

"Would you have me believe that Boyse left Mrs. Strokum's rosy bower at six in the morning, went off to drink himself nearly blind so as to conveniently find Mr. Millward and hear his tale?"

"I am only saying that the matter is not as cut-and-dried as you would believe it."

"Nothing is. But, Sir Walter: if Boyse had told Mr. Heddison about an early-morning meeting with Mr. Millward, would he not have done so first thing in the morning? But they did not come to arrest Anne d'Aubigny until early that evening. Because he did not think to invent the story until that afternoon. I only wish I knew why he wishes to implicate my client—who has, God knows, suffered quite enough already. He might have come up with a story which was more convincing upon its face."

"Miss Tolerance." Sir Walter leaned forward and regarded her earnestly. "Sarah. There may be a good deal to what you say, but I am not certain you will receive a fair hearing from Heddison. He trusts Boyse—however ill-advised that might seem to you, a magistrate must trust the men who work for him—and he does not trust you. If you will let me make my own inquiries—"

"But that is all I ask!" Miss Tolerance felt nearly giddy with relief. "I assure you, I am quite aware that Mr. Heddison dislikes me. If you can use your influence to persuade him—"

"I have no influence at all with Heddison. I can make some inquiries of my own, and I will do that. I cannot promise that I will reach the same conclusions."

"You will," Miss Tolerance said with assurance.

"There is one thing more," Sir Walter said gravely. He was truly worried, Miss Tolerance realized. "What is it you think to achieve by impeaching Boyse?"

"Anne d'Aubigny's release from prison, of course."

"You must understand that impeaching Boyse may not achieve that end," Sir Walter said. "She remains Heddison's most likely suspect. I understand that she is your client, and you may like her, but that alone is no reason to acquit her of murder."

Fifteen

I do not acquit her of murder because she is my client—you of all people must know better than that! I acquit her because—" Miss Tolerance considered. "I acquit her because it makes no sense to believe her the murderer. It is against reason."

"One might as well say it goes against reason to believe the Earl of Versellion was a murderer," Sir Walter said quietly.

Miss Tolerance felt suddenly breathless. Sir Walter looked apprehensive, as if he had crossed a line with her and was not sure what she would do. She was not certain either. Nor could she determine the nature of the strong emotion which flooded her: one moment it felt like rage, the next, deep hurt, the moment after, frustration. She clenched her hands.

"I beg your pardon," Sir Walter said. "Please—I only meant that in my experience anyone is capable of murder under the right circumstances."

Miss Tolerance un-fisted her hands and strove to keep her voice even. "Capable of murderous thoughts, indeed. But you have only to look at the woman to know she is not the murderess. She could not overpower her husband, indeed, she was terrified of him, with good reason. You have not met her, and perhaps cannot take my word in the matter—" she waved away Sir Walter's attempt to reassure her upon this point. "But Mr. Heddison has spoken with her often, yet appears unable to see no farther than his mechanical notion that she must be guilty because she was in the house—"

"Heddison may not be a man of great imagination, but he is thorough, and according to his lights, fair. Are you accusing him of bias? And to whose advantage?"

"Oh, for God's sake!" Miss Tolerance put her cup on the table, carefully. "I am accusing him only of prejudice and lazy thinking. I believe he made up his mind that my client was guilty on the day he was first called to the house."

"If the evidence—"

"The only evidence I have heard of that points to the widow alone is that which Boyse provided, and I have thrown a grave shadow upon that. And all of a sudden Mr. Heddison seems to be moving at great haste: Anne d'Aubigny has been in custody for only a day and already they are threatening to press her to bring her to trial—"

Sir Walter frowned. "It is very likely a threat only—I cannot believe Heddison would use the press until he had exhausted all other options. I do not see how it can be helped."

Miss Tolerance glared at her friend. "You are mighty easy about it, Sir Walter! A gently reared woman of three and twenty years, shut up in prison and threatened with the press if she does not confess to what she has not done—is that what you would wish for a daughter of yours? For a wife?"

Sir Walter's eyebrow crooked. "If the wife were also my murderer, I'm sure my scruples would be less fixed upon the point."

If he had thought the jest would distract her, Sir Walter was mistaken. "You are pleased to joke," Miss Tolerance said coldly. "I tell you that your colleague has judged the case without regard to the character of his suspect. How probable is it that a woman who comes barely to my shoulder should be able to dash out the brains of a man of whom she was terrified? It makes me wonder if there is a bias in the law, or at least among the magistracy, against women. You were quite eager to believe that I was guilty of murder, when first we met."

Even as she said it, Miss Tolerance knew it was a comment that would bring pain. Sir Walter frowned and took up his teacup between his fingers.

"Eager I was not," he said gravely. "But my feelings were the last evidence I could trust. I had no other suspects, and there were several things which suggested your involvement. You will recall that I was very happy to find you were innocent."

"Shall I thank you for your faith in me?" Miss Tolerance inclined her head. "But the evidence of your own judgment was not sufficient to speak for my character."

She became aware that her voice had risen. Across the room three elaborately pretty women—actresses—had turned from their conversation to stare at Miss Tolerance and her guest. She lowered her voice and sat back. "I beg your pardon," she said.

"And I yours," Sir Walter said. "I do not deny your experience, but my own tells me that the simplest solution is most often the correct one. That evidence is the surest aid to a true verdict."

"But the evidence in this case is tainted! And you are saying, it seems to me, I cannot rely upon my judgment but must accept evidence I know to be false."

"I am telling you to consult the same faculties which told you the Earl of Versellion was capable of murder, despite your feelings for him."

Miss Tolerance shivered. "I should think that as I was able to set aside my feelings for Versellion, to bring him to Bow Street and to testify against him, you would have a higher regard for my judgment."

Sir Walter studied his cup. "I have the highest regard for your judgment. But is it not possible—" He hesitated. "Is it possible that it is you whose mind is made up?"

"You are accusing me of bias? But I have no reason to care more for Anne d'Aubigny any more than any other client. I have a professional interest, but that is all. I cannot help, of course, feeling sorry for her situation—" Miss Tolerance broke off to take a note which a liveried boy offered to her on a salver. Somewhat relieved to have an excuse to break off a conversation which was becoming more and more painful, Miss Tolerance took the note and read it quickly. Her anger was forgotten.

"Josette Vose is dead," she said. "You will doubtless hear of it when you return to Bow Street. Beaten, and her throat cut. Mrs. Lasher sent a note to Mrs. Brereton's, and they forwarded it here. I must go."

"You believe it connected to d'Aubigny's death?"

"She was one of the last persons to see the chevalier alive, and I always thought she knew more than she would tell me. Perhaps someone else thought so, too."

"Is there anything I can do to—"

"You offered to inquire after Boyse and his 'Millward' testimony. I would be very grateful if you would do so." Miss Tolerance put Mrs. Lasher's note into her reticule.

"Of course," Sir Walter rose. "But is there any way I can help you?"

"I require nothing, Sir Walter. Happily, no one can suspect Anne d'Aubigny of this crime: she is safe in gaol." Miss Tolerance rose, bid Mandif good afternoon, and had left the Ladies' Salon before he could return the courtesy.

M iss Tolerance went at once to Mrs. Lasher's house. She found the house little disturbed by what had happened, although the man who admitted her confided that the madam was in a right fuss about something. It was a sign of the household's disarray that the man merely told her in which chamber Mrs. Lasher was to be found, and let Miss Tolerance direct herself. She found Mrs. Lasher in the room on the first floor in which they had first spoken. The madam was bent over a writing desk, scribbling something with fierce attention; her face, when she looked up to greet Miss Tolerance, was bare of paint and looked its full complement of years.

"How did you learn of Mrs. Vose's death?" Miss Tolerance asked, once they had greeted each other and exchanged pieties.

"The constable come and asked me questions. Not that I had much I could tell 'im. Wanted to know where Josie'd spent last night, and in course I couldn't tell 'im. Not for certain."

"But you said last night she was with the Duke of Cumberla—"

Mrs. Lasher put her finger across Miss Tolerance's lips to seal the name inside. "You want to get yourself killed? Or me? Beside," she added. "I don't know, not for certain. Josie called him 'the duke,' and 'my royal,' and ''Is Grace of C.' Could as easy have been the Duke of Clarence or Cambridge, or Cartwheels, come to that."

Miss Tolerance was not in a mood to be patient. "You told the constable you had no idea where she had been?"

Under stress, Mrs. Lasher's aitches fled. "They don't need me to tell 'em where she was. Found 'er dead in Cleveland Row, just a jump from the palace. With evidence, if you please. A note from 'Is Royal Such-and-Such, crested stationery and all, clutched in 'er 'and. Constable said Josie was dressed for a party, but cut up and beat." Mrs. Lasher shook her head wisely. "Lost control of 'isself, I'd say. They do, sometimes; 'tis why we generally 'ave someone near by, just in case. But 'ow would you stop a royal person . . ." She put her finger to her own mouth this time and looked at Miss Tolerance archly.

"Lost control and cut her throat? And then left her with a note that implicated him? I don't think much of the duke's aides, if that's the case. Did your constable give you any idea of what the note said?"

"Oh, lovey-dovey stuff, promising undyin' devotion and that sort of thing. P'raps 'e took a partiality to 'er, and when 'e couldn't 'ave 'er, cut 'er throat?"

"Couldn't have her? Even if their association had to this point been blameless, I was under the impression that money carried all for Mrs. Vose; surely a royal duke would be able to come to an arrangement."

" 'E lost 'is 'ead and cut 'er throat, like some of 'em do," Mrs. Lasher suggested again. "Cut 'er throat and 'ad 'er thrown out into the street. At least it was a prince, and not some bully-boy she met on a street corner."

"Being killed by a prince makes one no less dead," Miss Tolerance said practically. "In any case, a body clutching an incriminating note seems far too convenient for Bow Street, and far too inconvenient for the duke. Whatever his faults may be, I have never heard that His Royal Highness was a fool. Rather the opposite, in fact."

"A man in 'eat—"

"I agree. A man in heat might do anything. Cumberland is said to have the Devil's own temper; I could believe him capable of *crime passionelle*. But that man's advisors would not let the servants toss the body of his mistress into the street with a love note in her hand! Cumberland has already survived one scandal this year."

"Killed 'is valet," Mrs. Lasher agreed. She gave the final word a hard *t*. "Proves 'e's of a killin' disposition."

Miss Tolerance wondered if Mrs. Lasher had been bribed to support this theory so rigorously. She shook her head. "The Coroner's jury cleared him of involvement. A jury with several notable Whigs on it, they'd not have cleared him had there been evidence against him. Mrs. Vose's death points too conveniently to Cumberland, at a time when all the royal dukes are under scrutiny. I don't believe it."

"Who'd kill 'er? You think it's to do with the chevalyer?"

"I don't know. Perhaps. Perhaps she was killed to put Cumberland under suspicion."

"What, kill someone to make someone else look guilty of killin' the first party?" Mrs. Lasher shook her head. "That's too clever for me, and too cold-blooded."

Miss Tolerance rose. "Cold-blooded it is. I am sorry—" she had remembered that Mrs. Lasher was in mourning, after a fashion. "I am sorry Mrs. Vose was killed."

"Well, it does you out a witness, don't it?" Mrs. Lasher said practically. "And we shall 'ave to wear black gloves 'ere. We was as close to family as I s'pose Josie 'ad."

Miss Tolerance curtsied. "Then permit me to condole with you, ma'am. If you hear anything more, you will let me know?"

"I suppose I will, though it seems to be a dangerous business, givin' information to you. Your Mrs. Smith's settled right in," she added, not at all off the topic. "Alice is teachin' 'er to mend linens."

At the door Miss Tolerance remembered a last question for the madam. "Was Mr. Beauville here on the night the chevalier was murdered?"

"You don't think *he* had aught to do with it? They was friends, and Beauville is such a well set-up gent."

"He and the chevalier were as thick as thieves, you said."

"Well, he wa'n't here," Mrs. Lasher said firmly.

"That is very helpful, ma'am. I need only to ascertain that he was not in any other of London's five thousand houses of joy. As I have my work cut out for me, I hope you will excuse me." Miss Tolerance curtsied; already Mrs. Lasher had returned to peering at her papers.

Miss Tolerance went down the stairs, enough absorbed in her thoughts that she did not, at first, realize that someone was calling her name softly. She looked for the source of the summons. It came from a little woman in a wrennish brown dress, who might have been the apprentice of the severely dressed woman Miss Tolerance had met in the house a few times. Only her bruises, and her toothless smile, made her recognizable as Betty Strokum.

"A word, miss?" Mrs. Strokum gestured down the hall with her chin, winced, and led the way until they stood just under the stair.

"You have something new to tell me?" Miss Tolerance asked.

"Only I want to know how long I got to stay here." The bathing Mrs. Strokum had been subjected to had scrubbed away a quantity of dirt and the worst of her unpleasant odor; her bruises were livid, but less spectacular than they had been the day before.

"They are not mistreating you?"

"I suppose not, if you don't count making me 'em their sheets. But it's dull as ditch water; can you believe when the girls ain't occupied one of 'em *reads* to the others? I can't chat up the gentlemen"—she wrinkled her nose—"because I don't come up to the standards of the establishment! How long do I have to stay here? You ain't turned Boyse in to no one yet?"

"Not yet. I need to make my case as convincing as possible. You have nothing else to tell me?"

"I told you all I have to tell." Mrs. Strokum shrugged and winced, looking sideways at Miss Tolerance in a manner ill calculated to inspire trust.

"If I go back to the Duke of Kent and speak with the barman there, will his story agree with yours?"

"Oh, 'im. 'E's got no reason to love me. God knows what he'll say."

Miss Tolerance felt her patience teetering precariously on the brink of outrage. "Mrs. Stro—Smith. If there is any detail, anything else you can tell me about Boyse's contacts on that night, I require the absolute truth from you. You've already been beaten—it might mean your life if you hold back from me."

Mrs. Strokum recoiled. "*You'd* not hurt me?"

"I?" Miss Tolerance said blankly. "Of course not. But another woman in this case is dead because of what she knew. I should dislike to find you had joined her. Tell me simply, without varnish: did you see Mr. Boyse speak with a Mr. Millward on the evening of the seventeenth?"

Startled by the force of Miss Tolerance's tone, Mrs. Strokum shook her head.

"I thank you. Did Mr. Boyse speak to *anyone* that evening?"

"The barman." Mrs. Strokum frowned. "You ain't asking about 'Keep it down over there, you' or 'Outta my way, damn your eyes,' are you?"

Miss Tolerance shook her head.

Mrs. Strokum closed her eyes; her tongue crept into the corner of her mouth.

"'E asked Jerry Conway about 'is boots," she said at last. "What polish 'e used to get 'em so shiny. And said a word or two to that bitch Molly Purse. A Frenchman come and said something to 'im, quick-like, but I never 'eard what it was. But those was all quick bits, not a long jaw."

Miss Tolerance felt a flush of excitement. Her voice trembled when she asked, "Can you describe the Frenchman?"

Mrs. Strokum shrugged. "Middlin' height. Light hair. Fancied 'imself a bit, I think: that nice in his dress, and his hair cut just so. Nothing so special about 'im but what he thought of 'isself."

Henri Beauville to the life. "And you heard nothing of what he said to Boyse?"

"Nothing. Frenchy pulled Boyse aside and muttered a few words in his ear, then off he goes, and Boyse come back to me like nothing ever happened. You don't think *that* was Millward, do you?"

"It would be very interesting indeed if he were, but I don't think so. If you saw the Frenchman again, would you recognize him?" Miss Tolerance asked.

"Aye, I would. But I won't risk my neck—"

"Then stay in your room while you're here," Miss Tolerance counseled. "The man I'm thinking of has been a customer here in the past. If he comes and you see him, get word to me at once. Your life may depend upon it, do you hear?" She was conscious of the melodrama of her words, but feared that anything less than fear for her life would not spur Mrs. Strokum to cooperate. The whore took Miss Tolerance's assurances at full value; when she left the room she looked both ways as she crossed the hall, as if to ensure that neither Beauville nor his agents could have crept in to the building while she was occupied.

M iss Tolerance took a chair to Manchester Square, deep in thought. Beauville knew Boyse? From what Mrs. Strokum said, the two men had not talked long enough for Beauville to have told the long story that Boyse said he'd heard from "Mill-ward." And Mrs. Strokum had spoken as though the men knew each other, but the Duke of Kent did not seem like Beauville's venue, nor John Boyse one of Beauville's regular companions. Which suggested—in the wake of her conversation with Sir Walter, Miss Tolerance was careful not to leap to conclusions—that their association was an irregular one.

And there was the question of Beauville and the fire in her cottage. The image of Beauville, watching the blaze from one of Mrs. Brereton's windows, came to her unbidden. Fire was no trivial threat in London; the Great Fire was still spoken of, stories passed from mother to child as a warning to be careful with the coals. If Beauville had something to do with burning her cottage, it suggested that he believed that she knew something which would endanger him.

Could the exchange of words at the Duke of Kent have been Beauville hiring Boyse to set the fire? When she thought the matter out, she discarded the notion: Beauville had spoken to Boyse on the seventeenth—the same evening she had been attacked. The fire had been two nights later, on the nineteenth. Why hire such a thing done on an evening when he himself was at Mrs. Brere-ton's? Had he wanted her dead? Was the fire meant as a warning?

The action of a Village Simple who loved the sight of a blaze? Miss Tolerance closed her eyes and envisioned the pile of table, chairs, ledger, her writing box—

An idea came to her with such force that she nearly upset the chair in which she was riding. Miss Tolerance apologized to the chairmen and sat back again. What if Mrs. Brereton had been, in some fashion, right, and the fire was meant to destroy something? Not a record of a past case, but evidence in this current one. But if that were so, it was evidence Miss Tolerance herself did not know she had.

The only things which had been burnt beyond recovery were her ledgers, two chairs, and her writing box, of which only the bottom panel survived.

Her writing box, in size and shape, closely resembled the box taken from the privy house in Half Moon Street, in which the chevalier kept implements for inflicting pain upon his sexual partners.

If I were a blackmailer, what a splendid hiding place that would be for my evidence! If I were the blackmailer's victim, might I know of the box but not recognize it and mistake it for the one in my cottage?

Miss Tolerance gave orders for the chairmen to turn back to Half Moon Street.

The d'Aubigny household, already in mourning, seemed haunted. The crowd which Miss Tolerance had formerly seen there was gone now; perhaps Anne d'Aubigny's arrest had satisfied their vulgar gawking; perhaps they had relocated to Farrington Street outside Cold Bath Fields Prison, to keep their morbid vigil there. The door was opened by Peter Jacks, the footman, who greeted her as a familiar of the household, and asked at once if there were any news.

"Nothing definite, but I am in hopes to have your mistress back with you in a day or so," Miss Tolerance was pleased to tell him.

"We're grateful, miss." Jacks looked down at her from the doorway with an expression of bewilderment.

"May I come in, Jacks?"

"Oh. Well, yes, miss. Only—" Jacks stepped back to permit

Miss Tolerance to enter. "There's no one to call upon. With Madam away, and the chevalier dead—"

Miss Tolerance apprehended Jacks' dilemma. "Oh, I have not come to call. I came to look for something which may help to bring Madame d'Aubigny home."

"What is it, miss?"

"Evidence, Jacks. Will you trust me to look about where I will?"

"I'll fetch Mr. Beak." In default of his mistress, Beak was clearly the one who would make weighty decisions. Miss Tolerance waited for a few minutes. The hall was chilly, and there was neither the noise nor the scent of a fire in either of the near rooms. What she could see was clean and in order, but Miss Tolerance suspected that the servants were spending most of their time in the servants' hall by their own fire, waiting word of the household's fate.

Beak, roused from belowstairs, had apparently struggled into his livery coat and attempted to tweak his collar into place; the top button was not fastened, and his hair was rumpled. Jacks followed him down the hall, watching his superior with concern.

"Good evening, miss. Jacks says you need to make further inquiries?"

Miss Tolerance nodded. "I need a word with Sophia if I may."

Beak signaled Jacks to find the mail.

"Perhaps I may use in the chevalier's office?"

From the expression which passed over Beak's long face, Miss Tolerance could see that intrusion into his late master's privacy troubled him, but concern for his present mistress's welfare won out. He nodded and led Miss Tolerance into the chevalier's office.

"Shall you have the door closed, miss?" The drip at the end of the old man's nose trembled. Miss Tolerance could not judge whether it was with indignation or excitement, and in any case she did not intend to indulge the manservant's curiosity or territoriality.

"I think so, Beak," she said firmly. "You needn't fear; we shan't disturb anything."

At that moment Sophia Thissen arrived, and there was a brief confused flurry of motion as Beak stepped aside to permit her to enter; Sophia curtsied to Miss Tolerance; Miss Tolerance inclined her head as she attempted to reach around the maid and ease the door shut. Beak coughed and stepped back into the hall, and Miss Tolerance pulled the door to.

"Pardon, miss, but how does Madam?" The maid looked anxiously at Miss Tolerance, as though she had been summoned to receive bad news.

"I saw her this morning, and I believe she goes on comfortably, although of course she wishes to be home with you all. You have not been to visit?"

Sophia shook her head. "Not since that night I brought her there, miss. It's an awful place; breaks my heart to think of Madam there." Sophia's affection for her mistress appeared to be quite genuine, but not quite strong enough to outweigh her fear of the prison. Miss Tolerance could hardly fault her for that.

"Sophia, the day that the constables came for Mrs. d'Aubigny, there had been some ado in the kitchen, do you recall? Someone had left a box—"

"In the privy house. Yes, miss, I recall."

"I need to examine that box. When last I saw it, it was in your keeping."

Sophie nodded. "Master's box," she said slowly. "When them men come to take Madam, it clean drove every other thought out of my head. But when I come home that night and smelt something—everyone'd forgot it. I cleaned it up and put it away." Miss Tolerance, remembering what condition the box had been in when last she saw it, nodded appreciatively.

"Please fetch it," she said firmly.

Sophie still appeared unwilling. "Madam said—"

"Sophie, I would not ask if I were not hopeful of finding evidence to secure your mistress's release. *Please.*" Miss Tolerance sought the maid's gaze and held it. "I know the use to which it was put, and I shall not speak of that to anyone."

A moment's thought appeared to decide the matter. Sophie nodded and left Miss Tolerance alone to examine Etienne d'Aubigny's office.

Aside from the painting of the late chevalier above the fireplace, there was little about the room to distinguish it from similar rooms in the homes of any number of well-off gentlemen in London, or indeed, anywhere else. A desk stood before the heavily draped window, its pen-box, sanding jar and inkwell lined up with military precision along the right edge of the desktop. There was one handsome cabinet containing three shelves of books which, by their look, must have been bought for the handsomeness of their bindings. Two armchairs faced each other in front of the fireplace, under the chevalier's painted gaze. Two smaller paintings of oddly proportioned horses at graze hung on the wall by the window. The effect was one of masculinity unleavened by any degree of imagination, a room seldom used.

As a matter of form, Miss Tolerance ran her fingers around the edges of each picture frame, but found nothing jammed there. She examined the books and found only one whose pages had been cut. Miss Tolerance had some experience of peculiar hiding places; it seemed to her that a cut book in a showcase library must have some significance, but a few minutes' inspection convinced her that the man who never read his books had not imagined hiding anything within them, either. She opened the desk drawers and found nothing more interesting than writing paper and a Bible. The last seemed so unlikely an object for the Chevalier d'Aubigny to possess that it immediately begged closer inspection. She pored over the book, going so far as to pry up the endpapers in case something had been hidden under them, but she found nothing. She ran her hands along walls and examined the floor, but found nothing resembling a safe or locked box in which the chevalier might have hidden blackmail evidence.

At last Sophia Thissen returned, apologizing for the delay caused by having to explain her errand to Beak, with the chevalier's box held in front of her as if it might explode. She placed the box on the chevalier's desk and turned to close the door behind her.

The reluctance with which Miss Tolerance examined the box had nothing to do with its smell, for it had been thoroughly cleaned, and now smelled only of turpentine and beeswax. It was the contents and their associations which repelled her. She found herself lingering over her examination of the exterior, running careful fingers around the edges of the box, checking for the catch of a secret drawer. Likewise she examined the carving on the sides. She found nothing more than a splinter in her finger, caught on a rough edge.

Miss Tolerance took a breath, stiffened her resolve, and opened the box.

She removed the scarves and the cat-o'-nine-tails and the six tiny pearl-handled knives in their case one at a time, arranging them carefully on the desk. There was another whip at the bottom, a few cords, and a fold of black cloth which, when unfolded, proved to be a domino—an old-fashioned masquerade mask. When the box was empty Miss Tolerance picked it up and shook it, but nothing rattled, nor did anything drop out when she turned the box upside down.

She examined the handles of the scourge and the whip, looking for sign of an endpiece she could unscrew or flip back to reveal a hiding place. There was nothing. Gingerly she replaced the whip on the desk and looked up. Sophia was watching with a solemn expression.

"Sophia, when the chevalier—" Miss Tolerance faltered, less from squeamishness than from lack of the proper vocabulary. "When the chevalier used these objects with Madam, was it you who cared for her afterward?"

The abigail nodded. Her mouth was pinched.

"How often—"

For a moment it seemed Sophie would not answer. Miss Tolerance was about to explain how vital frankness was to Madame d'Aubigny's case, but it appeared Sophie had arrived at that conclusion on her own.

"Not so much in the last while. When that—Mrs. Vose was with him, he didn't much bother Madam. And sometimes, if Madam was sleeping, he'd give up after a time if he couldn't wake her. That was one reason she took the sleeping draught. As for how often he and Mrs. Vose—you might ask *her*."

Miss Tolerance shook her head. "I cannot. She had her throat cut in an alley last night."

Sophia shrugged. "Not a surprisin' end for summat like her."

"You did not like Mrs. Vose."

"I didn't not like her. 'Tis as I said: when she was with him, Master didn't hurt Madam. But she did like to make out like she was summat more than a whore. Talkin' like she was better than us as keeps our knees together and goes about our business!"

The abigail put her finger to her lips as if she had just recollected to whom she spoke. After a moment, "Don't mean I'd wish her dead. Do they know who killed her, miss?"

Miss Tolerance shook hear head. "Someone went to a good deal of trouble to make it look as if a very great man had killed her in a passion, but I don't believe it."

"Don't you, miss? Then who?"

"I don't know. But as you say, such an end was not entirely surprising for such a woman as Mrs. Vose." Miss Tolerance turned her attention to the box. "Have you any idea how this came to be in the privy, Sophia?"

Sophia's round face flushed. She examined her knuckles as if an answer might have been written upon them. "I put it there, miss."

"It was your idea to do so?" Miss Tolerance's tone was carefully sympathetic.

"No, miss. Madam asked me to do it, that morning, after the constables left. Couldn't bear the sight of the thing, she said, and with Master dead there was no reason to keep it."

Looking at the objects arrayed before her on the desk, Miss Tolerance could not but sympathize with Anne d'Aubigny's impulsive act, however much she might deplore it as a stratagem. This also explained the widow's shock when the box reappeared in her kitchen in the hands of the goldfinder. But was not Mr. Heddison, apprised of any of this, likely to attach some sinister significance? Decisively, Miss Tolerance swept up the scarves, bonds, and implements and dropped them into the box.

"I must examine the box at my leisure," she said. "I will take it with me and keep it safe. I think Madam would probably like to have it out of the house."

For half an hour more Miss Tolerance took advantage of the peculiar freedom which Anne d'Aubigny's absence permitted her in the house. She visited the widow's bedchamber, in which a neatly arranged fire was laid, unlit, awaiting Madam's return. There was nothing of note to the room: bed, clothespress, writing table and a chair, a shelf which bore a few novels of an improving rather than a sensational nature. Miss Tolerance wandered from there up the stairs to the servants' quarters, which were in no way remarkable. Finally, with Beak hovering in the doorway, distressed by her lack of respect for the deceased, she went over Etienne d'Aubigny's bedchamber as she had five days earlier. Beak fairly quivered as he promised that no one had disturbed the chamber since her last visit.

"We've had more important things to think of, miss," he said dourly. Miss Tolerance restrained herself from pointing out that she was thinking of freeing Anne d'Aubigny from prison.

"Will you ask Jacks to call a hackney coach for me, Beak?" she asked instead. "My work is almost done here."

Beak left. When he was out of sight Miss Tolerance knelt by the fireplace. The bit of white stuff she had found wedged in the grate on her last visit was still there. As she took out her pocketknife and began to prize at it, she worried that perhaps this was all that remained of the blackmail proofs she believed d'Aubigny to have had hidden. What then?

With a slip, the thing came loose from the grate. Miss Tolerance, hearing Beak returning down the hall, pocketed the white object and her knife and was respectfully closing the door when Beak came to tell her that her coach was waiting in the street.

Miss Tolerance took up her Gunnard coat and the chevalier's carved box and rode back to Manchester Square with the box upon her lap. She had the coach leave her on Spanish Place at the side entrance to the garden, and entered Mrs. Brereton's house through the kitchen door. She proceeded to her temporary lodgings in the yellow room unnoted by any but Cook. If someone had set fire to her cottage in order to destroy a box he thought was this one, she did not want to tempt a similar assault upon Mrs. Brereton's house. With the box hidden and a good deal to think about, she went downstairs to ask a question of Marianne Touchwell.

"You know I will not tell you that," Marianne replied. "Mrs. B's most cardinal rule—"

"If it were not a matter of importance you know I would not ask it," Miss Tolerance answered earnestly. "But the man's alibi begs corroboration. If he was here, I'm sure he would prefer to have you say so and remove him from the list of suspects."

"And if he was not?" Marianne shook her head. "I do not stand upon ceremony, Sarah, nor follow rules to their letter unless I see a reason for it. And the reason for this," she continued, without giving Miss Tolerance a chance to counter her argument, "is that Mrs. Brereton has sworn that any of us who discuss the who, when, or how of her clients will be thrown out on the street. I've no ambition to find another house and a less pleasant situation for myself. If you say Mr. Beauville would like us to provide his alibi, I do not doubt it's true. Let him come and ask us in Mrs. B's hearing."

Miss Tolerance sighed. "Perhaps Lisette—"

"No." The voice came from the doorway of the small salon in which they were sitting. Hearing it, Miss Tolerance was distracted from her query by surprise and pleasure. It was Mrs. Brereton herself. She and Marianne were at once upon their feet, welcoming the older woman into the room and settling her by the fire. A shawl was arranged across her shoulders, another over her knees, and so much solicitousness expressed by both women that at last it appeared to oppress Mrs. Brereton.

"Enough," she said. "You were inquiring about one of our clients, Sarah?"

Miss Tolerance recalled the circumstances of her last conversation with her aunt, and the heated suspicion that lady had voiced then. "'Tis nothing of importance, Aunt. In my desire to see my own client cleared, I stepped over the line and asked Marianne for information which she quite properly would not give me."

Mrs. Brereton nodded. "Good girl." She acknowledged Marianne with a regal nod. "Now, you surely have something else to do? Go and do it."

With a look to Miss Tolerance which was eloquent of dismay, concern, and a little amusement, Marianne rose, curtsied, and was gone.

"That was surely a little abrupt, Aunt."

"I have said before, Sarah: since you have no interest in learning to manage this business, you have no reason to worry how I treat my employees." As if to take the sting from her words, Mrs. Brereton raised an eyebrow mockingly.

"As you wish, Aunt Thea. But are you certain you are well enough to be downstairs?"

"I am not only well enough, I should have gone mad with boredom if I stayed in my room one moment longer. I have no objection to giving Marianne a little responsibility—she did not do badly while I was indisposed, overall. But this is my house, Sarah. Never forget that. It requires my touch."

"I do not forget it, Aunt. I am delighted to see you downstairs." What pleased her more was that she saw none of the wildness which had characterized her aunt's expression in their last meeting. Other than the continued weakness on her left side, expressed in a slight limp, Mrs. Brereton appeared very much her usual self.

"I am pleased myself. Now, Sarah, you were asking about one of our guests."

Miss Tolerance nodded. "You need not tell me that I should not have asked. I will not—"

"What did you want to know?"

"If a Mr. Henri Beauville was a visitor here on the evening of the eighth of November, Aunt. But I—"

Mrs. Brereton shook her head. "Hush, girl, and let me speak. I have had some time for reflection in the last week, as you may imagine, and it seems to me that you . . . are right. I have been overly rigid in the past, and had I not placed more importance in my rules of confidentiality than in your discretion, poor Matt might yet be alive. Perhaps. In any case, I am prepared to amend my rule. You may not go to the girls or the servants for information, but you may come to me. If you can persuade me that it is in my interest to share what I know with you, trusting in your discretion, then I shall do so. Is this agreeable?"

Had King George suddenly appeared sitting opposite her, in full possession of his faculties and professing the infallibility of the Roman Pope, Miss Tolerance could not have been more surprised. And, after a moment, touched as well. She took her aunt's hand.

"It is altogether agreeable, Aunt Thea. I shall do my best to honor your trust in me."

For a moment Mrs. Brereton appeared moved. Then she drew

her hand from Miss Tolerance's. "There is no need to become tragic about the matter, Sarah. Now what is it you need to know about Mr. Beauville?"

"He told me he was occupied in a brothel that night, which gives him an alibi for—a crime I am investigating." In the face of her aunt's new generosity Miss Tolerance felt uncomfortable in her own reserve.

"I see." Mrs. Brereton thought. "If you will go upstairs to my room, in the bottom drawer of the wardrobe you will find several books, bound in black cloth, without stamping. If you will bring me the topmost?"

Miss Tolerance went at once to fetch the book. When she had returned and given it to her aunt, she resumed her seat.

"Sarah, you will promise me your most solemn oath on your honor—which I know you hold very dear—that you will never look into this or any other of my books without my expressed permission." Mrs. Brereton regarded her niece with great seriousness. Miss Tolerance was as serious as she gave the promised "On my honor." Mrs. Brereton opened the book and leafed through. Miss Tolerance had thought she was inventing a pretty fiction for Mrs. Lasher when she spoke of her aunt's ledgers, but it seemed she had unwittingly spoken the truth. Mrs. Brereton peered at the pages, running one finger down the first column.

"November eighth. He was—yes, he was here. With Lisette. He arrived at half past ten and stayed until shortly after midnight. Which was as well, as Lisette had a regular caller who came soon after. Beauville came without appointment—well, he has not been such a regular as to know how we like to do things here."

Miss Tolerance thanked her aunt seriously.

Mrs. Brereton closed the ledger with a snap. "I have one other request to make of you, my dear. In the event that something should happen to me—I am no longer a girl, and this stupid influenza seems to have frightened even Sir George Hammond into a state of rare concern!—will you promise me to destroy these books?

Miss Tolerance nodded.

"Well, then. I trust this gives you the help you needed?"

In fact, like so many things in this case, this new information came as both a blessing and a curse. When Mrs. Brereton's information was combined with Henri Beauville's own statement, it was clear that he had no alibi for the time of Etienne d'Aubigny's murder. However, if she was to keep her aunt's house out of the matter, Miss Tolerance could not use the information to free Anne d'Aubigny.

Sixteen

D oes this help you?" Mrs. Brereton asked.

"It does." Miss Tolerance was already trying to devise a strategem to convince Mr. Heddison of Boyse's perjury, all the while keeping both Mrs. Brereton and Mrs. Strokum out of the matter. It would take the work of four women—herself, Mrs. Brereton and Mrs. Strokum, and Anne d'Aubigny—to undo the mischief of one man; of course three of those women were of equivocal status and would very likely be assumed by the law, in the person of Mr. Heddison, to have lost their wits and honor along with their virtue. And the fourth woman could be set aside as having too much self-interest in the case to tell the truth. It would be better, she thought, if she could provide some masculine evidence for her tale.

Mrs. Brereton talked on unattended to, until a name caught Miss Tolerance's attention.

"I beg your pardon, Aunt?"

"I said the most enthusiastic teller of the tale appears to be that poisonous woman you showed some interest in last week."

"I was woolgathering, Aunt. Forgive me. Who? What tale?"

"Camille Touvois, whom you once styled my competitor. Did

you hear nothing of what I said? A woman has been found murdered in an alley, and it is being loudly asserted by La Touvois that it was Prince Ernest who killed her. I know that Cumberland is not much loved, and his politics are exactly opposed to my own, but this seems to me the—"

Miss Tolerance sat up, her attention fully upon her aunt. "But how did you hear all of this, ma'am? Mrs. Vose was only found dead in the small hours of this morning. I'm surprised Madame Touvois should know of it, let alone be circulating rumors."

"And I thought I would be bringing news to you." Mrs. Brereton tilted her chin up, piqued. "As to how I learned of it, I cannot say."

By which Miss Tolerance understood that Mrs. Brereton had acquired this *on dit* from a patron who had visited that day. With the suggestion of Royal involvement, and Camille Touvois's endorsement, rumors concerning Josette Vose's untimely end would be certain to have penetrated every layer of London society by day's end.

"So Madame Touvois is telling the world that Cumberland is a murderer? Whatever can her motives be?"

"Perhaps she believes it. Or perhaps she is just trying her power as an opinion-maker. I take it you do not believe the rumor?"

"I know that Mrs. Vose is dead. For the rest—" Miss Tolerance explained her understanding of the circumstances in which Mrs. Vose had been found. "Cumberland is said to be arrogant, but surely even he must balk at murdering his mistress and leaving her for anyone to find, with incriminating notes upon her person. To do so would move one from the realm of arrogance to that of stupidity."

"Perhaps one of his aides—"

Miss Tolerance shook her head. "Would hang out a shingle inscribed with his master's name and direction? Not with the regency question on everyone's lips and Cumberland's War Support Bill yet to be voted upon. There are so many better ways Mrs. Vose's body might have been disposed of; the Thames is a very forgiving receptacle."

"So it is. You think that someone wants Cumberland implicated? But what business is the matter to La Touvois? Perhaps if she was one of his castoffs—but she is not in his style at all. And he is too well known a Tory, and she too vocally liberal. The duke will be a very different man than I think him if he can brook contradiction from a woman."

"And yet His Royal Highness met Mrs. Vose under Madame Touvois' roof. She told me he came because he wished to understand the liberal mind, but I must say it looked as if he had come to choose a woman. It appeared to me that Madame Touvois had made sure a good number of women of pliant virtue were available to him."

"So Cumberland and Touvois were acquainted. And she procured a woman for him. She does not sound like an embittered lover; more a woman of business. That is not in itself a reason to accuse the man of murder; we who procure do not, in general, like to see our clients kill our employees or die themselves. It casts a pall upon business."

"I don't doubt it does," Miss Tolerance agreed.

"I should think, by that reasoning, that La Touvois believes Cumberland is the culprit, whatever your opinion in the matter."

"It is more her desire to spread her accusation about town that troubles me. I should have thought Madame Touvois far too canny to risk the enmity of a man with as much power as Cumberland."

"Perhaps grief for a friend?" Mrs. Brereton suggested.

"Perhaps," Miss Tolerance said. She did not much believe it. And what, if anything, did these questions have to do with the death of Etienne d'Aubigny? "Perhaps I had best go and make some inquiries."

Mrs. Brereton nodded. "Do, then. If you learn anything of interest I should be delighted to know what it is. If you can trust me with it, of course," she added pleasantly.

Miss Tolerance bent to kiss her aunt's scented cheek. "Do not stay downstairs for too long, Aunt. It would not do to tax your strength."

The fall of snow was thickening, and the night was dark; Miss Tolerance thought briefly of her breeches, boots and Gunnard coat—and her smallsword as well. She could hardly forget that she had been the object of two attempts in less than a week. But she could not reasonably be expected to gain entry to a drawing room in breeches and top boots, regardless of their warmth or defensive value. Miss Tolerance put a pistol in her reticule, bundled herself well while Cole summoned a hackney coach for her and at last asked the driver to set her down in Audley Street.

If Camille Touvois wished to appear as a woman grieved by the violent death of a friend, or her household as one in mourning, she had not considered the matter very thoroughly. Miss Tolerance found a small party in progress when she called upon Madame Touvois. The maid who took her coat appeared to find Miss Tolerance's appearance, unescorted and uninvited, to be a little shocking. For a moment it seemed she might refuse to escort this intruder into her mistress's sight, but Miss Tolerance overawed the girl with her best impersonation of bland assurance.

"Miss Tolerance, ma'am," the girl announced, and fled.

Madame Touvois was seated on a low-backed sofa, talking animatedly to an audience of men—no other woman had ventured out on so unpleasant a night—who stood around her in attitudes ranging from appreciative to adoring. She smiled equally upon all of them, speaking quickly and laughing often, clearly enjoying her power to captivate. The effect upon her of Miss Tolerance's name—and Miss Tolerance's self, as well, it must be assumed—was subtle. Miss Tolerance was certain that her hostess was vexed by the introduction of a rival into her circle, but Madame Touvois did not frown; she rose and extended her hand as if Miss Tolerance were an awaited guest.

"My dear Miss Tolerance! How pleasant of you to call upon us."

Miss Tolerance took the hand offered her. "Thank you for making me so welcome, madame. I trust I do not interrupt?"

Her hostess gave an exaggeratedly Gallic shrug. "What is there to interrupt? A few friends taking a cup of wine and discussing the news of the day. It is very cozy here by the fire. But what has brought you out on so inclement a night?"

"I came to condole with you upon the death of your friend, Mrs. Vose."

Miss Tolerance had not expected to see Madame Touvois flinch at the name; her estimate of the Frenchwoman's *sangfroid* was too high. Indeed, she did not flinch, but cast down her eyes in an impersonation of sorrow. "It is very kind of you, mademoiselle. It was a great shock to us all."

"Will you go into full mourning, or will black gloves do?" Miss Tolerance's tone was dry as dust.

Camille Touvois pursed her lips. "I have never much liked the dress of mourning, nor do I expect she would have wished us to depress ourselves with it. Ah, I was very fond of Josette."

Miss Tolerance was sure that, had she been able, Madame Touvois would have produced one or two tears: just enough to be effective ornaments, not so many that her powder would have been compromised.

One of the men who stood behind the sofa coughed softly. They, more than Madame Touvois, appeared troubled by Miss Tolerance's sudden arrival. Madame smiled equally upon her admirers but did not introduce Miss Tolerance to them, or they to her.

"Where are my manners? Mademoiselle, will you not take a glass of wine with us?"

She gestured, and a glass of Madeira was produced for Miss Tolerance. Turning her back on the gentleman, Madame Touvois linked her arm through Miss Tolerance's own and began a leisurely circuit of the room. It took them out of earshot of the men, Miss Tolerance noted. Did La Touvois have something to say which she did not want them to hear?

"I feared that I would find you prostrate over Mrs. Vose's death," Miss Tolerance said at last.

"Prostrate?" Camille Touvois sniffed. "My dear Mademoiselle, I was very fond of Josette, but extravagant grief is so . . . extravagant. I find it as unconsoling as wearing black gloves. Did you think to find me swooning?"

"You do not strike me as the swooning sort, madame. But I did fear that you might feel some complicity in her death. It concerned me greatly."

Madame Touvous stopped and turned to Miss Tolerance. However mild her expression, her gaze was acute. "How could *I* be complicit in Josette's death?"

"It was in your household that she first encountered His Highness, the Duke of Cumberland, was it not?"

"So? What do you suggest?"

"Nothing, ma'am. Not the least thing in the world. Only that I had heard that you believe Cumberland was the murderer." Miss Tolerance touched her lips to her wine glass. The Madeira was syrupy and overly sweet. "I wondered at the time how it was that Cumberland was a guest of yours. It seemed very unlikely. Surely he was not ever a connection of yours, madame?"

"You ask if Cumberland was my lover? I am still French enough to call a card by its face name, mademoiselle. No, he was not. I believe I told you, on that other occasion, that he came to see what the opposition had to offer."

"Offer in what way, madame?"

"Offer in every way, mademoiselle. Of course, I am always delighted when my guests form pleasant attachments."

"Or unpleasant. Which would seem to be the case, if Cumberland murdered Mrs. Vose."

"Can there be any doubt?" Madame Touvois' dark eyes were disingenuously wide and serious. "The poor thing, found with her finery rent, her throat cut, and a note from His Highness in her hand!"

"Damning. Perhaps a little too damning." Miss Tolerance put her glass down. The woman did not care whether Miss Tolerance believed her; she was aiming for a far broader audience, and clearly did not consider that Miss Tolerance could do anything to affect that audience's belief. "The matter has not yet appeared in the newspapers, and yet you seem to know all the details. I wonder how that happens?"

"My visitors, of course. Some are kind enough to tell me the latest news."

"Of course. And you were so fond of Mrs. Vose."

"Why should I not be? We got on well together, Josette and I." Madame Touvois smiled.

"And it prospered her," Miss Tolerance agreed. "It is a considerable jump, to go from being the mistress of a civil servant like d'Aubigny to a prince of the blood. You achieved quite a coup there, madame."

"The coup was entirely Josette's, Miss Tolerance. And look what a sad pass it has brought her to. But it might have been any woman. It might have been you, my dear."

"I don't believe so, ma'am," Miss Tolerance said coolly.

"Oh, but of course. *You* brought your noble lover down, did you not?" Madame Touvois smiled sweetly. "But if you had not been so foresighted, he might have brought you down instead."

Miss Tolerance regarded Camille Touvois without comment for the several moments it took to bring her emotions into check. The two cases were very far from being the same, she reminded herself.

"Are you suggesting that the Duke of Cumberland feared that Mrs. Vose would bring him down? Or—" Inspiration struck. "Or was it you he feared could do such a thing?"

With no perceptible change in her face, Madame Touvois' smile hardened from sugar to flint. "I? How could I do such a thing?"

" 'Tis an interesting question," Miss Tolerance murmured.

Her hostess had herself in hand again. "I shall not cry if this brings Cumberland down," she said. "How should I? Poor Josette died at his hand. But even were he guiltless, my sympathies are well known: I wear Whig colors. The thought of so deep-dyed a Tory as Cumberland controlling the destiny of this great nation is . . . repugnant."

"I do not care for the prince's politics either, but I would not wish a friend dead simply to keep him from the regency."

"You think someone arranged for Josette's death in order to compromise Cumberland?"

Miss Tolerance shook her head. " 'Tis too much. Why bother to bring down a candidate for the regency whom neither party is likely to support?"

Madame Touvois shrugged again. "To create chaos, I suppose. There are some who relish the disarray of powerful nations. Does that seem grandiose to you? Well, you are young, Miss Tolerance. You have considerable force of character, but despite your history I find you rather naive." She spoke the last word as if it were the *coup de grâce* after a long fencing match.

"I prefer to think of it as principled." Miss Tolerance was conscious of a sense of breathlessness.

A burst of masculine laughter from the knot of gentlemen grouped around the sofa startled both women. Madame Touvois looked toward the men and sighed.

"This is such a charming conversation that you have persuaded me to neglect my other guests, and that will not do. You have not yet told me, mademoiselle, what brought you to my house tonight."

"Indeed I did. I came to condole with you upon Mrs. Vose's death," Miss Tolerance said again. "And having done so, I will beg you to return to your other guests, madame. Thank you for the wine."

Miss Tolerance set her glass, almost full, on a table, and inclined her head. Madame Touvois put a hand on her sleeve and stopped her departure.

"But you have not told me, mademoiselle, how poor Josette's death is connected to that task which I believe you had undertaken: to find the killer of the late Chevalier d'Aubigny."

"That is simplicity in itself, ma'am. Mrs. Vose was involved with the chevalier, and now she is dead. How very convenient a thing for whoever killed the chevalier. For my part I dislike it very much when my witnesses die. It inevitably means more work for me."

Again Miss Tolerance inclined her head in lieu of a bow. This time her hostess did not stop her from leaving.

M iss Tolerance shouldered her way into the eddies of snow on Audley Street. What was she to do now? She had left Madame Touvois' rooms as she arrived, strongly persuaded that the Duke of Cumberland had not killed Josette Vose. Equally she was convinced that Camille Touvois meant to brew up as much scandal and rumor to the contrary as it was possible for her to do. Why? It was not impossible that La Touvois was simply trying her power, seeing how much trouble she could stir up. Her character appeared to be one which delighted in mischief: where Miss Tolerance believed her own testimony against the Earl of Versellion to have been a painful matter of principle, Camille Touvois clearly viewed it as a very good joke on established authority.

But the nation was at war, and playing practical jokes upon royalty and law served no purpose other than to give aid and comfort to the French and their enemies. Madame Touvois' lies should be stopped. However little Miss Tolerance liked the Duke of Cumberland's politics, she liked Bonaparte less.

It took some time to locate a coach to take her to St. James's Palace, and considerably more time to persuade the porter to call a footman who would take a note to Cumberland. She could not be certain that the duke would read the note, or that he would take the warning seriously if he did, but she felt she must try.

> *Your Highness*, she wrote.
> *I hope you will forgive my forwardness, and beg you will believe that I act only from a disinterested concern for the good of Crown and Nation. Rumors are being circulated in the city, implicating you in the death of a Mrs. Vose, who I believe was known to you. These rumors are not the inevitable murmurings of the London populace, but part of a deliberate campaign of whispers intended to blot the reputation of the Crown itself. I beg Your Highness will take measure to combat these rumors in the strongest possible way. If it is not stopped, this scheme can only cast the nation into confusion at a time when the war, and the question of Regency, depend rather upon clear thinking.*
> *Please believe me, I am*
> *Your respectful servant,*

She signed the note, sealed it, and gave it to the footman. She would have departed then, but the footman asked that she wait for an answer, if any. She sat in a small, barren chamber off the hall from the porter's room, which was not warmed by fire or cheered by anything other than a pair of chairs and a rickety table. Miss Tolerance sat, feeling her toes slowly go numb in the cold.

The door opened. The man who stepped into the room was very tall and very thin; Miss Tolerance had expected to see a footman or perhaps an aide. This was the duke himself. She bowed deeply.

"I have heard of you," Cumberland drawled. "From my brother Wales. He is much impressed with your enterprising nature, and seems to feel it quite overrules the questionable nature of your morals. I am not so impressed." Cumberland approached her, looking down. Miss Tolerance, tall herself, was not often looked down upon; she suspected the duke used his height to intimidate. She did not in the least wish to be intimidated; it occurred to her to point out that Prince Ernest was not always so particular in dealing with women of flexible morals—but she had not come to pick a quarrel with a member of the royal family. She set her features into a semblance of polite submission.

"I am sorry to have troubled you, sir, but I do believe the matter of considerable importance. Someone apparently wishes to implicate you in the death of—"

"Yes, yes." Cumberland waved a hand impatiently, acknowledging Mrs. Vose's death. "The rumors have begun anew. The populace cannot keep their grubby fingers from the coats of their betters."

"But it is not the populace—" Miss Tolerance began. Cumberland cut her off.

"My valet attempted to assassinate me, and the rabble insisted I had slain him. In the end, they could not touch me. As to this matter, I regret the woman's death. She was *obliging*." He dwelt upon the word with a peculiar emphasis which made Miss Tolerance think of the contents of the Chevalier d'Aubigny's wooden box. "A great waste. But I will not dignify rumors by responding to them. The populace can go to Hell."

"I felt it my duty to tell you what I had learned. What Your Highness does with that information is, of course, entirely your affair."

She could not leave until Cumberland dismissed her or left himself. It seemed clear to her that the audience was over, but Cumberland stood, looking down at her. From his expression, Miss Tolerance surmised he was trying to imagine what feminine shape might be hidden under her masculine clothing. It was an expression with which she had some familiarity; was he wondering if she would submit to an advance? Or perhaps deciding if persisting past her resistance would be worth the effort?

The minute or so during which Miss Tolerance submitted to this scrutiny was decidedly unpleasant. Then Cumberland nodded to her. "You have given me your message. If there is nothing more that you require to tell me, you may go. Unless, of course, you dislike to go out into the snow. I am sure we could find some place for you to weather the storm."

A number of barbed responses came to Miss Tolerance's mind. Common sense won out. She thanked Cumberland again for his patience, bowed again, and left. However gratifying it would have been to explain to His Highness the several ways in which his proposition repelled her, royalty was royalty, and a woman with her own way to make must practice tact. She stood for a moment in the falling snow, letting cold air clear her head. Then she went to find a carriage to take her back to Manchester Square.

M rs. Brereton's house was filled with custom, the snow having apparently an aphrodisiac effect upon a number of London gentlemen. The building glowed with light in the midst of snow, and Miss Tolerance was conscious of a grateful sense of homecoming. She made her way upstairs to the yellow room, where she rang for hot water and, after a moment's thought, brandy. Her visits to Madame Touvois and the Duke of Cumberland had left her with a sense of unease which even hot water could not entirely scrub away. Clean and clad in a nightshift, she poured a glass of brandy and climbed onto the bed with a writing board, paper and pencil to hand, and spent a quarter hour bringing her accounts up to date. That done, she took up a fresh sheet and began to make lists of what she knew, hoping to diagram what, if anything, connected Mrs. Vose's death to that of the Chevalier d'Aubigny.

She wrote on one side of the paper: *d'Aubigny's Death*. Immediately under that she wrote: *Josette Vose—visited d'Aubigny, failed to come to terms, left before midnight, working*. In parentheses afterward she wrote: *source: Mrs. Lasher*. Then she wrote: *Anne d'Aubigny—laudanum, asleep*. Which explained not only why she did not awake when d'Aubigny was murdered, but how she had slept through the hue and cry which followed the discovery of the body. *Source: A d'A; servants*.

She listed each of the servants: *Beak, Jacks, Mary Pitt, Sophia Thissen: all in their quarters at the rear of the house. Door locked upon retiring by Beak. Source: A. Beak. Mrs. Sadgett: in her own home. Source: servants' testimony*. And nothing she had uncovered gave any of the servants a reason to want their master dead. Miss Tolerance might think the man unpleasant, but servants often had to deal with unpleasant employers. Murdering the master was too drastic a solution for so common a problem.

Miss Tolerance chewed the end of her pencil.

Henri Beauville, she wrote. *With d'Aubigny earlier in the evening. At Mrs. Brereton's from 10 p.m. until half past midnight. Afterward? Source: Beauville, Brereton.*

Finally she wrote: *Camille Touvois.* And there she stopped. Her instinct was that the woman must be involved somehow—if only because she had ties to d'Aubigny, Vose and Beauville—but she had found nothing whatsoever to implicate her. Whatever games Madame Touvois was playing, they were too many and too deep to be easily discovered. Which might make her a perfect target for blackmail by Etienne d'Aubigny, Miss Tolerance reflected. If only she could find evidence that d'Aubigny had been blackmailing anyone!

A thought niggled at her; she got down from the bed and retrieved from the pocket of her Gunnard coat the white stuff she had prised from the chevalier's grate. Examined closely, it was a roughly triangular scrap of fine lawn, with a bit of white thread which might have been embroidery on one edge. It seemed a strange thing to find in a gentleman's fireplace; it was not a cleaning rag, although it was smirched with ash and soot. Alas, it told her nothing useful. She put the scrap into her wallet.

Turning back to her paper she wrote *evidence found on the scene: damned little.* After she had spent another half-hour staring at the paper Miss Tolerance sighed, put the paper and pencil aside, and retired to her restless bed to lie awake, listening to the distant sounds of venery, and pondering blackmail.

Seventeen

Snow in a great city creates an unaccustomed hush. Some of the usual sources of clamor—sellers hawking milk or blacking or silver sand—are inconvenienced by ankle-deep drifts. The clatter of wagon wheels on cobblestones is muffled; a soft whisking sound marks each corner, where the crossing-boys mar the pure snow, brushing it out of the path and mixing it with the unmentionable contents of the gutter. Miss Tolerance had lain awake for some hours the night before, her mind turning as her body attempted to rest. At last, lulled by the snow-borne quiet, she slept. She woke to find a fire, kindled in the grate while she slept, which made the room invitingly warm. It was only at last, and with reluctance, that she rose.

Miss Tolerance washed, brushed and put up her hair, and dressed in her respectable blue twill walking dress. It had not required Sir Walter to make her aware of Mr. Heddison's prejudice against her; there was little point in antagonizing the magistrate with reminders that she was not a respectable female. Better to be cold and successful in feminine dress than warm and a failure in top boots and greatcoat.

The Public Office in Great Marlborough Street was thronged with people of all conditions, albeit rather more of the meaner working class and the underemployed than their betters. The benches which lined the walls were already filled with visitors, witnesses and complainants, most of whom seemed to have brought children, livestock, and property of various ages, sizes, and degrees of cleanliness. The din was powerful; the smell only slightly less so. Despite the inadequacy of the heating (coals glowed sullenly in grates at either end of the hall) the room was uncomfortably warm, and highly redolent of human animal.

Mr. Cotler, the clerk who had been on duty on the night of Anne d'Aubigny's arrest, was in his place this morning. He wore the extremities of fashion approved by the dandy set: high collar points, large brass buttons on his blue coat, and a neckcloth tied in an elaborate, slightly grubby knot, as Mr. Cotler had apparently forgotten to wash his hands. His boots were shined, his hair pomaded, and his expression that of a man who feels himself superior to his surroundings. Miss Tolerance greeted him as an old acquaintance and requested a few words with Mr. Heddison. Cotler stared at her, clearly trying to recall who she was.

"You must see so many people every day," Miss Tolerance said sympathetically. "Will you permit me to remind you? I am the woman who accompanied Mrs. d'Aubigny's maid when she was brought in the other night. And I need very much to speak with Mr. Heddison."

Cotler shrugged. " 'E's busy, miss. Don't know that I can call him away from the business."

Hoping for a bribe, Miss Tolerance diagnosed. Well, it was her own fault for having paid the boy the other evening. "The matter I am come upon is business, too. Will this help to assure that my message is brought to him?" she asked, and slid a half-crown along the edge of Cotler's desk with one gloved finger. The clerk's gaze followed the coin's progress from left to right and back again; his own finger extended to take the coin. Attempting a fashionable wardrobe—even one bought secondhand—must take rather more money than Mr. Cotler's wages provided.

"Do you want to write a message out, miss? Or shall I just tell 'im what you have said?"

Miss Tolerance said that she trusted him to convey the sense of her message, and returned to the benches to wait a summons. It was not quick in coming. A number of people came and went as she watched, transacting business, making promises and threats, scuffling among themselves once or twice. Miss Tolerance gave up her seat to a woman far gone with child, who rested a toddler on her knee; mother and child stared into the hopeless distance with a gaze that did not include their immediate surroundings.

After more than an hour Mr. Cotler, who had risen from his desk half a dozen times since their conversation, waved Miss Tolerance forward. "Mr. 'Eddison's compliments, miss, and could you talk to one of the constables instead? 'E's very busy today."

Miss Tolerance shook her head. "Given the delicacy of my information I can speak only to Mr. Heddison. I am afraid I cannot trust his constables."

Cotler raised an eyebrow. "Not trust the constables? 'E ain't going to like that."

"I did not imagine he would. I do not like it myself. Please tell him, Mr. Cotler. Neither the day, nor my client, nor I am growing any younger waiting here."

Whatever Heddison's reaction to her second message, it was another hour before she was again beckoned forward.

"Secon' door on the left," Mr. Cotler instructed her tersely. She gathered, from his expression, that he expected her discussion with Heddison to go badly. Miss Tolerance felt some qualms herself, but followed in the direction Cotler's ink-stained finger had indicated.

Mr. Heddison sat at a large, well-ordered desk to the left of the door. Neat stacks of paper lined shelves on the wall behind him, each stack held down by a miscellany of rusty iron objects: bootmaker's lasts, bent horseshoes, a carpenter's wedge. Five straight-backed caned chairs were lined against the right-hand wall; none appeared to have been moved out for the accommodation of visitors very recently.

"Thank you for seeing me, sir." Miss Tolerance dropped a curtsy, which salute forced Mr. Heddison out of his chair to bow in return. As he had favored her with the response due a gentlewoman, Miss Tolerance was hopeful that his attention would be as respectful.

"I hope you will not need much of my time, Miss—er—" the magistrate said.

"I shall be as brief as possible, sir," Miss Tolerance agreed. "It has come to my notice that there may be some inaccuracies in information which I believe was brought to you by one of your constables with regard to the death of the Chevalier d'Aubigny."

"And how would you know that?" Heddison asked. His gaze had returned to a paper on the desk before him.

"I researched the matter," Miss Tolerance said simply. "As I have only one investigation to follow, it is perhaps easier for me to devote my entire attention to finding a witness such as Mr. Millward—"

The name Millward brought Heddison's head up. "I shall not inquire how you came to learn that name. Have you located him?" he asked. "Boyse has had very little luck, and I want to ask some particular questions—"

"I am afraid that will present some difficulties, as Mr. Millward does not exist."

Heddison looked at Miss Tolerance in silence for a full minute. "Just because you have not been able to locate him—"

"Not at all, sir. I have been told that Millward was an invention."

"Nonsense. My constable must have received his information from somewhere—"

"I think that the information must likewise be an invention, sir. If there is no Millward, whom would my client have approached to murder her husband? Have you not wondered how a woman like Anne d'Aubigny could be expected to find a man like Millward without causing considerable notice? The kindest construction I can put upon the matter is that Mr. Boyse was so eager to see my client convicted that he invented a bit of damning evidence."

Heddison's wide mouth thinned until he looked like a dyspeptic lizard. "You accuse an officer of the law—"

"I do, sir. I do not do it lightly."

"No more lightly than turn in a peer of the realm as a murderer," Heddison said flatly. He peered at her to see if his barb had struck home.

"No more lightly than that," Miss Tolerance said coolly. "My governess suggested that acting rightly would not always be agreeable, and I think I may say that I have proved her right. If you think Versellion's trial gave me any joy, Mr. Heddison, you are quite wrong. But on this present matter: Mr. Boyse claims, I believe, to have been approached by this Mr. Millward on the evening of November seventeen, between the time when you and he visited Mrs. d'Aubigny in Half Moon Street and the next day, when Mrs. d'Aubigny was taken in for questioning. I have witnesses who place him at the Duke of Kent in Oxford Street, in the company of a who—a woman known to be an intimate of his. The barman at the Duke of Kent remembers that he was there from half past eight to one in the morning, and says that no one approached Mr. Boyse there for more than a moment."

"That does not mean that this Millward could not have spoken to him before half past eight. Or later, after he left the public house."

"The woman Mr. Boyse was drinking with, and with whom he subsequently spent the night, was a Mrs. Strokum. He was with her until morning. The barman will attest that she was with him at the Duke of Kent. It was she who told me that Millward was an invention. She did her best to shield Mr. Boyse, sir, telling me at first that there was a man named Millward but that Boyse had never spoken to him—I think she meant to provide an alibi to your constable. Later, after Mr. Boyse had beaten her—"

"Beaten—That is quite enough! Can you prove any of this? I should have Boyse in to refute it."

"I can provide the barman and Mrs. Strokum, sir. She is in hiding just now, not caring to invite another beating by Mr. Boyse, who threatened to kill her if she gave any information about Millward or himself." She held up a hand to forestall another interruption. "Mrs. Strokum said that Mr. Boyse did speak to one man that evening, but only long enough to exchange a few words, not the involved story your constable told you. From her description I am quite certain that the man Boyse spoke to was a Mr. Henri Beauville, who was an intimate friend of Etienne d'Aubigny."

Mr. Heddison's mouth pursed. He stared at Miss Tolerance for a moment.

"What do you expect me to do with this information?" he asked at last.

"I hope you will see that your chiefest evidence against Anne d'Aubigny has evaporated, and you will secure her immediate release from Cold Bath Fields Prison. For the rest—I have the greatest respect for the magistracy and should dislike to have any of Mr. Boyse's transgressions become public. I leave that matter entirely to your judgment."

Heddison smiled sourly. "That's mighty kind of you. But even if you can prove any of this, it still does not remove Mrs. d'Aubigny as a possible murderer. What motive could Boyse have to produce such a fabrication?"

"You must ask him, sir. Or ask Mr. Beauv—"

With startling speed Heddison took up a walking stick that leaned against his desk and swept it in a furious arc. Miss Tolerance jumped back; her hand went automatically to her left hip for the sword she was not wearing. The head of the stick breezed past her and hit the door with a loud crack.

Cotler's head appeared in the doorway. "Yes, sir?" He appeared to find this mode of summons nothing out of the ordinary.

"Fetch Mr. Boyse in here. At once."

Miss Tolerance bit her lip, letting her racing heart slow.

"Did I startle you?" Heddison asked. "My apologies. Take a seat, if you will."

Miss Tolerance doubted the sincerity of the apology, but took a chair from those along the wall, pulled it before the desk, and sat. For the next several minutes neither she nor the magistrate spoke. It was not a comfortable silence.

The door opened and Mr. Boyse stood there, filling the space with his height and girth.

"Have you had any luck in finding your man Millward, Boyse?"

Boyse looked from Heddison to Miss Tolerance and back again. "What's she been saying to you, sir?" He stepped into the room until he was beside Miss Tolerance's chair. It was like having a furnace set beside her; his size and heat were palpable. Miss Tolerance was certain he meant to intimidate her with his proximity; she looked up at the constable, nodded coolly, and looked away.

"You will answer the question, Mr. Boyse. Have you been able to discover anything about this Millward whom you say Mrs. d'Aubigny hired to kill her husband?"

"Tried to hire, sir. He refused the job, if you'll recall. No, I h'ain't found hide nor hair of 'im. Vanished clear off the face of the earth." Boyse turned and smirked at Miss Tolerance. She smiled politely.

"Did your Mr. Millward give you any idea of how Mrs. d'Aubigny found him, or why she thought he would accept her offer to employ him as an assassin?"

Boyse shrugged. "Barman told her 'e'd be likely to do a bit of work for her."

"So there exists a barman who could testify that Mrs. d'Aubigny approached Millward?" Heddison asked sharply.

Boyse realized his misstep; if he could not find Millward, surely he should be able to find this barman. "That's what Millward tol' me, sir."

"And when you spoke to Millward—have you any idea at what hour the conversation took place?" Heddison asked.

Boyse shrugged. "Somewhere's between I was dismissed—round about seven—and midnight, I'd say. Of course, I'd have time to get myself properly pogy," he added confidingly. "Say it was p'raps ten or so, sir."

"And this took place where, this conversation?"

Boyse shrugged again. "As I said, I was fair mystified. Don't recollect the location. Somewheres in London."

Heddison nodded. The purse of his lips became more pronounced.

"There appear to be witnesses who state that you were at—the Duke of Kent?" He turned to Miss Tolerance, who nodded. "The Duke of Kent, that night, where you are well known, and left with a woman—"

"Betty Strokum told a tale on me, sir?" Boyse's menacing affability slipped. "She didn't ought to do that. Of course, you can't trust whores, sir." He turned and looked meaningfully at Miss Tolerance.

"Or barmen, Boyse?"

This appeared to confuse Boyse. "Barmen, sir?"

"Are barmen less reliable sources of information?" Heddison sighed. "How did you know it was Mrs. Strokum I meant? She was beaten the other day, and accuses you of—"

"What, beating her? Whores need a good thumping now and then, sir," Boyse said. "Wouldn't you say, miss?"

Miss Tolerance kept her eyes on Heddison, who was in no way as sympathetic to his constable's humor as Boyse seemed to expect. The magistrate turned to her.

"At what time did the barman at the Duke of Kent say Boyse arrived there, Miss Tolerance?"

Miss Tolerance took a notebook out of her reticule and paged through it. "About half past eight o'clock, sir."

"Eight o'clock? That would certainly allow a few hours for him to become inebriated, as he says. The question arises: where was he in the hours before that?"

"Was he not working for you?" Miss Tolerance asked with some surprise.

At almost the same moment Boyse leaned forward confidingly, as if hoping to convey some information to his employer without including Miss Tolerance in the communication. "When I brung you the evidence, your honor, we talked about my—my deereeliction of duty. That I stepped out on that 'ere assignment."

"And I had assigned you to—" Heddison paused, as if in recollection. "We did discuss it. Your dereliction started at what time, Boyse?"

The constable stared at his employer. "Beg pardon, sir?"

"At what time did you start drinking, man?"

"Oh. Maybe six of the clock, sir."

"And you never foll—got to the piece of business I had assigned you?"

Boyse's eyes shifted from left to right, from Mr. Heddison to Miss Tolerance. "No, sir. I went straightaway to drinking."

The men were speaking around a piece of information Miss Tolerance did not have. It was not a sensation she liked. "The barman at the Duke said that Boyse was not drunk when he arrived, sir. He arrived—" she looked at her notes again. " 'Sober and full of himself,' I was told."

Boyse put out his hand as if he might take the notebook from her, then thought better of it. The hand, his left, dropped to his side, just by Miss Tolerance's shoulder. Miss Tolerance felt unnaturally aware of the meaty hand so near to her. Uneasily she turned back to Heddison, to see what he made of all this. His expression was quizzical.

"Do you know Mr. Beauville, Boyse?" Heddison asked.

The warmth which had radiated from Boyse's body abruptly faded. Miss Tolerance looked up at the man and saw his gaze still fixed upon her. His smile looked like a mask behind which an animal was trapped. He did not answer, and the quiet in the room became both oppressive and communicative.

"Perhaps we ought to put all the cards upon the table," Heddison suggested. "Miss Tolerance says that there never was a Millward, Mr. Boyse. She claims to have testimony—from people who are readily available—to this effect."

Boyse turned his head and spat.

"If you cannot provide a better account of your whereabouts on that night, I will be forced to give more credence to her evidence. When you left my company on that evening your instructions were clear, and the only reason I absolved you of negligence in leaving off the task to which you had been assigned was that you chanced upon evidence in the case . . ." Heddison trailed off, looking at his constable with concern.

"I should very much like to know what this task was to which Mr. Boyse was assigned," Miss Tolerance said. Both men ignored her.

"I hope I have not been mistaken in you, Mr. Boyse. The law allows us some latitude in how we achieve justice, but where there is testimony to counter—"

Boyse, still standing uncomfortably close to Miss Tolerance, seemed to be on the verge of explosion. His pocked face was very red, and he rubbed his fingers together as if the friction might discharge his anger. She sat poised on the edge of her chair, ready to leap away from him if necessary.

"What, Betty's word? The word of a whore? I told her if she said anything I'd have her by the throat—"

"You beat her? A *witness*?"

"A witness? That drunken bunter? If I did beat her she'd never 'ave noticed it. They get used to it in your line of work, don't they, miss? Whores? Looks like you and Bet got more'n one thing in common."

Without volition Miss Tolerance found that her hand had moved to her cheek, where the shadowy bruises of her own beating were still visible. She looked up at Boyse with horrified fascination, and something slid into place in her mind.

"What hand do you sign your name with, Mr. Boyse?"

Both Heddison and Boyse looked at her as if she were mad.

"Your left, is it not? And you lead with your left, don't you, sir? Did Mr. Beauville ask that you beat me, or did you decide to do it on your own?"

"*What*?" Mr. Heddison rose from his seat, leaning forward over his desk as though he could not tell at whom to aim his outrage. "WHAT?"

Miss Tolerance could see Boyse's chest heaving under the red waistcoat he wore in imitation of the Bow Street constables. His large, square hands flexed at his side, nearer to her neck than she liked. She spoke to Heddison, but did not take her eyes away from Boyse.

"Was *I* the task to which you assigned Mr. Boyse that evening, sir? As you can still see, I was accosted and beaten that evening, and when I consider it, my assailant had a remarkably similar fist to that of the man who beat Mrs. Strokum. He was a very big man, and one who led exclusively with his left—as I am bruised on the right. Did you assign Mr. Boyse to follow me, sir? I cannot believe that you would have authorized a beating."

Boyse was almost glowing with rage. His hands flexed as he glared back and forth between his employer and his accuser. Miss Tolerance continued.

"I was followed from—from an interview in Balcombe Street. I was frankly tired and not so careful as I might have been. My assailant was well muffled against the cold and rain, so I could not make out his face. I am not sure if his object was my death, but it certainly seemed that way at the time."

"You're here, ain't you?" Boyse snarled.

"Allow me some skill at what I do, Mr. Boyse. Had I not been likewise bundled against the cold I would have had my smallsword out, and the ending would have been very different. You had a lump on the back of your head that was bothering you the next evening when you came for Anne d'Aubigny, didn't you, sir?" Miss

Tolerance's smile was calculated to enrage the constable. If Boyse attacked her, would Heddison make any effort to stop him?

"Did Mr. Beauville ask you to kill me? Was he afraid I would come too close to him?"

"He 'ad nothing to do with it!" Boyse bellowed. "I thought you'd caught a bloody eyeful. Thought you knew who was followin'. How was I to know you couldn't see my face?"

"You were about the law's business!" Heddison barked. "What could the woman have done but come and complain to me, and I'd have sent her away with a flea in her ear!"

"I just—she didn't—Christ, sir! Look at her! Whore. And wearing men's clothes. Her so full of herself, needed takin' down a peg. I—" Boyse choked.

"You don't like me," Miss Tolerance finished for him. "So you beat me—then went off to a public house where you were known, to establish the best alibi you could. But what did Beauville have to say to you that night?"

Boyse looked again at Heddison. Miss Tolerance thought he saw no help there.

"He just wanted to know what progress on the case—'e was paying me to tip 'im the gen because he was a friend of the dead. I tol' 'im I couldn't say just then. That's *all*, sir!" He turned to Heddison again.

"But you did tell him later?" Heddison asked.

"Aye."

"Told him what?"

"Only that we'd been to the widow's that afternoon and found this one with 'er. That she—Miss Tolerance—said summat about the doors bein' locked or unlocked. I don't recall precisely. That I'd followed her to some whore's place in Balcombe Street—"

Miss Tolerance drew in a sharp breath.

Heddison looked back at Miss Tolerance. "What?"

"The woman who was found dead in Cleveland Row yesterday morning, sir. With evidence incriminating a man of some importance. Until a month or so ago, she was also Etienne d'Aubigny's mistress."

Heddison sank back into his chair.

"I do not know what to make of this," he said at last. "There is too much—I must think about what it all means."

"Yes, sir," Miss Tolerance agreed. "But while you are thinking, I hope you will arrange to have my client freed from Cold Bath Fields Prison? I have exploded one piece of evidence against her, and provided you with a few new suspects."

Heddison shook his head. "I must hear from the witnesses of which you spoke, Miss Tolerance. I cannot release a prisoner on the say-so of—"

"Of, sir?"

"Of an interested party. As for you—" Heddison turned to Boyse. "If Miss Tolerance does not prefer charges against you for assault—wholly outside of your authority as an officer of the law—perhaps this Mrs.—" he turned to Miss Tolerance to supply the name.

"Betty Strokum."

"Perhaps this Mrs. Strokum will."

Mr. Boyse, who had stood mute and defeated since the revelation of Mrs. Vose's identity, leaned over the magistrate's desk to protest. Heddison, his cane still in hand, rapped sharply on the desk, which brought Boyse to attention.

"You have no one but yourself to blame for this, Boyse. Beating *women*—of whatever condition—who by the nature of their frailty should be most liable to your protection."

"What, her?" Boyse did not look at Miss Tolerance. "I should have bloody killed 'er when I 'ad the chance."

"But you did not," Miss Tolerance said.

The thought of what might have been was apparently too much for Boyse, who rounded on Miss Tolerance with a roar and would have taken her throat in his grasping hands had she not rolled away from him and come up, awkwardly, behind her chair. Miss Tolerance dimly noted Heddison roaring at his constable to stop, but she was more engaged in evading Boyse's attack. She picked up the chair she had vacated and used it to keep Boyse away, but Boyse grabbed the seat and began to wrestle the chair from her. Miss Tolerance was weighing her next action when Boyse suddenly dropped and curled up on the floor, keening. Behind him,

Mr. Heddison stood, red-faced, with the knob-headed walking stick in his hand.

"Thank you, sir," Miss Tolerance said breathlessly.

Heddison gave no reply, but banged the stick against the door again. Mr. Cotler appeared at once, and was instructed to send in Mr. Greenwillow and any other of his colleagues who should be in the house. Cotler took one look at the scene before him: magistrate with cane in hand, Miss Tolerance still holding the chair before her, and Boyse curled on the floor; whistled, and closed the door.

Mr. Heddison shook his head. "If assaulting the very people whose protection we have undertaken was not bad enough, it seems you have been taking money to relay the course of the investigation! I am saddened beyond my ability to say it."

Mr. Greenwillow and another man appeared in the doorway.

"Detain him. Assault and abuse of privilege," Mr. Heddison said curtly, indicating Boyse with a nod of his head.

Awkwardly, the two constables stepped forward and took Boyse by the arms. Boyse looked wildly a the two men. "Teddy," he implored his former partner. Greenwillow looked everywhere but at Boyse's face. As the three men started out the door Boyse glared at Miss Tolerance.

"You whore. You bitch. I should have kilt you."

"But you did not," Miss Tolerance said again.

M iss Tolerance left the Great Marlborough Street Public Office with a sour taste in her mouth. She had promised Heddison to provide Mrs. Strokum at her earliest opportunity, and to send the barman at the Duke of Kent to him as well, to corroborate her story. To her own mind Boyse had convicted himself, but if was not her mind which must be satisfied upon the score if Anne d'Aubigny was to be released.

Mrs. Strokum had to be persuaded with gold and assurances to leave the safety of Mrs. Lasher's house and call in the Great Marlborough Street Public Office. When Miss Tolerance explained how matters stood with Boyse, that he was in custody and unlikely to be released, Mrs. Strokum appeared very pleased, particularly when Miss Tolerance made it clear to her that the beating she had suffered was one of the crimes for which he was being held.

"Prefer charges? I should damned well think I shall!" Dressed in the dark stuff gown which she had worn at Mrs. Lasher's, the whore looked surprisingly respectable except for her bruises, and that lascivious toothless grin.

With only a little concern for what the magistrate would make of Mrs. Strokum, Miss Tolerance escorted the whore into his offices and left to walk to the Duke of Kent and inquire after the barman there. She was in luck: the man himself was behind the makeshift bar, indifferently polishing a stack of tankards. The afternoon custom was not heavy; a serving boy was engaged in swatting the flies that buzzed around the stew pot on the hearth. The barman did not at first recognize her. Once she had persuaded him that she was the same "young gentleman" who had come sniffing around for information about John Boyse, her luck stalled. The barman—his name was Joseph Dake—had no interest in making even a brief appearance before the magistrate.

"I'll lose my custom if they think I'd hare off to the authorities at every chance I get, to tattle on who's been drinking here the night before," he said flatly. "Not that I have any love for Boyse— good riddance to 'im, if they can keep hold of 'im, which I doubt."

"They can keep hold of him if you can attest that he did not arrive here on that evening until after eight. He has as near given himself up as—"

"Then why do you need me?"

Miss Tolerance shook with impatience. "There is a woman— young, quite blameless—in prison on false evidence that Boyse provided. The magistrate won't release her unless I can prove that Boyse could not have been at an unknown drinking house talking to an imaginary informant, because he was here, drinking with Betty Strokum."

Mr. Dake regarded her stonily.

"I can ask Mr. Heddison to keep your name from the public record—I cannot assure that he will do, but I can try. And—" she put a hand to her reticule suggestively. "You will be rewarded for your time, and for telling the truth."

At last Mr. Dake untied his apron and tossed it onto the bar.

"You, Jackie!" he called to the boy who had been swatting flies. "Take the bar. And mind you get good coin while I'm gone, or I'll tan your hide for you!"

Near dusk Miss Tolerance arrived at Cold Bath Fields Prison with a warrant for Anne d'Aubigny's release. She had sent a note to Mr. Colcannon and had expected to find him waiting there, but he had not arrived yet, and Miss Tolerance was too impatient to see her client released to wait. She was taken into the warden's office; he was delighted to arrange for Madame d'Aubigny's freedom—when Miss Tolerance recalled that her client had paid a week's extortionate garnish for the amenities of bed and board she enjoyed, but was being released after only four days, she understood his enthusiasm. And there were the exit fees to be collected as well. The warden held the warrant up to the lamp and squinted at it for several minutes, assuring himself of its validity. At last he bowed to Miss Tolerance and called for someone to take her down to Madame d'Aubigny's cell.

A warder, a fat, wheezing fellow, had been called away from his dinner and did not share the warden's enthusiasm for Mrs. d'Aubigny's release. He led Miss Tolerance through the odorous hallways, breathing heavily and muttering under his breath. When they reached the cell Miss Tolerance slipped some coins into the man's hand, which somewhat improved his mood. With a flourish of keys he opened the door and let it swing wide. He grinned, bowed, and stepped back to let Miss Tolerance enter first.

The widow, sitting in near-dark, looked up anxiously as the door opened. It appeared to take her a moment to recognize her visitor. Then she rose to her feet and extended a hand in supplication.

"Miss Tolerance, have you any new word for me?"

"The best in the world, ma'am," Miss Tolerance said. She smiled broadly. "You are released."

"Now, missus, if you'll just let me unlock your fetters?" The gaoler got laboriously to his knees. "That's right, ankles first.

Good. Now them bracelets? Fine." Wheezing a little more, he got back to his feet. "Shall I send a boy in to carry out your trunk? Thank you, ma'am." He left at a brisk waddle, jiggling the coins Miss Tolerance had given him with one hand and his set of keys with the other.

Anne d'Aubigny looked around her uncomprehendingly.

"We should pack your things," Miss Tolerance suggested gently. "I would not trust anyone here to do it."

"Oh. No. Of course." Madame d'Aubigny did not move. "Free? Where are they taking me?"

"I am taking you home. Back to Half Moon Street. The evidence against you is exploded, ma'am. Even Mr. Heddison's suspicious nature could not stand against our witnesses."

"Then they have found someone else? Someone who killed Etienne?"

"Not yet. I don't think his investigation has gone that far." Miss Tolerance had begun to gather up the widow's personal items from around the room and pack them into the trunk. "I suspect Mr. Beauville, and have made Mr. Heddison a present of some suspicious information regarding that gentleman. But my first aim has been to secure your release. Now I shall have time to dig more deeply into the fellow's life."

"But—Josette can surely tell you—Mrs. Vose, that is—"

Miss Tolerance shook her head. The widow, of course, would not have heard this news. "I am very sorry. I know you had some regard for her. Mrs. Vose is dead."

Madam d'Aubigny sank back on the chair by the window.

"I am sorry," Miss Tolerance said again. "But—here is the boy for your box." Miss Tolerance cast a quick eye around the cell for any stray belonging, but nothing remained. She paid the boy to take the box to the prison gate and guard it until she could find a hackney carriage to take them back to Half Moon Street. Then, her sympathy mingled with impatience, she drew Anne d'Aubigny to her feet and helped her into her coat, arranging the fur collar around her chin. The widow allowed herself to be led like a child through the halls and down to the prison gate, where they found William Colcannon and the warden himself, who had come out to shake her hand and congratulate her on her release. The warden's cheer had doubtless been increased by the fact that Colcannon had paid the exit fees while waiting for his sister.

"I shan't ask you to come and visit us again," he said cheerfully. "There's many that do, but I don't suppose one like you will! Well, Godspeed, madam!"

Eighteen

The ride back to Half Moon Street was a mixed triumph. Miss Tolerance, full of pardonable pleasure at her victory, had imagined her companions would join in her enjoyment. Mr. Colcannon did; he was almost puppyishly delighted by his sister's release. But Anne d'Aubigny was as subdued as one who has sustained a final, finishing blow. Perhaps, Miss Tolerance thought, her look of sad bewilderment was owing to the shock of sudden release following hard upon the stress of incarceration and, before that, of her husband's ugly death. The cramped quarters of the carriage prevented Miss Tolerance from taking Mr. Colcannon aside to suggest he temper his joy until his sister had more stomach for it. He, finding his expressions of pleasure met with silence, gradually slipped into sullen quiet.

The carriage had reached Picadilly when the widow spoke.

"Do you think it was Josette?"

"I beg your pardon?"

"Did *Josette* kill my husband?"

"I do not think so," Miss Tolerance said. "You did not use to think so either. Has something changed?"

The widow shrugged. "She is dead. That would be an end to it. I should so much like there to be an end to all of this."

"I understand." Miss Tolerance reached out to pat Mrs. d'Aubigny's slight hand. "But a false solution is really no solution at all. I think I must look a little closer at Mr. Beauville—"

"But he was Etienne's friend! And Josette, she endured all of Etienne's—" her glance flicked to her brother, who was looking out the window sulkily. "His habits. Perhaps she could not tolerate any more. She called upon him only a day or so before he died, you know. Perhaps—"

"Mrs. Vose was paid to endure, as you put it. When your husband no longer could pay her, she ceased to visit. But that is a curious thing . . ."

"What is?" In her widow's black Mrs. d'Aubigny, slumped into the seat opposite Miss Tolerance, was almost invisible.

"Mrs. Vose admitted calling in Half Moon Street the night of the murder, but denied making a visit on the day before."

"But she would deny it if she had murdered him, would she not?"

"A visit at a time unconnected to the death? I can think of no reason for it. This visitor: are you certain it was Mrs. Vose, ma'am?"

Madame d'Aubigny shook her head. "I heard someone below, and Sophia told me Mrs. Vose had called for my husband."

"So you did not see her yourself?"

"No." Her face lit with inspiration for a brief moment. "I know it was her, for she was wearing a cloak of mine I'd given her, brown wool banded with black sable."

"I see." Miss Tolerance felt a moment of annoyance; each time she thought she had the end of the question in sight, some new obstacle loomed up. Mrs. Vose's call upon the chevalier might have nothing to do with anything—except that the woman had denied it.

"I am so tired, I cannot bear much more of this," Anne d'Aubigny said tearfully.

Mr. Colcannon, called out of his sulks by his sister's obvious distress, turned to comfort her, clucking as comfortingly as a nursery maid. Miss Tolerance turned away to look out the window.

Miss Tolerance only stayed a few minutes in Half Moon Street. Mrs. d'Aubigny, greeted with subdued acclaim by her staff, was bustled off to her salon with Mr. Colcannon following after. Miss Tolerance stopped Sophia Thissen for a brief word; the maid confirmed that she had told her mistress that Mrs. Vose had called upon the master—because she had recognized Madam's cloak, and because Jacks had said so. When she had given this information Sophia bustled off to minister to her mistress; Miss Tolerance suspected there would be a struggle for dominance between Sophia and Mr. Colcannon, and would have laid her money on Sophia.

When she turned to leave it was Jacks himself who stood ready to open the door.

"Mr. Jacks, I understand that a woman called upon your late master a few days before his death?"

The footman stood with a gloved hand upon the door latch. "A woman? Yes, miss, I recollect it."

"And you are certain it was Mrs. Vose?"

Jacks frowned. "Certain, miss? How should I be certain? That was the name she give me."

"I could give the name Queen Charlotte at your door, Jacks, and you would not believe it." Miss Tolerance smiled to take the sting from her words.

"No, miss, of course not. Mrs. Vose had a veil wrapped round her bonnet, so I didn't see her face, but I recognized the cloak—"

"The cloak. I see." Miss Tolerance had begun to hate this inoffensive piece of clothing.

"To tell the truth, miss—" Jacks looked over Miss Tolerance's shoulder as if to see if Beak were in earshot. "I didn't inquire too deep when Master had female visitors. But how shouldn't it be that Mrs. Vose? That was the name she give, and master didn't scold me for giving the wrong name. 'E would have done, you know. He never kept back ringing a peal over your head."

Miss Tolerance nodded. "Did you mention this visitor to Mr. Heddison and his constables?"

Jacks shook his head. "I didn't think to, miss. Nor 'e didn't ask."

Miss Tolerance thanked him and descended into the evening street.

In Manchester Square Miss Tolerance begged a cup of soup from the kitchen before she retired to her room. A lavish supper was generally laid out in one of the parlors later in the evening, but she had no particular desire to mix with Mrs. Brereton's customers. After dining with cordial informality in the kitchen, watching Cook put the final touches on an elaborate tower of French pastries, Miss Tolerance took the back stairway upstairs, balancing the inevitable teapot, a taper, and a tray of little cakes, and settled in to darn stockings. She found this homely activity remarkably useful for focusing the mind.

After the stockings, Miss Tolerance took up her other mending, and was occupied for nearly an hour. As she repaired a tear in the lining of her Gunnard coat, tucking the raw edge under and whipping a row of tiny stitches to finish the edge, an idea began to stir in her. Finished, she hung up the coat, put away her workbag, and took down from the wardrobe the box she had removed from the d'Aubigny house. The box's contents still gave her a frisson of distaste, and she thought perhaps she had not looked as closely at it on her first inspection as she might have done. Now she sat on the bed next to the box on her knees, took her candle in one hand and examined the exterior of the box closely, running her fingers along its carved surface, seeking anything like a catch or secret drawer. A quarter hour of diligent inspection produced nothing.

Miss Tolerance poured herself another cup of tea, then opened the box. The contents she removed one by one, with close inspection. With each handling the flail and bonds and other paraphernalia grew more repugnant—perhaps, she reflected, because with each handling she imagined a little more about their use. With the contents in a pile beside her, she pressed against the inside and outside of the box's floor, but there seemed no room for a drawer or false bottom. The red silk lining was worn and spotted, as she had previously noted. She tested the join between lining and wood along the top with one fingernail, but found no separation.

However, the fabric on one side wall rustled when she pressed it. Had it done so the last time she looked at it? Why had she not looked further? Because the fabric was old, because she had been looking for a *device*, something crafted as a hiding place. Miss Tolerance pressed again; it seemed there was something between the lining and the box's wall, but the upper edge was firmly glued in place and showed no sign of recent tampering. The bottom edge disappeared into the join with the padded lining on the bottom. Carefully Miss Tolerance probed at the velvet, running her fingernail along the bottom edge of the inside wall. The fabric wrinkled slightly. She pried more urgently and a loose thread appeared. With a little more pressure several threads—the edge of the velvet—pulled out from the corner where they had been tucked. Excited, Miss Tolerance made herself work carefully: the space was only a few inches long and very narrow; in order to find and extract the paper which was hidden underneath she had to go slowly.

Before she opened the paper Miss Tolerance reminded herself that the box was old, and that what she had found might well be a love letter from another generation.

There were two papers, flimsy and creased but unyellowed. Miss Tolerance unfolded the first of them and laid it flat; she put the box to one side and surveyed her find with mounting excitement. The note was written in French.

B—
   You are right. Public opinion will not suffice to control Pr. E. He is not much loved, but there is a difference between lack of love and his utter discredit. Tell S that if he cannot provide some way to embarrass his master, he will force me to move against his family in Corsica—that should provide ample motivation. If S can give us nothing useful, we may have to take the more drastic course. R wishes it done soon, before more support for W can be rallied. A day or two will decide it.

C

What was she to make of that? Who were B and C? Pr. E? S and R? She took up the second sheet. It was written in a different hand, and in English. This was dated the twentieth of October, only a fortnight before d'Aubigny's death.

CVT—
> *I have hit upon another plan to deal with Pr. E as you would like, but I shall have to rely upon you to bring him to the point. You may tell him you have several women who might be suitable to his taste, if only you can get him here. If he complains of the company, tell him to stop his nose and come anyway. I believe I can persuade J to break with hers—he has been entirely uncooperative in providing information, so is small loss to us—and she would be the very thing for our purpose. When she has Pr. E in her toils we can manage the affair to your pleasure.*

It was signed *B*.

Miss Tolerance stared at the letter for a few minutes, then laid the two pieces of paper out before her. Here was high treason, spread across her counterpane. Certainly it would have made excellent leverage for blackmail. And quite certainly it was an excellent motive for murder.

The hour was late, but Miss Tolerance took up pen and paper, wrote a short note to Mr. Heddison, and folded the two papers into it. This packet she entrusted to Cole for immediate dispatch to the Great Marlborough Street Public Office. Then she dressed and asked Keefe to call a carriage to take her to Audley Street.

The windows of Camille Touvois' rooms were lit to a dull glow in the dark of the quiet street. Miss Tolerance paid the carriage driver and stepped up to the door. She could not be certain what she would find upstairs—although from the quality of the light above it appeared that Madame Touvois was not entertaining tonight. Miss Tolerance had dressed for a confrontation, in breeches, boots and coat, with her sword in its hanger on her left hip. She entered the building and climbed up to La Touvois' rooms on the second floor. No one answered her knock. Miss Tolerance knocked again and listened for the approach of a servant.

After a moment she realized that there was no sound at all; not of maid or footman coming to the door, not of voices in conversation. She pushed on the door. It was unlocked and unlatched, and swung halfway open. Miss Tolerance, considerably piqued, entered, on her guard.

The rooms were empty. As she had noted from the street, candles were lit in each room; they were not more than an hour burnt down. Miss Tolerance advanced through the first and second rooms and came at last to Madame Touvois' bedchamber. There was no one there. Most of the furnishings were in place—tables and chairs, rugs dotting the polished floors—but the personal belongings were gone. The wardrobe doors hung open with nothing inside. Across the back of a chair a brown cloak was draped; there was no other sign of an occupant.

Madame Touvois had run, and very recently, but left the rooms with candles burning, to give the impression that she was still in residence. Silently damning her luck, Miss Tolerance continued to prowl through the rooms, looking for a clue to where the woman might have gone. Her servants might know, but by the time Miss Tolerance found them, Camille Touvois was likely to have disappeared beyond recovery.

From one of the outer rooms there was a noise. Miss Tolerance turned, hand on the hilt of her sword, as a masculine voice called out.

"Camille! Devil take it, where are you?"

Miss Tolerance stepped into the front room, hand still on her sword hilt, and bowed ironically to Henri Beauville.

"A very good question, sir. I don't suppose you know the answer?"

In the silence of the moment, several emotions appeared to pass over Beauville's face: surprise, apprehension, and, at last, amusement. His blue coat was spotted with rain; his sugarloaf hat he carried in the crook of his arm. He spoke to her, but his gaze went from one side to the other.

"It appears, mademoiselle, that she has left us both."

"Indeed it does, sir. May I ask what brings you here?"

"I came—" He appeared to consider what was wise to tell her.

"I came to reclaim something of mine that Madame Touvois was . . . holding for me. And to give her some news I thought she would be glad to know."

"It appears that she had already heard your news, sir. If what you meant to tell her was that Mr. Boyse was in custody and had implicated you—and thus herself—in the plot to incriminate Anne d'Aubigny."

Beauville stared at her blankly, then began to laugh. "A plot to incriminate the little widow? Is that what you thought?"

"There is more, of course," Miss Tolerance said coolly. She watched Beauville closely; his face was turned to her, but his eyes were moving around the room. Seeking something, she thought. Seeking something very urgently.

Public opinion will not suffice to control Pr. E. The words danced in her memory. The note had been addressed to "B."

"You will not find the letters here, Mr. Beauville. Were you working with Madame because she was blackmailing you, or did she keep the letters as insurance of your continued loyalty?"

Beauville's eyes snapped to Miss Tolerance. His laugh was hard and without humor. "What do you think?"

"I think, sir, that Madame Touvois was working for the French as a spy, and that you were her cat's-paw. I think that Etienne d'Aubigny learned of Madame's plots against the Duke of Cumberland—I presume to discredit the War Support Bill and his bid for the regency?—and was blackmailing *her*. Did you kill d'Aubigny for the letters?"

Beauville took a step backward. "You don't know—"

"Oh, I think I have at last pieced it together, sir. You will tell me where I err, of course. Madame Touvois was a spy, and had been given the task of discrediting the Duke of Cumberland. She threatened Sellis, the duke's valet, with harm to his family in Corsica if he did not brew up some scandal—we know how that turned out. And then she needed some other plan. So poor Josette Vose broke with d'Aubigny a-purpose to seduce Cumberland. And you throttled her, did you not? Was the plan always to murder her and attempt to pin the blame upon Cumberland?"

"You cannot prove it," Beauville said hoarsely.

"Perhaps you should sit down," Miss Tolerance offered. "I

would suggest a glass of wine, but it appears that Madame took all with her."

Beauville again looked around the room.

"You may search the entire of the apartment, sir. You will not find the letters Madame Touvois wrote to you."

"The Devil," he muttered. "You have them?"

"They are safe," Miss Tolerance said noncommittally.

"Where were they?"

"In the chevalier's box. The one we spoke of."

Beauville stared at her for a long moment, then began to laugh so hard that it appeared to Miss Tolerance that he was in danger of choking. "The box. The bloody box. And I was too dainty to look inside!"

"They were indeed very well hidden," Miss Tolerance said sympathetically. "It took me some time and diligence to discover them."

"I congratulate you. I suppose you will find it necessary to give the letters over to the authorities?" Beauville's tone was pleasantly regretful. His eyes did not leave her face.

"I have already done so." Miss Tolerance's tone matched his. "I know that you attempted to burn my house down, and me with it. I believe that Mr. Boyse's attack on me was his own idea—"

Beauville gaped at her.

"He admitted as much to Mr. Heddison, who I suspect is eagerly looking for *you*, sir."

"Bitch," Beauville said, low. "Christ, which of you is the worse? At least Camille was as honest as a woman can be. She was vicious and made no secret of it. She enjoyed having power and she enjoyed using it. And—"

"And it appears that she has left you to bear the blame and take the punishment. High treason in a time of war. If you wished to lose your head, sir, you might as well have stayed in France."

Beauville paled for a moment, then recovered himself. "You speak metaphorically, mademoiselle. England does not use the guillotine."

"No, sir. But hanging leaves one just as dead. I do hope the money you and Madame Touvois realized was worth your life." Miss Tolerance kept her eyes on the man's face. He was again looking over the shoulder; likely calculating how much force would be necessary to push past her and make his escape. She put her hand lightly on the hilt of her sword.

Beauville shook his head. "I made a good sum, of course. Camille did better, but it was never a matter of money for her."

"What, then? Loyalty to la Belle France? I should not have thought it of her."

"Loyalty? Camille? *Control*. This employment gave Camille the upper hand with a number of powerful men; she could make them dance to her tune. She enjoyed that." Beauville smiled. "But I see you have a sword, mademoiselle. I hope you will not think to use it on me."

"Only if you plan to escape, Mr. Beauville." Miss Tolerance returned his bantering tone, but did not take her hand from her weapon.

"I should hate to have to offer violence to a lady, however peculiarly dressed." Beauville had shifted his stance, moving to the balls of his feet as if poised to move suddenly in one direction or the other. Miss Tolerance altered her own stance. "You are intrepid, my dear. I should hate to kill you."

Miss Tolerance nodded. "Indeed, sir, I should hate to—"

She had no time to finish. Beauville rushed at her, clearly intending to startle her into dropping back, giving him a clear path to the door, the street, and escape. She did not oblige. With the distance between them so small, Miss Tolerance had not room to draw her sword; instead she ducked under the path of Beauville's attack, head down and right shoulder lifted, forcing the man to roll forward over her back, landing with a painful thud behind her. Miss Tolerance spun around and stepped a few paces ahead of Beauville as he scrambled to his feet, putting the door to the street behind her again.

Beauville was panting, more from surprise than exertion. Miss Tolerance had drawn her sword and held him *en garde*. He eyed the point of her blade, which hovered on a level with his heart.

"That was not what I expect from a lady," he said at last.

"But I am no lady," Miss Tolerance scoffed. "I hope you will not force me to more unladylike behavior."

Again Beauville looked toward the door beyond Miss Tolerance's shoulder, and then back at her blade.

"I do not suppose that you would yield to bribery?" he asked politely. "No, I suppose not. It seems we are at a standstill."

"Do you think so, sir?" Miss Tolerance stepped in, the point of her blade rising until it just touched the folded linen of Beauville's neckcloth. Beauville did not look down, but kept his eyes upon Miss Tolerance's face, compelling her own gaze to meet his. Then his eyes flicked over her shoulder and widened in surprise. Miss Tolerance's own eyes went for a moment to the side.

Beauville swept her blade aside with his left hand, stepped back, and drew his own blade. He had cut the meaty outer edge of his hand in throwing off her sword, but he ignored the welling blood of the wound and made his attack upon her.

Miss Tolerance found herself on the defensive for a moment, parrying rapid thrusts to her shoulder and hip and beating his sword away from her own throat with a determined hand. Then she returned the attack. Beauville was a flashy fencer who could not resist flourishes Miss Tolerance had long ago discarded from her own style as extraneous. The overall effect was an ornamented style with less power than precision. Still, he was strong and, over the course of the first few exchanges, abandoned the notion that his opponent would offer no challenge. Beauville made a series of thrusts to Miss Tolerance's shoulders—left, right, right—which she parried easily. She made her own cut to his right shoulder, was parried, and thrust to the left. He beat her sword away and thrust for her throat, stepping sideways in a circle which would have put him again closer to the door. Miss Tolerance, to counter him, threw his blade off to the left and stepped right, again interposing herself between Beauville and the door.

They broke for a moment, breathing heavily. The fluted cuff of Beauville's shirt was soaked with blood from his initial injury. He looked at the wound thoughtfully. "May I bind this up?"

"Certainly, sir. If you put your weapon up," Miss Tolerance said politely.

"That is hardly sporting, mademoiselle."

Miss Tolerance's smile hardened. "I do not fence as a gentleman's sport, sir. If I draw my sword it is in earnest. Nor will appeals to womanly delicacy help you; I should prefer not to kill you, Mr. Beauville, but if I must do so I shall."

"Kill me, Miss Tolerance? Do you really think you could?"

"I have killed a man, sir. 'Tis not an accomplishment I prize, but I am a practical woman."

"Ladies and their accomplishments! It appears that your life has been far more exciting than mine," Beauville said dryly. He bowed and returned *en garde*.

Poised upon the moment, both fencers hesitated. Then Beauville moved to attack, mixing thrusts with sweeping cuts with a speed which allowed Miss Tolerance no time for thought, only instinctive response. She parried each cut economically, beating a cut to her hip away strongly; she thrust, and caught her blade along Beauville's side. He reeled away from the scratch and, enraged, slapped the flat of his blade against Miss Tolerance's left arm. It stung like a whip. Miss Tolerance pulled her blade back, out of the entangling folds of Beauville's coat, and shook her left arm, which was numb with pain. For his part, Beauville gingerly tested the wound on his side with his bloodied left hand.

"We must finish this," he said. He had abandoned amused condescension. "Give way or I will kill you."

Miss Tolerance shook her head. "I regret I cannot, sir."

"Very well." Beauville swept a cut at her head; Miss Tolerance parried and returned the cut with one to his shoulder. Beauville danced to the side, seeking to maneuver Miss Tolerance away from the door. Miss Tolerance stepped in to his attack and kept herself between him and his escape. When one of the rugs rucked beneath her feet Miss Tolerance kicked it blindly away. Beauville was distracted for a moment, then snapped his eyes back to Miss Tolerance's face. He swung his sword in a wide, elegant moulinet which, unfortunately for him, telegraphed his intent to slice his opponent's head off. Miss Tolerance ducked beneath his blade and lunged, making an upward thrust which came in under his guard. Beneath her foot the carpet slid again, just enough to give her arm extra momentum. The sword pierced Beauville's coat and waistcoat, stopped for a second upon a rib, then slid in deep. As she felt the sword slide into resisting flesh Miss Tolerance knew it for a mortal wound.

Beauville made a sighing noise of pain and surprise.

Miss Tolerance pulled back at once and tried to support Beauville as he slumped forward.

"Lie back, sir. Here, let me make you more comfortable." Miss Tolerance eased Beauville's weight onto the floor and, after a glance around the room, pulled one of the drapes from the window, rolled it up, and put it under Beauville's head. She took up the cloak she had seen before—brown with sable trim—and covered him with it.

Beauville gasped; there was a wet, sucking sound to his breath.

"I should—should have believed you," he said.

"Hush, sir. Don't try to talk. I will summon someone—"

Beauville shook his head. "By the time they come I will be dead, I think. Who taught you to fence? I should like to give him my compliments."

Miss Tolerance was winded and near tears. "'Twould be difficult, sir. He died some years ago."

"Ah. Well, perhaps not so difficult after all." Beauville coughed. "What was his name? If I see him in Hell I will tell him you do him credit."

"His name was Charles Connell, sir. Lie quiet; you do yourself no good to keep talking."

Beauville ignored her warning. "You will use this to free the little widow, mademoiselle? My death?"

"She is already free, sir. With Mr. Boyse's testimony exploded and the link to you—"

Beauville gave a ghastly, coughing sound Miss Tolerance realized was laughter.

"I had Boyse lie, it is true, but—"

"But?"

"Mademoiselle, I am much of what you think of me. I set the fire in your little house. I killed Josette—Camille demanded it, and Josette could have linked me to d'Aubigny's death. She went there that night a-purpose to leave the door open for me, all by Camille's design. I do not think she cared to be in another's power—she preferred to be the one holding the reins. She paid him one time, visited him another, hoping to steal the letters away then. But no—" Beauville paused and gave a long shuddering sigh. "I was to kill him and retrieve the letters. But d'Aubigny was occupied"—he gave the word a peculiar emphasis—"when I arrived. I heard him, and the woman's noises. So I waited in the hall, behind a cabinet. I—" another horrible laugh. "I fell asleep for a time. When I woke, all was quiet. She was gone, Etienne was dead. The bloody box." He laughed again. "The one place I would not look."

"Who was the woman, Beauville?"

"Am I to do your work for you? Who else could it have been?" The man stared over her shoulder at someone or something or someone invisible to Miss Tolerance. "Christ, in the box. The bloody box, the bloody box, why did I not . . ."

He drifted into silence, still panting.

Miss Tolerance went to the stair, called for the porter and gave the alarm, asking for a surgeon and the watch. In an afterthought she sent to Great Marlborough Street for Mr. Heddison as well. Then she returned to sit by Beauville's side as he fought a solitary, hopeless battle with death.

Nineteen

The surgeon was the first to arrive. He was a tall, gaunt man, several days unshaved, with a spill of snuff on the cuff of his black coat. He introduced himself, in a strong Welsh accent: "I am the surgeon, Jones. A man is dying here?" Miss Tolerance directed him to his patient; Jones cast one impatient look at the disarray of the room—candles guttering, the smears of blood on the wall and the floor, and the bloody cloak with which Miss Tolerance had covered Beauville—and went to work. He spoke bracingly to Beauville, but aside, with Miss Tolerance, he was grave.

"He will be lucky to last the night," the surgeon said. "Was he lying thus when you found him?"

"When I—" Miss Tolerance would have corrected Mr. Jones, but an elderly man, wrapped in so many disreputable scarves that they nearly covered his caped coat of office as well as his face, wheezed into the room. The watch, Miss Tolerance surmised, and would have advanced to explain matters to him, but he was seized by a fit of coughing so profound that Mr. Jones went to offer assistance, and Miss Tolerance returned to Beauville's side. Jones had apparently explained his mistaken idea of the situation to the watchman, for as soon as his coughing had stopped the man reeled away out the door, muttering rather thickly that he was going to fetch "the authorities."

"Gin," Mr. Jones diagnosed tersely.

Miss Tolerance nodded. There was little to say. She and the surgeon sat quietly, watching the wounded man. Beauville had sunk into a kind of sleep; his breathing was wet and shallow.

Miss Tolerance was roused from her thoughts by the percussive sound of boots on stairs. Mr. Heddison, with Greenwillow at his heels, was at the door. The boy who had fetched them lingered in the doorway, gratified to play even a small part in so glamorous an event. The sudden commotion was too much for the surgeon, who began to scold, explaining that his patient was unlike to last the night unless he was untroubled. Heddison, identifying himself, in turn explained to Mr. Jones that as Mr. Beauville was like to die in any case, a declaration must be obtained. The two men glared at each other in a wordless battle between the flexed muscles of the legal and medical professions; Jones gave way first, with a muttered warning to Heddison that *he* would not be responsible for the outcome. Heddison nodded, paused long enough to direct Miss Tolerance to stay, and bent over Beauville.

Miss Tolerance took a seat and composed herself. She had told Beauville the truth; she did not fence for sport, but in defense of herself and her clients. She knew from experience that it would be several days before the physical memory of the fight faded: she would suddenly feel again her sword point penetrating her opponent's resisting flesh, see the surprise in the other's eyes and smell the warm, coppery blood. She knew as well that the emotions of the event would take far longer to dissipate. She had disliked and distrusted Beauville, but in dying he was showing a bravery that she could not but admire. She could not think of his imminent death with anything but regret.

The law would have its say in regard to Beauville's death as well. Miss Tolerance was fairly certain that any honest verdict would be in her favor. The two swords which lay in proximity to Beauville's body attested to the fact that she had not attacked the man unprovoked. For a moment she was distracted by the idea of the affair written up in the *Gazette*'s Dueling Notices: *By the sword*, *fatally, Mr. Henri Beauville, engaged with Miss Sarah Tolerance in a matter of treason.* Beauville murmured unintelligibly to Heddison across the room.

At last Heddison left Beauville and joined Miss Tolerance.

"I had only just finished reading your note and the materials it contained when your second summons arrived," he told her. His wide mouth turned down. "Beauville says you fought to keep him from escaping."

Miss Tolerance nodded.

"He also says he has no idea whence Mrs. Touvois has fled. Before you go, please give Greenwillow a description of the woman. Perhaps she may be stopped at a port—she must try to leave the country. Dover or Southampton, most likely."

"Indeed." Miss Tolerance waited, feeling strongly that there must be something more to be said, either about the plot she had unearthed or her own participation in it.

"Well, it is late. I will not keep you, but be prepared to make yourself available." Heddison bowed curtly and beckoned Greenwillow forward. He gave instructions to his constable, then went back to Beauville. Greenwillow, with a notebook and a stub of pencil, waited until Miss Tolerance had given Madame Touvois' height and hair color, then followed his master's lead in dismissing Miss Tolerance into the night.

She went home to Manchester Square, exhausted and depressed.

S he was wakened by Jess, carrying a tray of coffee and rolls, with several of the London papers upon it. The hour was very advanced—the light had dropped to the western side of the house and Miss Tolerance judged it must be nearer to one than noon.

"Ma'am said she thought you'd want to see these, miss," the maid explained. "She said I was to bring you your breakfast up, seeing as you might be wanting to celebrate."

"Celebrate?" Miss Tolerance said blankly.

"That's what she said, miss." Jess settled the tray before Miss Tolerance and poured out her coffee. "Good morning, miss." She curtsied and was gone.

The papers were filled with news, much of it characteristically muddled. The story in brief was that a vile plot against a royal person had been uncovered—unfortunately too late to save the lives of several persons who had been involved in the treasonous actions, including, Miss Tolerance was fascinated to read, "a beautiful innocent who was murdered solely to implicate the Royal Person in her death." Josette Vose had given a fair impersonation of beauty, but innocent? She had been innocent of nothing except, most likely, conniving at her own death. She was similarly interested to learn that the Chevalier d'Aubigny featured in the reports as a patriot who had died because he had uncovered the vile plans of Madame Camille Touvois and her lackey, Mr. Henri Beauville. Mr. Beauville's death was attributed to unknown persons, and an urgent entreaty was made to the public to be on the watch for Madame Touvois, a woman of middle height and full, fine figure, with hair a light red and curling, and eyes brown, not beautiful but handsome, thought to be traveling disguised.

There was no note in any of the papers of Miss Tolerance's role in uncovering the plot.

She was happy to have it so; notoriety was not an asset in her profession, and she had received far too much publicity in testifying against Versellion. Still she was bemused at how totally Mr. Heddison (who, she suspected, had called in the press as soon as she had left Madame Touvois' rooms) had taken credit for the resolution of the case. One thing pleased her: two reports mentioned that discovery of the treasonous conspiracy had completely removed any suspicion in her husband's death from the poor Widow d'Aubigny, who had been taken up for questioning before the direction of the investigation had been changed and the true culprits discovered.

Miss Tolerance sipped her coffee and ate her bread and butter. When she had finished her meal she prepared to go out. She must give her reckoning to William Colcannon and return the chevalier's box to Anne d'Aubigny. The box might well go into the privy house again, but that was none of her affair. Miss Tolerance washed leisurely, put her hair up, and laid out her blue twill walking dress. She was putting on her stockings when Jess appeared at the door with a letter on a tray.

"Just delivered, miss. By a important footman, Cole says." *Important*, coupled with the rolling of Jess's eyes, suggested *pompous*.

Miss Tolerance thanked the maid and asked her to request Cole to bespeak a hackney carriage for her. She finished dressing before she took up the envelope. It was of heavy laid paper, uncrested, addressed to her in a uniform copperplate which suggested a secretary's hand. Perhaps an offer of new employment, she thought. With the Widow d'Aubigny's business all but finished new employment would be welcome.

But the envelope contained a brief note in language that was unexceptionable and noncommittal, expressing the gratitude of His Royal Highness the Duke of Cumberland. From the number of banknotes which had been enclosed with the note it was clear that the note intended less to convey thanks than to insure silence. Miss Tolerance sat for some minutes looking at the banknotes spread across her lap, weighing practicality against scruples. The amount she was being offered would have kept her quite comfortably for a year. She folded the banknotes into her reticule, took up her coat, and descended to the waiting hackney.

When she applied at Cumberland's apartments in St. James's Palace she was put again in the blank, chilly room where she had last waited. Miss Tolerance had resolved to be, quite against her mood, as bland and pleasant-spoken as she could be with the duke. It was not the duke who joined her, however. This was a neatly dressed man of middle height and build, with close-cut brown hair of a medium shade, and features so unremarkable that one might forget what he looked like, almost while looking at him.

"Miss Tolerance?" The forgettable man bowed.

She curtsied. "Yes, sir? And you are?"

"You may call me Mr. Smith," he drawled. Miss Tolerance had his measure by the end of the sentence: a man who believed that her equivocal position licensed insolence. She would not rise to the bait.

"Smith is not your true name, I take it?"

"No more than yours, Miss Tolerance. It will do for our purposes. Will you tell me why you have come?"

Miss Tolerance opened her reticule and bought out the packet of banknotes. "I received this from His Highness this morning. I preferred to return it myself, to ensure no farthing went astray."

Smith looked at the money. "Was it not enough?" he drawled.

Miss Tolerance spoke with a politeness which ought to have inspired anxiety in the forgettable Mr. Smith. "You mistake me, sir. It is far too much. I will be quite adequately paid for my efforts by my own client." She extended the notes to Smith. He did not take them.

"The money is an expression of my master's gratitude. You have no reason to return it."

"Nothing I have done has been in your master's service."

"But what you have done has turned out very well for my master, and he wishes to thank you."

"Turned out well? With his mistress murdered in the street?"

"Ah, but you found the persons responsible, did you not? And my master is now regarded by the public with some sympathy—a novel situation, you must admit—both as a bereaved lover and as the target of that wicked plot."

"According to the newspapers I had nothing to do with the resolution of the case," Miss Tolerance said drily.

"If the men who run this nation were made to rely upon the newspapers to know the truth, England would be in a sad case, Miss Tolerance. The papers are for manufacturing opinion, not telling the truth. My master is well aware that it was you who—" Smith paused. "It was you who removed the obstacles the French had thought to throw in his way."

"Obstacles. To His Highness's bid for the regency?"

"Of course. More immediately, obstacles to the passage of an important bill he supports."

"The Support Bill." Miss Tolerance's distaste was obvious.

"Indeed. With the passage of the Support Bill the army will be given the money it requires to extinguish the French menace from the face of Europe—"

"At the cost of stirring up revolution here at home? If I have helped secure passage of that bill, I will take no pride in it, sir."

"You disapprove, Miss Tolerance? Well, we are fortunate that policy is not made by women. Your soft hearts do not accord with the resolve necessary to statecraft."

Miss Tolerance closed her eyes and drew a long, deep breath. When she had subdued her temper she smiled.

"Mr. Smith, I killed a man last night. Please do not condescend to speak of my resolve or the softness of my heart. You may give His Highness my condolences upon his loss when you return his money." Miss Tolerance regarded Smith's bland face and could not resist the impulse to disturb its smiling arrogance. "It is particularly convenient for His Highness that the branches of amour in which Mrs. Vose specialized did not become known to the public."

The effect of her words was everything she could have wished. Smith's bland smile vanished. He had all the appearance of a man on the brink of outrage. "Do you suggest that you would make known—if the money is not sufficient to guarantee your discretion—"

"Mr. Smith, I am not a blackmailer, nor am I given to plots and intrigues. My *soft heart* feels for the people who will suffer if your master succeeds in his object—and for the late Mrs. Vose. Your master has nothing to fear from me: I shall make nothing public. I shall continue to think, and feel, a great deal, however. As I remarked to him upon the last occasion when I called here, the mere fact that some of my services may be hired does not mean that I can be bought entire."

Smith bridled. "You would have me believe you are insulted by the money?"

"You will believe what you like, sir. If there is nothing else to discuss, I will take my leave."

"Not without assurance—"

"I have said I will make nothing public. I am not in the business of publishing scandal, Mr. Smith. Your master may congratulate himself for getting something for nothing." Miss Tolerance pushed the folded banknotes across the table toward Mr. Smith. She was agreeably aware, as she left the room, that Smith had not moved to take up the money.

Miss Tolerance had walked several streets, pulling on her gloves, breathing the icy air and composing damning ripostes, before her common sense caught up with her. She had let her temper get the better of her, and only hoped she might not live to be sorry for it. She used the walk to Manchester Square to regain her composure, went in the house long enough to fetch the Chevalier d'Aubigny's box and, in anticipation of a happier interview, turned her steps toward Half Moon Street.

William Colcannon, looking as much at ease in his sister's house as she had formerly seen him uneasy, greeted Miss Tolerance effusively as the Savior of the Household, and offered to pay her twice, even thrice her agreed-upon fee. With the interview with Mr. Smith so recently past, Miss Tolerance found the idea of overpayment oppressive, and informed her client that the fee agreed upon, plus her remaining expenses, would be sufficient. "The amount of money I have expended in your behalf, on bribes and incentives, is likely to make you open your eyes," she said. "You are soon to be married, and it is likely your sister will need your generosity as well; pay my fee, Mr. Colcannon, and we are quits."

Colcannon thanked her again, three or four times, before noting that Miss Tolerance carried a good-sized wooden box under her arm.

"Your late brother-in-law's property, which I am returning to your sister," Miss Tolerance explained to him. "Is Mrs. d'Aubigny in seclusion, or may I speak to her for a moment and congratulate her upon her freedom?"

"She will be delighted, honored—" Mr. Colcannon's vocabulary failed him before his enthusiasm did. He took Miss Tolerance up the stairs to the little room in which she had spoken to Anne d'Aubigny before. What a difference there was today: the dark drapes had been pulled and the afternoon light and a good fire made the room a very pleasant place.

"Anne, see who is here to see how you do! Your savior, Miss Tolerance!"

Anne d'Aubigny shook her head at her brother with amusement and affection. Her former pallor was much relieved. Even in her unflattering blacks there was a warm color in her cheeks, and the sunlight danced in her pale blue eyes. She had several books in her hands, but put them down to come forward and take Miss Tolerance's hands warmly.

"My brother is right, Miss Tolerance. I have so much to thank you for. Please, will you take a glass of wine with me?"

Miss Tolerance thanked the widow and said she would be delighted. Colcannon took his leave of the women, and Miss Tolerance, before she took the chair Anne d'Aubigny had directed her to, put d'Aubigny's carved box on a table.

"Perhaps you will not want to keep this, but it is yours," she began.

Mrs. d'Aubigny was suddenly pale again. She put one hand up to her mouth in a gesture which should have been theatrical but was not. For a moment she appeared to be at a loss for words. At last she whispered, "What am I to do with it?"

Miss Tolerance felt a pang of impatience.

"I think we have seen that the privy is not a successful resting place for it," she said drily. "It is fortunate, indeed, that the box turned up again, for the solution to your husband's murder rested within it."

"It did?" Mrs. d'Aubigny sat down. She had lost all of the animation of a few moments before; of course, Miss Tolerance thought. The widow still saw the box as the repository for the chevalier's implements of pain. She knew nothing of its other secrets, which had assured her freedom.

"Your husband kept documents hidden in the lining of the box which will serve as the basis for the Crown's case against Madame Touvois—if she is caught."

"My husband was a *spy*?"

Miss Tolerance shook her head. "No, ma'am. Not a spy, although what he was doing was not much more savory. He was blackmailing the true traitors. It was a clever hiding place; even Mr. Beauville said he would not touch the box on the night of your husband's death."

"Did he?" Anne d'Aubigny took up a handbell and rang it twice. "Poor Mr. Beauville. The paper said he was killed trying to escape."

"Yes." Miss Tolerance found herself explaining the circumstances of Beauville's death and her part in it.

"How brave you are, Miss Tolerance," the widow said at the end of the tale. "It is a horrid thing, to kill someone, I imagine. For a woman. Men are more used to . . . to wars, and hunting and . . . I am sorry you were forced to it on my behalf."

Miss Tolerance could not think what to reply, and was happy for the appearance of Jacks, with the tray, decanter, and glasses, and Sophia Thissen. For a few minutes there was a domestic bustle of clearing the table for the tray and pouring out the wine. Sophie took the box away with instructions to have it broken up and burnt in the kitchen fire.

"What shall you do now?" Miss Tolerance asked when both servants had departed.

With the box gone from the room its hold upon Mrs. d'Aubigny's imagination seemed to be lifted, and she regained her earlier animation. She gestured at the books she had left upon the desk. Miss Tolerance saw a box nearby and realized she had interrupted the widow at packing. "I am going away. London has too many painful memories. My brother suggested I go to my cousins in India. Perhaps I can outstay the awful notoriety here."

Miss Tolerance agreed that this was an excellent solution. Mrs. d'Aubigny began to enthuse upon the wonders she expected to see: she was evidently an avid reader of travel books. Miss Tolerance sipped her wine and listened.

Despite the warmth of the fire and the wine, and Anne d'Aubigny's soft voice, Miss Tolerance could not relax and enjoy the completion of her work. Rather, she found herself becoming distracted, not listening to the widow but chasing a shadow of thought. At last she caught it. She felt a pang of pleasure and panic and raised her eyes to meet Anne d'Aubigny's.

"The bloody box," she said.

Mrs. d'Aubigny stopped short in her praise of Madras. "I beg your pardon—"

Miss Tolerance was seized with too much wonderment to apologize. "Beauville called it the bloody box, and I thought he meant it as a profanity. He was being purely descriptive. The bloody box. He was here the night of your husband's murder, you see. There

was a woman with chevalier, so Beauville hid in the hallway and
dozed off. When Beauville woke the woman was gone, and he
went in to find the chevalier dead. And the box was there.
Smeared with blood and brains, I don't doubt. That is why you
had Sophie drop it into the privy, isn't it?"

Anne d'Aubigny looked at Miss Tolerance quizzically, as if she
could not think of the proper way to respond. Did she hope to
win her accuser's sympathy? Was she marshaling defenses that,
with Beauville's death, she had put aside? But perhaps she did the
widow an injustice. Anne d'Aubigny finally nodded, as regal as
any doomed queen.

"Will you tell me what happened that night?"

The widow, entranced, stared at some picture only she could
see, and began to speak. Her words were not rushed but irrepress-
ible, as if she would not rest until the last of them was spoken.

"My husband had gone out and I had thought myself safe for
the night. I went to bed—Sophie brought me my sleeping draught,
and I slept. I do not know how much later it was—everyone in the
house was abed—when Etienne came to my room and woke me.
He pulled me down the hall to his room; I was very addled with
the laudanum, and very tired. He said Josette was gone, that he
might as well have me as her. And he . . . he did." The widow
looked up at Miss Tolerance seriously. "I knew to submit. He
went a little easier with me, so. But I was so tired, and stupid with
the laudanum. Sometimes the drug made it easier; either Etienne
would go away when he found me asleep, or it would help me not
to mind. But sometimes when I'm roused from a deep sleep it is
worse. It was so, that night. When Etienne was done with me he
pushed me off the bed and told me to go, to get out of his sight."
She laughed harshly. "He rolled over and was asleep at once. And
I—I was bleeding, my nightshift was bloody and I felt near to
swooning. I saw the box. Do you know the way in which one en-
dows a place or a thing with some sentiment or history, Miss Tolerance? *Look, my love gave me this ribbon,* or *see, that is where we
danced* . . . I saw the box and it was every cruel thing Etienne had
ever done to me. I picked it up and thought, if I could destroy it he
would not hurt me again. But then I thought: he will get another
box. And he will punish me . . ."

The widow's voice was high and thin at the memory. Miss Tolerance released a breath she had not known she held.

"Afterward I did not know what to do. I wanted to wash my hands but I could not bear to stay in the room with . . . him. I am not a person accustomed to action, as you are. I was not thinking very clearly. I ran back to my room to wash. I do not know what I was thinking; the rest of me was—there was—my nightshift was more befouled than before. Then I heard a noise in the hallway which scared me."

"Beauville," Miss Tolerance said.

"Did he know it was I who—"

Miss Tolerance shook her head. "He may have suspected it, but he did not say so to me."

The widow nodded thoughtfully. "When I heard that noise I was certain that Etienne had risen up and was coming for me. Even with what I had done. His blood and his brains . . ." Mrs. d'Aubigny faltered for a moment over the memory. "It will sound foolish to you now, but I had to see if he was really dead. It hardly seemed possible to me that Etienne's life could be so fragile. I waited until there was no further noise—no one had raised an alarm—and went back to his room. It was horrid, but he was dead. It sounds cold to say it, but you cannot imagine the comfort that was to me, Miss Tolerance."

The widow sat in her chair like a child, hands in her lap, her eyes fixed upon Miss Tolerance.

"Do *all* your servants know—?" Miss Tolerance asked. She felt overwhelmed by what she had uncovered, and uncertain what her own feelings were. Was the murder justified? An act of passion? How was she to act now?

Anne d'Aubigny shook her head. "I don't think so, not even Sophia. When I went back to my husband's room the laudanum had begun to wear off and the meaning of what I had done came to me. I felt so free. And so frightened! When I was taken to prison I thought it was only my due. Only today, when I felt safe, did I begin to think I might have a chance at the sort of normal life I expected when I was a girl."

Miss Tolerance kept her sympathy in check. She must hear it all first.

"When you returned to your husband's room what did you do?"

Mrs. d'Aubigny regarded her steadily from watery eyes.

"I knew I must remove any sign that I had been there. I took off my shift and wiped—everything—off the box. That was dreadful. Then I threw the shift into the fire and let it burn."

"Ah." Miss Tolerance's eyebrows went up. "Ah, yes, of course." She took out her wallet and extracted from it the scrap of white fabric she had taken from the chevalier's room. She laid the fabric on her knee, smoothing it carefully. "I found this in the grate. It is a bit that did not burn, I take it."

Mrs. D'Aubigny agreed that it must be. "I thought I had destroyed it all. I took the box back to my room and put on a new shift and went to bed. In the morning I told Sophia to get rid of the box."

"By throwing it in the privy?"

The widow nodded. "Sophia knew what Etienne did to me. It was she who salved my bruises and bound up the wounds. She understood what the box meant and why I would wish it destroyed."

Miss Tolerance sat speechless. She could not tell if she were more outraged or saddened by the tale.

"You understood," Anne d'Aubigny said with certainty. "From the first, you said—"

"I recall. I said I knew what it was to be mistaken in whom I loved. Did you imagine that meant that you should deceive me, or use me to make a mock of the law?"

"The law! The law permitted my husband to make a mock of our marriage vows!" Anne d'Aubigny's gaze locked with Miss Tolerance's. All meekness and submission had disappeared; the widow did not appear angry, only resolute. "What will you do?" she asked.

Miss Tolerance examined her own hands and considered. Had Anne d'Aubigny not murdered her husband, Henri Beauville would have done so, and for less cause. Beauville had not scrupled to direct suspicion to the widow; he had used Boyse to encourage that suspicion and remove it from himself. The law now appeared to be ready enough to fix the guilt in d'Aubigny's murder upon Henri Beauville, who had, God knew, enough guilt for the death of Josette Vose; and with Camille Touvois, whom Miss

Tolerance was certain would never be returned to London to hang. The matter could be resolved very easily.

And yet Miss Tolerance felt uneasy with the idea. Anne d'Aubigny had done murder; should she be permitted to escape punishment? A reasonable jury might well decide that she had acted to defend herself against further violence. A reasonable jury might well feel that she had been punished in advance of any crime, and ought not suffer further. And the law—Miss Tolerance stopped. *The law permitted my husband to make a mock of our marriage vows!* Was the law likely to make concessions on a charge of petty treason?

What if Anne d'Aubigny went free? Miss Tolerance could not believe that she, with sullied honor and no standing in society, found herself in the position of judge and jury. But, as the widow had said, she did understand what it was to be mistaken in the man she loved.

"Miss Tolerance?"

"You would never do it again," she said, half to herself.

Anne d'Aubigny appeared shocked by the notion. "I will give you my oath! I would never—"

Miss Tolerance held up her hand. "Yes, I know. I hope you will forgive me; I need to consider the matter. When do you plan to leave?"

Madame d'Aubigny's lips trembled. There is a ship sailing in a few days. The *Lucy Singer*, for Madras."

"Then I suppose I must make my mind to tell the law what I know before that time, or lose the opportunity to do so."

In the silence of the room the fire popped and the chimney whistled faintly. Anne d'Aubigny regarded Miss Tolerance steadily. At last she said, "I understand. And I thank you for your consideration, Miss Tolerance."

As well you might, Miss Tolerance thought. She took a sip of her wine in a silent toast to the Widow d'Aubigny and her future.

Twenty

Miss Tolerance spent the evening in a reflective mood, quietly playing cards with her aunt. She had felt some guilt over her neglect of Mrs. Brereton in the past week; she might excuse that neglect by saying, truthfully, that she had no gifts as a nurse, but the fact was that it had been easier to be away on Anne d'Aubigny's business than to stay home fretting uselessly. If she had thought to wait upon an invalid, however, she had the wind taken out of her sails at the sight of her aunt, elegantly dressed and coiffed, with the Cent deck in her hand and an agreeably rapacious look in her eye. Mrs. Brereton's fine complexion had regained a good deal of its well-tended clarity, but there was still a papery quality to the skin about her eyes, and a tentativeness in her manner, as if her illness had reminded her of a mortality she had successfully ignored for many years. But the worst of Mrs. Brereton's illness was past, and the d'Aubigny matter was resolved. Miss Tolerance was happy to be able to sit talking amiable commonplace and playing piquet for paper points.

"But ought the *Times* not make some mention of the role you played, my dear?" Mrs. Brereton declared a blank and laid down five cards. "It was your investigation brought all to light."

"There is no ought about it, ma'am. And Mr. Heddison is far

more adept a player than I am; he made sure that the credit, and the reward as well, I do not doubt, will go to the Great Marlborough Street Public Office. I don't doubt he plans to deal with Mr. Boyse on his own, with as little public notice of the corruption in his office as possible. I would lament more, but I have been handsomely paid by my client." Miss Tolerance saw no reason to mention the Duke of Cumberland's attempt to bribe her. She suspected her scruples would make no sense to Mrs. Brereton, and dreaded the discussion that would ensue. "And what use is public notice to me? Versellion's trial put me in grave danger of becoming a familiar figure. How could I do my work if every man on the corner recognized me as I passed?"

"So you will keep your involvement a secret?"

"I propose merely to say nothing unless asked, and then to exercise discretion. I believe that is ten points to you, Aunt."

"So it is." Mrs. Brereton smiled. "Cole tells me that the whitewashing in your cottage is finished. Will you return?"

"I certainly shall. What excellent news! I will ask Frost to have my clothes carried back tomorrow."

"You need not go, you know. The yellow room is not needed. You are not discommoding anyone." Miss Tolerance thought she discerned a note of anxiety in her aunt's voice.

"You are very kind to offer it, Aunt, but you know I like my privacy. And you are always taking on new women—to say nothing of the fact that you haven't replaced Matt. Do you mean to do so?"

"I haven't yet found a boy that suits the house; molly-whores are tricky—"

"I miss him too," Miss Tolerance said quietly. "But my point is really that you will need that room again. I ought not to occupy it if I cannot put it to use the way the rest of your staff does." She put a gentle hand on her aunt's. "You need not a fear a resumption of our former coldness, Aunt. I am sorrier than I can say that we allowed a stupid quarrel to estrange us. And indeed when I have my own place we are the better friends for it."

"So you say," Mrs. Brereton said. "Well, I know better than to argue with you. Perhaps I will give the yellow room to Marianne. And my ruff is—" she peered at her hand and totaled the cards in her best suit. "Twenty-four."

"I'm sure Marianne will like it," Miss Tolerance said. She declared twenty-seven points.

" 'Twill make it more convenient when she needs to ask a question about how things are being done." Mrs. Brereton watched her niece from the corner of her eye. "You were right: she has a good sensible head upon her shoulders, and managed the house while I was sick, as well as keeping up with her callers. She deserves some sort of notice."

Miss Tolerance smiled with real pleasure. "I am delighted to hear you say it, Aunt. I think Marianne will be a great help to you."

"You might have been," Mrs. Brereton said, with the air of one who expects to be scolded but cannot keep from making a remark.

"I might have," Miss Tolerance said mildly. "But my heart would not have been in it, and you and I should have quarreled."

"Well," said Mrs. Brereton, "we have had quite enough of *that*." She laid down a set of four. "Match that!" she said with pleasure.

The next morning Miss Tolerance saw the return of her belongings, and a few pieces of borrowed furniture, to the little house behind Mrs. Brereton's. Despite the fresh whitewash there was still a smell of charred wood, an unpleasant acrid scent that pinched the nostrils and soured the throat. The house was very cold and damp; Miss Tolerance lit a fire and bustled about, putting things away, making note of what she would have to replace. Looking at her list she thought for a moment of Cumberland's bribe, which would have bought her new furniture instead of used, with a nice nest egg remaining. She was sitting by the fire with some darning when Keefe brought a letter to her.

The paper was heavy white laid stock, with her address written in a Continental fist tightly looped and back-slanted. The handwriting was unfamiliar to Miss Tolerance.

"How did this come?" she asked.

"A boy—a crossing-boy by the look of him—brought it. Didn't wait for a reply, just took to his heels and run. Now you come to say it, miss, it don't look like the sort of message normally received from a street urchin."

"Paper this fine usually requires livery and a senior footman,"

Miss Tolerance agreed. "Perhaps someone prizes his anonymity too much to advertise the letter's origin. And it may be new employment for me. Thank you, Keefe."

She waited until the servant was gone before she turned the letter over. It was double-sealed with red wax, without frank or stamp. If it was a new inquiry, why address it to her here instead of Tarsio's? She shook her head: *I really must let go my squeamishness about my privacy.* She ran her fingernail under the wax blots, lifted them, and read the letter with astonishment. It was written in the same back-slanted hand, poorly spelled and altogether confounding:

> *Dear Miss Tolerance*
>
> *I am sorry we could not continue our excelent coversation, but as you better than anyone else will be aware, circumstanses make it necesary that I remove myself from Londron for a time. I hope you were not too distresed by my absense when you called—but I hear that poor Beauville met you there and gave you some exerxise. You must not repine at having killed him. He was really a very useles man: not one thing that I set him to do did he do properly. The French will not miss him and nor will I.*
>
> *I supose you are congratulating yourself for your cleverness at having unraveled the whole busines. Indeed, you did very nicely to a point, but you must not expect to know the whole. Like you, I am a woman with my way to make, and like you, my goals change with my employers. I have done most, if not all, that I hoped to do, and can leave England with a light heart.*
>
> *And that I must now do, as Mr. Smith has been at my door these five minutes, and says the yaght must sail by the next tide.*
>
> *Please believe me that I remain your admiring friend,*
>
> *Camille Veronie Touvois*

Miss Tolerance's hands trembled. She had the powerful impulse to throw one of her remaining pieces of crockery across the room. When the immediate impulse had passed she read the letter again, marveling at Madame Touvois' nerve—although a far earthier term occurred to her. After several minutes in this uncomfortable state of admiration and rage Miss Tolerance asked herself why Camille Touvois had sent the note at all. What was its purpose? To thumb her nose at a bested adversary? Would someone bent on escaping English law stop to write such a note, the emotional equivalent of one nursery-child crying "Nyahh!" to another?

Miss Tolerance read the letter again, putting aside her outrage and simply parsing the words. On this reading the import of the last paragraph struck her: "Mr. Smith has been at my door these five minutes, and says the yaght must sail by the next tide."

"You may call me Mr. Smith," Cumberland's aide had told her.

Smith was a common enough name. That had been the point of the man's transparent lie.

So: were the Smith she had met and Madame Touvois's Smith one and the same? Touvois hinted at it—else why add that last paragraph? If her Smith and Miss Tolerance's were the same man, then Camille Touvois would be leaving the country under the Duke of Cumberland's protection. But that could not be. Whatever his faults, the duke would not ally himself with the French—and in her first paragraph La Touvois had made it plain that she and Beauville had been in the pay of the French.

Could Touvois have cozened the Duke of Cumberland into protecting her? Miss Tolerance wished that she had not left matters so badly with Sir Walter Mandif; she would have liked to show the letter to him and see what he made of it. She read the letter again.

"No," she murmured. Whatever she thought of Cumberland, he was not a stupid man. He would not have been tricked by some act of Camille Touvois' into believing her a wronged innocent. Touvois's name and the list of her crimes had been blazoned in the newspapers. If she were indeed under the duke's protection—which the letter certainly implied—Miss Tolerance could imagine only two reasons for it. The first was blackmail. But what hold could Touvois have upon him? The Sellis matter, her first attempt to destroy Cumberland and his reputation, had been exploded by a Whig jury which had been sufficiently unbiased to acknowledge that the duke had not slain his valet.

What else might be held over Prince Ernest's head to compel him to protect Camille Touvois? A bastard child? Just another FitzHanover among the many. More florid sexual indiscretion? Possibly—but Cumberland had been rumored to have fathered a child on his youngest sister, the Princess Amelia: what worse could be said of him? Sodomy? Not impossible to believe, but to have survived this long with no whisper of it seemed unlikely. Brutality of the sort practiced by Etienne d'Aubigny? Mrs. Vose would have known that answer. Smith had said that matters had turned out very well for his master; that Mrs. Vose's death cast Cumberland in a sympathetic light. A very convenient death, if it not only gained him sympathy but hid a brutal nature as well.

Would Cumberland not hate Camille Touvois, who had constructed the plot to discredit him with Mrs. Vose's death? Or would he perhaps have been grateful to her? Miss Tolerance read the second paragraph of the letter again: *Like you, I am a woman with my way to make, and like you, my goals change with my employers.*

Miss Tolerance drew a breath.

Could Camille Touvois be telling her, in so many words, that the French had indeed been her masters in arranging the Sellis affair, but that Cumberland himself had paid her to arrange the *affaire Vose*?

Miss Tolerance rose and began to pace the length of the room, weighing obligation against risk. The answer she reached was always the same. Miss Tolerance looked about her and recalled that the box in which she had kept her pens, inkwell and paper had been destroyed in the fire. She threw on a shawl and crossed the garden to her aunt's house to beg a sheet of paper and pen, and sat down at once to write.

An hour later, after several false starts, she had completed a letter to the Prince of Wales. It was not entirely outrageous of her to write to Wales; she had met him at Versellion House, and Cumberland himself had told her that Wales not only remembered her, he had been impressed by her enterprise. Wales might feel that the letter she proposed to send to him, detailing everything she knew and everything she conjectured about his brother Cumberland's involvement with Camille Touvois and Josette Vose, was presumptuous. But she could not in good conscience keep treason a secret. She had promised that she would not make Cumberland's secrets public; she had not said she would not tell the duke's brother.

> *I would not approach Your Highness with this matter but that I feel most strongly it has a bearing upon the security of the Nation. If Prince Ernest has indeed authored a plot to make himself sympathetic, the better to achieve backing for the War Support Bill or his own ambitions, he has done so at the cost of at least two lives. If my conjectures are wrong, I shall be glad of it. But I felt I must lay the whole before Your Highness, in hopes that whatever steps you think best should be taken. If Your Highness has need to speak further upon this matter, I am at your service. You have my earnest promise that I shall not speak of this matter except to yourself.*

Having finished the note, sanded and sealed it, Miss Tolerance took it across to Keefe and asked him to have it brought to Carlton House.

"I'll take the note myself, miss," Keefe assured her. "I can use a bit of air." Miss Tolerance, noting that it looked to snow soon, thanked Keefe very much. She returned to her cottage.

Nothing, it seemed, had been what she thought it.

S he returned to the comfortable tasks of making her house a home again. She kept the fire in the grate burning steadily and rejoiced to feel the damp chill recede to the furthest corners of the downstairs room and then from the bedchamber upstairs. She brushed and hung her clothes, polished her boots—not with champagne, said to be the polish of choice among the wealthy, but with plain harness wax—and took out the bag of rags from which she hoped to fashion a new rug.

Dusk found Miss Tolerance sitting by the fire, drinking tea and braiding rags, thinking of Anne d'Aubigny and wondering what the widow would find in India. She hoped the widow would make the most of her second chance; it was not a thing given to every troubled woman.

Later Marianne rapped at Miss Tolerance's door and was invited to take a glass of wine.

"Not working tonight?" Miss Tolerance asked.

"I've been working, well enough, but not on my back. I've been sitting with Mrs. B, looking over the ledgers."

Miss Tolerance cast her friend a look of purest astonishment. "The ledgers? As well to say you have been given the keys to Heaven!"

Marianne laughed. "Felt like it, indeed. First, of course, I had to sit through half an hour's rant upon why what she was going to show me must be kept a secret—from the patrons and the other girls and—"

"From me? I don't doubt it. I gave up my chance at the keys to Heaven, and I think I must have hurt my aunt a bit in doing so. But I am glad to see them going into your competent hands."

"So Mrs. B said. I should say thank you, but I imagine my privileges will be bought with a great deal of work, ciphering and writing and fretting. All this atop my regular responsibilities," she added with an emphasis that made it plain she was quoting from her employer. "Yesterday I had employment and a following. Today, it appears, I have a career."

Miss Tolerance raised her glass. "To your career!"

Marianne hesitated. "You are certain you don't mind? You're all the family Mrs. B has, and she would leave you the whole—"

"What would I do with the whole? No, Marianne, I am delighted that my aunt has had the sense to do this. You will do a far better job than I would."

Marianne lifted her glass. "Then, to my career. And yours."

The wind wound around the house with a thin, cold wail. Marianne rose at last and said it was time she returned to the house. "I've a gent coming in a bit." She picked up the garden-cloak in which she had made her journey across the garden and threw it over her shoulders. With her hand on the latch she turned her head to bid Miss Tolerance good night, and stopped.

"There, and I haven't given you this, which was my whole reason for being here!" she exclaimed. She slid her hand into a pocket of the cloak and took out an envelope. "This came for you. I'm that sorry I forgot it. The pleasure of your company, I expect."

Miss Tolerance saw her friend safe across the garden, then opened the letter. It was from Wales. He thanked her for the information she had shared with him and asked her to call at Carlton House at noon the next day to discuss the matter further.

R oyalty may be early or tardy, as it pleases. Commoners do well to be prompt. Miss Tolerance arrived at Carlton House at five minutes before noon the next morning, again wearing the steel-blue walking dress and her most demure bonnet. She was shown directly into a tidy little study, decorated in the Chinese style, with a good fire burning. She sat on a chair upholstered in red fabric embroidered with a profusion of yellow and blue birds, and looked around her with interest. The room had a chaotic elegance that was just short of being cluttered; there was a small sofa, three chairs, and several cabinets which held many Oriental curios.

Within five minutes of her arrival the Prince was with her. His protuberant blue eyes were both affable and sharp as he raised her from her curtsy; his corsets creaked unmistakably. "You know far too much about my family's dealings to stand upon ceremony, Miss Tolerance," he said pleasantly. "Thank you for coming. May I ask you to tell me again the extraordinary information which you outlined in your letter?"

Miss Tolerance did so. Wales interrupted from time to time to ask her to elaborate upon a point. He had clearly considered her information, and its sources, carefully.

"There is no direct link between Madame Touvois and my brother?" he asked at last.

"None but the letter, sir. Which I have brought to put into Your Highness's keeping." Miss Tolerance took Camille Touvois' letter from her reticule and placed it upon the round inlaid table by her elbow. "The only true link is that which I forged in my own mind, and that I would reveal only to you."

Wales nodded. "Ernest is not stupid. He would not commit anything to writing. But this Frenchwoman, Madame Touvois—"

"The letter? It appears to give credence to her role as a French spy. But I recall something Mr. Beauville said of her: that she delighted in causing mischief, particularly among the power-ful." Miss Tolerance smiled sourly. "I imagine her, cozily situ-ated somewhere on the Continent with a very good deal of money from your brother and from the French as well, laughing at all."

"What am I to do, then, with my brother? This was a kind of treason. A plot against the process of law, certainly. And people died for it: that Beauville fellow, and the woman, my brother's wh—mistress." The prince looked at Miss Tolerance fixedly, his rheumy eyes shrewd. "I must ask a telling question, and trust that you will be honest with me, Miss Tolerance. You are *certain* my brother himself did not murder the woman?"

"Yes, sir." Miss Tolerance was pleased to reassure him. "Beauville told me as much before he drew his sword and forced me to defend myself."

Wales breathed a long, gusty sigh which smelt sweetly of cloves and snuff. "My brothers and I have shown an ample talent for tarnishing the reputation of the Crown without deliberately conniving at the matter. Miss Tolerance, you have all my thanks. I regret I cannot do anything more public—"

Miss Tolerance shook her head. "That would not serve your purpose or mine, sir. I am happy to have been of service."

Wales took her hand and bowed over it. For a moment Miss Tolerance was afraid he would kiss it. He did not, but she was aware of the royal eye upon her, assessing her. He gave no more than a chaste regal salute, to Miss Tolerance's relief. "If there is ever any way in which I may be of service to you, madam, I hope you will let me know." He released her hand and tugged a square-cut emerald ring from his little finger. "I am quite in earnest; if you have need of my assistance, send this ring to me and I will understand."

Miss Tolerance curtsied, murmured her thanks, and tucked the ring into her reticule. *Like something from an opera!* she thought. A handful of guineas would have been more useful, but she did not say so. She would never use the ring: a Fallen Woman does not summon royalty.

"If you will excuse me now, Miss Tolerance? It appears I must have a talk with my brother Cumberland." Wales smiled. "Although I can never be king, it seems I must still act the head of the family. Your pardon, madam, and again, all my thanks."

When Miss Tolerance rose from her curtsy the prince was gone. As she left the room a footman joined her to escort her from the house, and at the doorstep she found a hackney carriage had been summoned for her.

"Miss, His Highness desired I give you this," the footman said. *This* was a leather purse, gratifyingly heavy. As the carriage pulled away from the curb, Miss Tolerance opened it just far enough to disclose the cheering glint of gold. These coins, at least, she need not scruple to accept. She gave the driver Tarsio's address.

M iss Tolerance ordered a bottle of burgundy and the news-papers and sat in the Ladies' Salon. The whole of Anne d'Aubigny's case, from the death of her husband to her detention at Cold Bath Fields Prison, to her triumphant vindication, was recapitulated over several weeks' issues. The more conservative the paper, the worse Anne d'Aubigny's supposed crime was painted at the outset, the more fervent the outcry against the godless French when the "treasonous plot" was exposed. The *Times*, in particular, which had early on suggested that Mrs. d'Aubigny was "the most horrid and unnatural of criminals, a woman who slays her rightful master," did an about-face that was almost dizzying. With Beauville dead and Camille Touvois named as the author of the treasonous plot, Mrs. d'Aubigny now figured as "the gently reared and much-abused relict of a man who early sought to warn this Nation of French perfidy, and paid the ultimate price in horrid murder!"

Miss Tolerance dropped the *Times* in disgust and took up the newest number of the *Gazette*, leafing through to the Dueling Notices. The gentlemen of London, she noted, had not been behind-hand in attempting their mutual slaughter:

By the sword, fatally, Mr. John Wantage, by Lord Desston.

By shot, Sir Walter Coigne, by an anonymous gentleman.

By shot, fatally, Alan, Lord Bennis, by Mr. Hottyn, in a matter of family honor.

Miss Tolerance thought of Henri Beauville and turned the page.

She passed over the shipping news, then went back and read the departures carefully. The *Lucy Singer* had departed that morning for Madras. Among the passengers, a Miss Anne Colcannon.

Miss Tolerance raised a glass to the *Lucy Singer* and its passengers.

A glance out the window demonstrated to Miss Tolerance that the evening was well begun, although it was only a little past five o'clock. The Ladies' Salon had become lively with noise, and Miss Tolerance was not in a mood to listen to the effusions of her sex. She collected her coat and left, standing for a moment on Tarsio's steps; the dank chill of the air was redoubled, and wisps of sour yellow fog were thickening near the ground. Then Miss Tolerance pulled the collar of her cloak a little tighter and hailed a hackney carriage. She had one more task to accomplish, and thought she had best do it now, with several glasses of good burgundy to give her courage.

Sir Walter Mandif had a comfortable red-brick house on Gracechurch Street; the windows at the front gave a cheery light in the misty darkness, and the brass doorplate and knocker shone with reflected light. She was admitted to the house by a very young man, not much more than a boy, whose attempt at dignity was largely overmastered by the high spirits of his age. Miss Tolerance explained her errand and he bounded off, puppylike, to see if Sir Walter would permit her a few words. He returned a moment later to bring her to a comfortable office paneled in light wood and well lit around the desk. There were shelves along two walls, filled with books; more books were stacked upon a marble-topped sideboard next to the door. On the floor along the wall to the right of the desk a long line of ledgers stood. There was a tiled fireplace and a small fire in it which cast warm shadows on the backs of two chairs arranged to face the desk. *A very pleasant work place,* Miss Tolerance thought. *How is it I never visited here before?*

Sir Walter sat at his desk surrounded by half a dozen large books, writing in a ledger which appeared to be a fellow of those that stood on the floor. He seemed both focused and relaxed, as if concentration were a comfortable state for him; only the slight pursing of his lips suggested that he was taking pains with his work.

The only sounds were the snap and lick of the fire and the scratch of Sir Walter's pen upon the ledger pages. "Miss Tolerance, sir," the boy said.

Sir Walter looked up from the page and smiled.

Miss Tolerance examined that smile and saw in it a genuine pleasure which touched her. She also thought she saw caution. Did he think that she had come to quarrel?

"I am happy to see you," he said simply, rising from his chair. "Please, sit. Will you take some wine?" He called the manservant back. "Michael, the claret and glasses, please."

Miss Tolerance watched the boy go, then took one of the winged chairs that faced the desk. She licked her lips, annoyed with her own nervousness, and looked squarely at Sir Walter.

"I have come to say I am sorry," she said simply. "To apologize for what I have said, and what I have thought. I hope you can forgive me; I do not have so many friends that I can afford to squander their goodwill." Her voice was low and quiet.

Sir Walter shook his head. "It was I—" He stopped as a slight rattle announced that Michael was returning with the wine. The boy carried the tray with an energy that made Miss Tolerance fear for the decanter; when all was safely settled on the desk Michael grinned as if it were perfectly natural that the world should appreciate his success. Mandif thanked the boy and dismissed him, then took the time to pour out two glasses of claret. He presented Miss Tolerance with one and sipped from his own before he continued.

"I presumed too much on our friendship, I think. I underestimated—" He paused. "These last months, indeed the whole summer, have been hard ones for you. A difference of opinion with a friend must have seemed like a judgment upon—"

"But you were right," Miss Tolerance said.

"I beg your pardon?"

"You were right," she said again. "It is part of what I have to tell you, and I hope you will understand why I waited as long as I did, when I have told you the whole."

Sir Walter looked at her in surprise. "Right about what? The newspapers—Heddison's statement said—"

"An agreeable fiction. There are certain things I learned only after Mr. Heddison had announced his triumph: blame a dead spy and free a brutalized woman. But in the matter of the Chevalier d'Aubigny's death, the spy was blameless. Anne d'Aubigny killed her husband."

The magistrate sat back. "Perhaps you will explain."

Miss Tolerance nodded. Carefully she explained the circumstances of Anne d'Aubigny's marriage, and the events which had led to d'Aubigny's death. "Once she began to strike him she kept on until she saw his brains upon the sheet, because she was not certain he would die otherwise. She seems to have believed he had nearly superhuman strength."

"Then the tale of letters implicating Beauville and Touvois—"

"It was true: Beauville was meant to kill d'Aubigny and steal the letters, but he never found them. Anne d'Aubigny knew nothing of them."

"If all you tell me is so, the chevalier appears to have reaped what he sowed," Sir Walter said. "I am all a-maze. But why are you apologizing to me?"

"Why would I not? You said it was the wife, and you were right. I could not keep my feelings from coloring what I saw. I believed Anne d'Aubigny was innocent for no better reason than that I wanted her to be. I saw her as a woman betrayed by the man she loved—"

"Which appears to me to be an accurate reading of the facts. You seem to me to have been correct about most of the facts in the case." Sir Walter rose from his chair, wineglass in his hand. He did not approach Miss Tolerance; instead, he paced along the far wall, speaking thoughtfully. "We disagreed, and that was not pleasant. That will happen among colleagues. But you seem very intent upon finding yourself guilty." Miss Tolerance looked at him sharply. Sir Walter said, very gently, "I think you have mistrusted your own judgment for some time. Since last spring, or at least since your testimony at Versellion's trial."

"Do you think I have no reason to do so?"

"I think that if you expect your judgment to be entirely unaffected by your prejudices, you may next expect to achieve sainthood. So you were not entirely right about Anne d'Aubigny. You were not entirely wrong, either."

The fire snapped. Miss Tolerance could not find her voice to reply, and was suddenly aware that tears stood in her eyes, ready to fall.

"My dear, if you find your errors intolerable you will have a very hard life."

Miss Tolerance's shoulders began to shake. She was perhaps as surprised as Sir Walter to discover that, despite the tears which had rolled silently down her cheeks, she was laughing. It took her some minutes to regain her composure, during which time Sir Walter watched her with an expression of amazement.

"Sir Walter, I hope I never again quarrel with you," she said at last. "You have a perspective—and a way of stating it—which is . . . tonic." She briskly took her handkerchief from her reticule.

Sir Walter poured a little more claret into her glass.

"So: Madame Touvois and Beauville were involved in treason and in the death of Mrs. Vose; the chevalier was a blackmailer; and Anne d'Aubigny, with some justification, it seems to me, dashed her husband's brains out. Is there anything else you wish to tell me?"

Miss Tolerance thought guiltily of Cumberland, but shook her head.

"Well, this leaves me with the interesting question of how I am to act in this matter."

Miss Tolerance shook her head. "I think I have spared you that problem." She was not sure how Sir Walter would take her last bit of news.

"Spared me? How so?"

"Anne d'Aubigny sailed for India this morning."

Sir Walter opened his mouth and closed it again. He nodded to Miss Tolerance as if in acknowledgment of a point well played. "I could, of course, send a letter to the authorities in India. But from what you tell me it appears that justice, if not the law, has been served."

Miss Tolerance nodded. "I truly think it has."

A clock on the mantel ticked through the seconds. Miss Tolerance turned her wineglass between her fingers but did not drink. She was in great anxiety to know Sir Walter's mind—and his feelings toward her.

At last, "Do you know Shakespeare, Miss Tolerance?"

She blinked. "I beg your pardon, sir?"

"Mrs. Siddons is appearing in *Macbeth* at New Covent Garden Theatre tonight. Would you care to see it? Her Lady Macbeth is accounted very fine. I often find, when I am puzzling out human behavior, that recourse to Shakespeare's plays can make things clearer. I don't believe there was an emotion or motive that the playwright did not at some point touch upon. Do you find it so?"

Miss Tolerance recognized an olive branch when one was presented to her. "I know but little Shakespeare, Sir Walter. Romeo loved Juliet, I believe, and Hamlet was a melancholy prince. Further than that I dare not venture. I was an indifferent student with an uninspired governess in my schoolroom days."

"I find that hard to believe," Sir Walter said.

"'Tis all too true," Miss Tolerance said. "But I hope I have somewhat mended my ways."

"Then you will accompany me?"

Miss Tolerance smiled and sipped her wine. "I would be very happy to, Sir Walter. It is always my pleasure to learn something new."

History and Appreciation

In the real world—and friends of the English Regency period will know at once that the world of *Petty Treason* does not take place within the realm of real history—there was an attempt on the life of Ernest, Duke of Cumberland, in May of 1810. Cumberland's valet, Joseph Sellis, was later found in his room, an apparent suicide, and an inquest found that Sellis had been the assassin and, failing of his object, had taken his own life. However, there were persistent rumors that Cumberland had killed Sellis, either to hush up an affair with Sellis's wife, or to quash rumors that he had made homosexual advances to the valet. I have, in the self-serving way of writers, twisted the whole business to suit my story, and painted Cumberland darker than he was—although he appears to have been unpleasant enough. A high Tory, he was virulently anti-Catholic and reactionary; he detested the common folk, and they returned his dislike with interest. Mothers were said to have chided their wild daughters by telling them that the Duke of Cumberland would come for them if they did not behave; there were even rumors that he had fathered a child with one of his sisters, the princess Sophia. Cumberland was generally considered to be the real black sheep of the family, but there is absolutely no evidence that he connived at anything so byzantine as the plot I have laid out here. I will say that the history of George III and his children is filled with the sort of family dysfunction that could keep a panel of psychiatrists busy for years.

English law at the time of *Petty Treason* was less friendly to the accused than American law (or current English law) is. A suspect did not have the right to confront his accusers; he (and his legal representatives) were often unable to find out the nature of the charges or proofs against them; hearsay was quite acceptable evidence; and the suspect did not have the right to testify in his own behalf. There was no such thing as a not-guilty plea, but you could not be tried without your consent. However, prisoners who "stood mute" and did not give consent to trial were frequently *pressed:* laid on a stone table, naked, and piled with stones until they confessed or consented to trial . . . or died. At a time when the death penalty was commonplace for theft of anything worth more than a shilling, and the last burning on the charge of petit treason was only a couple of decades past, justice depended largely upon the goodwill and common sense of the people administering it. There were no London police per se at the time, either: individual parishes were protected by the Watch, elderly men who patrolled the streets at night. The Public Offices, modeled after the Bow Street magistrate's office, were an early attempt to put a crime-fighting force in London, but the major tool of law enforcement was the informer, and informers were paid well.

England in 1810 was at war—a condition in which the country had existed off and on for almost thirty years—and a series of bad harvests, coupled with the financial demands of the war and growing industrialization, wrought havoc with the nation's economy. At this point, there was a growing political tension between those who, like Cumberland, felt that the French (with their frighteningly egalitarian policies) must be vanquished at all costs, and those who believed steps must be taken to ease the pressure on the people of England, who were, after all, supporting the war, and sometimes starving for it.

The more I learn about this period, the more I find there is to learn. While my mistakes and inventions are my own, I have had enormous help and support from a number of people, and I couldn't have gotten anything right without them. Andrew Sigel not only enthusiastically embraced Sarah Tolerance and her world, he was invaluable in helping me think out what-ifs of my particular branching off of history. He supplied books, made comments, and was generally a Prince of the Blood. Likewise Greer Gilman, Sherwood Smith, eluki bes shahar, and Gregory Feeley. As always, my thanks to my fencing teachers, Richard Rizk, David Brimmer, T. J. Glenn, Duncan Eagleson, and M. Lucie Chin, whose grace and style have a huge impact on Miss Tolerance's own. The members of my writers group, as always, were not only supportive but constructive, catching the Big Errors before I made a fool of myself in print.

My thanks and a wave to the staff at Starbucks (Ninety-third and Broadway in New York City) for cheery greetings, a comfortable space to sit and write, and keeping the coffee coming.

More thanks: again and always to Patrick and Teresa Nielsen Hayden and Anna Genoese, for their generous enthusiasm and editorial acumen; my agent, Valerie Smith, and my publisher, Tom Doherty, for making so many things possible. More thanks to Tor's design, production, and marketing departments, all of whom labor long and hard in the service of Tor Books (and thanks, in particular, to copy editor S. B. Kleinman, who manages to juggle the antique language in this book with a fine eye for typos, inconsistencies, and momentary lapses on the part of the author). They all make me look good. To my best bud, Claire Eddy, who always seems to have time to help me gnaw on a bit of plot, and to Melissa Singer—both of whom are not only editors but fellow travelers on the working-mom road—the usual love and appreciation. To Steve Popkes, thanks for years of being out there and keeping me honest.

And always, my love to my husband, Danny Caccavo, and our girls, Julie and Rebecca; life with them is always an adventure.